A
Cowboy
to Remember

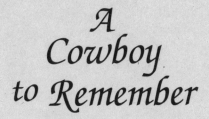

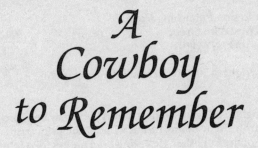

A Cowboy to Remember

REBEKAH WEATHERSPOON

Dafina Books

Kensington Publishing Corp.

www.kensingtonbooks.com

DAFINA BOOKS are published by

Kensington Publishing Corp.
119 West 40th Street
New York, NY 10018

All Kensington Titles, Imprints, and Distributed Lines are available at special quantity discounts for bulk purchases for sales promotions, premiums, fund-raising, and educational or institutional use. Special book excerpts or customized printings can also be created to fit specific needs. For details, write or phone the office of the Kensington special sales manager: Kensington Publishing Corp., 119 West 40th Street, New York, NY 10018, attn: Special Sales Department, Phone: 1-800-221-2647.

Dafina and the Dafina logo Reg. U.S. Pat. & TM Off.

ISBN-13: 978-1-4967-2540-0
ISBN-10: 1-4967-2540-9
First Kensington Mass Market Edition: March 2020

ISBN-13: 978-1-4967-2543-1 (ebook)
ISBN-10: 1-4967-2543-3 (ebook)

10 9 8 7 6 5 4 3 2 1

Printed in the United States of America

For Russell and Jackie,
who have always welcomed me home.

Acknowledgments

I would like to thank the following Black Women:

Beverly Jenkins
Brenda Jackson
for showing me the way.

Patti LaBelle
Aretha Franklin
for the soundtracks and the legendary shade.

Lizzo
for the Juice.

Leona
Alyssa
for the incantations.

Edna
Olive
Jackie
Miss Kim
for the blue print to my own body and soul.

And Esi
for understanding the importance of a puppy
on the page and all my Beyoncé references.

I'd also like to thank my agent Holly Root
for giving me the time I needed to try again.
You are one heck of a cheerleader.

Chapter 1

Evie blinked, then discreetly cleared her throat before letting a natural smile settle on her face. She could do this. All she had to do was listen. Smile and nod and listen. For the first time in months, she wasn't being asked to perform, with bright lights and no less than four cameras covering her and her co-hosts from different points along a hundred-and-eighty-degree arc. She couldn't say she wasn't *on*. Any time she left her apartment, she was Chef Evie Buchanan, the culinary princess of New York and star of the hot new morning show *The Dish*.

And at the moment, she was standing in the middle of the famed Holiman Library, elbow to elbow with well-respected food critics Elester Morger and Peter Hector. She was definitely on. Her agent, Nicole, and Nicole's girlfriend, Jane, rounded out their current little cluster. Conversation and alcohol flowed freely. Evie was trying her best to embrace the former and avoid the latter. The last thing anyone needed to be when stepping back out onto New York's slushy December streets was completely wasted.

No, the conversation wasn't the issue at all. From the moment Evie walked through the doors, she'd been greeted warmly as the unofficial guest of honor. It wasn't the conversation or the company. It was the music. The best holiday hits from oldies to today's covered classics. Evie loved the concept of Christmas until the music started playing in the hours following Thanksgiving, when an unmistakable lump lodged itself at the top of her throat. That same lump usually made an appearance twice more throughout the year. During the first few hours of her birthday and on the anniversary of her grandmother's passing.

Evie was grown now, established, accomplished, starring on a freaking TV show, but the first notes of any rendition of "This Christmas" always left her struggling to keep the tears at bay. Which would be fine if she could take a minute to hide and regroup in the ladies' fitting rooms in the middle of a crowded Macy's, but right now? She was on. If she could only find this mysterious, hidden DJ booth or the person holding the aux cord and ask them to maybe switch to the latest pop hits or some smooth jazz. Or maybe if she could find Blaire. Her best friend and roommate said she was taking a quick trip to the restroom, but that was over twenty minutes ago. Evie could excuse herself to go find her, but ditching two of the most respected men in her profession so she could cry in the bathroom with her friend about how much she missed her nan was a bit excessive.

Evie swallowed again. She could do this.

"I understand trends. I really do. But sometimes a

grilled cheese is just a fucking grilled cheese, and I'm not schlepping out to Brooklyn more than once to pay seventeen dollars for something my seven-year-old mastered last week," Peter said. They all laughed, Evie included. She'd been to T_G and tried one of their grilled cheeses, on the house. It was not worth the trek.

"I have to agree with you there. A little steep, but Donia is delightful," Evie added.

Peter swallowed a swig of his Pinot, nodding deeply. "That's why I gave them a B-plus with an asterisk. Donia is easily the sweetest woman in New York. Present company excluded."

The light burst of laughter that came out of Evie was a little more genuine this time. "Thank you, Peter."

"I get such a kick out of your asterisks," Elester said.

Peter shrugged and finished off the last of his wine. "Hey, it helps me to be a little more diplomatic. Some people ride that asterisk. I saw Michael Lowell last week—"

"From Montin. Newish place down in Alphabet City," Evie added for Nicole and Jane's sake.

"Right. I gave their shrimp carpaccio a D with an asterisk. He said they were booked up for weeks after the review dropped."

"What was the asterisk for?" Jane asked.

"They only play Springsteen, Joel, and anyone with an association to Clapton. I mean, there's a lot I'll put up with if you're pumping the room full of the Boss."

"Season two, Evie. Start every segment with 'Dancing in the Dark,'" Jane teased.

"Yeah, they like me in production, but they don't like me that much."

After being crowned the first Black winner in *Supreme Chef* history, Evie had returned to the city, prize money and a copy of *Fine Dining Magazine* with her face splashed across the cover in hand, only to discover she no longer had a job. Yeah, she'd been gone for over two months, but her former bosses at Nighly had told her that her skills were unmatched. With her running the kitchen, another reality-show win would only drive more customers through Nighly's overpriced doors. She'd seen proof of it after she'd won on the less involved, but equally popular Food Channel show, *The Chopping Block*.

But even though her presence alone had been enough to boost business, they weren't looking for an executive chef who was more interested in a chance at fifteen-minute increments of reality TV fame than the food. Evie would never forget the way Alexander, one half of the team who'd gotten the Manhattan hot spot off the ground, had leaned on that idea—that she didn't care about the food, which was especially absurd, since food was the only reason she'd moved her whole life to the city. Luckily friends of a friend had hot yoga'd with Nicole, who had some hot intel about a new daytime cooking show being shopped to the networks. Former NFL star Troy Smith-Wilson, the driving force behind the concept, was eager to get himself back into the spotlight. Soon, Evie had found herself doing camera tests with Troy and a rotation of two other hopefuls before they settled on interior designer Ashley

Simms and one of Evie's long-time idols Chef Mitchell White.

With season one only halfway complete, they had already received word that they had been renewed for two more seasons. And though she wasn't exactly sure she believed it, the producers had told Evie in no uncertain terms that she had been the key ratings draw. Evie liked to attribute it to the chemistry that the four hosts shared in front of the camera, but she couldn't deny how much her social media following had exploded. She was definitely popular, though maybe not enough to tell the producers what music they needed to play.

"If you ladies will excuse us, I see my darling friend Laurence," Elester said, nodding toward the far side of the room. Peter lightly kissed Evie on her cheeks and disappeared behind Elester through the crowd. When they were a safe distance away, Evie let her shoulders sag just a little.

"They love you," Nicole said.

"I know. They are both great," Evie replied before she nearly reconsidered her night's ban on alcohol. "Can I tell you something?"

"Yeah, of course." Nicole edged a little closer. Jane followed. She was so chill, Evie didn't mind her being in the inner circle.

"I'm having fun. Really, I'm having a good time."

"I get it. A work party is still a work party and you're a little zonked."

"You don't think I'm totally ungrateful?"

"No. I think you've been working nonstop for months and I know those shoes are uncomfortable as hell." Nicole glanced at her phone, forever clutched in her hand, before she looked up and gave the open mezzanines above a quick glance. "There are plenty of places to hide in here. Take a breather. Come back. Give me one more hour and then we'll all flee into the night."

"You're a saint. I'll be back."

As another of her grandmother's favorite Christmas classics ramped up, Evie took off for what looked like a side exit. She wasn't sure she was going to make the whole night without crying. She was too overwhelmed and too overstimulated by the music, the crowd, the tightness of her dress and, yes, the sexy but painful-as-hell high-heeled boots she was wearing. The little green sign came into clear view as she gently made her way past clusters of people. She could almost taste the sweet freedom of the freezing-cold night when a hand gripped her wrist. Evie stopped, and just as she was about to call on all her PR training to prevent herself from telling whoever it was to let the fuck go, she realized she was face-to-face with Blaire.

"Girl," her roommate said, drama dripping off the word.

Evie answered right back. "Girl."

"Okay. Once again, thank you for being a really good cook and thank you for being on TV and thank you for being my roommate and not kicking me out after you could afford to live alone and thank you again for bringing me to this party. Tops every faculty holiday party ever. I just ran into Kata and Rina in the restroom and they both said I look amazing."

Evie laughed, picturing Blaire and the pop duo

gushing over each other's outfits. She reached up and tucked the end of one of Blaire's faux locks back into the massive bun piled atop her head. "You do look amazing."

"Thank you." Evie smiled at her friend as Blaire tipped her chin skyward with the tip of her freshly painted fingernail. The smile didn't hold, though, and Blaire immediately noticed. "Hey, you okay? I know what Stevie's Christmas hits do to you. I can ask them to switch it up. I'm sure they'll do it for the princess."

Blaire's display of fierce friendship only made matters worse. If they had been in the comfort of their own apartment, Evie would have allowed herself a brief but good cry on Blaire's shoulder, but now was not the time and definitely not the place. Not to mention she'd spent nearly an hour in the makeup chair. Her makeup artist's go-to brand of mascara was waterproof, but she doubted her whole face could stand the rainstorm brewing inside of her.

"Yeah, I'm fine. Just a little stuffy in here. I'm just going to pop out into the hallway and get some fresh air."

"Okay. Text me if you need to fly the coop. I will go and see if I can find Raquelle." Evie had lost track of her assistant shortly after they walked through the door, which Evie didn't mind. Raquelle knew how to balance professionalism and play just fine. Still, one of them should check on her.

"Oh yeah. Please see if you spot her. Chef Pool is here and he's grabby."

"Eww. Okay, yeah, I'll find her." Evie squeezed her

friend's hand, then turned and made her way back toward the side exits. Before anyone could stop her for even the smallest of small talk, Evie pushed her way through the fire door, into an empty stairwell. She checked the door to make sure it wasn't about to lock behind her and then started to make her way up to the top floor. She got about halfway there before her feet started to protest. Five floors up would have to do. She took a deep breath and looked down at the nearly full champagne glass and the small cocktail napkin she still had in her hand. Rushing without spilling, a skill she'd learned in her first kitchen.

She took another deep breath and tilted her head back. She'd use gravity to hold her tears at bay if she had to. This was what she wanted. She'd leveled up, from baby prep cook, eager to prove herself, to reality-show star, and now she was on one of the most popular shows on television. This was what she wanted. She'd given up everything she had to get this far. She just didn't think this place would feel so lonely. She regretted the thought as soon as it flitted through her mind. One would think after more than ten years she'd have come to terms with the fact that she had no family. And that she had processed the even harsher truth that certain members of her family of choice had pushed her away.

Ten years, and still, on the heels of almost every thought about Nana Buchanan, there was his face. Zachariah Pleasant. Evie knew childhood crushes stayed with you, but this one refused to fade the slightest bit, even with thousands of miles and years of silence between them. She hadn't forgiven Zach for pretending he was breaking her heart for her own good, but there were times when she wished things had gone differently. Especially when she needed a break from work and the city. What she wouldn't give to be back on the Pleasant family ranch, enjoying the holidays under the warm California sun. Even if she could go back, it wouldn't be the same. Nana was gone, and Zach and his brothers had moved on with their lives. Still, for a split second Evie day-dreamed about what it might be like to join them for one more Christmas brunch and ride up to the canyon.

One tear managed to escape and Evie knew she had to pull it together. Delicately she dabbed under her eye, careful not to smudge her eyeliner. "You'll be in Barbados in three days. Pull it together," she said to herself. "Ten days of sun and relaxation. And nothing close to the smell of horses." Okay, she was able to make herself laugh. The one thing she didn't miss about home was those damn horses. Evie blew out another breath and gave herself a good shake before she started to make her way back down the stairs. She'd made it just a half flight down when she heard the door at the bottom open and close. She moved a little faster, gripping the banister so she didn't eat shit in her heels and go ass-over-Spanx down the stairs.

Evie hated being spooked in quiet places so she called down, announcing her presence as a courtesy. "I'm on my way out. Stairs are all yours." But there was no response. She moved a little faster.

When she reached the third floor, she came face-to-face with the absolute last person she wanted to see, especially on a night like this. Chef Melanie Burns stood there, leaning against the railing, an unlit cigarette between her lips. Evie could just picture her grandmother shaking her head, telling her that now was not the time to finally strangle her former castmate. In the shadows, toying with her lighter, she looked like a damn Disney villain.

Evie was too familiar with this type of behavior from Melanie. After all, they'd been together for six weeks before Melanie had been eliminated from *Supreme Chef.* It only took Evie a few hours to realize that her former castmate was a terrible person. There was a four-step process to dealing with Chef Melanie Burns. Step one: Listen. Step two: Simply say "okay." Step three: Walk away. Step four: Get on with your day.

"Melanie. Hi."

"Yvonne! Hello. What are you doing up here? Dark and dank stairwells are no place for a girl like you."

Evie let a faint smile cover her grimace. She wanted to ask Melanie what in the hell she was doing in the building, let alone the same dark staircase. Melanie was a thorn in so many sides. Evie had no clue how she'd managed to get an invite. Evie had submitted her own short list of friends and colleagues she wanted there. She couldn't imagine anyone wanting Melanie on their list. She was so damn unpleasant.

"Great party," Melanie went on. "But you knew that. Only the best for you, right?"

"For me? No. I think the season is the reason for this little soirée. It's a holiday party. Nothing else."

"Oh please. I came with Tim Malick. He told me how you are just killing it up in Studio F. This is definitely all for you."

Evie was going to have to have a chat with their production accountant. He clearly had no clue how disliked Melanie was.

"Melanie, you know this holiday party is for the cast and crew and friends of the show," Evie said calmly. The truth was like a tripwire for Melanie. It didn't take much of it to set her off.

"I saw the pictures you posted from Tiffany's wedding. Looked like the gang was all there."

Tiffany Lam and Evie had been roommates on *Supreme Chef* and ended up in the final two slots. Not only had Evie been the first Black woman to win, but with her and Tiffany in the lead it was the first time two women of color had been the ones to bring it home. Melanie hadn't been invited to Tiffany's wedding for pretty obvious reasons. There was nothing more to it.

"I dropped her a little note. Told her it would have been nice to be invited. I mean, she even invited the PAs from our season."

And that did it. For the first time in years, Evie actually saw red. Rage heat flashed all over her body. Evie resisted the urge to toss back the rest of her champagne or smash the flute over Melanie's head. Instead she finally said what was on her mind.

"That is so fucked up."

Melanie jerked back like she had been slapped.

"For *weeks* you were so cruel to Tiffany. Why on earth would she invite you to her wedding?"

"Cruel?! More like I told her the truth. Truth she needed to hear. Some of us don't need people like you kissing our ass all the time."

"You told her she reminded you of your friend from camp, only your friend from camp was skinnier. What grown woman insults another woman's weight for no reason? What grown woman is still bringing up camp?!"

"Whoa, look at you! All this time, so prim and proper. So calm, so collected. Who would have thought all you had to do was get Chef Yvonne Buchanan away from the cameras and her adoring public and the real bitch comes out?"

Evie hadn't realized she was raising her voice. She swallowed a different kind of knot that was now blocking her throat, and straightened her shoulders.

"Ah, there we go. TV-ready Evie. You're like damn pageant robot. No wonder the judges loved you. So lifelike, who'd think she was a real human?!" Melanie said with a harsh burst of laughter.

"Goodnight, Melanie." Evie turned to leave, but stopped when Melanie grabbed her wrist. She instantly shook her off.

"Wait, we're not done here."

"Oh yes, we are. I'm going to say this in the nicest way I can. Stay away from me, Melanie. And please," she added with more than a hint of disgust, "leave Tiffany alone. Excuse me."

Evie turned again and started down the stairs. Later she'd have a faint memory of the words "self-righteous bitch" practically seething from between

Melanie's clenched teeth and the feeling of both of Melanie's hands connecting with her back in a forceful shove. You could always count on Melanie's reactions to any and all situations to be outsized and hellishly dramatic, but pushing someone down a flight of stairs was way over-the-top, even for Chef Melanie Burns.

Chapter 2

Nicole took her ID back from the nurse at the reception desk and followed her instructions toward the elevator. The sound of her boots squeaking across the tile floor mixed with the sound of her heart thudding in her ears. She'd never been this stressed before. Maybe an indicator of how charmed a life she'd led up to this point. All of her clients were amazing, talented people who shared her desire to aim as high as possible. Evie Buchanan was the best of them all.

Which is why it hit her extra hard when they found Evie unconscious in that stairwell.

Evie was a private person. Like Nicole she was excellent at drawing an appropriate line between the personal and professional, but after Evie had once let it slip just how difficult the holidays were for her, Nicole understood why Evie might need a short break from the joyful spirit of the evening. When an hour passed and no one had seen Evie, Nicole knew something was wrong. She tried to keep her unease about the situation under wraps, but as the clock ticked closer to one a.m. and Evie still wasn't picking up her phone or responding to texts, Nicole decided it was time to have a conversation with security.

She cursed the gods for the fact that by the time they found Evie and the ambulance arrived, the bulk of the guests had moved on to more exciting after-hour activities. Nicole's first priority was making sure Evie got the medical attention she needed and then she was going to find out what the fuck happened in that stairwell. Getting answers was made exponentially harder with the party guests scattered to the wind.

Nicole found the elevator and waited for two nurses and a man pulling on his trench coat to step off before she stepped on and hit the button for the tenth floor. Evie had been in the ICU for over forty-eight hours. She was breathing on her own, but even though the doctors were able to sew up the nonfatal gash on the side of her head, she remained unconscious. Nicole had almost dropped her coffee when the text from Evie's roommate, Blaire, popped up on her cell. **She's awake.**

"Come on." Nicole used her knuckle to mash the door-closed button before checking her phone. She'd told Blaire to update her if anything changed on her way over to Presbyterian. Thankfully, her phone was bone dry. When the elevator finally hit the tenth floor, Nicole paused long enough to read the floor directory mounted on the wall before she turned left and took off at a run. Around another corner she found Blaire pacing outside an open door, tears running down her face. Their eyes met and Nicole's knees almost gave out. Blaire froze and then, realizing what Nicole was thinking, waved her over.

"What it is?" Nicole asked, her chest feeling tighter.

"The doctors—something's wrong. She can't remember anything." Nicole peered inside the room and felt the air rush out of her lungs. There was Evie, looking pretty worn-out and ragged, but alive nonetheless. She sat up in the hospital bed listening carefully to the doctor. She glanced at Nicole for just a second before turning her attention back.

Blaire wiped her face. "She woke up, so I called the nurse, but then as soon as I started talking to her I knew something was wrong. She just kinda froze and stared at me. It was eerie."

"Who's in there with her now?"

"That's Sophia, the nurse on call, and Dr. Manzo came in to consult. There was another doctor around here somewhere, but he wouldn't talk to me. Just the nurse."

"Great."

"Raquelle went to our apartment to get Evie's glasses. She said she couldn't see."

"She wears contacts?"

"Yeah."

"Did they kick you out?"

"No. I kinda lost it when she said she didn't know her name, so I kicked myself out. I'll go back in when I can keep it together. I can't believe this."

Nicole reached out and gave Blaire's upper arm a firm squeeze. "She's awake. That's what matters. Let's just wait and see what the doctor says."

"Okay." Nicole watched Blaire as she seemed to pull it together. It took a lot to bring Nicole to tears, but she didn't blame Blaire one bit. Nicole was doing her best to hide her own internal freak-out. Evie would be okay. She'd be fine.

"I think we have some friends of yours out in the hallway," Nicole heard the doctor say to Evie. "I'd like to invite them in and maybe we can talk about this together. Would that be okay with you?"

"Yeah, okay," Evie said as she looked back in their direction. Nicole could really see it now. There was something off about Evie's voice and not just the tone of it. She was such a polite person. Most of her sentences included some form of *please* or *thank you.* She was never this dry. Dr. Manzo stepped out into the hall and quietly introduced herself. Nicole filled the doctor in on her role in this situation.

"It appears that Yvonne is experiencing some memory loss. This sometimes occurs with head injuries." Nicole nodded, biting the inside of her cheek. She had to let the doctor speak before she peppered her with questions. "Just to clarify, neither of you are family or her significant other."

"No," Blaire said. "She's an only child and there's no boyfriend or girlfriend. And—no immediate family either. Everyone passed away. Wait!"

"Yeah?" Nicole urged.

"There was a guy. Shit, I can't remember his name. Evie grew up on a ranch and the people who owned the place—she made it sound like they were cousins or something. I think Raquelle knows."

"Okay. Why don't you come in, introduce yourselves, and we'll hold off on asking her any questions. Memory loss can be a little scary and very confusing.

It's best if we keep from distressing her any further. How does that sound?"

"We can do that," Nicole replied before she glanced over at Blaire, who appeared to have pulled it all the way together. She nodded before adding her own confident, "Okay."

"Good." Dr. Manzo dipped her chin and motioned for them to head on into room. Just as they were about to start their introductions, Raquelle hurried into the room, flushed and out of breath.

"Here, I'm back. Sorry. Here are your glasses," Raquelle panted. Nicole wondered for a moment if she ran up the stairs instead of waiting for the elevator. Dr. Manzo waited until Evie slid the thick pink frames on her face before continuing.

"Is that better?"

Evie blinked, looking around at her captive audience. "Yes. That's much better."

"Good. Why don't you go ahead," Dr. Manzo said with another dip of her head in Blaire's direction.

"I'm Blaire. Best friend, roommate, not ride-or-die, but ride-and-never-let you-leave-the-house-in-shoes-that-don't-really-go-with-your-outfit. I teach AP history at Hope Academy in Harlem. Oh, um. We've lived together for four years. It's been a good four years," Blaire said with a little laugh. Evie's lip lifted a bit at the corner, but it was far from a full smile.

"Evie, I'm your agent," Nicole said. "You have a career as a chef and you cook on a morning show. I've been representing you for a little over two years."

Evie nodded and uttered a quiet "Hello," but that was it. Nicole could see it in her eyes. Evie had no idea who any of them were.

"And I'm Raquelle. I'm your personal assistant. I do, like, everything you need and I help run your social media accounts. I'm your right hand, really." The girl was working up to a serious ramble, but Nicole didn't stop her. "You're allergic to kiwi, but it won't kill you. It just makes you sick. You're mildly allergic to strawberries, but you eat them anyway. Your dirty secret is how much you love Kraft Mac and Cheese. When Fenty Beauty dropped, you requested an extra sample kit just for me and that was the coolest thing ever. Definitely landed you the best-boss-ever award. Oh and you're a Pisces. Also you just got a new IUD so you don't have to worry about that for a little while."

The nurse piped up, giving Evie a warm smile. "These three ladies have been by your side day and night. You've got your own fairy godmothers right here."

"That's right." Dr. Manzo gave Evie a little pat on her arm before she turned to the nurse. "I think we should get Miss Buchanan in for another MRI. We'll definitely want to keep an eye on you for at least a couple more days. I don't want to get any hopes up, but we'll try to get you out of here in time for Christmas."

"You, um—you had a trip planned, but I'll contact the airline and see if we can get your money reimbursed or get you a flight voucher or something . . ." Raquelle trailed off, withering under Dr. Manzo's intense focus. Right now the less information they threw at Evie the better.

"Why don't we get out of their way and then we can check in with Dr. Manzo later," Nicole said.

"I'd like to stay. If I can," Blaire said. "I called out for the rest of the week anyway."

"Me too," Raquelle added. "I mean Evie's my boss. This kinda is my work."

"Can they stay?" Evie said, taking the whole room by surprise. She'd barely said a word.

"Absolutely," Dr. Manzo replied with a warm smile. "There's a cafeteria down on three. We'll send someone by as soon as we're finished."

"Okay. I'll head down with you," Nicole said. She stepped into the hallway and waited for Blaire to grab her bag before the three of them headed to the elevator. They all stood there in silence, as if they'd made some private pact to wait until they were safe in the elevator before they said another word.

"Fuck," Nicole said under her breath before saying it again, a little louder. "Fuck!"

"Yeah," Blaire added.

"So we just wait?" Raquelle asked. Nicole looked over at the twenty-three-year-old. She'd come on as Evie's assistant two months after she'd signed with Nicole. The three of them had been through a lot together in such a short period of time. A traumatic brain injury was not something she wanted to add to their group bucket list. Nicole let out a short breath, then turned to face them.

"Okay. Both or either of you stay as long as you can, but I think you should take turns and one of you should go home and try and get some sleep. We're no good to Evie if we're dead on our feet."

"I can't sleep. Sorry. I'm too wired," Blaire said.

"Same." Raquelle sighed.

"I'll probably crash out later, but now—"

"Yeah, no, that's fair. I feel like I'm crawling out of my skin," Nicole admitted. The door dinged on five. An elderly black man stepped on and pressed the button for the ground floor. Nicole would have to wait to lay out the rest of her game plan. When the doors opened on three, she ushered Raquelle and Blaire out into the hallway and found a quiet corner next to a vending machine.

"Okay. Protocol stands. If anyone has any questions you direct them to me." Nicole hated to sound so calculated, but the narrative was everything. The police had spoken to as many of the party guests as they could and still no one had a clue how Evie had wound up so badly injured in the stairwell. With no real facts, folks were left to gossip.

If people thought Evie couldn't handle her booze or keep her balance at a simple holiday party, that could cause problems for her extremely clean image that, in her case, reflected the real thing. Evie had worked way too hard for her career and her brand. The last thing Nicole wanted was a set of loose lips screwing things up with Evie and the producers on *The Dish.* "Has Evie's phone quieted down a bit?" she asked Raquelle.

"Yes, and I did like you said. Ignored all the general texts expressing concern and responded as myself to personal friends. She slipped when one of her heels broke and bumped her head."

"Excellent. For now. Evie is doing much better. She's just going to lay low for the holidays and get some rest. Got it?"

Nicole watched Raquelle's throat work as she processed her instructions. When she nodded,

Nicole went on. "I'll let the network and production know she's up and about and will be ready to go when we're back from the break. I have to run back to the office. I have a meeting at four, but 9-1-1 text me if anything else comes up. I'll swing back by tonight. You going to be okay?" she asked Blaire. Tears were lining her eyes again.

"Yeah, I'll be fine. I'm just worried about her. She had no idea who we were."

"I know. Let's just think best-case scenarios for now. Her memory could come back in the next few hours. We panic when we need to panic. Try to at least take a nap. You're a good fucking friend, Blaire, but you can't be there for Evie if you can't stand up."

"Okay. I'll get some sleep. I promise."

"Oh! What was that business about the ranch? The cousins or something."

"Right! Raquelle. Evie told me you have all her in-case-of-an-emergency info saved, right? There was some guy she grew up with on that ranch. He knew her grandmother?"

"Oh yeah. Um . . . the last name was Pleasant. I have it my docs. Hold on." They waited as Raquelle's finger flew across her phone screen. "Jesse Pleasant. He uh . . . hold on one sec. Big Rock Ranch, Charming, California."

"That's it!" Blaire said with a loud snap of her fingers. "I knew she was from some town that sounded extra cutesy."

"But she told me literally only to call him if she dies," Raquelle said.

"Okay. Well, she's not dead," Nicole replied. "But let's keep that number in the top of the contacts."

"Why? What are you thinking?" Blaire asked.

"I'm thinking about what we're going to do if her memory doesn't come back."

Evie snapped out of a deep sleep, her whole body jerking. Her eyes blinked open as her heart thudded in her chest. It was so much so fast, she closed her eyes again. Her head still hurt a little. She'd been dreaming and she wasn't ready to wake up. She knew she was in the hospital. She'd spent almost a whole day being subjected to tests. There had been an accident and she'd hit her head and now she couldn't remember a thing. But she wasn't alone. When she'd woken up the first time, the woman named Blaire, who was apparently her best friend and roommate, had been by her bedside and she'd stayed there most of the day. Blaire answered her questions and helped make a little more sense of what she was missing.

She was a chef who starred on a morning television show. There had been a holiday party and she'd fallen down some stairs. Blaire had showed her pictures they'd taken while they were getting dressed for the party. She now recognized Blaire with her luminous brown skin, beautiful hair, and bright smile, but the woman next to her in the photo was a complete stranger. When Evie asked to see a mirror and was presented with Blaire's cell phone camera so she could look at her face, she still felt like she was looking at a stranger, but this time the stranger wore glasses and had bandage on the side of her head. Not knowing her own face—hell, being unsure of her own name—filled Evie with a kind of unease that she couldn't put into words. But something told her at the very least she could trust Blaire.

When she wasn't having her body's metrics taken or subjected to various scans, or listening to Blaire, she slept. Three times throughout the day and all through the night, she slept hard. Every time she'd had a weird dream. Bits and pieces of each dream still lingered. She remembered this most recent dream so clearly, she felt like she was still working her way through it.

It made no sense to her, but somehow there were two suns. One blazing overhead. She'd forgotten her bandana and her cowboy hat, and the sun was beating down on the back of her neck, beating down on the crown of her head. The other sun was setting in the distance, painting the sky purple and pink. She made her way toward the horizon on the back of a large brown horse, but she was riding backward. She could still see the horse's tail flicking rhythmically as they made their way down the trail.

And then there was this man walking beside the horse. A gorgeous Black man wearing a black cowboy hat and a Lakers jersey. Kobe 8. When she saw him, she realized the heat she was feeling wasn't from the sun. It was the heat radiating from the smile on his face. She could feel that heat coming up from her stomach and spreading all over her cheeks and down the back of her neck. She could still hear his voice. He laughed at her, teased her. They were going to be late. She wanted to tell him to stop making fun of the way she was riding, but her tongue wouldn't work. It didn't seem to really matter, though. Deep down she didn't want the teasing to stop.

Evie tried to open her eyes again and this time her body was better prepared. Carefully she tried to sit up, pushing herself up against the thin pillows.

"Hey. You're up?" Evie looked over at the chair beside her bed. Everything was blurry, but she had heard the owner of that voice enough in the last twenty-four hours. It was Blaire. "Here. Here are your glasses." Evie took the pink frames Blaire placed in her hand and slid them on her face. Much better. Her room was dim, but she could see. Blaire was wrapped in a blue hospital blanket, her legs stretched out in front of her.

"Hey. How are you feeling?" she asked.

"Okay," Evie tried to say. She cleared her throat and tried again. "Better. Thank you. Did you sleep here all night?"

"In the hospital? Yeah. One of the nurses pointed me toward an empty room. I got to spend a couple hours not in a chair. How'd you sleep?"

"Okay. I think. I had a weird dream. I was riding a horse backwards." She didn't mention the man.

"Oh wow. That must have been some dream."

"Did I ride horses? Do I?" Evie asked.

"Um, I don't know for sure, but maybe. You told me you grew up on a ranch. Maybe they had horses. You don't talk about your childhood much, actually. Did the dream make you think of anything? Any memories?"

Evie paused a moment and tried to get back to her dream. Bits of it were already fading. All she could see—and almost still feel—was the horse under her and the man. She could still see his smile and hear his laugh, but there wasn't much else. She remembered yesterday. Meeting Blaire and the other two women, her agent and her assistant. She remembered the MRI and how nice Dr. Manzo had been and the sweet nurse who brought her double dessert, but whose name she didn't catch. That was it. Nothing before waking up in the hospital.

"No. I can't think of anything."

"The doctor said it might take a few days. It'll be okay." Evie didn't have any response to that. Instead she just watched Blaire as she started fiddling with her phone, before holding the screen for Evie to see. "Does this guy look familiar to you?"

Evie looked at the picture of a large, muscular Black man in a suit, black cowboy hat in his hand. She thought back to her dream, but this was a different man. "No. Who is he?"

"His name is Jesse Pleasant and you grew up with him. Nicole and I were talking and we think we might give him a call. He might be worried about you. I found a Jesse Pleasant Sr. who is also kind of a stone-cold silver fox, but he's much older and he's an actor on some BBC cop show. This is your guy."

"Is he an old boyfriend or something?"

"I don't think so. You never mentioned him like that, but he's fine, isn't he?" Blaire said with burst of laughter. Evie looked at the phone screen again.

"He is handsome."

Evie tried to ignore the frustration she felt when

Blaire's smile faded a bit. Maybe *handsome* wasn't the word Blaire wanted to hear.

"Anyway, so yeah. We were thinking since—ya know, before—you told Raquelle this guy was your last-line-of-defense type of emergency contact, we could call him and let him know what happened, let him know you're here. And then we can go from there."

"Okay. Yeah, that makes sense. Is he family?"

Blaire's expression really dropped this time. She reached out and took Evie's hand. Her fingers were warm, so Evie did her best to hold still. "No, honey. Remember yesterday we mentioned it was just you and your grandma, and your grandma died about ten years ago. But let's call Jesse. He might as well be family. Maybe. I think it would be good to at least talk to him. And maybe all together we can look at all of our options for when they are ready to release you."

"Right. Since I can't remember anything."

"Right. But don't worry. I got you, boo." That little laugh was back again. A knot tied itself in Evie's throat. She wished she could laugh with Blaire and share in whatever relationship she was sure they had, but there was nothing. Just Blaire's warm hand on hers and lingering thoughts of an unknown man.

Chapter 3

Zach Pleasant did nothing to hide his smug smile. Once again, he got exactly what he wanted. His grandmother reminded him constantly that it wasn't polite to gloat, but when he knew how much it annoyed his older brother Jesse, he didn't see the point in reining it in. Their ranch foreman, Felix, wasn't helping the situation either. His own grin of amusement tipped up the corners of his thick mustache as he glanced between the Pleasant brothers. All three of them stood around the large mahogany desk in the center of Zach's office. They just had to finalize a few details and the deal would be done.

"So you want to confirm delivery for the first Saturday in January?" Zach said.

"Yeah, let's go ahead with that. I'll have a sit-down with Arnie and the boys. We'll aim to have him down at your place that morning." Don Milcher's voice came through the speakerphone loud and clear. The Pleasants had done several deals with the quarter-horse breeder over the years. They'd been very pleased with everything Don had brought to the table and today was no exception. "I'm almost sad to part with him. My granddaughter's in love."

"That's exactly why I want to get him out here. We need a little something to bring that sparkle back to the youngins." Zach had no Southern accent to speak of. He was born at Cedars, right in the middle of Beverly Hills, and raised in SoCal his whole life. Didn't stop him from pulling out a fake accent every now and then for dramatic effect.

"Alright. Alright." Don laughed. "Now you're laying it on a little thick. He's already yours, Pleasant."

"Don, I'll have everything handled by noon," Jesse said.

"Perfect. Always a pleasure, boys."

"Would you say it was a *pleasant* experience?" Zach added.

Don let out a loud groan that rolled into more deep laughter. "Felix, give him a shot to the chops for me, will ya?"

"I wish I could, man. I wish I could, but he cuts my checks."

"Can't mess with a man's money. Until next time." They said their goodbyes and Zach ended the call. He leaned back in his chair, stretching his arms behind his head.

"You happy now?" Jesse asked.

"Brother, you know I am."

It was the start of another stellar week at Big Rock Ranch, Southern California's most exclusive luxury dude ranch. Christmas was just days away and they were completely booked with families and couples who wanted to do something a little different this holiday season. The ranch was even booked for a

large New Year's Eve wedding to close out their year.
And now Zach was about to be the proud owner of a
gorgeous black-and-white paint foal whose sire he'd
not so quietly coveted for years, the perfect Christmas present for himself—and the ranch.

"I'm going to head back out. You need anything
else from me?" Felix asked, looking between Zach
and Jesse.

"No, I don't think so," Zach replied just as his
office door popped open. His baby cousin and assistant, Lilah, poked her head in the door.

"Sorry to interrupt, but Jesse, there's a Nicole
Pruitt on the phone and she said it's urgent. Something about someone named Evie Buchanan." she
said. At the mention of Evie's name all the air was
sucked out of the room. There wasn't a day where
Evie didn't cross Zach's mind, but there was a
strange, unwritten rule amongst his family and any
staff member who had been on since the days of
Amelia Buchanan—no one mentioned Evie's name.

The sound of Felix's Stetson slapping against
his thigh snapped Zack out of his state of shock.
"I'll let you boys handle this." Felix knew better than
to hang around for this conversation. With a nod to
both Zack and Jesse, he made a break for it, giving
Lilah a fatherly squeeze on the shoulder as he went.

"What the—" Zach's gaze flashed back to his
brother. To strangers Jesse came off as calm and
cool, but Zach knew all his tells. He didn't miss the
way his brother's throat worked. A thousand questions ran through his mind, and from the look on
Jesse's face, Zack knew he had the answers. Zack
stood up so fast he almost knocked over his chair.

"Did she say what it was about?" he asked Lilah, but Jesse spoke up before she could answer.

"Tell her I'll be with her in a moment. You can put her through to my office." Jesse made for the door, but Zach was quicker than his brother, who had at least four inches and fifty pounds on him. He vaulted over his desk and blocked Jesse's exit.

"What are you doing? Move," Jesse said.

"What is going on?"

"That's what I'm trying to find out, so unless you're going to WWE me to the floor and stop me from taking this woman's call, I think you better get the hell out of my way."

"Fine." Zach moved from the doorway, but followed Jesse as he marched across their shared reception area, by the sleeping form of Jesse's dog, Clementine, and back into his private office. Jesse glared at him as he rounded his own desk, but Zach didn't give a shit. He sat right down in one of the available leather chairs. "Put it on speaker."

This time Jesse gave in and hit the speaker button at the bottom of his landline phone. "This is Jesse Pleasant."

"Jesse, hi. My name is Nicole Pruitt. I'm Evie—Yvonne Buchanan's agent. Yvonne's assistant had you down as her emergency contact."

"Hello, Ms. Pruitt. I'm here with my brother Zachariah. Is Evie okay?"

"She's alright, but we have a bit of a situation." Zach looked up and he could see the fear clamping down on his chest reflected in Jesse's eyes. "There was an accident." They both listened carefully as Nicole Pruitt detailed what had happened to Evie at the holiday party for the cast and crew of *The Dish*. Zach's bedroom DVR was filled with episodes of the daytime cooking show, but he had only made it through one episode. Zach tried not to dwell on why that was as Nicole Pruitt went on to detail how Evie had been unconscious for nearly two full days and how she was now rolling through her third day of complete memory loss.

"Why didn't you call me when it happened?" Jesse asked.

They could both hear the hint of annoyance in Nicole's voice when she replied. "Mr. Pleasant, I found my client bleeding from a head wound at the bottom of a flight of stairs this weekend. I apologize if I didn't think to reach out to a man that Evie has never mentioned before. She told her assistant only to call you in the case of a fatal incident. I needed to be sure calling you was the right thing to do."

Zach and Jesse looked at each other. There were some details missing. Jesse let out a deep breath and rubbed his bald head. "Okay, well, what can we do now? How can we help?"

"Gentlemen, I'm willing to admit when I'm in a little over my head. The hospital is going to discharge her in a few days and I know Christmas is right around the corner, but she—"

"She still has no memory and you don't have a game plan," Zach said.

"Exactly. The doctors are optimistic that her memory will at least partially return, but I'm trying to think long- and short-term here. I'm thinking about her health and her career. She's too recognizable and well-known to be walking around Manhattan with no clue who she is. And if we make it through the holidays without further incident, she has to be back on the set of a cooking show the second week in January, and I'm not sure if she remembers how to cook. Or how to play for the cameras."

"Damn," Zack let slip.

"Yeah, damn is right. And I know this is all kinds of wishful thinking on my part, but I'm hoping seeing your face might bring something back from her childhood. It's not everything, but it would be something."

"Understood," Jesse said. "I'm going to send you back to my assistant, if you can give her the details. I'll be on the red-eye tonight."

"I'd appreciate that. Evie would too."

Zack watched Jesse as he transferred the call back to Lilah. "You're Evie's emergency contact?" he asked.

Jesse grabbed the black Stetson his father had gifted him for Christmas a few years back. Zack had a matching hat in tan. "We're not talking about this right now. You got things covered here? I should only be a few days," Jesse said as he made for the door.

"Hold the fuck on. Answer my question."

Jesse gestured toward his phone, his eyes flashing wide with exasperation. "Clearly I'm her emergency contact. And clearly there's more important things for me to deal with right now than me explaining this all to you."

"Alright, well, I'm coming with you."

"Zach."

Zach sucked his teeth. "Man, nah. Don't. Don't act like *I* don't know what's going on between me and Evie. Or what isn't. But you just said, Evie is the priority now. And I want to be there. Plus, which one of us do you think has a better chance of shocking her memory back?"

Jesse sighed and Zach knew he had him. All three of them, their baby brother Sam included, had been close with Evie, but Zach and Evie had history.

"Fine. I'll get with Lilah and handle our flights and everything. You can go talk to Delfi and let her know she's steering the ship while we're gone, and then you tell Miss Leona that we might not be back by Christmas morning." With Sam off with his latest girlfriend and their parents deciding not to return to the States for the holidays, the plan was for the two of them to spend Christmas with their grandmother and their baby cousin, but it looked like that plan was about to change.

"Why are you acting like she won't understand? She loves Evie. Hell, she might want to come," Zach said.

"Just go talk to her."

"I will. I got it covered."

Jesse started for the door before he paused and turned back toward Zach. "Whatever you're thinking," Jesse said. "Whatever you're feeling, it stays here. You might want to be the one to swoop in and save the day, but that's not going to work this time. And if Evie does remember you—"

"I know."

"All that bullshit, Zach. I mean it. It stays here. And if you can't handle that, then I'm leaving your ass behind."

Zach just nodded. Their dynamic had been set in stone the moment Sam learned to talk. Jesse was the brains, Zach the mouth, and Sam the charm, but now he heard Jesse loud and clear. Jesse would pull rank for Evie's sake if he had to. Zach had screwed up big-time and pushed Evie away when she needed him most. Now was not the time to try and mend that fence, but that wouldn't stop him from being by Evie's side. This time he was going to be there for her, whether she knew him or not.

Zach usually had the ability to fall into the deepest sleep seconds after takeoff. But it was long after they'd reached cruising altitude on their red-eye flight to JFK and he was still wide-awake.

Evie Buchanan. Holy shit. Back when they were kids he didn't fully understand the way he'd felt about her, but now that he was finally a grown man he could admit that Evie had been the first girl to really stir something in him. When she arrived at Big Rock to live with her grandma, she'd been awkward and shy, but it didn't take long for her to break out of her shell.

She'd followed Zach and his brothers all over the small valley town they called home, trying to keep up with them at every turn. They may have been the same age, but for a long time Zach looked at her as a little sister. They had a good time running from one end of the ranch to the other, and Zach had even better time teasing the shit out of her.

He wasn't sure when her obvious crush on him

had gone from just that to full-blown infatuation, probably around the time her grandmother had made it clear that she didn't want them left alone together anymore. Teenagers were sex-crazed hormone monsters, drawn together by the powerful magnets anchored in their genitals, according to Amelia Buchanan, but *lustful* wasn't the way Zach would describe the situation. For him it had been a gradual thing. Slow, burning feelings (that, he could admit, did lead to Evie making more than one appearance in his teenage fantasies). By the time he realized what he felt for Evie was definitely more than just friendly affection and teenage horniness, she was gone.

He became a master at explaining his feelings away. Charming was small. There weren't many girls his age to begin with. Proximity was the problem. On more than one occasion, their mother had assured all her boys that they'd probably meet their wives in college, but deep down a part of him wondered if Evie had been the one.

Ever since they'd gotten off the phone with Nicole, all Zach could think about was their last night together. He'd fucked up. He'd fucked up real big. So big that what he hoped would be his attempt to comfort and reassure her that he'd always have her back, ended with Evie in tears, begging him to stay out of her life. At first Zach had stopped himself from calling or texting Evie, because he wanted to respect her wishes. Weeks turned into years, and when he didn't hear a word from her he knew she'd meant business. She truly wanted a Zachariah

Pleasant–free life. He'd be lying if he said it didn't bother the shit out of him.

He glanced over at Jesse, who was taking full advantage of the extra legroom first-class had to offer. "I know you told me to chill, but I gotta ask."

Jesse let out a quiet groan. "Can't help yourself, can you?"

"Listen, we touch down in New York and you won't hear another word about this from me."

Jesse opened one eye and peered at his smart watch. "Fine. You have five minutes."

"We don't land for another three hours."

"And you think I'm talking to you about Evie for the next three hours? You are out of your mind."

"Fine. I just have one question anyway. Why you?"

"Why me what?"

"Why did Evie have you down as her emergency contact?"

"You sure you want to know?"

Zach paused a moment and ran through all the worst-case scenarios. The one that topped the list had his brother and Evie in a sexual relationship that they somehow managed to keep under wraps for ten years. Luckily, even though Jesse could keep some secrets, he rarely left Charming. A secret affair was out.

"Yeah, tell me."

"I didn't know she made me her emergency contact. She didn't tell me."

"But you know why she did. From where I'm sitting, I don't see the difference between her putting down you or Sam. Or Miss Leona."

"Are you saying if there was an emergency you'd call our baby brother, who is available two months out of the year, or our eighty-year-old grandmother before you called me?"

"'Course not. You're my emergency contact. Then Lilah. Then Pops."

"I answered your question. This little chat is over."

"I have a few more minutes and you're still not being all that slick. Why you?"

"I'm going to tell you and then you are immediately going to let this shit go. I would like to at least get an hour of sleep before we land."

"Fine. Go."

"We've kept in touch."

"This whole time?"

"Yeah, this whole time."

"Wooooooooow," Zach said as he leaned back against the headrest.

"Now. Let it go."

"You mean to tell me—"

"That since you broke her heart and she decided she couldn't deal with your wishy-washy noncommittal crap—"

"Noncommittal?!" Zach hadn't meant to disrupt the peaceful quiet of first class, but his brother was on some first-class bullshit.

"Hey, maybe don't get us arrested as soon as we step off the plane."

"Sorry." They might be wealthy, but Zach couldn't forget they were still flying while tall and black.

"Anyway. You couldn't decide whether you had feelings for her or not, and she was the one who ended up getting hurt. End of story."

"That's not what happened."

"Right now, man, I don't really care. We have to do what's best for Evie *now*. You have to deal with your revisionist history on your own time."

"Whatever."

"Your time's up. Watch a movie or something."

Zach just grunted in response. A movie wasn't going to distract him. "When you say you kept in touch, how often are we talking? Like birthdays and holidays, or do you and her have a group chat with Sam and you're just yukking it up seven days a week?"

Jesse opened his eyes and leaned against the armrest between their seats. He fixed Zach with the glare he'd learned from their father. The glare that meant if they pushed one more step they were going to get worse than a spanking. Luckily the glare had been so effective, none of them had had a chance to experience Jesse Sr.'s full wrath firsthand. Not that Zach thought his brother would actually fight him mid-flight, but he didn't really wanna see what pushing Jesse to the limit meant for him. Fired up Jesse and the Hulk had a lot in common.

"Drop it, Zach."

Zach searched his brother's eyes for a moment. Jesse wasn't playing this time. "Jesus, you're just like Senior."

Jesse sat back and stroked his beard as he closed his eyes. "I know. It's why he left me in charge."

"He left *us* in charge. Check that FAQ on our website."

Jesse finally cracked a small smile and Zach knew that order had been restored. Sensing sleep still

wasn't in the cards, he pulled out his phone and
connected to the inflight network. He'd distract
himself with unread emails instead of dwelling on
just how many times he'd wished a new text alert
from Evie would appear. He couldn't think about
the fact that in a few hours they would finally be
back together, face-to-face, and she would have no
clue who he was.

Chapter 4

Evie couldn't climb out of the ravine. Nana had told her more than once not to chase after the boys, but Evie didn't listen. She followed them down the narrow path on the promise that they had something cool to show her, but now she was all alone, trying to scale the smooth diamond-coated walls that lined the shallow stream.

"You want a boost?" Evie heard the familiar voice say, and for some reason an angry heat spread out over her face. She looked over and there he was, squatting beside the water. He picked up three pink acorns and skipped them all at once to the other side. Hot tears bit at the back of Evie's eyes.

"No. I don't want a stupid boost. This is all your fault."

"I know, and that's why I'm trying to help you. Come on." He came closer and laced his fingers together. All she had to do was step in his waiting palm and he could hoist her up, but the wall was too high. Even with his help she would only be able to reach halfway. "Hop on, Buck."

"No. I got it."

"Yvonne! We gotta go!" Evie looked up and saw Nicole in a puma mascot costume standing on the ledge above, the furry fierce head tucked under her arm.

"I'll be right there."

"Just let me help you." He chuckled some more.

"No. I got it." But she didn't have it. She tried and tried, but her cowboy boots couldn't find purchase on the slick diamond wall. She tried once more, jumping as if her quad strength would propel her some twenty feet in the air. It didn't. She fell and kept falling, the desert floor swallowing her up. When she landed she was on a rainbow parachute, sprawled out on the floor of the old barn. A dirty green Coke bottle in the middle was pointing to her, but the barn was empty, except for him.

"I guess it's your lucky day," he said, with that damn chuckle.

Evie felt herself frown, but that didn't stop her from crawling across the parachute. *"Just kiss me and get it over with,"* she grumbled. She closed her eyes and leaned in, but she felt nothing. When she opened her eyes, he was gone.

"Okay, now wipe your lips with this." Evie took the damp paper towel from Blaire and wiped the sugary, exfoliating crystals off her lips. Instantly her mouth felt better. She rubbed her lips together, marveling at how soft and smooth they suddenly felt.

"Good, huh? Now put on this lip balm. Shanny recommended it, and we always trust Shanny."

"She does my makeup?" Evie asked before she used her finger to apply a bit of the fresh-smelling balm. It had been three days since she'd woken up in the hospital. The doctors were somewhat pleased with her progress. She felt better moving around for short periods of time and she didn't feel like she needed to sleep most of the day. Her head still ached, but the area around her stitches had stopped throbbing. Still, her memory hadn't returned. Dr. Manzo had assured them all that Evie would be fine, but the more time she spent with Blaire and Raquelle, the more complicated she realized total memory loss was.

She knew nothing about her best friend or her assistant, nothing about the people and things they mentioned to her, nothing about herself. All she could do now was rest and heal, and pray her brain did what she needed it to do. If not, she'd just have to build new memories, learn new things, and possibly start her whole life from scratch. She couldn't think about her career at the moment. That was too much to consider.

Nicole had sent out a press release, stating that Evie was doing just fine and resting, but requesting privacy at this time. It didn't stop people from sending tons of texts to Evie's phone, texts Raquelle was thankfully managing. It also didn't stop people from sending dozens of bouquets of flowers to her hospital room. Evie was overwhelmed by the continuous deliveries.

"Right."

"And she sent the white and yellow roses."

"Yup. You're good at this!"

Evie tried not to sound disappointed with her pitiful progress. "Who are those from?" She nodded toward another bouquet of flowers on her bedside table.

"Let me see." Blaire snatched up the tiny white envelope. "Oh, these are from Tiffany! You two are really good friends."

"Does she live in New York?"

"I think she's actually in Spain right now. That's where her husband is from." Evie knew sometime soon she was going to have to leave this hospital, and while Blaire had been amazing, she wouldn't be able to hold Evie's hand every day, filling the gaps and explaining the ins and outs of Evie's personal and professional relationships, who was friend or foe. If Tiffany was a good friend, the idea of seeing her and not knowing who she was didn't sit well with Evie, even if it was outside of her control.

"They got married a few months ago. You were a bridesmaid. You looked amazing." Suddenly Blaire's phone made that little chirping noise that signified she had a text. She'd shown Evie how her phone worked and how she usually silenced it when she was in her hospital room, but they were waiting to hear from Nicole. Evie watched as Blaire's fingers moved quickly across the screen before she tucked the phone back into her sweater pocket. She offered Evie a warm smile.

"That was Nicole. She just met Jesse at his hotel. He came with his brother Zach. They should be here soon."

Jesse Pleasant. The name had been rolling around in her head since Blaire had shown her a picture of the California rancher she apparently had family ties to. She'd asked to see his picture a few more times and found herself straining to place the man in the dark cowboy hat with the man who was now making a constant appearance in her dreams. It seemed like every time she closed her eyes, wherever her sub-conscious mind took her, the man and that brown horse seemed to be there.

The horse felt more like an accessory, but the man, his smile, Evie was now convinced he meant something to her. Every time she saw his face behind her eyes, an unexplainable warmth filled her chest. But while Blaire and Raquelle seemed to have a pretty comprehensive list of all of Evie's friends and coworkers, this man remained a mystery. Maybe meeting Jesse in person would help her connect the dots. He might not be her mystery man, but at that moment he was the only person in her life who might know anything about that horse.

Not that the man or the horse was the most pressing issue of the moment. Jesse was coming to see her for a very specific reason. Nicole had done her best not to stress Evie out, but she saw things very clearly. If Evie's memory didn't return right away—or worse, ever—she needed a safe and private place to recover and rebuild, and that place wasn't her Manhattan apartment.

Blaire couldn't keep an eye on her forever, and *babysitter* was outside of Raquelle's job description. Evie was worried about running into friends and not knowing their faces or their names, but she also knew how bad it could be for her, both personally and professionally, if she ran into someone looking to do her harm. They needed a plan of action, and there was a good chance that plan would involve Jesse Pleasant.

"What should I say to them?" Evie asked.

"What do you want to say to them?"

"I have . . . questions, but I guess I should just see how it goes. You and Nicole and Raquelle have been amazing. What if they aren't nice?"

"If either of them doesn't treat you right, we'll kick them out."

Evie swallowed a lump that had suddenly appeared in her throat. "I guess I should ask them about my parents and my grandmother."

Blaire reached over and took her hand. "Just take it slow. Remember what Dr. Manzo said. Overwhelming yourself with information all at once won't help." Evie knew she was right. Every time there were breaks in her conversations with Blaire and Raquelle, Evie felt exhausted. So many names she tried to connect with pictures of faces. She didn't even know her own address. And then there was the whole other list of questions the three of them simply couldn't answer, like how she'd gotten the very noticeable scar on her forearm. All she wanted to do was remember. Asking Jesse to dump her whole life story on her in one sitting might not be the best way to go.

They went back to their match game, putting names and faces to the most recent floral arrangements. As Blaire was doing some digging online for an Armand Waller who had sent Evie a dozen red roses, Nicole sent another text.

"They're on their way up. Don't be nervous. Nicole said they seem perfectly chill."

"I'm not nervous," Evie said. "I'm just—back to what Dr. Manzo said. I have to take my time. I want to know everything they know, but asking someone to tell you everything they know might not be the best thing to do."

"I'm sure they'll do their best to fill you in. Don't worry." Again, Evie knew Blaire was probably right, but as soon as she accepted that fact, another type of inexplicable unease settled in Evie's stomach.

"I know this sounds silly, but do I look okay?"

She'd looked at at least a dozen photos of herself in the past few days. She had no idea what Jesse and his brother were expecting, but she knew there was no way she looked as put together as she did on her social media. She wore makeup in her "dressed down, hanging at home" photos on Instagram.

"For real?" Blaire cringed.

"Yes."

"You look like you got hit by a car—but! The glasses are helping. Those frames are so cute. You should wear them more often. The cuteness is balancing out the shock of the bandage. Plus I can see a difference after you exfoliated your lips. Your lips look great."

Evie reached up and gently touched the protective gauze on the side of her head. They'd had to shave a chunk of her hair to get through the tracks of her sew-in just to clean the wound and suture her up. Her lips wouldn't work as a distraction. Not that she had anyone to look good for. "I'm being silly. It doesn't matter what I look like. I just need to talk to them."

"It's okay. You're meeting guys for the first time since your accident. And cute guys. I mean, Jesse is fine and I bet his brother is fine too. Actually." Blaire jumped up and checked her shiny locks in the mirror. She looked great. She pouted her lips and reapplied some shinier gloss before she jumped back into her chair. "You look fine. Don't worry about it."

"Okay." Evie swallowed again, worrying.

"Here." Blaire handed Evie her glass of water. She took a deep sip. She had no reason to be nervous. That didn't stop her heart from counting out the seconds it took before she heard footsteps coming toward her room.

"Right in here," said Nicole's now familiar voice. She entered first. Behind her was one of the largest men she'd ever seen. Jesse Pleasant towered over Nicole, ducking his head under the doorjamb as he walked in. He was more attractive in real life. Dark brown skin, bald head, a nicely manicured beard, broad shoulders in a nicely tailored, dark green suit jacket. She noted the black cowboy hat in his hand for a moment, but then another man stepped into the room behind him.

Evie assumed it was Jesse's brother, Zach Pleasant. She knew—for a fact—he was the man from her dreams. Not as tall as Jesse, but still large and broad, Zach was extremely handsome. He had a crisp haircut; shaved on the sides, thick dark curls on top, and he also had a wonderful beard. His suit jacket was dark blue. Evie couldn't take her eyes off of him.

"How you doing today, gorgeous?" she heard Nicole say.

"I . . . I'm feeling better. Thank you," she managed to say. "Hello."

"This is Zach and Jesse. This is Blaire Edwards."

"Evie's roommate." Blaire stood and shook hands with them. Zach was carrying a cowboy hat too. As far as Evie was concerned he was the most handsome man in the world. Yes, she'd only seen pictures of men on Blaire's phone and the few male members of the hospital staff who'd been tasked with her care, but she was confident Zach was it. He was the ideal man. And then she heard his voice.

"Looks like an FTD showroom in here," he said

with a short laugh. She knew that voice. She'd heard it teasing her in her dreams.

"Yeah, a lot of people are worried about our girl," Blaire replied.

"I believe it."

"Are you comfortable?" Jesse asked suddenly. She didn't know him—not like she should—but she could tell something was wrong. For such a large, imposing man his voice sounded so unsure. She tore her gaze away from Zach and looked at Jesse. He stood at the foot of her bed nearly blocking out all the sunlight from the window.

"I'm sick of being in this bed, but I'm okay. Thank you for asking."

"Why don't Blaire and I give you guys a little space. I'll go out and try to sneak you in something better than whatever they're going to serve you for lunch," Nicole suggested.

"I'm gonna call my mom, but I'll be right outside. Unless you want me to stay," Blaire said.

Evie glanced at the looks on Jesse and Zach's faces, both expectant and wary. Trust seemed like a strong word when it came to men she had just met, but she did want to speak to them, maybe with a few less people crowding in her hospital room. "It's okay," Evie said. "You can go."

"I'll be back in a few minutes," Nicole said with a tight smile.

Blaire leaned over and squeezed Evie's hand again. "We'll be right back."

"Okay."

Evie watched as Blaire and Nicole walked out of the room and instantly it felt like they took all of their comfort and ease with them. Not that she was afraid of Jesse Pleasant or his brother Zach. Clearly Jesse was important to her if he was her emergency contact. But once again, she was with complete strangers who somehow knew her better than she knew herself. They were all silent for a moment.

"Man." Zach let out an odd chuckle, shaking his head. Then he looked right at Evie before sitting on the edge of her bed.

"What is it?" Evie asked.

"Nothing."

"Please tell me. Dr. Manzo said that it's best if people don't assume I'll get an inside joke or be able to read their cues. I can't. You know things that I don't remember." Evie felt awful for the way the warm smile on Zach's face immediately dropped, but she knew she was right. There was so much she didn't remember.

"Shit. I'm sorry. You're right. Nicole mentioned that. She said that you didn't seem like yourself and she was right."

"What's missing? What's the most obvious thing?" Evie asked.

"Well, for starters you would have asked me what the hell I was doing here the moment you laid eyes on me."

"Why?" Evie asked.

"We can talk about that later," Jesse said, a bit of authority reinforcing his voice. Evie wanted to question him again, but from the way Zach clammed up she figured she should drop it for now. "How have they been treating you here? How are you feeling?" Jesse asked.

"Well. Better. The nurses are very nice and Dr. Manzo has been very patient with me. They've been letting Blaire stay beyond visiting hours, so that's been nice. I don't feel so alone."

"Man!" Zach sprang up with another laugh and slapped his tan cowboy hat against the side of his free palm. "This isn't weird to you?"

"You're not helping," Jesse said, his voice sounding dangerously tight.

"This isn't weird to *you*? I'm not talking about her. I'm talking about all of this." He motioned between the three of them. "When have the three of us ever had a conversation this tense and tight. Nicole said don't confuse her. She didn't say we should act like damn robots around her."

"I don't want that. Please be yourselves around me."

"See?"

Jesse threw up his hands in surrender and leaned against the corner of the windowsill. Zach seemed to take that as some sort of cue. He sat back down on the bed, closer this time. Evie could feel the warmth of his leg pressed up against hers through the thin hospital bedding. It reminded her of the warmth from her dreams. She looked up into his dark brown eyes and was shocked all over again at the familiar feeling. He meant something to her.

"You look like hell, Buck," he teased. It made no sense, but something in his perfect smile triggered something deep inside and Evie started to cry.

Chapter 5

So much for not fucking things up. Before Zach could let an "Oh shit" slip, Jesse had shoved him out of the way and Nicole and Blaire came flying back into the room, rushing to Evie's bedside.

"What happened?"

"What's wrong?"

"I'm fine." She sniffled before letting out another hiccup that turned into a sob. Zach's chest started to ache at the sound. It had been almost a decade since he'd been face-to-face with Evie Buchanan. Nicole had prepared them for the shock. Evie wasn't herself, she'd told them more than once. Plus, she was still pretty banged and bandaged up. She'd warned him, but he wasn't prepared for how weak and fragile Evie looked in that hospital bed. The glasses and the fact that she hadn't cussed him straight the fuck out the minute he walked into the room had thrown him off too.

The tears were something else though. The Evie he knew was too proud to cry in front of him, or anyone for that matter. He looked at her, stunned, as more tears squeezed out of the corners of her eyes. She didn't know him, but something he'd said had set her off. Maybe it jogged a memory.

"Here. Move." Jesse shoved Zach against the other wall and handed Evie a box of tissues.

"Thank you."

"Are you okay?" Nicole asked.

"Yeah, I—I just thought . . ."

"You thought what?" Zach asked.

"Nothing. I think I've been a little overwhelmed and it just caught up with me, having new visitors. I didn't mean to—"

"You don't need to apologize," Jesse said. "Maybe we should come back later. Let you rest some more."

"No! No. Please stay. Blaire said you might be the closest thing I have to family."

"That . . . is true," Jesse said.

"You don't remember anything about growing up with us?" Zach asked, watching her face closely.

Evie carefully shook her head. "I've been having dreams about horses and the desert, kind of, but none of it makes sense. I can't connect any of the pieces."

"We're in town as long as you need us," Jesse said.

"Yeah. We're not going anywhere until we get this all sorted out. We don't have to talk about anything now. We can just kick it with you for a little while."

"No." Evie sniffled again, but now her tears seemed to be under control. She wiped her face with a fresh tissue. "You didn't come all this way just to hang out with me."

"We don't mind. Do we, Jess?" He turned to his brother and was given the firm nod of confirmation he and Evie both needed. This meet and greet had gone to shit, but Zach didn't want to leave Evie's side.

"It's whatever you want," Blaire chimed in.

"I'm sorry. I hate stressing you all out."

"Nonsense," Nicole said. "We're here for you."

Zach watched Evie's face as she focused on the edge of the bed for a moment before she looked up. "Can I speak to Zach alone for a few minutes?"

Her request was music to Zach's ears, but he didn't miss the storm cloud that passed over his brother's face as he leaned away from the window. Jesse's brows drew together, a warning, before the expression dropped and he looked back in Evie's direction. "I'll go with Nicole and grab you some lunch."

"Thank you. I have questions for you too, but maybe one at a time will be easier."

"Absolutely."

Blaire made a little motion with her hand, reminding Evie that she'd be right outside on the phone. Once they were alone, Evie's eyes were back on him. There was so much Zach wanted to say, so much he needed to say, starting with "I'm sorry." But he waited.

"Do you want to sit down?" she asked. Her voice was the same, but it had this odd, gentle lilt to it, like she was working so hard not to offend him. Zach sat down on the edge of the bed, his leg pressing against hers. He carefully placed his Stetson on the other side of her bed.

"It's good to see you," he said.

"Even like this?"

"Yeah. Well—it'd be better if you weren't in a

hospital bed, but yeah. It's good to see you, even like this. I was pretty convinced that you'd never speak to me again."

"Why?" she asked. He was terrible at this not-confusing-her thing. Zach took a deep breath and knew he had to come clean. She might kick him out, but it was her choice.

"I fucked up after your grandmother died. I was trying to comfort you and I said the wrong thing. Or a dozen wrong things, and you told me to stay out of your life."

She frowned, like she was trying to do a difficult math problem. "What kind of things? What did you say?"

"That you'd be better off without me and our two-horse town, but I think what set you off was when I stopped you from kissing me."

"Oh." Then Zach saw it. Evie made a face, eyes popping wide with stunned understanding. He knew that face and knew the laugh that usually followed it. She didn't laugh this time, but the expression was enough to give him a bit of hope. Evie just needed some time. She'd be back to her old self. And if he knew the old Evie she wouldn't waste a moment cussing him smooth the fuck out whenever the time came. But for now . . .

Zach moved a little closer and took Evie's hand. "So, talk to me, girl. What else do you want to know?"

"Were we ever . . . were we ever a thing? Were we ever together as a couple? I know there's probably more pressing information, but I want to know."

"What makes you ask?"

"I've seen you. Before now, in my dreams."

Zach coughed and did his best to redirect his train of thought, but it was already speeding down a certain track. Evie had no memory of anything, but somehow, he'd made it through the haze of her amnesia. He wasn't going to let it go to his head, but he was pretty sure Jesse had one hell of an *I told you so* coming his way.

"No, we were never together, but we had a thing."

"What kind of thing?"

Jesse was going to kick his ass. "It's not important right now."

"I understand that you probably have your reasons for not wanting to tell me, but I think it's Nicole's plan to possibly send me back to Charming with you. You may know me, but I don't know anything about you. You can see how that puts me at a disadvantage. If something happened between us, I have the right to know."

She had a point. She was surrounded by people who were a thousand steps ahead of her. It was only fair that she be given a chance to catch up.

"I'll give you the abridged version because I don't want to make you more upset. You had a crush on me when we were kids and I didn't really understand how I felt about you until you moved away for culinary school. When I saw you again, I thought it was—I don't know what I thought, but I said and did the wrong things. We fought and we haven't spoken since."

"This was—"

"About ten years ago," Zach admitted, hardly believing it had been that long. He'd missed Evie like crazy, but now that they were back together—forget her injury—it felt like it had been no time at all. He ignored the wave of conflicting emotions that threatened to crash over him and settled for giving her hand a gentle squeeze. She returned it even though she was clearly busy trying to sort things out in her mind.

"So, we haven't spoken in ten years?"

"Yep."

"But I've talked to Jesse. My assistant, Raquelle, found some texts in my phone." Irrational jealousy heated Zach's face.

"He mentioned that you two had been in touch. What happened in these dreams?"

"Um, we were usually somewhere hot and there was a brown horse."

"Ah, maybe you were remembering Chestnut."

"Is that your horse?"

"No, that was your Nana Buck's horse, your grandmother. You learned to ride on him." Zach pulled out his phone, but before he pulled up a picture of Amelia with her beloved quarter horse, he thought twice about it. "Blaire didn't tell you about your nan, did she?"

"No, she never met her. She just repeated back a few of the things I told her over the years, but it wasn't much."

Zach tried not to think about the years following the funeral. The Christmases, the birthdays when Evie should have been back in Charming or at least gotten to video chat with the whole gang at the ranch, and how she'd been alone, because of him.

"I'm not sure this is the best idea, but do you want to see a picture of her?"

"Yes," Evie said without hesitation. Zach fished out his phone and googled a picture of the acclaimed horse trainer who had made herself a fixture at Big Rock Ranch long before he was born. There were pictures of Nana Buck in his grandmother's home, but over time they'd faded into the background. It had been a while since Zach had really looked at her sharp brown gaze and her welcoming smile. He handed Evie his phone and waited as she took in the image of her grandmother.

"What happened to her?" she asked.

"She had a heart attack."

Evie was quiet for a few long moments, just looking at the screen. Zach sat quietly, fighting the urge to break the silence with a joke or distraction.

"She's not what I expected."

"Oh yeah?"

"All the pictures I've seen of myself I'm so dolled up. I figured if she raised me, I got some of that from her."

"Nah. You were a tomboy through and through. I think the glamour is just for the cameras."

Zach half expected Evie to roll her eyes or suck her teeth, but she just kept staring at the phone.

"What about my parents?" she finally said.

"You lost them in a car accident."

"You probably don't have any pictures of them."

"No. They passed away before the internet was really a thing. You did post a picture of them on your Facebook a long time ago, but after you started the show you deleted your personal account." Not that Zach had gone to look her up a dozen or so times.

"Oh."

"Hold up. You said I was in your dreams and then you asked if we'd been together in real life. Were we *together* in your dreams?"

Evie stared at him for a minute and Zach saw it again, that trademark stubbornness. The Evie he knew was definitely in there. She drew herself up, straightening her shoulders and letting out a deep breath. "No, there was just—there were things I'd rather not discuss right now."

Zach couldn't hide his smile this time. "That's cool."

"Can you tell me about your family? What's the ranch like?"

"Sure thing. Let's see, there's me, and you met Jesse, and we have a younger brother named Samuel. You and Sam got along great."

"Do you have a picture of him? Sorry, I just have so many blanks. It's all blank. Blaire keeps telling me about people and I keep hoping something will come to mind and there's just nothing."

"Nah, don't apologize. Here." Zach moved to the chair beside her bed and pulled up the private family Instagram account his baby cousin had put together. Lilah had done a great job as unofficial family historian even though things were a little tense between her and her parents at the moment. Zach hadn't taken enough time to appreciate how much she'd done to keep track of their accomplishments and everyday moments. He showed Evie pictures of Sam and his horse, Majesty.

"He's an actor. He hooked up with this girl on his last film and now he's spending Christmas with her family."

"Do you like her?"

"She seems alright. Here's Lilah. She works at the ranch for me and Jesse." He swiped through to more pictures of Lilah and a few of their other cousins, Penny, Wiley, and Sage. By the time he got to the pictures of Senior's last birthday party at the ranch, Evie seemed more comfortable. Her tears had dried for real and she was actually smiling as Zach told her how pissed his mom had been when his dad ruined his own birthday surprise.

"Are you close with your parents?" she asked.

"Ah, yeah . . ." Zach said, trying to think of how to explain the relationship there. He knew how lucky he and his brothers were. They had two loving parents who only wanted the best for them. It didn't change the sting of his father walking away from their family business. Zach and Jesse had proved themselves more than capable of running Big Rock. Still, it was something they thought they'd be doing *with* their father. He only had himself to blame for the shattered expectations there, and that annoyed him even more.

"You don't sound so sure." Evie dipped her head a little, forcing him to look her in the eye.

"Nah, my dad's great. I just—we—" Zach stopped himself as soon as he heard Jesse's voice in the hall. "Actually, let's maybe get into that another time."

Jesse and Nicole walked into the room, bringing the smell of hot food with them. Nicole held up the plastic bag in her hand.

"Grilled chicken salad and some coconut cake for you, and a grilled cheese for Blaire."

"Here, let me." Zach hopped up. He took the bag from Nicole and started setting up Evie's lunch on her bedside table.

"Thanks. We saw Dr. Manzo on our way up," Nicole said.

"What did she say?" Evie asked.

"She'll be by to check on you in a bit, but she's pretty sure they are going to discharge you the day after Christmas. I know spending the holiday in the hospital won't be fun, but Blaire—"

"She said she's going to come by as soon as they open presents," Evie said. Zach could tell she sounded a little disappointed, he just didn't understand why.

"Do we have some other plans?" Zach asked Jesse.

"I—we'll be here."

"Great. I have to go visit my folks," Nicole said. "But I'll be back in time to see you off."

"You should spend time with your family. Raquelle showed me how to use the video chat on my phone," Evie said. "I can just call you. You don't have to rush back."

"Nonsense. I'll be here. Don't worry. You should eat your lunch while those leafy greens are fresh. You gotta get your strength up," Nicole said. She flashed Evie a smile that turned ice-cold as she turned in his direction. "Uh, Zach, can I have a word?"

"Yeah, sure." Zach had known Nicole a whole two hours, but he knew what a woman's friend who was getting ready to drag the hell out of him looked like. He slid Evie's dining tray into place over her lap, then followed Nicole out into the hall. She closed the door behind them.

"Hey. Hi," she said, getting right to it.

"What did Jesse tell you?"

"He didn't tell me anything. She started crying the minute you opened your mouth."

"Listen—"

Nicole held up her hand to silence him. "I get it. You two have history. Do you still have feelings for her?"

Zach answered as honestly as he could. "Yeah, there are feelings."

"Is there a woman or many women waiting back in Charming?"

"No. Jesse and I are very focused on the ranch right now. We both decided that work and our family are the priorities for now."

"Jesse's single too?"

"Yeah. Why?"

"Just thinking." Nicole let out a quick breath, then looked Zach dead in the eye. He spoke up before she could really lay into him.

"I get it. Evie is your client. You're just looking out for her, but she is family to us. Yeah, it may have been a while, but we wouldn't have dropped everything, including our grandmother, on Christmas Day, flown out here for someone we didn't care about. It's freezing outside." That made Nicole laugh. "We'll take good care of her."

Nicole considered him for a moment, her eyebrow arching up.

"You don't trust me."

"I don't trust guys who look as good as you. Evie's under enough stress. She feels untethered as hell. She doesn't need a guy whose smile reduces her to tears, stressing her out even more. Did she remember you? Did she tell you anything?"

"Apparently I've been popping up in her dreams. Me and her grandmother's horse, but she didn't know who I was. Just that I felt familiar to her."

"Oh," Nicole replied, shocked.

"I didn't jog her memory, but something about me is trying to get through."

"Well, that's something. Dr. Manzo will want to know."

"We'll let her know."

"Yeah. I didn't know your grandmother was Leona Lovell." There were no secrets when it came to Miss Leona. Just a little digging and you could find her connections to Big Rock, but none of that was as interesting as the Oscars, Grammys, and the few Tony awards she had under her belt. Most people his age knew her best for her recurring role as Althena George on the hit medical drama *Rory's War*, Thursday nights at nine, only on ABC.

"She loves Evie too. She's already offered to—"

"I know. Your brother said."

"I know how fucked up this all is, but we got her. Trust me."

"Fine. But do me a favor and turn the charm down about four hundred percent. I'm gay as hell and I can see why she's having dreams about all this," she said, motioning toward the general area of his face.

Zach laughed, flashing her his thousand-watt smile. "I have no idea what you're talking about."

"Yeah, I'm sure. Let's go back in there."

"After you."

Blaire came back a few minutes later and the four of them kept Evie company until Dr. Manzo and one of the nurses came by to check on her.

"Oh look, the gang's all here!" Dr. Manzo said. "I'm gonna have to ask you to excuse us for a few minutes. I try not to do exams in clown-car settings."

"Sure thing." Nicole assured Evie that they'd be right back, then led the whole gang to a small waiting area on the floor below.

"So," she said.

"You said be prepared, but I wasn't prepared. I'm seeing glimpses of the old Evie in there, but she's not herself," Zach said.

"She'd be best off staying with our grandmother. We all live on a private cul-de-sac, but our grandmother's home has plenty of room to accommodate her and any private staff we bring on to assist. Private garden. The works," Jesse added.

"Yeah, that makes sense. I don't—I'm just at a loss here, fellas. I'm covering for her with the network, but that'll only work for so long."

"You worry about her job and we'll take of everything else. If Evie's on board, day after Christmas she's coming back with us," Zach said. "It's doesn't have to be permanent thing, but you were right. We can't send her back to her apartment like this.

And, Blaire, we know you need to get back to your life soon."

"I wish I could stay," Blaire replied with a grimace. "But yeah, my school only offers so much PTO."

"I imagine your grandmother has decent security at the ranch," Nicole said.

"Yeah, we have high fences, cameras, half a dozen loud dogs between our houses," Zach said. "Most people don't know she has a place in Charming though. Why?"

Nicole took a deep breath. "There's something else. I'm not entirely sure Evie fell."

"What, you think she was pushed? Why didn't you tell us that before?" Jesse demanded. Zach didn't blame him one bit.

"Yeah, there's a big difference between an accident and a murder attempt. How's the security been here?!" Zach said.

"I didn't say anything about attempted murder. I just know Evie. She wasn't drinking, and even if she tripped, I'd expect her to pop up with a skinned knee, maybe a broken wrist. You didn't see her when we found her. I just don't think it was an accident."

"You told the police?" Jesse asked.

"Of course I told the police, but do the police in California do hardcore investigations of living victims they think just got a bad bump on the head?"

"Okay, you have a point," Zach admitted.

"As soon as she woke up, they officially didn't give a shit, and I can't tell the network to make a fuss because they'll replace her immediately if they hear anything about memory loss. Something just smells fishy as fuck and I'd rather be safe than sorry. Who knows, her memory might come back in two days and she can tell us everything that happened, but in the meantime, I don't just want her to have some place to rest. I—"

"You want her to go into hiding," Zach said. Nicole nodded, before her whole body trembled with a stressful sigh.

"Does Evie know?" Zach asked.

"No. She's already hypervigilant, which is good, but the memory loss is enough. I don't want to traumatize her even more with a hunch."

"No one's been by to see her but us, and Raquelle hasn't noticed any weird texts or comments on her social media," Blaire said.

"Okay. Here's what I need." Jesse rattled off a list of things he wanted to make sure Evie had for her trip and everything Blaire and Nicole would need from her in her absence, like her half of the rent. "I'm sure she has more than enough to cover her bills, but just to take the stress off you, we'll handle it for now. She can pay us back later if she insists."

"I'll call Raquelle and between the two of us we can pull that all together," Blaire said. "Actually, let me just head back to my place now. I'll call you guys in a few hours."

"Thank you."

"You know, anything for our girl." She kissed Nicole on the cheek, then took off for the elevator. They waited a few more minutes before heading back up to Evie's room. They caught Dr. Manzo on her way back down the hall. She answered the few administrative questions Jesse had about arranging an outpatient nurse for Evie when the time came, and then she suggested they cut down their get-well group. Evie was overwhelmed.

Zach and Jesse could agree there. Plus, it was Christmas Eve. Blaire and Nicole had gone above and beyond and now it was time for them to get back to their families. Zach and Jesse had it from here. They exchanged numbers and agreed to check in with each other over the next twenty-four hours.

"You guys know how to get back to your hotel?" Nicole asked, as she pulled her scarf out of her purse.

"Yeah, we're good. Thank you for everything. I think we're gonna go catch some shut-eye and then one or both of us will be back for visiting hours tonight."

"Good deal. I'll talk to you soon." She nodded to them both, then headed down to the elevator.

"Why don't you go in and sit with her for a while," Zach suggested, pulling out his phone.

"What are you doing?"

"Looking for the closest Macy's. We need to get Evie some Christmas presents." When Jesse didn't come back with some sleep-deprived order or demand, Zach glanced up from his phone. "She has to spend Christmas Day—"

"I wasn't gonna argue with you. You go. I'll stay here."

"Thanks, man."

The minute he stepped outside he realized two things. One, he didn't have a proper winter coat.

Two, he really didn't know his way around Manhattan. Didn't matter. He donned his Stetson, which shielded his face from the falling snow, then caught the first cab that stopped for him and went to straight to Macy's. Everything was pretty fucked at the moment, but at the very least, he could finally step up and be there for Evie.

Chapter 6

When Evie fell asleep, Jesse had been at her bedside. After he'd paced back and forth at the foot of her bed, explaining their plans following her discharge, he'd stuffed himself into the blue hospital chair and did his best to keep her entertained. Apparently, Zach had to run out and grab something he'd forgotten. Jesse was on bedside-companion duty. He told her at length and in very boring detail, everything he could about Big Rock Ranch. Like how many staff the whole property employed and the seasonal schedule they had to keep during the winter due to the weather. It was difficult to trail ride after a heavy rain.

Jesse took his role as the ranch's co-owner and financial manager very seriously, which Evie appreciated, but he was, if Evie was being kind, maybe not the best at explaining the more captivating details. When Evie stopped asking follow-up questions, he took the hint and decided to download one of his favorite stories called *The Night Before Christmas*. After he read it out loud, Evie asked if they could watch something on TV. Jesse was very sweet, and

Evie could tell he was trying his best, but Blaire was definitely better company.

He found some movie called *Love Actually* and they watched it in silence until Evie fell asleep.

When she opened her eyes again, it was still dark, but she could tell it was morning, and now there was a different California rancher beside her bed. She reached for her glasses and turned to face Zach.

"Merry Christmas," he said, flashing her a sleepy smile.

"Hello. Where's Jesse?"

"We're doing shifts. Not sleeping for over twenty-four hours and changing time zones? Not a good idea. He's catching some shut-eye back at the hotel, but he'll be here in a few hours."

There was so much Evie wanted to say. She wanted to tell him she'd missed him last night, which made no sense. She didn't know him. Not really, but when she looked at him in the dim light coming from the far side of the room, all she could feel was the warmth from her dreams. She'd spent a few days in a row with Blaire, but in some ways Zach just felt more familiar. She couldn't say that she felt comfortable around him. Comfort didn't come with the odd flutters that rippled through her stomach every time she thought about him, flutters that compounded themselves now that he was in the room with her. She couldn't explain it, but she liked having Zach around.

"We have more stuff for you back at the hotel, but I got you a little something." Zach reached into a bag at his feet and handed her a thin rectangular box wrapped in festive Christmas paper. A silver bow was tied around one corner.

"I didn't get you anything." Evie realized how ridiculous that sounded the moment the words left her mouth.

"I think it's okay. It's the thought that counts. Open it."

Evie turned the box over and gently pulled the tape loose on the blue and white snowflake wrapping paper. When she opened the lid to the box inside she found a pink diary with a sparkly white unicorn on the front. Beside it were two new pens tied in a bow, a tiny lock, and a set of small keys. The lock didn't look like it would provide any actual security, but the set was very cute.

"I don't know if you still journal, but you went through like five diaries a year when we were kids. You had one like that when you moved to the ranch."

Evie searched her mind for a memory, but came up blank. She picked up the diary and turned it over in her hands. She didn't know what to say, but she didn't mind when Zach filled the silence.

"You're on one hell of a ride. Might be good to have somewhere to write down your thoughts."

Evie thought about her dreams. Maybe keeping track of them would help. "This is—this is wonderful. Thank you."

"How'd you sleep?"

"Okay. I don't like this bed. It's not very comfortable."

"Miss Leona will hook you up. The beds in her guest rooms are comfortable as hell."

"Miss Leona is your grandmother. That's what Jesse said. I'll be staying with her."

"Yeah, if you've decided to come with us."

"I don't think I really have a choice."

Zach frowned as he moved a little closer to the bed. "Yeah, you do. Nicole came up with a good plan and none of us want you out walking the streets of New York like this, but you have a choice. We can hire a nurse for you. Whatever you need."

"Jesse mentioned that too."

"But . . . ?"

"I think coming back to the ranch might be the best idea. Jesse told me more about it last night. It sounds nice."

"You loved it there. I think you'll enjoy coming back. Did you have any more dreams?"

"About you?" Evie said. She felt herself glaring at him as that same tightness from her dreams flared through her chest. The crush she'd had on him was real and, apparently, so was the way he loved teasing her. She hated it. Kind of.

"Hey, I didn't say anything about—"

"What did you dream about?" she asked him right back.

"I didn't dream about anything. I was so tired, I hit the sheets in the hotel and it was a wrap. We'll get you out of here and into a nice, soft bed and you'll know that good sleep."

It sounded heavenly, but that wasn't the answer she wanted. "You like giving me a hard time, don't you? You're just like this in my—"

"In your dreams. You can say it. I won't be mad."

Evie sighed and tried not to roll her eyes.

"Here's how I see it. Something about me is trying to make it through the fog in your memory."

She didn't want to give him the satisfaction of agreeing with him, but what he said had some truth to it. Something in her mind was showing her bits and pieces of her life, of her past, and for some reason all of those bits and pieces included Zach. "That's a good way to describe it."

"You cried when I called you Buck. You've had more than one dream about me, but you didn't recognize anyone else in the pictures I showed you. I think that only means one thing."

"What's that?"

"I am a vital part of your recovery."

It was too early in the morning to have this conversation, but Evie couldn't stop herself. "You like giving me a hard time and you're full of yourself. If I come back to the ranch, how much time do I have to spend hanging out with you?"

A stuttered cough that turned into a laugh burst out of Zach, and Evie realized how quietly they'd both been speaking.

"Give me crap if you have to, but I think it's only fair if you admit how much you've been thinking about me," she said.

"Every day for the last ten years, and there might have been a few dreams in there too," Zach confessed, and then for a moment all his bravado seemed to leave the room. Evie sat still as his eyes roamed over her face, and finally settled on her mouth. Her lips were still smooth, from the day before. She's taken

Blaire's advice and applied more lip balm before
she'd gone to sleep. If her lips looked as good as
they felt, maybe Zach might try to kiss her.

But she wasn't ready for that.

"I have to use the restroom," she said. She set aside
her new journal and started to slide to the edge of
her bed.

"Oh, shit. Sorry. Do you need me to call a nurse?"

"No, just help me up." Zach gently took her elbow
and held on as she shuffled to the small private
bathroom she had in her room. "I got it from here.
Thank you." She slipped inside and used the facili-
ties, then slowly made her way back out. She needed
to be up and walking more. Her legs felt terrible.
Zach was waiting right outside the door when she
opened it. She gladly let him help her back into bed.

"Nicole asked me if I still have feelings for you,"
he said as she straightened her covers over her feet.

Evie ignored the fresh wave of heat that rushed
over her chest. "What did you tell her?"

"Absence and distance, all that shit," he said with
a shrug and a smirk, but Evie wasn't in on the joke.

"What?"

"I do. Nothing changed."

"Except ten years and a critical head injury. What
if I start to develop a whole new personality and you
don't like it? That's one of the risks of memory loss."

"What scientific journal says that Zach Pleasant
will no longer find Yvonne Buchanan appealing?"

"That's not what I meant. What if we spend more
time together and I don't like you. What if—"

The door popping open interrupted their back-

and-forth. Nurse Lyle entered. "Good morning, Yvonne. And Yvonne's friend."

"Good morning," she replied.

Lyle stopped and looked Zach up and down. "I heard some real deal cowboys had come to see you, and I see the rumors are true." Zach was wearing jeans and suit jacket, but his cowboy hat and his boots probably gave him away.

"How do you do?" Zach said with a sudden twangy accent. He touched his fingers to his forehead and winked at Lyle.

"Well then." Lyle pretended to swoon. "Deep from the heart of Texas."

"He doesn't even talk like that!" Evie said, shocked at her own annoyance and even more shocked at how quickly it melted away when Zach turned that smile back on her.

"I'm Zach. Nice to meet you," he said in his normal voice. "From SoCal, not Texas. But a cowboy all the same."

"I'm Lyle. And I can see you're trouble. If you'll excuse us, I just want to check Yvonne's stitches."

"By all means."

Evie held it together as Zach tossed another wink her way and backed out the door, his hat gripped in his hand.

"Whew, girl. You are in trouble," Lyle said as soon as they were alone. "No one should be that fine this early in the morning."

"Please," Evie said. "Don't rub it in."

* * *

Nicole knew she was overreacting. It had been over a week and Evie was doing much better. Nothing suspicious had happened in the days since her fall. All over her social media there was nothing but well wishes, and the executives at *The Dish* had agreed to find a short-term replacement for Evie until her doctors cleared her to return to on-camera work. Who didn't love a guest host? They sent their version of love and support, but Nicole knew both came with an expiration date. Nicole held Evie's contract in the back of her mind, the only assurance that for at least the next six months Evie still had a job.

She spent Christmas Day helping her mother cook and only snuck away once to watch *The Dish*'s pretaped Christmas special.

Early the next morning she drove back into the city and went straight to the hospital. She took the elevator up to Evie's room and the whole way she reminded herself to breathe. Evie Buchanan was one of the best in the industry. A talented chef with a pure heart, and a dream client. Professional and a pleasure to be around. This was business, Nicole knew it. She tried to remind herself, but it was too late. Evie was a friend now, and Nicole cared. She was worried.

She reached Evie's floor and found she was the last to join the farewell party. Jesse and Zach were standing in the hall with an orderly who was waiting with a wheelchair.

She pushed down the lump in her throat before she spoke.

"Everything all set?"

"Yup, they're just having their final debriefing," Zach said.

"We have a car waiting downstairs," Jesse added.

Worry still poked at Nicole, but she found comfort in how efficient and competent the Pleasant brothers turned out to be. She poked her head in the door and saw Evie surrounded by Blaire and Raquelle. Nurse Lyle was helping Evie into her coat.

"I wrote down everything," Raquelle said. "The passcode to your phone. The password to your laptop. The password to your Instagram, but don't bother with that. I'll take care of it until you're ready. I have dozens of cute holiday food posts, throwback recipes ready to upload. The works. I will keep your adoring public busy until you're ready to come back."

"I packed all your favorite clothes. Favorite pajamas," Blaire said. "You have like a three-month supply of contacts in there if you get sick of your glasses, and I gave Jesse your prescription if you want to order more."

Nicole turned to Jesse. "Anything else you need from me?"

"Not that I can think of. We'll cover Raquelle's paycheck and Evie's part of the rent until we're out of the woods, and then we can revisit."

"You guys—" Nicole started, but Zach waved her off.

"Don't worry about it. You have the network to deal with. We'll handle everything else."

"Okay. Keep me updated. I sent you my assistant's number too, just in case."

"Yup, we both got it."

"She's in good hands, Nicole."

"I know. I know. Just—you know, the fear and un-certainty. Amnesia seems so much more fun on TV."

"I'll call you every day when I get home from work and you can text me whenever you want," Blaire said before she stepped back into the room, pulling Evie into a tight hug. "I want to hear all about the ranch and all the beautiful horses."

"Oh, that reminds me." Nicole turned back to Zach. "Maybe don't parade her around the ranch. I mean, I don't want people to know where she is, but I also don't want your guests trying to photo-graph her."

"Already on it. Don't worry. We got this. Nothing but private moonlit tours. If she wants them." There was no hint of planned seduction in Zach's voice, but that didn't stop Nicole from turning her laser focus right to Jesse.

"Don't let him take her on moonlit tours."

"Don't worry. I won't."

Zach's quiet chuckle filled the hall.

"Get in here, Nicole," Blaire said, waving her over. Nicole didn't miss the tears lining Blaire's eyes as she stepped into the room. She walked right up to Evie and fixed the edge of her fur-lined hood.

"You won't need this jacket in California, but it'll keep you warm on the plane. Take this time to rest and heal. Don't rush it, be kind to yourself. Your memory will come back. I know it."

"Thank you," Evie replied.

"You can call me anytime."

"I will."

Nicole stepped a bit closer then, and lowered her

voice. "Please, for the love of God, watch out for Zach. I know he's a sweet-talker with a megawatt Colgate smile, but the last thing you need is a messy friends-with-benefits situation right now. Trust me."

"Oh no," Raquelle whispered. "Definitely sleep with him. Like, you have to. Make him wear the cowboy hat when you sleep with him."

"Yeah, sorry, Nicole. I'm with Raquelle on this one," Blaire said with a bright smile. "When you're feeling up to it, you should definitely sleep with him. I'm sure they have a hayloft. That's an experience I think you need to have. A new memory."

"I don't even know if I like him. I'll figure out what I want to do if my memory doesn't come back first, and then I'll decide if starting any kind of relationship with any man is a good idea."

"See, that's the Evie I know and love. Career and self first. Tumbles in the hay second," Nicole said as she tried to force a smile. "Come on. Let's get you out of here."

They said their final round of goodbyes and then Evie was off, a pair of comically large sunglasses and an oversized hat giving her a bit of privacy—or drawing way more attention than necessary. Nicole, Blaire, and Raquelle hung back as she was wheeled to the elevator, the Pleasant brothers following close behind. One who clearly had a thing for her and one who would do anything to protect her. For now all Nicole could do was wait and hope and try to hold on to Evie's job.

* * *

Evie tried to sleep during the six-hour flight to Southern California, but she was wide-awake. Her private nurse, Tilde, sat beside her, working on her second novel of the flight. An older White woman with an interesting accent, Tilde wasn't as warm as Sophia and Nurse Lyle, but Evie chalked that up to the early hour. After a very formal introduction, she offered Evie her e-reader and one of three paperbacks she had in her carry-on, but Evie settled on looking through Instagram. Raquelle had given her a quick tutorial of all there was to discover, and while slime and soap-carving videos had worked for the first two hours, Evie was starting to get antsy. She knew why, but she refused to admit it to herself.

She wished she were sitting next to Zach. He and Jesse were right across the aisle in their own comfortable first-class seats. Jesse took the aisle seat, giving him enough space to stretch out his long legs. It made sense, but now there was an aisle and almost seven feet of California rancher between her and Zach. She hadn't fully wrapped her mind around what it would mean to sleep with a man, but she couldn't stop thinking about the kiss they'd almost shared Christmas morning. Every moment she had to herself had been spent thinking about Zach and a whole realm of what-ifs. Nicole was right, her health and her future came first, but couldn't her future involve a relationship with a man? Not that that man had to be Zach Pleasant, but of course Nicole didn't expect Evie to stay single for the rest of her life, did she?

Blaire had done her best to catalogue Evie's past relationships and lovers. The list was pretty short, since Evie had spent a large part of her twenties traveling for work. The most recent suitor had been Armand Waller, the man who had sent the red roses. Blaire realized she knew him as Banker Boy, but before the accident, Evie had mentioned that she was convinced that Armand was hiding a wife—or worse, a wife *and* kids—in Connecticut. Blaire wasn't sure if Evie had officially kicked him to the curb, but they both agreed ghosting him was the right call. And then Blaire explained what ghosting meant.

Evie was glad to hear that a few years ago she had at least enjoyed sex with another chef named Lincoln Carter, but that just left her wondering what sex felt like. The downsides to memory loss where complex and frustrating to say the least.

In any event, Evie was currently single. Sure, she had just reached the point where she could recite her own date of birth from memory without having to pause, but one day, dating would be back on the table. Would Zach wait around that long? Did she want him to wait around? What about the awful fight they'd clearly had? It had to be pretty terrible for Evie to have avoided him for so long. Could she hold a grudge she didn't even remember? All of these questions bounced around in her head just before Jesse suddenly sat up. Evie thought he was asleep, but he must have been resting his eyes. He undid his seat belt, then eased out of his seat. He crossed the aisle and leaned in close.

"How are you doing?" he asked quietly.

"I'm okay."

"Good," was all he said. Then he turned and headed in the direction of the restroom. Evie could not figure him out. Clearly they'd been friends, but he barely said anything that didn't have to do with the logistics of running the ranch or her general well-being. As soon as the bathroom door closed, Evie saw Zach undo his seat belt and ease across the aisle. He knelt beside her and lightly took her hand.

"How ya holding up?" he asked.

"I'm fine. I'm not sure I enjoy flying though. The engines are so loud. Is Jesse okay?"

"Honestly?"

"Yeah."

"He's just worried about you, but he's not big on displays of emotion. I think he'll relax when we get back to Charming."

"How are you doing?" she asked.

"Me? I'm fine. How you doing, Tilde?" he said, peering around Evie to her seat mate.

"I'm well, Mr. Pleasant. You really shouldn't be out of your seat. I have everything under control here."

Evie felt herself smile at the small laugh that escaped Zach. "She's right. We'll talk when we land."

"Okay."

Zach winked at her, then went back to his seat. He buckled his seat belt just as Jesse came out of the bathroom. Evie didn't hate the idea of being with Zach, but maybe she needed to slow that train of thought down. Maybe first, she should spend some time with him outside of a hospital.

Chapter 7

It was early afternoon when they landed at the Ontario airport. Zach explained that flying into LAX would have added a solid two-hour drive back to the ranch. Evie was grateful for the direct flight to a closer airport. The flight wasn't exactly unbearable, but somewhere around the five-hour mark, Tilde could tell how squirrely Evie was getting. She couldn't imagine sitting another two hours in a car.

The flight crew allowed Evie and her small entourage to exit first. Once they were outside, Evie was shocked by the change of scenery—and the heat. Without asking, Tilde took her coat as they made their way to the large navy-blue SUV waiting for them at the curb.

A White man in a blue-and-green plaid shirt and a white cowboy hat hopped out the driver's side and rushed around to open the passenger door.

"Zach, Jesse. Ladies," he said with a smile.

"Thanks for coming out, Bruce," Jesse said, clapping him on the back.

"Not a problem, boss. Had to run the Johnstone

party out to catch their flight. And it just so turns out your place is on my way."

"Evie, this is Bruce. He works at the ranch. This is Evie and Tilde."

Bruce tipped his hat in their direction with a smile, then started loading their bags into the trunk. From the way he seemed to accept Zach's introduction, Evie figured he was not a member of the staff who knew her when she was a kid. Zach and Tilde helped Evie get settled in the back-row seat, and when they were buckled in, Bruce pulled out of the airport. Evie looked out the window as they headed toward the Pleasants' home. She hadn't seen too much of New York City, just what she took in on their snowy trip to the JFK airport. California felt so open. No tall buildings. The sunny sky seemed to stretch on and on. With almost no traffic, they cruised along and Evie took in the rolling hills and flat expanses that lined the side of the road. Far off in the distance there were mountains.

She was so caught up in the sun-kissed landscape, she nearly jumped when Tilde's fingers patted her hand. "Zach is trying to speak to you."

She looked between them, startled, and was greeted by Zach's smiling face as he turned in his seat to face them. "I'm sorry. What did you say?"

"I said, welcome home."

"Jesse showed me pictures on the website, but this isn't what I expected."

"Different from life in the big city."

"Different from the tenth floor of Presbyterian."

"I'm glad we could spring you. We'll be at the

house in fifteen minutes. Miss Leona is psyched to see you."

Evie wasn't sure what to expect from their grandmother, who for some reason they referred to by her first name. Hopefully she and Evie got along. So far her recovery had been filled with kind, caring people, including Jesse and now Tilde, who weren't exactly the warm fuzzy type. She was sure at some point her luck would run out and she'd be faced with someone who absolutely did not wish her well.

After a while they did appear to roll into a small town with strips of shopping areas and restaurants. They drove by a massive place called Target that Zach said had just recently been remodeled and expanded.

"I'd take you there for funsies, but we'd run into at least forty-seven people from high school, and you don't want any of that right now."

"I ran into Jenny Yang there last week," Jesse mumbled from the front seat.

"High school crush. Broke his heart," Zach whispered. Evie filed that information away just in case she ever ran into Jenny Yang. Then she briefly wondered if she would run into any of Zach's ex-girlfriends as they drove into a quieter part of town. The retail area seemed to end and Evie noticed signs for different farms and fruit orchards.

"I'll show you around here, so more later. People think California is just desert and beaches, but we pump out half the country's produce."

"Oh wow," Evie said. They continued on, and seemingly out of nowhere, Bruce took a left and pulled onto a short but secluded road. They stopped at a high wooden gate and Evie realized the fence attached to it stretched for a pretty good distance in either direction. The gates swung open and Bruce drove the SUV down a road that seemed to go on for miles.

"This is Pleasant Lane. We basically have our own small neighborhood." Up ahead Evie could see three massive homes spread out around a central driveway. They passed two smaller buildings as they got closer, but Evie couldn't take her eyes off the sprawling mansion at the center. She spotted some movement and then four dogs of various sizes came running toward the SUV. Zach and Jesse didn't seem the slightest bit worried, and Evie could see why when all four of the dogs hit some sort of invisible line and started pacing anxiously.

"We also have a bunch of dogs. Black one's Clementine. Big shaggy girl is Sugar Plum. Euca's the spotted one and Poppy is the little yapper there. Don't worry. None of them bite."

"Oh. Okay," Evie said, unsure. Bruce pulled the car to a stop and Zach and Jesse immediately hopped out. Bruce followed, she assumed to grab their bags, but Evie was more focused on the elderly Black woman who had just emerged from the grand front entrance of the home in the center of it all. She was draped in jewelry, dressed in a flowing red top and matching flowy pants. Two other women were right behind her, but Evie was focused on the woman who must be Miss Leona Lovell. Jesse had explained that she was a movie star, had been for over sixty years, but Evie didn't know what it would feel like to be starstruck. Jesse immediately embraced Miss Leona as she kissed both his cheeks. Zach seemed to fall right in line and received the same warm welcome, before he jogged back over to the car and helped Tilde and Evie out of the back seat.

"You got this. She loves you," he whispered in Evie's ear as he offered her the solid support of his forearm. She could walk fine on her own, but her legs still felt like they needed a little more exercise before they were back to their full strength. Also it didn't help that the dogs were as excited to see her as they were to see Zach and Jesse. A large black dog with a red collar kept trying to lick her hand. "Just don't look her directly in the eye," he went on.

"What?" Evie stumbled as she caught Zach's teasing tone a minute too late.

"I'm just playing," he said with that damn chuckle that made it impossible for Evie to be even a little bit pissed off at him.

"Not funny."

As she made her way up the front steps, Miss Leona cocked her head to the side and looked Evie up and down. The flowing outfit and the beautiful butterfly pendant hanging around her neck and stacks of gold and silver bangles were accompanied by a face of full makeup—perfectly arched eyebrows and bright red lipstick—and what Evie thought was a gorgeous jet-black wig cropped in an angled bob.

"It's good to see you, baby." Miss Leona's voice felt like a warm hug.

"It's nice to see you, too."

"So no memory, huh?"

"No. Sometimes I think I feel bits and pieces of things, but nothing real."

"Mm, all the things I'd like to forget. Talk about a fresh start. Don't worry. We'll get you settled. We'll get you fed and then you can rest, rest, rest. Lord alive, we need to do something about your hair. Come on." Evie had hoped her butchered sew-in weave, which she'd draped over her shoulder, was less obvious with the bandage and the floppy hat she was still wearing, but Miss Leona saw through it all. She gave Evie two light pats on the back, then led her into the house.

"You know Corie. That's my goddaughter," she said, pointing to the plump Black woman standing on the front steps, and then she nodded toward a Black girl who had to be around Raquelle's age, standing beside her. "You haven't seen Lilah since she was a baby, but she used to come around when you were in grade school."

"Hi, Evie. Big fan," Lilah said with a little wave. She was sweet faced and soft-spoken. Evie found herself hoping they'd be friends.

"Go on. Move, Sugar. Euca, you other two. Corie, get these dogs out of the way."

Corie snapped her fingers and ordered them to shoo. It didn't work. Suddenly an ear-splitting whistle pierced the air. The dogs immediately froze. Evie turned around to see Jesse with his thumb and his middle finger still between his lips. He snapped his fingers, then pointed toward the far end of the porch. "Go sit," he said, his voice level. All four antsy pups went and lay down in the shade of the small lemon trees that lined the front of the house.

Still a little stunned, Evie followed Miss Leona into a beautiful sprawling kitchen/living room space where there was another surprise waiting. She recognized Sam Pleasant from the pictures Zach had shown her. He stood, feet spread apart and arms wide-open in welcome.

"Wazzup!"

"Oh snap! Oh snap! Oh snap!" Zach laughed as he eased around her and Miss Leona. She watched as he executed an elaborate handshake with his little brother, then pulled him into a tight hug. "'Sup, man."

"Just thought I'd hop on a flight and see what all the fuss was about. Hey, girl."

Sam had a combination of Zach and Jesse's features, all arranged in a sweet, high cheeked face. Evie figured he and Lilah were around the same age. He had Zach's same charming smile, but he lacked his brothers' facial hair and their massive height. He was still tall though, at least a whole head taller than Evie. He wasn't sporting the whole cowboy-in-a-business-suit ensemble that his brothers made work so well, but he still looked handsome in his Rams hoodie.

"Evie, this our brother, Sam."

"Nice to meet you," Evie said.

Sam's expression dropped and his gaze darted between Evie and his brothers and Tilde. "Oh shit— I mean shoot. Okay. So she really—okay. It's nice to meet you? See you?"

"Either is fine," Evie said. "I'm sorry I stole your brothers away for Christmas."

"Psshtt. They were right where they needed to be. Man, I haven't seen you in ages."

"How long are you in town?" Jesse asked as he made his way into the kitchen.

"I fly out day after tomorrow. I have to do this thing for *Variety* on New Year's Eve."

"Turning into Senior right before our eyes," Zach said, his mouth turning up at the corner.

"Checks are already better though."

"Geez, man," Zach said with a wince.

"Hey. Chill out," Jesse scolded.

"All of you go sit down. All in the way. Jamming up my kitchen," Miss Leona grumbled. "Be useful or move. Corie, can you show Miss Sweetheart here to her room?" Evie realized she meant Tilde.

"Absolutely."

"Actually, I got it," Jesse said. "And then I gotta head over to the ranch right quick."

"It's the Rock!" Sam shouted. Zach and Lilah laughed. Evie had no clue what they were talking about. Jesse rolled his eyes, then nodded in Evie's direction.

"You're in good hands. Listen to Miss Leona. Get some rest."

"Thank you, Jesse."

He nodded one more time, then led Tilde down the hall.

Sam laughed when he was out of earshot. "Man, *he's* turning into Senior."

"Said the same thing and then he threatened to toss me out of the plane at thirty thousand feet," Zach said. Evie must have missed that conversation.

"Evie, baby. Do you want something to eat?" Miss Leona asked.

"We have tons of leftovers, including my amazing chili," Lilah said.

Evie hated to turn down their hospitality, minutes after she walked in the door, but she was suddenly too overwhelmed. She was still getting to know herself, but she knew if she pushed herself any harder, and tried to force interactions with this many new people at once, she might cry again. And no one needed that. "Chili sounds good, but is it possible to see where I'll be sleeping? I think I might take a nap. I couldn't sleep on the plane."

"Of course, baby. You get your rest. Zachariah, we're gonna put her in the sunshine room."

"Excellent choice, Miss Leona. Come on with me." Zach took Evie's hand and she couldn't ignore the small thrill that ran through her the second their fingers laced together. They walked through first floor of the large house and stopped at a room near the end of the hall.

"You're in here. Miss Leona, Lilah, and Corie are upstairs," he said, just as Tilde came out of the room right beside them.

"I was going to lie down for a little bit," Evie said. She shook herself free from Zach's hand as if they'd been caught doing something wrong.

"Oh good. Let me just check your bandage."

Evie turned back to Zach. She wasn't sure what she wanted to say, but she felt like she had to say something. She felt like she was running. Miss Leona had already been so welcoming and she wanted to spend time with Lilah and Corie—and Sam, since he would be leaving town again—but between all the new names and faces and the dogs, a wave of exhaustion was overtaking all the energy she'd built up for the three-thousand-mile trip. She swallowed and tried to speak before Zach cut her off. "I—"

"Hey, I'm not going anywhere. The other house, right over there. That's my place. I'm gonna catch up with Sam, but I'll be around." *Yeah, but will we ever get some time alone?* she thought.

"Okay." They both hesitated a moment and then a moment longer until it was clear that Tilde wasn't willing to wait all day for Evie to come along. "Okay, bye." She followed Tilde into the bright, airy bedroom and sat down on top of the softest bed she'd ever felt. Of course, her remembered experience was thin. After Tilde completed her thorough examination and firmly encouraged Evie to drink a glass of water, Evie kicked off her shoes and made herself comfortable on top of the covers. She just needed a little nap and then she would rejoin the fun.

Zach knew a nap was probably a good idea, but he was too jacked up on caffeine and the weird effects of two cross-country flights in a few days. He knew he'd crash out as soon as he hit his bed that night, but for now he needed to clear his head. The more time he spent around Evie, the more eager he was just to be alone with her, to talk, to try to . . . he wasn't sure what exactly. But he knew he couldn't hang out on his grandmother's couch with Evie sleeping right down the hall. He walked back into kitchen, back into the chaos of a full house still dressed top to bottom in Christmas decorations.

"I'm gonna head over to the office. I left my laptop there. And I have to go say hi to Steve."

"He missed you," Lilah said. "I went and brought him some Christmas carrots and he looked me dead in the eye like *you're not my daddy*."

"I'm a deadbeat, I know."

"Hey, I'm coming with you. I took Majesty out for a long ride this morning, but I'll swing by the stables again." Sam hopped off his perch on the kitchen stool and kissed Miss Leona on the cheek. "We'll be back for dinner."

"If you go riding—" she started.

"We know. Bathe before we come back in this house."

"We'll leave the trail where we found it," Zach said. "Come on."

"Miss Leona told me you ditched her on damn Christmas," Sam said as soon as they stepped out on the front porch. Zach stopped and turned his face to the sun before he slipped his Stetson back on.

"I think checking on Evie was a reasonable excuse."

"I know why you went—"

"Now, listen—"

"Oh, I know Jesse gave you all kinds of shit. What the hell happened?"

Zach gave his brother the short version of Evie's accident according to Nicole as they walked back across the property to his house, the house he used to share with both of his brothers. Euca and Clementine followed, pushing their way past Zach's legs as he unlocked the front door to his place. He didn't like spending more than a few nights away from

Charming or the ranch. Forget leaving town for a medical emergency. His house had that strange stale feeling, like all life had abandoned it, taking any sense of warmth with it. It'd take a day or two to break the place back in, shake off the feeling of plane seats, unfamiliar hotels beds, and shitty plastic hospital chairs. Still, it was good to be home.

"Her agent thinks she was pushed," Zach said.

"Jesus."

"Yeah." Zach walked to his bedroom and Sam followed. He set his Stetson on his dresser, then went right to his closet and pulled out some fresh clothes.

"So she's hiding out here until—"

"I don't know. Until she feels well enough to leave."

"I talked to Mom and Senior," Sam said as he leaned against the side of Zach's dresser.

"I have to call them back. We Facetimed them Christmas morning, but they were rushing off to some show."

"Do they know you brought Evie back here?"

"Sure don't, sure didn't tell them. You know what Dad would have said."

"Usually it's the moms who want to marry their kids off," Sam said with a scoff.

"Listen, I don't agree with him, but I get where he's coming from. I keep trying to explain to him that those days of everyone getting married and starting a family before they turn twenty-five are over."

"He might be on to something though. To him, you and Jesse are old as fuck."

"How is thirty-two and thirty-four old as fuck!?"

"I don't make the rules, man. I'm just saying.

And there won't be any Pleasants from our line to leave this place to if one of you don't meet a woman at some point."

"Yeah, I'll ask Evie how she feels about the concept of heirs as soon as you fly Natalie over to—"

"Natalie and I . . ."

"You what? Oh! That's why you came back."

"Yeah, that's over. It was my first time meeting her parents, and the second we get off the plane she tells her mom she's expecting a proposal any day." That stopped Zach in his tracks. "That's what I'm saying!" Sam said, throwing his hands up in the air. "I very calmly told her that I wasn't there yet."

"You guys have been dating for three months."

"I know, man."

"Well, she tripped herself up there. Did you know Jesse was Evie's emergency contact?" Zach knew he should let it go, but the fact that his brother and Evie had been in touch this whole time was still working his nerves. What else didn't he know?

"No."

Zach pulled a fresh T-shirt over his head, then turned back to Sam. He knew when his brother was up to something. "But you've kept in touch with her too, haven't you?"

"Yes . . ."

"What the fuck?"

"Listen, that beef was between you two. We've been friends on Facebook and then Instagram this whole time, and then I ran into her at this thing in the Hamptons last year. She asked about you, but you know Evie. It was mostly shit-talking, and then she had to go kiss some network ass. What do you want me to say?" Sam laughed.

"Nothing. Just like your ass did this whole time. You and Jesse. Man, I swear."

"Oh, come on. What? We were keeping you from the love of your life?"

Zach spun on his brother and pointed a finger right in his face. "Exactly."

Sam laughed, shaking his head. "So you going to give it the old college try now? After how many years of acting like the idea of you and her was big nay-nope? Now that she can't freaking remember you?"

"One, she does remember me. Sort of." Zach told him about how he accidentally made her cry and she told him about the dreams. "She remembers parts of me."

"Yeah, 'cause she was in love with you."

Zach sat on the edge of the bed and tugged on some fresh socks. "Yeah, we'll see about that."

"You don't know how badly I wish I could stick around and watch you fuck this up."

"Yeah, she'll come around and stab me with a fork any day now. But in the meantime, let's ride." Zach clapped his baby brother on the back, then the two of them headed over to the ranch.

Chapter 8

A ride, even a short one, was just what Zach needed. He and Sam saddled their horses, then set out on Cooper's Trail, the wider, smoother trail that made it easier to ride Majesty and Steve side by side. Sam had stories and jokes, but they were both quiet after a while. Zach was indifferent to Natalie, but he couldn't pretend his brother hadn't just gone through a breakup, even if Sam had jumped off the subject faster than he'd brought it up. Natalie meant something to Sam if he'd agreed to go meet her folks for Christmas, and the breakup had to have been brutal enough for Sam to hop on a flight right back home. Zach made a mental note to check up on Sam over the next couple of weeks, even if his brother was busy doing his Hollywood thing.

They turned back as the sun started to set, and as they headed back to the stables, Sam told him more about some projects his management had lined up for him. It was a good distraction, hearing about his brother's career. It kept all his thoughts about Evie at bay for a little bit longer.

"I know I won't win shit, but I do want something

I can get a nomination for," Sam said as they finished rubbing their horses down. They stopped their conversation as a few guests kicked up a fuss, wanting to see the horses even though all equine activities were done for the day. He saved Kurt, Felix's right hand, the stress of persuading the guests to head back for dinner by offering to give them a quick tour himself.

Kurt finished up with Steve and got him settled in his stall while Zach took his sweet-ass time introducing the couple to nearly half of the over seventy horses they housed at Big Rock. He loaded the couple from Portland down with so much horse-related information they were anxiously eyeing the exit as he launched into the breeding history of draft horses and why, though they weren't as exciting as thoroughbreds, they still did an important job at the ranch, providing the literal horsepower to cart visitors on the extra-fun hayrides. He did this whole song-and-dance in a fake Southern accent, mind you.

When they finally excused themselves for dinner, Zach felt like he'd given them their money's worth. Distracted them from possibly recognizing Sam too.

When they got back to the truck, they picked up their conversation where they left off as they started the short trip back to the house.

"As I was saying before. There's nothing wrong with you wanting awards. Listen. If Miss Leona can do it, so can you. And I don't mean to downplay Senior's accomplishments. He's good. And he's got plenty statues of his own, but you've got that *it* that Miss Leona has."

"You're just—"

"No, I'm not just saying that." Zach pulled his truck to a stop in front of his grandmother's front door. They'd missed Jesse when they stopped by the office to grab Zach's computer, but he could see the lights on in Jesse's house. "I watched *Inferno* five times its opening week. You are fucking brilliant in it. You went from stunt rider to scene stealer in actual features, and you didn't use Miss Leona's name to do it. You made this happen."

"Man, I guess—"

"No 'I guess.' You know I'd clown you into next week if you were stinking up the screen. You're only twenty-six. You'll get there. You'll get that statue."

Sam was quiet for a moment before he looked over at him. Their relationship was built on 97 percent comedy, but neither of them had any issues telling the truth, and Sam knew it. "Thanks, man. I wish I could get you in front of the camera. I can't believe you do that accent with guests."

It had been a joke when they were on the rodeo circuit with Senior when they were kids. One way to cope with good ole boys who were still pissed that slavery had ended and even more pissed at how much prize money Jesse Pleasant Sr. and his sons used to walk away with every year.

"Hey, you know how it goes." Zach slid into the accent again. "You come all this way for a slice of country living, you expect a show."

"Shit, I'm glad Jesse decided to the raise rates."

"You and me both. Now get the fuck out of my truck. I need to shower."

"You coming back over for dinner?" Sam asked as he stepped down from the cab.

"Yeah, I'll be there in a bit. Don't eat it all."

"No guarantees."

Back at his place, Zach undressed and got right in the shower. He knew if he sat down or even looked at his bed he'd be out for the rest of the night. He needed to eat and, of course, he'd taken it upon himself to make sure Evie was settling in okay. It was nice to spend time with his baby brother, a nice break from Jesse's stone-faced demeanor, but as soon as Zach stepped under the hot spray he only had two things on his mind. His empty stomach and a certain chef.

Now that he was back in Charming and Evie was out of immediate danger, Zach couldn't stop thinking of all the what-ifs and what-could-have-been scenarios that might have popped up over the last ten years. Yeah, it pissed him off to no end that his brothers had carried on some type of relationship with Evie while he was left thinking she'd written off the whole family. As recently as a week ago Evie Buchanan still hated his guts, but he couldn't undo the truth of where they were now and what part he'd had in getting them there. Seeing the way she'd reacted to him in the hospital, the way she'd taken his hand as he'd shown her to her room, their almost-kiss, Zach couldn't give up on this.

As he rinsed the conditioner out of his hair, he had to wonder what would have happened if he had just taken a chance over the last decade. He would have altered Evie's career in some way, but would he have ruined it? There was no way for him to tell. All he knew for sure was how badly he missed her, how much downplaying not having her in his life had wounded him. He lost Nana Buck and Evie all at once, and he didn't handle either loss well. But he had to handle the situation right this time.

Zach knew he'd fucked up. He could still hear the way Evie's voice broke, still clearly remember the tears running down her face when he told her to go back to culinary school. He wished he'd said the right thing, even though he was too young to know what the right thing was at the time. It just never occurred to him that his brothers would carry on whole relationships with her and not say a word about it. Not even a single *I checked in on Evie. She's doing fine.* Nothing. A shitty voice in the back of Zach's head thought they might have been trying to protect Evie from him, but that couldn't be true.

Zach shook off all the speculation and hypotheticals when he realized he was just standing in the shower, wasting time. He got ready and headed back over to Miss Leona's place, which was oddly silent when he opened the door. Lilah was quiet except for when she sneezed, but when Sam and Corie got going you could hear them across the valley. He followed the faint sound of George Benson coming from the kitchen and found Miss Leona alone, putting away a pitcher of her holiday punch.

"Where is everyone?" Zach asked.

"Evie's turned in for the night."

"Where's everyone else?"

"Oh, I thought you only came rushing back here, drenched in cologne, just to see Evie," she said, pinching her nose.

"Drenched is a strong word. You told me not to come back into your house smelling like the horses."

"I didn't want the smell of a cosmetics factory either. Sam and Corie wouldn't stop cutting up, so I sent them to the movies. Evie and Tilde were trying to rest. They didn't need all that noise. Jesse turned in for the night too. You hungry?"

Zach double checked his phone. Little punk Sam didn't even drop him a text. "Uh, yes, ma'am."

"Go ahead and make yourself a plate." She nodded toward the covered leftovers on top of the stove. Zach made a bowl of Lilah's chili and corn-bread and then another plate of the ham and greens and mac and cheese Miss Leona had made. With all the houseguests and Jesse's daily caloric intake, the massive spread would be wiped out by the following afternoon.

Zach set himself up at the kitchen island, smiling at his grandmother as she sat down beside him with a glass of that hundred-proof punch.

"So what are you going to do now?" she asked as he swallowed his first bite.

"About what?"

"Don't play dumb with me, Zachariah. I taught you that smile. She's back. She's not all there, but I saw the way you looked at Yvonne and I saw how she looks at you. Time, distance, and a little forgetfulness—"

"This is a little more than forgetfulness."

"Don't interrupt me. It's rude. I was simply saying that I know you and I know that look. Evie could be back with us for good if her memory doesn't come back, and I know you're not going to just go on with your life like she isn't living next door."

Zach leaned back in his chair and gave up his

pitiful fight. Dragging his napkin across his mouth, he sighed.

"Can I ask you something?" Miss Leona said.

"Yes, ma'am. Ask away."

"What's the rush?"

"What do you mean?"

"She was released from the hospital this morning. You waited ten years. I won't get all up in your business about what you were doing all this time when you could have sent her a text message or gotten your behind on a plane or picked up the damn phone, but what's the problem with giving her some time to heal?"

"I—" Zach stopped himself. Miss Leona had a point. Evie had told him to leave her alone, so he had. Maybe he was in his own head, dealing with his own shit, but over time he had convinced himself that whatever feelings either of them had, had long since faded from both their minds. But he knew that wasn't the case. He knew it from the moment Jesse received that call from Nicole. He knew it from the way Evie looked at him the moment he walked into her hospital room.

The feelings were still there, but whatever he was feeling for Evie was only a part of the equation. He wanted her back in his life, but he needed to give her time to decide what she really wanted for herself and what she wanted with him. A short laugh escaped Zach's chest as he reconsidered his current plan of courtship. Or lack of a plan, if he was being honest.

"I guess . . . maybe I could pull back a little. I feel like—"

"You feel like you've found each other again."

"That's it. I didn't realize how much I missed her until I saw her sitting in that hospital bed."

"I understand. We're all worried and we're all glad she's back. I had to catch my breath when she got out of the car. Looks just like Amelia."

"You miss her, don't you?"

"Every day."

Zach looked at his grandmother and thought about what she must have been like at his age. She and Nana Buck had a tight clique, rounded out by Zach's grandfather Gerald Sr. and Evie's grandad, Justice. One by one, they'd all passed away, leaving Miss Leona to love her three sons, their wives, and thirteen grandchildren. She was surrounded by family and friends who loved the hell out of her, but it wasn't the same. He didn't want to consider how'd he be feeling if Evie's accident had turned out differently. Zach leaned over and a planted a kiss on his grandmother's temple.

"I hear you," he said.

"Good. I have a feeling Evie's going to be with us for a while, and I don't need you coming around here every hour on the hour asking if you can escort her to the box social. Let her come to you, if she wants to, in her own time. Don't be so damn thirsty."

A burst of laughter exploded from Zach. Miss Leona whacked him on the arm, shushing him.

"So loud. You're gonna wake up Evie and then Tilde is gonna come in here and I'm gonna have to remind her that she's a guest in my house."

"Oh no. What happened?"

"She asked me when was the last time we changed the water filter and then gave me a lecture about the 'menu' I'd have lined up for Evie, because nutrition is key to recovery and brain health." Miss Leona paused for dramatic effect and then slowly rolled her eyes. Zach chuckled and spooned up some more chili.

"She's out of here tomorrow."

"Good."

"Who taught you *thirsty*, Miss Leona?"

"Last season on *Rory's*, the finale," she said as she picked up her wineglass. She took a deep sip.

The parking lot of Charming High was covered in straw, but it all made sense. It was homecoming weekend and they needed horses for the parade. The sky was pink and black all at the same time. Streaks of green and blue outlined the clouds. Evie could hear thunder in the distance, but there was no chance of rain. It never rained in Charming. Not during homecoming. The lights of the stadium lit up Zach's bright red pickup truck.

Evie was cold, but she didn't care. She was too busy kissing Zach Pleasant. He sat in the driver's seat, his boots on the step rails, thighs open, leaving plenty of room for Evie to stand between his legs. She was so turned on as his tongue moved against hers. She knew they shouldn't be doing this. Especially right in the middle of the parking lot, right in the middle of the game, right in the middle of election night. She still had her I VOTED sticker plastered to the front of her jean jacket. Anyone could see them, but she didn't care.

She wanted to get closer. She knew they couldn't have sex, not right out in the open with people walking by and the game dragging into halftime. But maybe if she climbed into his lap, they could do a little something to help ease the throbbing ache that was starting to soak her underwear.

Evie broke their kiss and buried her face in Zach's shoulder to cover her laugh.

"What's so funny?" he asked, giving her side a little squeeze. A little tremor of excitement rushed all over her body. She'd been waiting to do this for a while.

"Nothing. I just told Nicole I wouldn't."

"Don't tell Nicole you did then."

Evie looked to her left at the hole that had been created in the back wall of the school. It had been like that for as long as she could remember, the library and part of the custodian's office exposed to the parking lot. Thorny vines grew up the walls of crumbling cinder block. Evie laughed even harder as she saw Mrs. Milenakis moving back and forth in the line, trying to avoid the thorns. She looked right at Evie and Evie knew she was going to get an earful the next morning, if she decided to go to homeroom. Which she wouldn't because she was an adult and she didn't have to report to homeroom. She had to be on set in the morning. Nicole was going to kill her.

"We're missing Jesse's game," Evie said when she turned back around, but Zach was gone. It didn't make any sense. She could still feel him all around her. She searched the truck. Tears pricked the back of her eyes and suddenly this strange pain tightened in her chest. It was happening again. It kept happening. She squeezed her eyes shut and tried to will the feelings away. She would be fine. She was fine.

When she opened her eyes she was standing in a dark stairway. More crumbled walls wrapped in thorny vines. Below she could hear music. Nicole was waiting for her. She started down the stairs, but every time she tried to take a step down, her foot would get stuck. Something was wrong *with her laces. Evie reached down and untied her sneakers and then she fell.*

Evie woke with a start. It took her a moment to re-alize where she was. She blinked a few times, trying to place the claustrophobic feel of her hospital room. Even with her glasses off she could tell the windows in front of her were too big. She leaned up in the comfortable queen-size bed, blinking some more, knowing the blurry scene around her wouldn't improve unless she put on her glasses.

She was in Charming, California, in the home of Miss Leona Lovell. She'd slept through the after-noon and would have slept through the night if Tilde hadn't woken her up to encourage her to eat some dinner and hydrate. She appreciated the inter-ruption to her deep, dreamless slumber, but as soon as she finished the delicious leftovers Miss Leona had sent to her room, she changed her clothes and went right back to sleep.

She felt for her glasses and pushed them up her nose. The digital clock across the room told her it was three thirty in the morning. She could still feel the edges of her dream. Her throat felt raw, like she'd just been crying, but the rest of her body was still in that kiss. Nothing about it was real, but Evie could still taste Zach on her lips and the throbbing ache between her legs didn't want to fade either.

She reached for her phone that Tilde had plugged in on the nightstand. Blaire had showed her how to use the *do not disturb* function. Her phone had been silent all night, but there were a few notifications on her screen. A text from Blaire and two from Raquelle. She'd been so tired and overwhelmed she'd forgotten to call them when she reached Miss Leona's home. She was sure Jesse had touched base with them after they arrived, but she wanted to text them back. She wanted to talk to Blaire and tell her everything about her journey cross-country. She wanted to hear Raquelle's bubbly voice. Both would have to wait. Even with the three-hour difference, something in the back of her mind told her that it was too early for social calls.

Evie turned on the bedside lamp and carefully made her way over to her bags. The journal Zach had given her was right on top of her things. She knew the diary was made for a kid, but that didn't stop her from writing down everything she could remember from her dream and how every detail of the dream made her feel.

The next time Evie woke up it was to the sounds of Miss Leona and Tilde arguing in the hallway. She wasn't exactly sure what they were saying, but it was suddenly quiet. A few minutes later Tilde entered her room. She checked Evie's blood pressure and her bandage, then told her to go back to sleep. Evie wasn't going to argue with that suggestion.

Hours later she woke and realized she'd slept the whole morning away. It was almost noon. In the leather armchair across from the bed she found towels, a washrag, and a fluffy robe. She knew she should find Tilde and at least let her know she was up and she was going to take a shower, but she wanted a little more time to herself. She took off her pajamas and slid into the robe.

The en suite bathroom had a large shower with a marble bench and a movable showerhead. It took her a few tries to figure out the knobs, but she successfully showered and got ready for her day on her own. She used the lovely scented lotions that Blaire had packed in her suitcase. She used the lip balm from Shanny too. There was nothing she could do about her hair, but for the first time in a week she was starting to feel more human.

She followed the soft sound of music back out to the kitchen, but halfway she stopped as she realized the hall leading to her room was lined with photos and clippings of the Pleasant family. She'd been so distracted by Zach the day before, she hadn't noticed the small family museum that went to the end of the hall, beyond the guest room where Tilde was staying. She followed the line of photos and found that the hall curved. It led to a large entertainment room with a big wall-mounted TV, a big couch that looked like it could seat least twelve people, and a pool table. This room was also filled with photos and there was a large case against the wall, filled with trophies.

Evie walked into the room and right over to the case. Dozens of trophies, some shaped like stars and others that were little statues of men on bucking horses. She looked at the names on the little plaques. Most of the trophies belonged to Jesse Pleasant Sr., but there were plenty with Zach's and Sam's names on them too. Evie didn't want to be caught snooping, so she headed back out into the hall, looking at the pictures on the wall as she slowly made her way back to the kitchen.

She only stopped twice. The first time was in front of a framed cover from *Essence* magazine. It was dated a little over a year ago. Zach and Jesse were photographed standing side by side, wearing their signature cowboy hats. The words *PRINCES OF CHARMING: How the Pleasant Brothers Are Changing the Face of Luxury Hotels* was printed across the left side of Jesse's lapel. Evie had to admit they both looked ridiculously handsome. She wondered what he was like as a boss, what it was like for him and Jesse to work so closely together.

She moved on, those questions still running through her brain until she came to a picture of a young Zach and Sam with her grandmother Amelia. Looking at her grandmother's warm smile and the confident way she stood with one hand on her hip and the other on the reins of a black-and-white horse that towered over her made Evie feel like maybe there was one side of this memory-loss thing that worked to her advantage. She couldn't remember a thing about her grandmother, or her parents. She couldn't remember losing them.

The music coming from the kitchen changed and she realized how long she'd been standing in front of the pictures. She found Miss Leona and Tilde both reading in the open kitchen/living room area—sitting as far away from each other as possible. Tilde was in an armchair near the fireplace, reading another paperback, and Miss Leona seemed to be flipping through a cookbook while she stood at the counter. A pair of reading glasses was perched on the end of her nose. Two of the dogs were sprawled out on the kitchen tiles. Only the big one bothered to look up as Evie entered the room.

"Good morning, baby," Miss Leona said with a smile.

"Good morning."

"Samuel had to catch a flight, but he told me to tell you he says goodbye and he'll check back in tomorrow to see how you're doing."

"Oh. It was nice to see him for a little bit." Evie felt an odd sense of disappointment. Sam was another stranger to her, but he seemed very sweet and very easy to be around. She looked forward to getting to know him. She looked forward to getting to know all of the Pleasants, but at the moment Miss Leona seemed to be the only one at home.

"He'll be back soon. He always comes home. How'd you sleep?"

"Very well. Thank you," she said, suddenly remembering her dream. She ignored the flash of heat when the sounds of Zach's laugh echoed in her memory. She didn't think it was a good idea to ask Miss Leona where he was too. "The bed is very comfortable. Much better than the one at the hospital."

"Hmmm," she said with a smile as Tilde made a bit of a grunting noise from across the room. Maybe she hadn't imagined the argument they'd had earlier.

"You hungry?"

"Yes, I am."

"Well how about some eggs. Come on." Miss Leona took Evie's hand and led her through the open French doors to the backyard. Evie almost gasped at what she saw. Miss Leona's backyard was a massive garden. A few fruit trees and rows of herbs and vegetables. There was a porch swing ring there, hanging over the back patio, and Evie could see that on the far side of the yard there were chickens. The bigger dog brushed by her and started poking around in the grass.

"I told Tilde to let you sleep. Sometimes a stay in the hospital does more harm than good, in strange ways. It's good to get back home." Evie glanced over in time to catch her wink.

"I don't have a real home here in Charming, do I?" Evie suddenly asked as Miss Leona led her over to the chicken coop.

"You always have a home with us, but no, you don't own any property here at the moment. You sold your grandmother's house and had everything put in storage."

"Is it—is it still there? Our things. Her things." Evie wasn't sure what she was asking, but she wanted to know. It was overwhelming to see Zach and his family, not even his whole family, but the select members who'd filled Miss Leona's kitchen the night before. It was overwhelming to know that she was the only member of her family left and she couldn't remember a thing about them. She thought of the picture Zach had shown her of her grandmother and that brown horse. Maybe if she could look at more of her things she would be able to remember something. Or at the very least, be able to connect some more dots from her dreams.

"All your things are still in storage over in Appleton. I believe Jesse has the spare set of keys. I'll have him take you over there."

"I'd appreciate that. Thank you." They stopped just outside the coop.

"In the meantime, I want you to think about your next move."

"I'm not sure I—"

"I didn't say you have to decide right now. You take your time, but I think it's important to move through this life with purpose. Do you understand me?"

"Yes, I think so."

"You will get well. This scar will heal," Miss Leona said, motioning to the side of her head. "And then you need to think about what's next. If you need help, some helpful suggestions, you come talk to me and we'll sort it out together. And in the meantime, you're gonna help me prepare tonight's dinner."

"Oh, yes. Please. Anything I can do to help out around the house," Evie said. She knew none of the Pleasants or Miss Leona were asking for a single thing in return for their outstanding hospitality, but she wouldn't feel right if she spent the upcoming weeks or months just sitting around. "When I'm ready I would love your help. Maybe I can find some sort of job in town or help out at the ranch."

"Oh no, honey." Miss Leona opened the gate to the large chicken coop and ushered her inside. Several chickens, brown and white and black, made little chirping and clucking sounds as they shuffled out of their way. "That's not what I meant by purpose. I'm going to teach you how to cook so you can get back on television."

"I can't ask you to do that."

"Who do you think taught you the first time?"

"You did?"

"Of course I did. Your grandmother couldn't cook for shit. You take your time, and you decide what you want to do from here on out, but if you decide you want your cooking career back and your memory doesn't want to cooperate, then you and I are going to start from scratch and all the clout and the fans you've already built up will get you the rest of the way. You just have to figure out what Yvonne Buchanan 2.0 is going to be like. Reinvention. It's how great women get by."

Evie didn't know whether to laugh at Miss Leona's vulgar language or cry at the revelation that she'd been so instrumental in Evie's success and how enthusiastic she was to help her with her journey all over again. Or whether to cry at the sudden connection she felt to Miss Leona. Jesse seemed to be acting out of a sense of duty. Zach—well, she had a feeling what Zach wanted—but this was something different. She just wanted Miss Leona to be kind, to like her. She never expected that Miss Leona would help her rebuild everything she'd lost.

"Thank you. I think that would be a good idea. I should at least try, right? My passion for cooking might help me get my memory back."

"From your lips to God's ears, my dear." Miss Leona flashed her a warm smile. "Let's get you some fresh eggs."

Chapter 9

After the delicious breakfast Miss Leona made, she told Evie to keep herself busy while she took a call. Evie had free rein of the whole house with the exception of Miss Leona's rooms at the other end of the house. Evie kept her journey to the entertainment room to herself. She figured it wasn't a bad idea to get the lay of the rest of the land, but she wanted to make a call of her own first. She went back to her room and called Blaire. The phone rang several times and just as Evie was getting ready to give up, Blaire answered.

"Hey!" Blaire's cheery voice came through the phone. "You called!"

"Yeah, I did. Hi."

"How's everything? How are you feeling? What's the grandmother like? Did Jesse change his robotic settings to human man? Have you had sex with Zach yet?"

Evie couldn't hold in her burst of laughter. It was good to hear Blaire's voice. "Things are good. I'm feeling much better. Hospital beds are the worst."

"I don't miss sleeping in that chair at all. Okay, tell me everything."

"Miss Leona is going to teach me how to cook," Evie said. It felt good to share that new development. It felt good to finally have news to share that didn't have to do with her health. "She showed me how to make a frittata this morning, but I just watched. Tomorrow I'm going to help make breakfast and dinner. I didn't know she was the one who taught me how to cook in the first place."

"I didn't know that either. Oh, Evie, that's wonderful. If anyone knows how to cook it's an old Black lady who lives on a ranch. That'll be awesome. Probably better than some stuffy culinary school and more relaxed than being tossed back into a fast-paced kitchen."

"Yeah, I'm a long way from any fast-paced kitchen, but hopefully I can get back there, some day."

"Do you want to cook?" Blaire asked.

"Yeah. I do."

"Good. You love it so much. I know you're going through a lot, but I hated the idea of you having to give it up, and I don't just mean the show."

Evie definitely didn't want to think about her actual job that was currently hanging in the balance. "Tell me about your day. This has been the Evie show, twenty-four hours a day. What's going on with you?"

"Thank you for asking, babe. I mean that. Well, things are much better now that I feel like you're settling in, but I miss you! The apartment isn't the same without you."

"I miss you too." Evie meant it. A lot was missing,

but it didn't take her long to figure out why she and Blaire had been best friends and roommates for so many years. Blaire was pretty great.

"So, let's see. I'm off for a few more days, but I need to prep for finals and OMG, I don't want to. My students are driving me nuts this year. Also, I think I have a date for New Year's Eve."

"With who?"

"Um, a doctor," Blaire admitted, sounding guilty for some reason.

"What's his name?"

"David. I ran into him a few times when I came to see you. He caught me on the way out after we sent you on your way. We talked a bit and then he asked me out. I'm kinda excited. He seems sweet and he's really hot. I don't think you can go wrong with a hot doctor."

"A hot doctor sounds amazing. You have to tell me all about your date when you get back."

"I will. Speaking of hot. Zach. Talk to me."

Evie thought about how nice it felt to kiss him, even though the kiss wasn't real. "There's nothing to say. I haven't seen him yet today. I think he's at work, at the ranch."

"Oh, but I bet you're dying to. That's so hot. He's like a real cowboy."

"I wouldn't hate seeing him, but I don't know what to say. Nicole had a point. I really need to focus on myself right now."

"Right, but there's focusing on yourself and cutting out all possibility for something to grow, and then there's focusing with an emphasis on putting yourself first, while also allowing a ridiculously fine man to show you how a little reverse cowgirl works out West."

"I don't know what that means, but it sounds sexual."

"It is," Blaire said. "Look it up—no wait, don't! No do. Yes, you're not a child. You need this information. Also, if you don't have sex with him you're gonna want to have those search results at hand, literally."

"I don't know. I'm . . . conflicted."

"About what? Tell me."

"I like him. I think, but obviously things were bad between us if I didn't speak to him for ten years."

"You want my opinion?"

"Sure."

"You were like twenty-two. I think about the dramatic grudges I've held since I was twenty-two and only like two of them were really worth it. If he wants to make things right and if he apologizes for what he did—"

"I don't even remember what he did."

"But he told you, right?"

"Yeah, but I—"

"Well, tell him he owes you an apology and then go from there. You don't have to stay angry with him if you don't want to. Tell him to apologize, and if you're satisfied with the apology and you want to see where things go, then I say go for it. Shit, you can always dump him if it doesn't work out."

Evie didn't like the sound of that last bit and that told her all she needed to know. She was unsure of how it would all work out or even if it would, but she wanted to give Zach a chance if he was interested. She needed to confirm that important bit of the equation too.

"Maybe I'll wait until your date with the doctor. You can tell me if you liked him and why, or if you didn't and why, and then I can compare notes to how I'm dealing with Zach."

Blaire let out a short chuckle. "Okay. But just an FYI, we have totally different taste in guys. I like them quiet and nerdy. You like them . . ."

"I like them like what?"

"Like Zach Pleasant."

After she finished her call, Miss Leona explained the plan for the rest of the day. Around five thirty, Jesse would arrive with her new full-time nurse, Vega. She and Tilde would swap intel on Evie's physical well-being and then Tilde would catch the red-eye back to New York.

Corie, who had been gone all day running errands for Miss Leona, came home a little after four. She broke up some of the tension between Miss Leona and Tilde with her bright personality. Evie tried to help her put away all the stuff she'd picked up at the store, but Corie wouldn't let her. Instead, Evie sat at the island and talked to Corie while she restocked some spices in the pantry.

"My mom is actually Miss Leona's goddaughter. My grandma used to be Miss Leona's body double back in the day."

"Oh wow."

"Later, we'll watch *Seeds of Sunshine*. The 1959 version."

"The only version," Miss Leona said from her seat on the couch.

"She's right. The 2017 version was terrible. The movie is literally about the Civil War and somehow they managed to downplay the war and *whoops* all the Black characters away."

"They made my character White," Miss Leona said. "I didn't go to the screening."

"I'd love to see your version," Evie replied. She enjoyed the few movies she'd watched in the hospital. It would be great to see one starring Miss Leona herself.

"Let me put the rest of this stuff away." Corie took off down the hall with two loaded-down bags and enough toilet paper for twenty. When she came back they sat on the couch and Corie brought up the movie. Evie noticed Tilde was still reading her book, which was fine, but somehow a little rude twenty minutes into the story of a group of women trying to aid, and then ultimately falling in love with, Union soldiers. More than halfway through, she finally put down her book and watched the film.

Miss Leona played Belle, a former slave whose current employer had set out to lend a hand at the battlefront. Her husband dead, she asked Belle to accompany her. Belle agreed, for a price. Evie was immediately sucked in by the love stories that were at the center of this epic tale of the Civil War. She knew it wasn't real, but she wanted so much for Belle and her sweetheart, Homer. She realized she owed so much of what she was feeling to layers of emotion Miss Leona was pouring into the character.

It was so strange to see such a younger version of Miss Leona on the screen and sort of amazing to see how well she'd aged. She still carried a certain fresh beauty that Evie had a feeling was unique to Miss Leona herself. The story was so dramatic and the performances so enthralling, Evie found herself moved to tears more than once. When the end credits rolled, she turned to Miss Leona.

"That was wonderful. *You* were wonderful," Evie said, unable to stop herself from gushing.

Tilde added her own grunt of approval. "It was an excellent film."

"Thank you. Both."

"How'd you know you wanted to be an actress?" Evie asked. Her wardrobe alone clued her in to the fact that Miss Leona had a flare for the dramatic, but you couldn't fake that kind of talent or the confidence that seemed to accompany it.

Miss Leona looked down at her lap and made a show of smoothing out her flowing top over her knees. "When we were little my father would make us sing for our supper. My sister and I started doing full dramatic productions. She would 'write' them and I would do the bulk of the performing. My father used to have me perform for our neighbors. I fell in love with entertaining even the smallest crowds."

"That's amazing. I can't wait to watch more of your films."

"There are plenty more where that comes from," she replied with a wink.

"May we check the news?" Tilde asked.

"By all means."

Evie didn't miss the way Miss Leona rolled her eyes.

As Corie turned to a local station for the start of the five o'clock news, Evie excused herself to the restroom. When she stepped back into the hallway, she heard Jesse call out his hello from the front door. Evie found him and Lilah in the living room, where he introduced them all to Vega Ro, a very beautiful, very petite brown-skinned woman in adorable rainbow scrubs. She was younger than Evie expected, no older than thirty. She had long, curly black hair pulled back in a loose braid and she had a beauty mark just below her lip.

"I am all packed up and I have stripped my bed. Would you like to see where you'll be staying?" Tilde said once all the hellos were exchanged. Everyone sort of froze and looked between Tilde and Miss Leona and Jesse and Vega. Vega shared a looked with Miss Leona, then cleared her throat.

"Sure. Lead the way."

"Evie, please join us."

"Yeah, uh, okay."

Tilde turned on her heels and marched right down the hallway. Clearly she and Miss Leona hadn't hit it off, but Tilde didn't need to make it so obvious that she was willing to disrespect Miss Leona in her own home. Evie was sure if Tilde wasn't leaving within the hour, Corie, Miss Leona, and maybe even Jesse might have had some choice words for her. Evie and Vega followed her down to the second guest room.

"Evie, if you'll sit." Tilde closed the door and launched into her debriefing. Evie sat on the edge of the now bare mattress. Vega snorted as she pulled a tablet out of her bag and came over to the edge of the bed. Tilde gave her a rundown of Evie's initial injuries and diagnosis.

"Yes, correct. I received her records yesterday and reviewed them," Vega said. "And you've been—"

"She's reported no dizziness. Blood pressure is normal. No pain beyond some soreness at the sutured area." Vega looked at Evie, eyes wide, lips pursed, then looked back at Tilde, who hadn't skipped a beat. "She has an appointment with Dr. Zordetski. She is scheduled for an MRI and if Dr. Zordetski approves she will have her stitches removed. You will speak to Jesse about transportation."

"May I see?" Vega asked Evie, gesturing her hand toward her bandage. Before Evie could answer, Tilde stepped forward. Evie automatically tipped her head to the side to avoid further injury and let Tilde remove her bandage.

"Oh, it's healing nicely," Vega said. "Is there anything else I need to know?"

"I'm concerned about the number of people there are in the house," Tilde said as she covered Evie's stitches. Evie was stunned silent. What the hell was she getting at?

"Have any of them hurt you?" Vega asked.

"No," Evie replied. "The opposite. I feel very welcome here."

"I mean regarding the noise," Tilde said like she was making complete sense and not being extremely rude and maybe a little bit racist.

Vega's mouth popped open, then closed again as she looked at Evie once more. Evie felt herself offer a matching look of shock mixed with confusion. She and Vega were on the same page. It was time for Tilde to go. Vega set down her tablet, then inhaled deeply. "I grew up in a noisy houseful of people, and being surrounded by loved ones did the body and the spirit just fine."

"I am also concerned about her diet. Miss Lovell cooks extremely heavy meals."

"Okay. I'm going to stop you there," Vega responded, holding up her hand. "I'm not sure if you know who Leona Lovell is, but half of her blog is about her vegetable garden and her fresh recipes. Did she drop you off at an Arby's and tell you to fend for yourself?" she asked Evie.

"Of course not. What's Arby's?"

"It's better if you don't know. I'm sure Ms. Lovell, Evie, and I can all get on the same page about her nutritional needs. Thank *you*, Tilde."

Tilde frowned, then turned to gather her things. After she shoved her last two paperbacks into her carry-on, she made a show of slamming her jacket over her arm.

"One last thing. I understand that Evie is an adult, but the other grandson, Zach, has been very forward with his interest in her."

"What?" Evie said. "No, he hasn't—"

"You might want to ask Dr. Zordetski to speak to her about rushing into sexual activity following such a severe head injury. You might also want to speak to—"

"I will . . . not speak to Evie like she's a child, but I'm sure she appreciates your concern. I think we've covered it all."

"Hmm." Tilde yanked the handle of her carry-on. "I wish you a speedy recovery, Evie. Goodbye." She didn't wait for Evie to respond, just marched right out of the room and apparently right out the front door. They heard it slam, then Corie's very clear, "What the hell was that all about?"

"Wow," Vega said.

"Miss Leona has not been feeding me unhealthy food," Evie scrambled to clarify. "We gathered our own eggs this morning."

"And what if she was. If I were in the hospital for over a week, I'd be mainlining junk food for another week at least, just to make up for lost time. Don't worry. I didn't think she handed you a bucket of bacon grease. Is there anything else *you* want to tell me?"

"Uh, I don't think so. I am feeling much better. I want my stitches out immediately. They are starting to itch."

"Should I be on the lookout for this guy Zach?" she said with a little laugh.

"Nothing is happening. I—I mean, it's a long story."

"Oh, I am so here for long stories, but long stories are not what the Pleasants are paying me for. How about this: On Monday we get you all checked out, and if the doctor says you are cleared for sexual activity, we will load you down with condoms and you will not hear another word from me about it. Sound good?"

"Yes, I can live with that."

"Great. Now. I'm just gonna say this. Woman to woman, 'cause I've seen your show before and I know you like looking like a ten-and-a-half on a bad day. Let's talk about your hair."

Two minutes later Evie was back out in the kitchen surrounded by Corie, Lilah, Vega, and Miss Leona. They needed to have a hair conference and Evie was happy to attend, but at some point during Tilde's dramatic exit they also managed to swap one Pleasant brother out for another. Jesse was gone and Zach was standing in the middle of the living room flipping through the program guide on the television.

She smiled when she saw him and he smiled back, but Operation Fix Evie's Fucked-Up Do was underway before they could greet each other properly.

They sat Evie down at one of the island chairs.

"I mean, they just cut right into her sew-in," Corie said. "I know those bundles weren't cheap."

"How are you feeling about your hair?" Miss Leona asked, pity dripping off her every word.

"Not great."

"Here's what I was thinking," Lilah chimed in with her sweet, low voice. She pressed her phone screen a few times, then handed it to Evie. "Considering where your bandage is, this would look super cute with the shape of your face and with your glasses." Evie looked at the pixie-cut style with the model's thick natural curls piled on top of her head, swooping forward. It would be a drastic change, but she liked it a lot. Zach came around the counter and looked at the photo over Evie's shoulder. Her body instantly warmed as his hand brushed hers.

"I like it."

Corie sucked her teeth. "Ain't no one care what you think."

"My bad. Let me just go sit down over here." Zach sat down on the couch and made a dramatic show of opening up the newspaper.

"I have to ask my agent, Nicole, first. If I end up going back to work, I don't want to get in trouble for changing my look."

"Go ahead and ask her, baby. I say do it. If they don't like it, I'll send you a whole line of wigs," Miss Leona said. "But if it'll bring you peace of mind, run it by your agent first."

"Here." Evie's phone chimed as Lilah sent the picture over. Evie immediately sent it to Nicole in a text. Thinking of this haircut. Will this get me in trouble with the producers at The Dish?

"Let's see what she says." Evie settled in to wait for Nicole's response, but before she could lock her phone, Nicole replied. First off, I freaking love it. Second, the producers will be fine with it. And if they aren't I'll tell them they can spin it as part of your recovery story. Win, win for everyone.

"She said yes."

"Great," Vega said with smile.

"Zachariah, call your barber and tell him you'll pay him extra for a house call," Miss Leona called across the room.

"Yes, ma'am," Zach said. Evie could see his thumbs-up sticking up over the edge of the counter. It was nice to see him again, but with the full house— Vega was great so far, but they'd hadn't reduced their number of live-in nurses—she was starting to wonder if she'd ever be alone with Zach again.

Chapter 10

Zach moved the porch swing with the toe of his boot, then put his foot back on the patio. He knew Miss Leona's rules applied to no feet on the outdoor furniture too. Zach should have known better than to think he was going to get a minute alone with Evie when he returned to Miss Leona's that night. He walked right into another girls' gab session, and before they could kick him out his uncle Gerald called. All things considered, he knew it was best to take the call outside. Poppy joined him, picking her way around the yard in the moonlight.

"I know expansion is possible, but I worried about the acreage—"

"And then the insurance," Zach said. Zach knew his cousins were struggling with their decision to walk away from their father's vineyard. He didn't envy them at all.

"Mm-hmm. I'm trying to give Thomas and Micah more time to get their business off the ground, on their own terms, but sometimes I wish they'd just take the damn check."

"Listen, Jesse and I took the damn check. Took the whole damn ranch. Doesn't make it any easier."

"Yeah, I know. I've been in my boys' shoes. I took Mom's investment but I did things my way. Senior had Big Rock handed to him and it had always been his plan to hand it off to you boys."

"And don't think we're not doing things our way. When we took over—you remember Ned?" The former GM of the ranch thought he was going to convince Miss Leona to sell Big Rock to him while Jesse and Zach were finishing up graduate school, but things didn't go Ned's way.

"I remember him."

"Ned was pretty pissed when Jesse showed him the books this summer. He thought we were going to follow his business plan into the sun, but he didn't understand just how good Jesse is at what he does."

"Didn't expect Mumbles to outshine him."

"Don't call him that." Zach tried not to laugh. Jesse had been over six feet since he was twelve, but his personality took a long time to catch up to his size. He was still quiet, mostly. But he wasn't shy and he wouldn't hesitate to fuck someone up.

"You know I'm joking. Jesse's a good kid."

"And Ned underestimated him. We had the amenities and the accommodations, but we were understaffed."

"I remember. You're not supposed to penny pinch and cut corners at a place like Big Rock."

"Exactly. Jess had the financial vision for it and it's paying off."

"I need him to talk to Thomas. Maybe he can

help them give Pleasant Brothers Construction the jumpstart they need. I'm glad you boys are holding it down."

"Me too. I'm not going back out on the circuit for cash. My body can't take it anymore."

"You're young. You can handle it."

"Yeah, tell my knees that. I did a simple dismount for some guests two weeks ago. Stood still, cheesing like a damn asshole until Felix got their attention so I could hobble away. My knee said *yeeet!*"

Uncle Gerald laughed, then abruptly cleared his throat. Zach knew what was coming. "How's my baby girl?"

"She's fine." Zach looked back in the window and could see Lilah showing Evie something on her phone. He almost mentioned Evie to his uncle, but thought better of it. "She's doing a great job. She's definitely getting a raise next quarter."

"Do you think she'll speak to me this time?"

"We can give it a try. Hold on one second." Zach opened the French doors and stepped back inside the kitchen. "Hey Li, you want to talk to your dad?"

"No." She didn't bother looking up. "Thank you."

"Alright then." Zach stepped back out onto the patio and closed the door.

"She say no?"

"Yeah. Sorry, Unc."

"It's okay. I'm fine since I know she's with you. Her mother cussed me out 'cause we had all our kids here except her. I wish I knew how to parent girls. Better."

"Well, step one, don't try to marry them off."

"Yeah, yeah."

Zach loved his aunt and uncle, but they were a little too old-school when it came to Lilah. He remembered the odd text she'd sent him in the middle of the night, asking him for the codes to the front gate. She'd taken the bus from her parents' house in Napa down to Charming. He'd been up the rest of the night with her and Miss Leona when they finally pieced together why she had literally up and run away from home. Neither of them could blame her.

That was almost two years ago. She'd been living with them in Charming ever since. She kept in touch with her mom over email, but she couldn't bring herself to speak to her dad. Zach knew he had to stay out of it. Especially when he and Jesse weren't all that far removed from their issues with their own father when it came to their lives and their family business.

"Just give her some more time. She'll forgive you eventually."

"Yeah. I hope so. Give Miss Leona a big kiss and a hug for me, and if you can try to convince Lilah to call her mother. She can be mad at me, but Denise misses her girl."

"I'll see what I can do."

Zach talked to his uncle for a few more minutes before they called it a night. He stood out on the patio a while longer, enjoying the cool winter evening. The temperature dropped in Charming the moment the sun went down, and though his brothers probably wouldn't believe him, he enjoyed these quiet moments at the end of the day, especially during Big Rock's busy seasons.

He'd been up at the ranch since dawn, catching

up on all the things he'd missed while they'd been in New York. They had a wonderful crew over at Big Rock. He trusted all his operations leads to make sure things ran smoothly day in and day out, but he was also pretty hands-on. Not because he wanted to micromanage, but because he loved the ranch.

Zach loved catching the look on a guest's face when they first stepped out of the shuttle cars in front of Big Rock Lodge. He loved the look on a child's face when they saw their first real horse up close and in person. He loved seeing a pissed-off teenager go from "Fuck this family vacation" to "Mom, watch me ride!" He'd seen his friends and even his cousins struggle with what adulthood held for them, but Zach was lucky. He was exactly where he needed to be.

And suddenly, in the last few days, it didn't feel like enough. Something inside him had been uncovered. The feelings he had for Evie, feelings he'd been denying his whole life, had come to the surface and there was nothing he could do to ignore them.

He turned his phone over in his hand and thought about how neither he or Jesse had mentioned Evie all day. It was fine with him. He wasn't in the mood for more of Jesse's lectures, but his grandmother's words still bounced around in his mind.

Zach needed to be more honest with himself when he thought about Evie and how badly he wanted to be with her. He wanted to see her, yeah, but he wanted to spend actual time with her, alone. He wasn't trying to make a move, he just wanted to be with her, talk, relax, get to know her as she was now. And he wanted to see how he could help her, see what she needed without Jesse or a doctor or even her agent, hovering.

But for now, he would definitely have to wait. He whistled for Poppy, then followed her back inside and sat down beside his grandmother on the loveseat. She was enjoying her nightly viewing of *Jeopardy*. He .hung tight, messing around on his phone through the rest of the episode. Through an episode of the *Wheel* and two reruns of *Rory's War*. He sat quietly by, listening to Corie and Lilah attempt to catch Evie up on all the seasons following Rory's career at Mercy General Hospital.

Vega sat on the other side of the room, knitting, but even she had her opinions on Rory's terrible choice in men. As the commercial breaks dragged on, Zach felt like he'd entered into some battle of wills between himself, Corie, and Vega. His grandmother went to bed at the same time every night. He could tell Lilah to beat it, and while Corie would eventually take a hint, Zach knew she'd give him an earful-and-a-half about how it was perfectly fine for him to go back over to his own house.

When the second episode of *Rory's War* ended, Miss Leona stood, groaning loud as she tried to cover a yawn. "I'm gonna watch the news in my room. Goodnight, my beautiful babies." She kissed Zach on the cheek, then made her way around the room saying her warm goodnights, with Sugar Plum tight on her heels. She even had a kiss on the forehead for Vega. "You need anything, and Corie will get it for you."

"Thank you, Ms. Lovell."

A few minutes later Zach saw Lilah listing a bit to the left. She caught herself before her head hit the arm of the couch. Her eyes sprang open. "Goodness. I should go to bed too. Do you need me tomorrow?" she asked in her soft voice.

"Nope, we said you're off until January fifth and we meant it."

"I know. I just know Jesse could use my help."

"No, he'll use you because you keep showing up. Take your days off. We'll have plenty for you to do when we get back."

"Okay, goodnight."

Zach wanted to ask her one more time to call her parents, but he'd do it when they were alone. He knew Lilah would talk to him about it, but she wouldn't want to open up in front of Vega or Evie.

And then there were four. Zach turned and looked Corie dead in the eye. She looked back at him and slowly shook her head. Zach's eyes widened and he slowly nodded. Evie was sitting on the other end of the same couch and he knew she could see the ridiculous stare-down playing out between them, but he didn't care. Finally Corie hopped off the couch and reached down for her shoes.

"Fifty dollars in my Cash App and not a penny less."

"Done."

"Nice doing business with you, chump," she said with a bright smile. "Night, Evie. Night, Vega."

Zach wasn't going to ask Vega to give them a minute, but something told him she wasn't going to drag this out. Sure enough, at the next commercial break, Vega packed up her knitting. "Evie, darling, I'm calling it a night. Don't stay up too late?"

"I won't. I'm going to head to bed soon."

"Good. Mr. Pleasant," she said with a little smirk and a nod.

"Nurse Vega."

Finally. At long last they were alone. Sort of. Poppy and Euca were passed out at Evie's feet. Poppy was down for the count, but Euca cracked an eye open and watched Zach get up from the loveseat and join Evie on the couch.

"Hi," Evie said.

"Hey."

"She's right. I shouldn't stay up too late. It's been a long day."

"You're right. I have to work in the morning," he said, but neither of them moved. Zach couldn't believe how badly he wanted touch her, how badly he wanted to hold her. He watched the emotions playing over her face as she looked down and started playing with the edge of her sweater. "Come on. I'll walk you to your room."

Zach stood and turned off the television before he turned and helped Evie up from the couch.

"I saw all of your trophies. I wandered down to the other TV room," Evie said as they walked down the hall. When he looked down he realized she was nodding to all the family photos and accolades that lined the walls. His grandmother had only mounted a fraction of them.

"Yeah, we're a—we're a busy family."

"An accomplished family."

"If you only went down to the den you didn't see

Miss Leona's awards. You'll have to ask her to show you her office. She has two Oscars in there. It's pretty impressive. But hey, the Buchanan legacy isn't too shabby either. Your grandpa was a rodeo champ and your grandmother could ride a horse while doing a headstand blindfolded. She had plenty of trophies under her belt. Taught me, Sam, and our dad everything we know. You aren't doing too bad for yourself either."

"Yeah," she replied, unconvinced.

When they stopped at her bedroom door, something in the air between them shifted.

"You owe me an apology for what happened between us when my grandmother died. Or maybe even before," she said suddenly. "Did you apologize before? At any point before my accident?"

Zach managed to fight off his initial reaction when it came to Evie: shock, which he would have usually downplayed, but he couldn't do that now. Not this time. No jokes, no turning on the charm. No bullshit. He scratched the back of his head, then let out a deep breath.

"In my mind I did, a thousand times. Five hundred of them this week alone, but no, I didn't apologize to you and I didn't apologize when I should have. I'm sorry, Evie. I was a dumb kid who didn't know what to do or what to say at the worst time of your life and I hurt you. I'll never stop wishing I could take it back. And I'm sorry that I never tried to make things right before now."

"I wasn't expecting you to say that."

"Yeah, I figured as much, but it's true."

"Everyone seems to think that you're trying to sleep with me," she said, shocking him again.

"Is that what you think?"

"No. I think you—actually I'm not sure what you want."

"I want you back in my life," Zach admitted finally. "Not sure how that's all going to work out, but a wise woman by the name of Leona Lovell told me that I shouldn't rush things and maybe I should give you some space."

"Hmm."

"Do you know what you want?" he asked, quietly. It was struggle not to reach out and touch her.

"I don't want to rush things either, but I don't think I want space."

"Oh? Alright." Zach tried not to sound too excited.

"But I'm not sure if I can trust you."

"Fair enough. Trust has to be earned. I just want to spend time with you."

"You were in my dreams again last night. And this time we kissed," Evie admitted.

"Oh word?" He couldn't help smiling this time. It was all he could do to cover up the fact that most of the blood in his body was now rushing to his dick. "Was it any good?"

"I'm not saying. It was a dream, so that part doesn't matter."

Zach laughed. "Okay, then."

"Blaire told me I should ask you about reverse cowgirl?"

Zach almost choked. "That's an interesting suggestion from Blaire."

"I think she was joking about asking you, but she did tell me to look it up."

"How about we look it up together. Here." Zach moved against the wall and sank toward the floor. Evie followed. They sat side by side on the painted tile as Zach pulled up the browser on his phone. The words *Sex position #150* were the first thing to pop up. "We will skip right over videos because I don't need to traumatize you right now." He clicked on the images tab and the results weren't much better. He scrolled past several awful memes before he got a pretty standard illustration. He clicked on it and handed Evie his phone. "There you go."

"I don't know why I didn't picture this. It's pretty self-explanatory. Do you like this position?"

Yeah, like Zach was answering that. "I mean, I don't think it would work between me and you."

Evie looked up at him, hurt in her eyes. "Why?"

"Because if you and I end up that kind of naked, I want to be able to see your beautiful face."

"I don't have your phone number," Evie said, her voice sounding a little shaky.

"Would you like my number?"

"Yeah. Let me get my phone." Evie stood up and slipped into her room. Zach followed and leaned against the wall as Evie grabbed her cell off its charger. "Here." Zach took her phone and saved his number into her contacts. "You can text me whenever you want. You can also call me. Even if I'm up at the ranch."

"I'll keep that in mind. I have a lot of work to do.

I have to become a master chef so I can take my show back."

"If anyone can do it, I know you can." The determination in her voice made his chest warm inside. He couldn't believe he'd missed so much of her rise to stardom.

"Did you ever watch my show?" she asked.

"I saw an episode or two, but I don't keep up with it." Zach was being honest. He may have left out the fact that he had every episode of television that Evie had ever appeared on saved on his DVR. She didn't need to know all that. "I had a feeling you didn't want me to watch."

"That might have been true. I don't know if I'm ready to watch myself," Evie replied with a yawn.

"Here. I'll let you get to bed."

"Before you go there's something I think I should tell you."

"What's up?"

"I've given it a lot of thought and I think we should kiss."

"Oh word? How much thought exactly?"

"If I'm being really specific, since maybe three thirty this afternoon, but it doesn't mean it wasn't deep, serious thought. We should give kissing a try."

"I agree—" Before Zach could respond further, she stepped in close and pressed her lips to his. Her mouth was so soft, softer than it looked, softer than he imagined. Zach wasn't going to waste this moment. He slid an arm gently around Evie's waist and pulled her closer, kissed her deeper, his tongue carefully sliding against hers.

She seemed unsure at first, but almost instantly she relaxed against him, letting her tongue respond. Zach hated everything he'd done wrong with Evie before, but he did not regret waiting for this kiss. There's no way his sixteen-, seventeen-, even twenty-year-old self wouldn't have fucked this up. But now he knew what he was doing and he knew what it really meant when a woman sighed into his mouth.

The kiss stretched on and Zach took in everything about those long moments. Evie's perfect breasts pressing against his chest, the way she was straining up on her tiptoes, the painful urge to scoop her up and throw her on the bed, how hard he was getting. When Evie pressed her thigh against his erection, he knew it was time to stop.

He pulled away, his eyes struggling to open. When he could finally focus on Evie's face, he reached up and lightly brushed her cheek. They were both breathing heavy and Zach had a feeling neither of them wanted this to be a one-off. This was only a preview of things to come.

"That what you had in mind?" Zach said, catching his breath.

"Yeah. I think that worked."

"Good. When you're feeling up to it, I'd love to show you the ranch," Zach said.

"I would love that. Maybe after I get my stitches out. I'm seeing the doctor on Monday."

"Monday night then."

"But I'll see you again before then?"

"I live right next door."

"All by yourself."

"Yep. All by myself."

"Good to know."

Zach lowered his head once more and lightly pressed his lips to hers.

"Goodnight," he whispered when he pulled away. She didn't say a word when he slipped out of her bedroom door, but that immature teenager in him hoped she'd send him a late-night text.

Chapter 11

Evie woke up to the sounds of her alarm. It was cloudy outside, but the sky was still bright. She slipped on her glasses and as soon as everything came into focus, she couldn't stop herself from smiling. She touched her lips, thinking about the way things had unfolded the night before. She'd kissed Zach, in real life, not in a dream. She'd been aroused in her dreams, but nothing close to how turned-on she'd been when Zach pulled her into his arms.

She picked up her phone off her nightstand and considered sending him a text, but she knew it was better to make him wait. She liked Zach, a lot. He was so handsome it hurt to look at him, and that smile of his was truly dangerous. She didn't blame everyone for warning her, telling her to guard her heart and her panties. But when he apologized without a sly smile and without a hint of sarcasm, she knew he was sincere.

Zach Pleasant was, at the very least, drawn to her, and whatever happened before, Evie knew it was more important to move forward and think about the future instead of dwelling on the past. Unless

Zach did something to make her feel some other way, Evie was going to follow her gut, and her gut told her it was absolutely okay for her to be crushing on Zach.

Evie pulled up the text conversation she'd been having with Blaire and sent her a new message. I think I'm ready to tackle reverse cowgirl.

She hit Send and then started to get ready for her day. When she got out of the shower she had a handful of text responses and one missed call. She dried off and applied a generous amount of this wonderful-smelling lotion Blaire had packed for her, all over her body. When she was dressed, she looked at the messages on her phone from Blaire.

WHAT??!?! DID YOU SLEEP WITH HIM?!

Evie thought about calling Blaire back, but she wasn't ready to have this conversation out loud. She started typing a response instead. No we didn't have sex, but I went for it and kissed him. We also looked up reverse cowgirl together on his phone. It does look interesting, but I don't think it's the first position I want to try. I hope I'm not terrible at sex.

Blaire was already responding. No, sweetie. I bet you're the best at sex. You're great at everything you put your mind to.

Evie laughed, thinking about how many man-hours she'd have to dedicate to becoming a master of sex. She started to reply when there was a light knock on the door.

"Are you decent?" Vega said.

"Yes, come on in." She sent Blaire a blushing emoji, then set her phone down on the bed.

"Good morning." Vega entered her room wearing a fresh pair of scrubs. Euca was right behind her, wagging her tail as soon as she saw Evie.

"Morning," Evie said before she gave the dog's head a little scratch. "And good morning to you, puppy."

Vega smiled, patting Euca's spotted fur. "She's a stage-five clinger, but it's okay 'cause she's a sweetie pie. It is miserable outside. I went for a short walk with Miss Leona and Corie this morning, and then it just started pouring. It's barely drizzling now, but it's still a perfect day to stay inside."

"That stinks, but I have a lot to do, so maybe it's for the best."

"Oh yeah? What's on the agenda?" Vega asked as she gently took Evie's wrist. Evie waited until she finished taking her pulse.

"I'm learning how to cook."

"Nice. How's your head?"

"Good."

"Just gonna check your stitches a half dozen more times, and then we can move on." She changed Evie's bandage and checked her pupils and they were done with their morning checkup.

"If you need a taste tester, I'm your girl," Vega added.

"That would be great."

"Let's do it."

Evie watched Vega as she made some notes on her iPad, and for some reason the words came tumbling out of her mouth. "You're not asking me about last night?"

Vega did an almost convincing job of suppressing her own smile. "Like I said. Miss Leona isn't paying me to get all up in your business, but is there something you want to share with the class?"

"I kissed him."

"You made the first move?"

"Yeah. He walked me down here and I kissed him."

"You're proud of yourself, aren't you?" Vega teased.

"A little bit."

"Well, I am happy for you. He is not hard on the eyes at all. Okay, ma'am, you are good to go. Is it time to get cooking?"

"I think so." Evie stepped into her slippers, then followed Vega down the hall with Euca by her side.

"First lesson. We eat with all of our senses," Miss Leona said. "Our eyes, our sense of smell, the textures that hit our mouths, the flavors that hit our tongues. They are all important. If someone can't see your dish, you want them to be drawn to the wonderful aromas. I'm going to teach you the basics and then you're going to practice making it pretty."

"Okay. I'm ready."

"Just what I want to hear," Miss Leona said as she handed Evie an apron. Evie tied it around her waist and walked over to the other side of the island to join her new teacher. "You're gonna make our frittatas. I already gathered some eggs. I want you to go into the fridge and grab the butter, then you're going to pick out two different vegetables to

include in your dish. Miss Vega, do you have any
food allergies?" Miss Leona asked as Evie grabbed
the butter.

"No, ma'am. Is it okay if I watch?"

"Absolutely. You cook?"

"Sort of, but I'd love to pick up some pointers."

"And Evie needs to get used to having an audience,"
Miss Leona added. "Make yourself comfortable."
Vega hopped up on a kitchen stool and they got to
work.

Evie grabbed some tomatoes and spinach and set
them on the counter next to a small onion Miss Leona
had already set out. For some reason she felt a little
unsure about her choice, but she stuck by it. "I know
we had tomato and spinach yesterday, but it was
delicious. I'd like to have it again."

"Lesson number two: Eat what you like. You also
cut down on food waste by actually using the ingredients you have on hand. Tomato and spinach sound
perfect to me. Any objections from Miss Vega?"

"My mom said diners can't complain when they're
eating for free."

"Your mom sounds cold-blooded, and I think
we'd get along great. Now Evie, I want you to cut up
that onion. Like this." Evie paid close attention as
Miss Leona peeled off the thin outer layer of onion
then started making small slices across the top, then
more slices in cross sections. She made one more cut
and neat little pieces of onion started piling up on
the cutting board. The smell of the onions burned
Evie's eyes, but she liked the aroma. Something about
it was familiar to her.

"You try, and don't rush. Slow is much better than

taking a chunk out of your hand. At some point you will cut yourself. It will not be the end of the world, and we have a lovely young nurse on staff, but let's hold off on the flesh wounds as long as we can."

Evie took the remaining half of the onion and mimicked Miss Leona's actions. She went slowly at first, but somehow her hands seemed to know exactly what to do. In no time she had what looked like a finely diced onion.

"Very good."

Evie felt her cheeks warm at the simple praise.

"Now, do you want diced tomato or tomato chunks?" Miss Leona asked.

"What are we doing?" Corie asked as she walked into the room. She took a seat at the island.

"Chef Buchanan is getting back in the ring," Vega replied. Evie glanced at Corie and didn't miss the way she and Vega were looking at each other. She'd have to think about that later.

"Um, which do you think will taste better?" she asked Miss Leona.

"That's not what I asked you, baby. Which would you like?"

"Let's try diced."

"Great."

Evie rinsed the tomatoes and then watched Miss Leona demonstrate the best way to dice them up. Evie followed her lead, cutting up the tomatoes into small pieces. It was slow going at first, but again her hands seemed to just know what to do. And so it went on. Miss Leona walked her through each step of the frittata. She was an excellent teacher. Calm and patient, and when Evie hesitated, her lack of confidence tripping her up, Miss Leona encouraged her not to be afraid.

"Worst thing that happens, you burn down my kitchen, and I have insurance. Let's keep going."

In the end, they had a beautiful breakfast, with enough food for six people. Miss Leona had Corie grab four plates and then Evie had the honor of serving her breakfast guests. Evie waited, the nerves setting off sparks in her stomach as Vega and Corie each took a bite.

"What do you think?" Evie asked.

Vega took one more bite before she answered, while Corie made a dramatic show of chewing extra slowly. "It's good!" Vega said. "Ten out of ten would eat again. It's really good."

"Could use a little salt," Corie said before a teasing smile spread across her lips. "I'm messing with you. It's good, Evie! Are you gonna try it?"

"Oh, I guess I should." Evie picked up her fork, took a deep breath, and then took a nice healthy bite. "Mmm," she said, shocking herself. Corie and Vega burst out laughing.

"What?" Evie chuckled a bit herself. She took another bite and another. "It is good."

"Don't be so surprised. You know what you're doing," Corie said.

"It's called muscle memory," Vega added. "You probably don't remember a lot of things, but your body does. That's great. With some practice you'll be cooking on your own in no time."

"I hope so." Evie didn't want to sound too eager, but that was exactly what she wanted to hear. She would get back in a professional kitchen if it was the last thing she did. No stupid head injury was going to stop her.

Miss Leona polished off her own slice, then leaned against the counter. "It was delicious, baby. Almost as good as mine."

"Thank you."

"As we go along I'll share what I know about wine pairings and table settings. Hungry people just want to eat, but presentation matters, especially in your line of work," Miss Leona said before she motioned to Corie and Vega. "Now you two. Do the dishes."

Evie helped with the cleanup, and after the kitchen was spotless and the remaining pieces of the frittata were packed away for Lilah whenever she got back from her trip into town, they all sat down to watch cooking shows on Miss Leona's streaming service. They settled on *Anita Bower: Fresh From Home.* The meals she created seemed difficult at first, but as Evie followed along, making notes in her head, they didn't seem impossible. She just needed the ingredients, a little moral support from Miss Leona and her taste testers, and a little faith in herself. Evie could do this.

Halfway through the second episode, where Anita was now preparing a meal of lobster salad, fresh rolls, and these elaborate fudge brownies for her dinner guests, Miss Leona's cell phone started ringing.

"Oh that's my son." Miss Leona left the room, answering the call as she went. A few minutes later she came back. "Evie, baby," she said from the hallway.

"Yeah." Evie looked around the side of the couch and saw Miss Leona waving her over. She followed her down to her wing of the house and stepped into what appeared to be Miss Leona's office. There was a comfy-looking couch and a large desk. Zach wasn't kidding. This room was also filled with photos and trophies, evidence of Miss Leona's accomplishments. Evie waited by the door as Miss Leona walked behind her desk. She motioned to a tablet that was resting against an ornate metal stand on the desktop. "My son, Jesse Senior, just wanted to say hello. He's off starring in a British procedural."

"Oh, okay." Evie came around the desk, and sure enough there was Jesse Senior on the screen. She recognized him from his pictures. Evie could see all three of his sons in his features and his broad shoulders. He also had a nicely manicured beard. She just had to pretend to know what a British procedural was.

"Hello, Yvonne." His voice was deep like Jesse's, but warmer, like Zach's.

"Hi, Mr. Pleasant."

"Heard you've had quite the holiday."

"Yes, sir."

"Is that Evie?" she heard a woman's voice say a moment before Mrs. Pleasant appeared over her husband's shoulder. She was absolutely glamorous in an ivory turtleneck sweater. Her hair was pulled back in a high bun and she was wearing the most stunning shade of red lipstick. Massive diamond earrings hung from her ears. Evie remembered seeing a photo of a younger version of Mrs. Pleasant in an evening gown wearing a MISS CALIFORNIA sash. Now on the screen she looked like she'd barely aged a day. Right when she laid eyes on Evie, her expression seemed to brighten as a smile spread across her face.

"Hello," Evie managed to get out.

"So glad to have you home," Mrs. Pleasant said. "Are you enjoying yourself?"

"Um . . ." Evie glanced at Miss Leona. "It's nice to be here with Miss Leona, yes."

"And the boys. I'm sure Zach is happy to see you," Mr. Pleasant added. Something in the way he said his son's name made Evie's stomach tense. She had the odd sense that maybe Zach's parents were the only two people not trying to keep them apart.

"Zach and Jesse have been very helpful and very welcoming. I look forward to spending more time with them both."

"We're in Paris right now, but we'll be back in the States at the end of spring. It would be good to catch up with you," Mrs. Pleasant said.

"I'd like that."

"Honey, we should go," Mrs. Pleasant went on. "We were invited to this over-the-top after-hours dinner party by one of the producers. Too much every which way, but the star has to make an appearance."

"You two have fun," Miss Leona said. "We'll talk soon."

"Evie, make sure Zach gives you a tour of Big Rock. He's really done a great job with the place. You'll see. You'll be real proud of him. He's helping to turn the whole town around."

"She'll love it, Jesse. I'm sure. You two get going."

Evie wasn't sure what to make of the weird tone of Miss Leona's voice, like she was trying to stop Mr. and Mrs. Pleasant from saying more. Evie remembered then the way Zach had avoided the topic of his parents when she'd asked about them in the hospital. Clearly there was some tension he didn't want to talk about. They seemed like perfectly nice people. She wouldn't push, but she was dying to know what was going on.

Miss Leona reminded Jesse Senior to check in with his sons and his own brothers, and then she ended the call. Her voice was still a little funny when the screen went black, but she laced her arm with Evie's like nothing had happened.

"You have to ignore Regina and Senior," she said. Evie realized she was still staring at the screen.

"Is there something I'm missing?" Evie asked.

"Senior had it in his mind that you and Zach were somehow destined to be. He saw you two running the ranch together. He just didn't bother to consult you or Zachariah. Meanwhile, your grandmother had other plans for you."

"Oh." Evie wasn't sure what to make of that information. Suddenly a wave of sadness washed over her. She glanced back at the computer screen; the dark window of the video chat and the desert wallpaper looked back at her. The image of Zach's parents was still vivid in her mind. A light squeeze on her arm snapped her out of the trance.

"You okay, baby?" Miss Leona asked.

"Yes, I—I just—talking to them I realized I haven't seen a picture of my mother. Of my parents. I don't know what they look like."

"Oh, Amelia had pictures of them all over the house. Dozens of pictures of your mother, since she was a little girl. Wedding photos, the works. No doubt in my mind they are in the storage unit."

"This is your office?"

"Yes indeed. These days I only use it for video calls, but yes."

"Zach mentioned all of your awards."

"My illustrious career." She walked over to the cabinet and pointed to one of her Oscars. "My personal favorite."

"'Leona Lovell, *Glory in the Night*, Best Lead Actress.'"

"I played a mail-order bride who was accidentally sent to a white man in Kansas. They eventually fall in love. What did the critics say? 'Lovell lights up the screen with her heartbreaking portrayal that shows us love is the most human emotion of them all.'"

"Who said that?" Evie asked as she continued to admire the statue.

"Don Lane at *The Hollywood Observer*, October 1967. I have the article around here somewhere."

"That's amazing," Evie said. She looked over as Miss Leona squeezed her hand.

"We'll find some pictures of your mom and dad. Don't worry."

"Thank you."

"Anytime, baby. Come on."

When they got back to the living room, they watched one more episode of Anita's show, and then after Miss Leona offered it up to a vote they decided it was time for Evie's first viewing of *Glory in the Night.*

Around four the sun broke through the clouds as it began to set. The forecast called for rain through the weekend and New Year's Eve. Zach figured they'd have to cancel the fireworks display, but the square dance they had planned would keep the participating guests plenty occupied. After he swung by the stables, he headed back over to the lodge to catch up with Delfi, their head of guest services and one of Zach's buddies since high school.

She'd been Evie's friend too, once upon a time, but they'd also fallen out of touch. In a more natural way. It was Friday and a new wave of guests were arriving. There was already a New Year's Eve proposal on the books, but another guest had decided he also wanted to propose at the dance. Delfi suggested they arrange something private in the couple's room. It took some convincing, but Delfi was able to work her magic. A private proposal would be more intimate and more romantic.

"I don't know what it is with guys and public proposals. I mean, I love this place as much as the next gal, but I'd be so pissed if Britnay proposed to me at a barn dance in front of a bunch of strangers."

"Well, you work here." Zach laughed. "I think you might feel a bit differently if she proposed to you at Disney World or in front of the Eiffel Tower."

"Zach. What part of no public proposals is difficult here?"

"Okay, okay. I get it."

"Hey, I know things ended on a weird note for you guys, but did you hear anything about Evie? Britnay follows her Instagram and she said she was in the hospital."

Zach didn't want to lie to Delfi so he gave her half the truth. "She's actually resting up with Miss Leona."

"Oh!? She's here in Charming?"

"Yeah, but on doctor's orders to rest."

"Well, that's good. It's much more peaceful here than New York City, I imagine. We'd love to see her when she's up for visitors."

"I'll let her know for sure. So you're good for the weekend?"

"Yes. Fully prepared to tell a bunch of grown people that no, they cannot go outside to play because it's raining. Spa appointments will triple. It'll be fantastic."

"Excellent. I'll see you later."

He headed through the back of the lodge and over to his office. He'd been trying really hard to keep all his Evie-related thoughts under control all day, but Delfi had to go and mention her name. Yeah, sure, Evie had been running laps through his mind since the moment he left her room the night before, but now there was an Evie-related smile plastered to his goofy face and he wasn't sure he wanted to get rid of it.

He had a few emails to answer before it was quitting time, and then he was driving his truck at the top legal speed back over to Miss Leona's. Evie hadn't sent him a text like he'd hoped, and when he'd considered sending a text of his own it was after midnight. All he could hear was his grandmother calling him thirsty, and thought better of it. But it didn't stop him from replaying that kiss over and over in his mind. It was better than he'd imagined, and all he wanted now was a repeat performance.

He opened the door to their shared reception area and bumped right into Jesse. He watched in slow motion as Jesse's phone slipped out of his hand

and skipped across the floor, narrowly missing the black Lab sleeping under Lilah's desk. Clementine looked up, then went right back to sleep.

"Shit! Sorry, man."

Jesse picked up his phone and inspected his screen.

"Is it cracked?"

"No, it's fine. What's up with you? You haven't been paying attention all day."

"What are you talking about?"

"You came in here whistling, and walked right into me. Didn't see me walking there?"

Jesse had a point. He blocked out the sun on a good day, but it was a simple accident. "I said, my bad."

Jesse looked up from his phone and fixed Zach with a cold stare, his eyes narrowing as the air between them stood still. "You just couldn't stop yourself."

"What?"

"You made a move on Evie, didn't you?"

"I did not make a move on Evie—"

"Jesus, Zach!" Jesse exploded. "What is wrong with you?"

"Whoa whoa whoa! What the fuck are you talking about? She kissed me."

"Don't act like you haven't been flirting with her nonstop since we got to the hospital."

"What the fuck—"

"You can't do this," Jesse said, like he was throwing down some royal decree.

Zach felt his neck snap back in shock. Jesse was the oldest, at the end of the day he called a lot of the shots at the ranch, but there was a difference between

offering brotherly guidance and tossing around de-
mands.

"Why are you acting like I'm some creep who's
going to fuck her over?" Zach asked.

"Because."

"Because what?"

Jesse was quiet for a moment and then he turned
and stormed back into his private office.

"Nah, man. We're having this out," Zach said,
following him. He was glad Lilah and Jesse's ac-
counting assistant Mylene had the rest of the week
off. They didn't need to see this. "What is your problem with me talking to Evie?"

"I know you."

"You do. And when have I ever gone around ruth-
lessly fucking women over?"

"I never said you fucked anyone over. You've been
going around flashing that *come here, ladies* smile at
every woman in the county since Sunny."

"Nah, you don't get to bring Sunny into this. Sunny
was ready to get married and I wasn't. And that was
a peaceful-ass breakup. She's seeing some other dude
now! I've been staying away from relationships—just
like you, might I add—because I didn't want to get
into anything serious."

"Exactly. You knew Sunny wanted to get married."

"What. Are you talking about. The minute she
told me, I pulled back."

"What makes you think you're ready to be serious
now. Evie needs—"

"Okay. You have got to stop speaking for Evie. I
know you guys kept in touch. I know you care about
her. I know you want to look out for her. And I know

she's in a really tough spot right now, but she is an adult. She's not a child that needs you to shield her from me. We had a good talk last night. We hashed some things out and then she kissed me."

"Bullshit."

Zach couldn't help but laugh. "Do you have feelings for Evie?" He had to know because Jesse was on some total bullshit right now.

"Of course not. I just know how this is going to end."

"Please enlighten me."

"Why, Zach?" He tossed his phone on his desk and crossed his arms over his wide chest. He looked like a fed-up grizzly bear, but Zach wasn't backing down.

"Have you talked to Evie about me once? This whole time? Like while she was in the hospital? Since we've been back."

"I—no."

"So you're just talking out of your ass because you think I'm incapable of holding down a serious relationship with someone, but you have no idea what she wants from me or how she feels about the situation."

"I—"

"You're talking out of your ass. Grab your shit and let's go."

"Where?"

"To our grandmother's house. You're gonna talk to Evie once and for all."

"No."

"No, fuck you. Let's go. I'm your damn brother

and you're trying to paint me like some silent-movie villain."

Jesse looked at him for a moment then snatched up his phone. "Fine. But I'm taking my own truck. Lock up before you leave." Jesse slipped on his jacket, then grabbed his Stetson off its hook. "Come on, Clem." The dog glanced between them, then followed Jesse out the door. The wall of the office shook as he slammed the door behind him.

Zach let out a deep breath and collapsed into a chair. What the fuck had just happened?

He knew everyone was touchy about Evie and her current state of health, but he never really knew how little his brother trusted him, when it came to her. He understood. Shit with women made Jesse uncomfortable. He'd pretty much given up trying to find a girlfriend of his own. And it wasn't for lack of interest. Women all over Charming had taken a crack at Jess, but nothing had worked out. Zach also understood how much Jesse cared for Evie. They'd been tight as kids and—

It dawned on him then. Jesse wasn't just trying to protect an injured woman from a situation that had potential to go left. He was trying to protect his friend. Sometimes Zach forgot how close Evie and Jesse had been as kids. They were all together so much he'd forgotten all the time he and Sam had spent riding, leaving Jesse and Evie alone. Jesse didn't have romantic feelings for Evie, but he loved her just the same. Zach knew he had to do right by Evie, but maybe it was time to have a serious conversation with his brother.

Zach took his time shutting down the office. He

and Jesse both needed some time to cool off, and maybe it would be better for everyone involved if they didn't come barging in to Miss Leona's house like two cavemen who'd lost their minds. He turned off the lights and grabbed his laptop bag, then locked up before he drove back to Pleasant Lane.

"Hello?" he called out as he walked into the kitchen. He found Vega, Lilah, and Corie watching TV. "Jesse been by here?" Zach asked.

"Yeah, he came in here all puffed up. Miss Leona deflated him a little, then sent him over to Super-Storage with Evie."

Zach thought about joining Vega and his cousins on the couch, but he was still a little on edge. "Li, can you text me when they get back?"

"Sure."

"Thanks." He thought about going to check in on his grandmother, but he knew she'd have another lecture waiting for him too. He slipped on his Stetson and went back to his place to wait.

Chapter 12

Evie wasn't sure what to say. Everything happened so fast. Jesse came storming into the house and before he could say a word, Miss Leona seemed to shut down whatever had him fired up with one look. Jesse stopped in his tracks and removed his cowboy hat, then took a deep breath. Miss Leona asked him if he still had the keys to Evie's storage unit. When the answer turned out to be a yes, she sent them off, but not before Lilah handed Evie a beautiful floral silk scarf.

With Vega's help they covered her butchered hair and tied the silk scarf in a beautiful twist at the top of her head. Evie checked herself in the powder room mirror and for the first time since she woke up in the hospital she felt kinda pretty. That glowy feeling lasted exactly as long as it took them to walk to Jesse's black pickup truck. Euca and the shiny black Lab whose name she couldn't remember followed them, but only the black dog jumped in the back of the extended cab behind the driver's seat.

Evie buckled her seat belt and tried to make herself comfortable, but five or so minutes later this

awkward silence had built between them. Evie
wondered if he was going to say a word to her at all.
She didn't know how long it would take to get to the
storage place, but the silence was not working for
her. She glanced in the back seat. The dog was sitting, happily looking out the window at the quickly
darkening sky.

"Is this your dog?" Evie asked.

"Yeah, that's Clementine. Got her from the shel-
ter last year."

"She's very beautiful."

"Thank you. She's a good dog."

"Do the other dogs belong to you too?"

"Just Clementine. Euca is Sam's dog and Sugar
Plum and Poppy belong to my mother, but they'll
follow pretty much anyone around," he explained.
His voice was still tight. Still, Evie could tell he was
trying to be polite.

"I spent some time with Euca and Sugar Plum
today. They are very sweet." Jesse just nodded. When
the silence dragged on, Evie finally asked," Are you
okay?"

"Not really, but I'd like it if we could talk about it
a little later."

"Okay," Evie said, and then she hesitantly asked,
"Are you upset with me?"

"No. I'm upset with Zach. I'll be ready to talk
about it in a few minutes. I just don't want—just give
me a few minutes. I'll be fine."

"Okay. I talked to your parents today. They seem
nice. Though I'm not sure your dad—" Evie stopped
herself before she brought up Jesse's father's comments about her and Zach.

"Our dad what?"

"Oh, nothing. He just wanted me to check out the ranch. He said you guys have done a great job with it. Do you want me to stop talking?"

"No," Jesse said. Evie got a sense he wanted to say something else. "You usually did most of the talking before. I don't mind it."

That explained a lot. "Well, I made a frittata today and then I got an intense lesson from Miss Leona on how to make the perfect BLT. I can see why I became a chef. Cooking is fun."

"Yeah, Miss Leona taught you and me both how to cook a bunch of stuff when Zach and Sam were out competing."

"I bet we had a good time."

"We did."

Evie realized that while she'd seen a few articles and photos of Jesse, she'd only seen proof of his former football career. Nothing that suggested he'd been involved in the rodeo.

"Do you ride horses?"

"Not usually. I got bit by my dad's horse when I was a kid and thought it was best if I admired them from afar."

"Make sense."

"Hmm," was all he said. Evie was quiet again, but luckily the storage facility wasn't too far from their house. They parked and Jesse rolled down his window a little bit before he hopped out. Evie followed him to a side entrance, glancing back at Clementine's face in the back seat.

"Will she be okay?"

"She'll be fine," Jesse said.

They stopped at a sliding glass door, where Jesse took out his phone and apparently pulled up a code that he entered into a keypad on the wall. There was a beeping sound and the doors opened and they walked into a large lobby area with dollies and hand trucks lining one wall. There was an elevator with a keypad and a door marked STAIRS with an identical keypad, but Jesse pointed to the right, down a long, dark hall.

"You got a first-floor unit."

Evie followed, relieved when Jesse found a light switch. She felt only slightly less terrified now that she could see down the corridor. About halfway down they stopped at unit 110. Jesse pulled a smaller key ring out of his pocket and opened the padlock on the door. It made a loud grinding noise when it opened. Evie was surprised to see that everything inside was in order. Jesse found the light switch inside and Evie could see how all the stacked boxes were neatly labelled.

Evie remembered then that these things had been sitting there packed away, for almost ten years.

"Jesse, who pays for this?"

"I do. We do. You had our Realtor sell Nana Buck's house, and then Miss Leona hired a crew to go through everything. You decided what you wanted to keep and what you wanted to sell."

"That's—your family is too kind to me."

"No such thing. You're family to us. The bed of my truck is still wet. We can fit at least two of these boxes in the back seat with Clementine."

"Okay. I'll pick two and then we'll come back."

"Good plan. Take your time." Jesse stepped back

out into the hallway. Evie thought he was going to leave her alone and go back out to the truck, but he just pulled out his phone again and leaned against the wall.

She turned back around and surveyed the storage unit again. There were dozens of boxes stacked on shelves all the way to the ceiling. In one corner, by the door, there were a few pieces of furniture: a couple rocking chairs and a sideboard. Obviously those would stay put. She walked over to the wall of boxes and was suddenly overwhelmed as she read the labels. They were typed up, laminated, and taped to each box. They made this a lot easier than having to open each box to figure out what was inside, but she realized the labels didn't really mean anything to her. She wouldn't have any memories of AMELIA'S PERSONALS or EVIE'S STUFFED ANIMALS, but maybe they could trigger something. She had no idea where to start.

"I want to see pictures of my parents," she said to herself, her eyes darting along the wall.

"Here." Jesse came up behind her and pulled down a box from the top shelf. FAMILY PHOTOS was printed on the front. He placed the box on the floor. "It's heavy."

"What's bothering you?" Evie asked.

Jesse reached for another box marked FAMILY PHOTOS before he responded. He sighed first too. "Zach and I got into it back at the office."

"You got into fight?"

"Yeah."

"I'm sorry." She was just about to ask what they were fighting about, but Jesse kept right on going.

"Did you kiss Zach last night? Or did he come on to you?"

Heat rushed over Evie's face and the side of her head suddenly started to ache. Kissing Zach wasn't a secret. She'd already told Blaire and Vega. She just didn't expect Jesse to know about it or to make it sound like it was the worst thing Evie had ever done. She swallowed and waited a few seconds for the aching to stop. It took a few deep breaths, but she found her voice. "He told you about that?"

"He didn't brag about it, but he said something happened when he knew damn well he should leave you alone."

"Why does the idea of Zach and me being together bother everyone so much? Everyone but your parents, apparently," she asked, more to herself. Then she looked up at Jesse. "Was I bad for him? Is *Zach* a bad guy? I know he's your brother, but you should tell me if he is."

"Wait, what about my parents? What did they say?"

"Nothing exactly. They just seemed very happy to hear that Zach and I were spending time together again. Then Miss Leona mentioned that your dad thought Zach and I would have made a good match once upon a time, but this sounds like more than that. What's going on?"

Jesse looked at her for almost a full minute and Evie waited. It was dead silent in the storage unit, but she refused to fill the silence this time. She'd rather wait for the truth than rush a lie. Jesse took off his hat and scratched the back of his bald head.

"Zach is a good man. He—he's a great brother and a great business partner."

"But he's shitty to women?"

Jesse was quiet again, thinking about what he wanted to say next. Maybe it had something to do with her grandmother and why she didn't see Zach and Evie together. Maybe . . .

"You're—I just think you deserve the world, and I know Zach could never put you first because the ranch comes first. It's why we're both single. It's our curse, I guess. We love Big Rock more than anything, but you deserve better than that. You deserve the best," Jesse said.

Evie felt herself frown. "I wish—I wish I believed that." She wanted the best for herself, but she couldn't picture a scenario where she was too good for Zach. She couldn't put her finger on it, but something felt really off about that.

"You don't?"

"I want to believe it, but, Jesse, I still don't know who I am. What if I was some asshole after I moved away?"

"You weren't."

"But, what—"

"You weren't. You're still the first person to reach out to me on my birthday every year. At midnight, wherever you are, you text me or call me."

Evie wanted to ask Jesse to take her off whatever pedestal he'd put her on, but that wasn't the problem. He sounded like he was trying to protect her in a very specific way, from Zach and maybe even from herself. She cocked her head to the side and looked up at his handsome face.

"You weren't talking to me a whole bunch in the hospital, but we were really friends, weren't we?"

"Yeah."

And then Evie realized. She'd been so flustered about how Zach and everyone else had been so warm to her, she never considered that Jesse's hesitation to get close to her could be about something else. Yeah, she had it bad for one Pleasant brother, but this Pleasant brother, this quiet mountain of a man, cared about her too.

"You're worried about me, huh?" she asked.

"I was. I am."

Evie couldn't stop herself. She stepped forward and wrapped her arms around Jesse's waist. His big arms came around her shoulders and squeezed her tight. They held each other for a moment before she stepped back.

"You're a sweet guy, Jesse."

He shrugged. "It hit us real hard when Nana Buck died, and when Nicole called, my damn heart stopped. I really thought we'd lost you too. I wasn't ready. And then I thought of all the years without you because you and Zach had been fighting—"

"Wait. I get why Zach and I were fighting, but you're a grown man, you could have come to see me. Why didn't you?"

"I—I guess—shit, I don't know."

"Some friend," Evie teased, giving his arm a little shove. "Well, I'm here and I want us to still be friends, if you'll give me a chance to get to know you again."

"Yeah, I think that works."

"Good. But you still don't trust me with your brother?"

Jesse shrugged again. Maybe he'd run out of steam. "That's not the problem. Sorry for bringing this up."

"I appreciate your apology, but we're working on twenty years of history between the three of us, four if you include your brother Sam, and a lot more if you include our grandparents. I've been back in your lives a week, and surprise, still no memory. We were bound to hit some speed bumps, but I still want to know. What does it matter if I kissed Zach first?"

"It doesn't matter."

"Apparently it does if you guys had a fight about it."

Jesse sighed, then gave in. "I came running back to the house because I didn't believe Zach, you know, about what happened between you two, and he said I could ask you for myself. He wasn't being serious, but I called his bluff. Saying it out loud though now, I see how ridiculous this all sounds."

At least he was smart enough to sound embarrassed. She didn't have siblings, but it sounded like they could drive each other crazy for no good reason. "Okay. That sounds so silly, but I don't want you two fighting about me. Let's finish up here and go back to Miss Leona's."

Jesse's nod was enough to end the conversation. She was glad they had talked. Zach and Jesse had made a whole lot out of nothing, but talking to Jesse had made the anxiety of going through the family's things fade a little. Evie faced the wall of boxes again with a bit more determination.

"We can fit two boxes."

"These aren't as big as I thought. We can cram three in there. Four if you don't mind Clementine sitting on your lap."

Evie thought back to the full-sized black Lab. "That's a lap dog to you?"

"I have a big lap."

Evie laughed. "We'll take three."

With Jesse's help they figured out which three boxes she wanted to go through most urgently. There was a box of pictures marked PHOTOS: YVONNE'S ROOM, one of the boxes marked FAMILY PORTRAITS and another marked YVONNE'S ROOM NOTEBOOKS. Jesse used his car keys to rip through the tape, and inside Evie found a bunch of her journals. Jesse grabbed a dolly and hauled the boxes out to the truck while Evie locked up. They both decided it made sense for her to keep the keys just in case someone else drove her the next time. Clementine was very happy to see them as they headed back to Pleasant Lane.

"That's Zach's place, right?" Evie asked as they pulled up the long drive. The lights in the house on the far end of their private cul-de-sac were on.

"Yeah," Jesse replied.

"It looks like he's home. Let's go talk to him."

"Okay."

He pulled up in front of Zach's house and when they hopped out of the truck, Evie walked around the front and grabbed Jesse's arm so he couldn't run away.

"I'm coming. You don't have to put me under citizen's arrest," he said.

Evie laughed but she didn't let go. Instead she

tugged him all the way to Zach's doors, Clementine following along at their side. Evie rang the doorbell and ignored the jitters in her stomach. She'd been wanting to see Zach all day. Under different circumstances, granted, but she was happy to be finally seeing him.

"It's Jesse and Evie," she called out. A moment later Zach answered the door. He was wearing a white button-down shirt with the sleeves rolled up and a nice pair of jeans. It was a simple outfit, but he still looked so damn handsome. He flashed her that killer smile.

"Miss Buchanan, a pleasure." Then the smile dropped and he glared at his brother over her shoulder. "Jesse."

"Jesse and I would like to come in and talk to you." Zach looked at the two of them before an odd chuckle bubbled up from his chest. "What's so funny?"

He shook his head. "Nothing. It's just like back in the day. Jesse would tell me not to pick on you, you'd tell me not to give Jesse so much shit. Somehow Sam always got off easy. Come in."

"Thank you."

Clementine took the invitation and pushed her way in.

Evie wasn't sure what she expected from Zach's house, but it was a smaller—but not small—version of Miss Leona's house. They followed him to the big leather sectional in this living room. He had some basketball game on and there were a few boxes of pizza on the coffee table.

"I was just about to tell Corie and the ladies to come over. Give Miss Leona some peace and quiet for a moment. Have a seat." He muted the TV and sat down in the middle of the couch. Jesse sat on the far end and Clementine wasted no time jumping up on the couch beside him. Evie took a seat on the other end so she could look at them both as they talked. She cleared her throat. She figured one day she'd have to get used to commanding a room again. Why not start with an audience of two.

"I think Jesse is worried that you're not going to give me your all," Evie said plainly.

Zach nodded firmly once. "Which I understand, but Jesse should trust me. We are business partners and brothers. But I understand that Jesse truly does care about you and is just looking out for you."

"Jesse, would you say that's an accurate representation of the situation?" she asked.

"Yeah," was all he grumbled.

"Okay, now. Vega reminded me that it's okay for people to mind their own business," Evie went on, ignoring Zach's snort of laughter. "So while I appreciate your concern, Jesse, it isn't your business to say what happens between me and Zach. *But,* I do want you and me to get back to being friends, and I do want you to have my back, just like I hope I can have yours—is that okay? If I'm supposed to get better, then I need you to trust me. I need to be able to make decisions for myself. Informed decisions, but still they have to be my decisions."

"Yeah, I get it."

"And just to clear the air, Zach has been a complete gentleman. I kissed him."

"Told ya, ya punk bitch," Zach joked.

Evie and Jesse both rolled their eyes. "Now is there anything you'd like to say to Zach?" she said.

"Sorry I popped off back at the office. I do trust you," Jesse said. "I'm just worried about Evie."

"And I want you to be," Zach replied. "We all care about her and I want her to make her own decisions too. But you know me, man. I'm not trying to mess with her. You know that."

"And Jesse, there's another thing you have to know: I could just be using Zach for sex."

"Okay." Jesse slapped his thighs and stood up. "I'm out."

"I'm just kidding," Evie said. "Please stay."

Zach laughed. "You gotta admit that was funny. A little fucked up, but funny."

Jesse sat back down in a huff, but he seemed to be more at ease suddenly. Zach must have been right. This was just their way. The jokes, clowning around, giving each other some shit here and there. Evie had to admit, she didn't hate it. She could easily see a friendship with both of the Pleasant brothers.

"Are we all okay?" Evie asked.

"Yeah, I think we're cool," Zach said, shooting his brother a genuine smile.

"We're cool," Jesse agreed.

"Great. Now, Zach, you said something about calling the girls over for dinner."

"Yeah, let me text Lilah."

"Jesse helped me grab some pictures and stuff

from storage. After we eat, can you guys help me go through them?"

"Sure."

"Of course," they responded at the same time.

"Here, I'll put the other box at Miss Leona's and bring the pictures in here. Stay put, Clem." Jesse headed for his truck and his loyal pup followed, clearly misreading the command to hang tight. Evie didn't mind though. She and Zach were finally alone. He looked toward the front door for a heart-beat or two before his gaze met hers. Evie was sure her glasses were going to start fogging up any second.

"Hey," Zach said.

"Hi."

He slid closer to her, closing the distance between them on the couch. He smelled amazing. Like manly soap. He reached up and lightly brushed Evie's cheek. It was nothing, just a simple touch, but the feeling of his fingers sent shock waves right between her legs. Everything she felt like she'd experienced with him in her dreams had been such a cheap sub-stitute. One touch and she thought she was going to melt right there on the spot.

"How was your day?" he asked.

"Good. How was yours?"

"Good. So, you're thinking about using me for sex?"

Evie swallowed, her gaze roaming over every inch of his face. She wondered if it would be weird to ask him if she could keep some recent photos of him in her room or on her phone, just in case. "I haven't decided yet," she said. "I've been considering my options all day."

"Let me know when you reach a decision. I'm

feeling the head wrap," he replied, even though his eyes were definitely focused on her lips. He moved closer and she could feel the warmth coming off his body. Hopefully Jesse and the girls took their sweet time making their way across the cul-de-sac.

"Oh, thanks," Evie said. Her fingers automatically touched the edge of the silk scarf. "It was gift from Lilah."

"You look beautiful," Zach whispered.

Evie wanted to thank him again, but they were too busy kissing.

Chapter 13

Though it put an end to their make-out session, moving their party of six over to Zach's house turned out to be a good idea. Once Corie and Jesse got going, things got a little loud and rowdy, and over at his place they didn't have to worry about bothering Miss Leona, especially as it grew later and later.

They finished the pizzas with ease while watching the basketball game. Evie enjoyed listening to them all talk about the players and various stats of both teams and the league in general. Even Lilah got in on the conversation, correcting Jesse and Zach about some guard who had recently been traded. Evie had no idea what the hell they were talking about, but it was nice just to be included. She felt better when Vega admitted she had no clue what was going on either.

"I haven't watched pro ball since Obama's first term. My ex-girlfriend was a Clippers superfan."

"Boooo," Corie teased.

"Yeah, Vega, you should have disclosed that information before I hired you," Jesse said. "This is a Lakers household. Get out."

"I didn't say *I* was a Clippers fan. They were just my last frame of reference when it comes to pro basketball."

At halftime Evie and Lilah sat on the floor and started going through the pictures. Corie grabbed an extra box to help Evie sort and keep track of what pictures she wanted to keep handy. She started with the box marked FAMILY PORTRAITS. Inside there were a dozen or so framed pictures.

She pulled out the first one, a picture of a little Black girl with box braids tied back in low pigtails with red polka-dot ribbons. The face was vaguely familiar. Evie saw some of her own features in the child's face, but there was no connection.

"That's you," Zach said. Evie looked up at the warmth in his voice. She could still feel the softness of his lips against hers. Not that she was going to rush into anything, but she really hoped the doctors cleared her for sex. Just in case. He stood, giving her shoulder a light squeeze before he moved around the other side of the coffee table. "Nana Buck had that hanging in your living room for ages. Taking a trip to the fridge. Anyone need a refill?"

Jesse held up a finger as he chugged the rest of the beer in his other hand. "I'll take some more water, please," Evie said before she turned to Lilah. "We can put this back in storage. It's cute, but not exactly something I need to hold on to. Right this minute."

"'Kay. Back in storage it goes." Lilah took the frame and carefully placed it in the spare box. Evie pulled out two more of her school pictures as Zach came back with their drinks. He handed off Jesse's beer and set down her water. She didn't expect him to take a seat on the couch behind her so his denim-clad muscular thighs were spread wide on either side of her shoulders, but she welcomed it.

"Watch her stitches there, Romeo," Vega said, pinning Zach with a hard look.

"I'll be careful. I promise," Zach replied. When it was clear no one else had thoughts on their new seating arrangements, Evie went back to their photos. There was one more of herself riding a small white pony. She must have been five or six years old. She handed that off to Lilah, then looked back into the box. The next picture was old too, two people standing near an old wooden fence. The man had a baby swaddled against his chest and the woman stood beside him with her arms wrapped around his waist. The woman was laughing.

Zach eased to the edge of the couch and started rubbing her upper arm. "Those are your parents," he said quietly.

She looked at the picture, not sure what to do or say. She knew their faces now, but if her memory didn't come back, this picture, and any others like it, would be all she had.

She closed her eyes and forced that thought away. There was no need to make this harder for herself.

"You okay?" Zach asked.

"Yeah. I just—I wish I remembered them. My mom was so pretty."

"I think we only met them once, but I do remember your mom being extremely kind."

"I'm sure Miss Leona can tell you more about her," Lilah said.

"I'll ask her in the morning."

"Let's keep this one handy," she said as she passed the picture to Lilah. She looked at it too for a few moments.

"I think my dad had a crush on her," Lilah said. "Her name was Sandy, right? Sandra Buchanan."

Jesse nodded. "Yeah, that was it."

"Yeah, my dad had a crush on her before he met my mom, but she moved away."

"God, I don't even know where we lived," Evie realized.

"Just up in LA. Your mom was a studio teacher for the Disney Channel and your dad was a camera guy, I think," Zach said.

"Yeah, that's right," Jesse added. "Your dad was . . . Jim?"

"Yeah, Jim Wright. I remember Nana Buck telling us one time that women in your family don't give up their maiden names for anything. Your great-grandma came up with the name herself."

Evie repeated their names in her mind. Jim and Sandra. Those were her parents and from here on out, she wouldn't forget. The next picture in the box was her parents' wedding portrait. She definitely could see the resemblance between her and her mom now. She was very beautiful, and on her wedding day, looked very happy and in love. And very eighties. The big hair and the lace headband and veil were a lot to take in. Her dad's mustache dominated his half of the photo—it was almost funny. She picked up her phone off the coffee table and took a picture of the photo. It was getting late on the East Coast, but she started a new group text with

Raquelle and Blaire. She attached the picture before hitting Send. **My parents!**

The last few pictures were more of Evie, one of a man they believed was her grandfather and a massive black horse, and a professional portrait she'd taken with her mom and her grandmother. She had to be around three years old. Evie decided to hold on to that picture, her parents' wedding photo, and the picture of her grandfather and the horse. Lilah suggested they clear off the window bench in the guest room, which would give Evie plenty of room to display the framed photos. She liked that idea. They carefully boxed up the rest of the photos to go back into storage, when Blaire responded.

Blaire: **Awww, babe. That's awesome. Look at your mom's hair!**

Raquelle: **I was just about to text you! They look so great. Holy Freaking 80s. Unrelated, does the name Melanie Burns ring a bell?**

Raquelle sent a picture of an angry-looking White woman with long black hair standing in the middle of a kitchen. She was wearing a long-sleeved chef's coat. She had tattoos on her hands and one creeping up the side of her neck. Evie wasn't sure if she was a real chef or someone playing pretend. Either way she didn't look familiar.

She turned her head and looked at Zach and then she looked at Lilah. "Does the name Melanie Burns make any sense to any of you?

There was a round of nopes, but then of course

Lilah came through. "Yeah, she's a chef. She was on your season of *Supreme Chef*. You beat her, of course."

Evie: Name and face don't ring a bell, but Zach's cousin says she's a chef.

Raquelle: Right. I didn't know if her face would trigger anything.

Evie: Why, what's going on?

Evie waited for a few minutes as the game came back on and the Lakers extended their lead, but after a while, when neither Raquelle or Blaire responded, she called Raquelle.

"Oh hi, Evie." Raquelle's voice sounded strange.

"Hey, what's going on?"

"Um, okay. It could be nothing, but I've been monitoring your InstaMessages, and she sent some kinda crazy stuff over the last few days. I didn't notice it at first because so many people message you."

"What kind of stuff?" Evie asked. "Did I have some kind of relationship with Melanie before?"

"Not really. You hated her and I'm pretty sure she hates you. Are you alone?"

"No. I'm with Zach and Jesse and their cousins and my nurse."

"Oh, put Zach on."

"Will you tell me what's going on?"

"Yeah, but Zach can get to the messages faster than me walking you through it. Give him your phone."

"Okay." She turned and handed Zach her phone. "It's Raquelle."

He frowned but took the phone. "Hey, Raquelle . . . Yeah, sure, hold on." Evie moved to the couch so she could sit beside him. He pressed a few buttons on her screen and opened up her Instagram messages. She had a few hundred unread, but at the top she could see Melanie Burns's face in a small circle next to the name FeelTheBurn. "Here." Zach opened the messages.

"Whoa. Raquelle, we'll call you right back," Zach said before he ended the call. He let out a sigh and showed Evie her phone. Melanie had sent three messages over the last few days, each more aggressive than the last.

I can't stand you.

Too high and mighty to fucking reply.

I should have recorded the shit you said. I'd fucking ruin you and your pretty princess image.

Evie blinked and adjusted her glasses. She couldn't believe what she was reading. "I—I don't—"

"It's okay if you don't remember," Zach said. It was exactly what she needed to hear. She didn't realize it at first, but she was racking her brain, trying to figure out what she possibly could have done to make Melanie Burns say such horrible things to her. But the truth was that she didn't remember, and it was pointless to try. She didn't remember Melanie's face, and the name was a mystery to her too.

If Melanie was also a chef and they had been on the same show, there were plenty of opportunities for them to have crossed paths. Jesse had said that Evie was a nice person and her friends and her agent seemed to agree, but what if they were wrong? She'd seen how polite Tilde had been before she went instant asshole toward Miss Leona, after Miss Leona had welcomed her so warmly. Maybe Evie had only been good to her close friends and her coworkers.

Evie was wondering when her luck was going to run out when it came to others and the kindness they extended to her. This, however, was not what she expected. Suddenly the room felt too small and her head started to throb. Zach's hand started to move up and down her back. It was a soothing motion, but she didn't like the way the room felt too still. She glanced up and everyone was quiet, looking at her, just waiting for her to react.

Vega hopped up from the armchair she had curled up in. She came across the room and took Evie by the arm. "Come on, mama. Let's go get some fresh air."

Evie didn't argue. She took Vega's arm and followed her outside.

Vega called it a panic attack. Evie's mind was racing and she felt like her chest was going to collapse in on itself. The fresh air did help calm her breathing and her nerves, but it didn't do a thing to ease her embarrassment. She thought the crushing, overwhelming feeling that had caught her off guard a few times in the hospital was a rare accident, but Vega explained that they were pretty common.

"We're just gonna go for a slow stroll. You take

some deep breaths and enjoy this cool night air."
They walked the length of the cul-de-sac twice, with
Euca tailing along, before Evie started to feel like
herself again. Vega didn't say anything, just walked
arm in arm with Evie while she focused on the cool
air and the sparkling stars in the sky. Every now and
then Euca would bump into her leg, and she found
a little comfort in patting the large dog's head. Evie
felt like she could breathe again, but she was oddly
drained. She didn't want to go to bed, but she didn't
want to go back into Zach's house to face him or
Jesse or their cousins.

"I think I might be done for the night," Evie said.

"Took the words right out of my mouth. I bet
Miss Leona has a banging tea stash. Why don't I
make you some and you can unwind in your room.
You've had a pretty full day. I'm sure this puppy here
will tag along if we let him."

Evie looked down and almost laughed at the
pleading look on Euca's face. She felt bad for ditching everyone. Especially Zach. She liked spending
time with him, and being near him helped ease all
the complicated emotions about her parents that
were swirling through her. The look on Evie's face
must have given her away.

"Don't worry about them. Or your photos. Jesse
and Zach will bring them over."

"Yeah, okay. Tea and bed sound good."

Evie went straight to her room, Euca following
after her. After she washed her face and changed
into her pajamas, Vega brought her a large cup of
tea. She had Evie's phone too, but she didn't hand
it over right away.

"Raquelle and Blaire texted a few times," Vega said, showing Evie her locked phone screen. Sure enough, there were a whole bunch of alerts crowding the display. "Again, you're an adult, and my business is your health. I'm not a therapist, but I feel like your mental health falls under my jurisdiction. If I were in your shoes, I'd at least give my phone a rest until the morning. Is it okay if I respond to them for you? Friends freak out when you don't text back."

"Yeah, I'm seeing that. Please text them back." Evie used her thumb to unlock her phone, then handed it back to Vega. She sent whatever texts she needed to send then plugged Evie's phone back into its charger.

After she helped Evie take down her hair and change her bandage, Vega offered to keep her company until she fell asleep.

"I think I'm okay now. I'm pretty tired."

"Okay. I'm right next door. Come on over or tap on the wall if you don't feel like getting up."

That made Evie smile. "I will."

"Come on, dog." Vega waved Euca over from her command post on the floor. They said their good-nights and Evie was alone. She sat on the edge of the bed and finished her tea.

Over an hour later she was no closer to sleep. She'd promised Vega she'd give her phone a break, but now she was just bored. TV would have to do. She found the Cooking Network and started a show called *Knifed*. Watching chefs try to do their best with secret ingredients from a basket was entertaining in a way, but not enough to distract her from the thoughts roaming around in her head. She wished she'd asked the guys to bring over the last box of pictures. At least sorting through the photos would give her something to do with her hands. She looked over at her phone and broke her promise. She pulled up Zach's number and sent him a text. Sorry I didn't get to kiss you goodnight.

As soon as she set her phone down it chimed with his reply. You don't owe me an apology. I'm sorry Melanie Burns is such a dick. You feeling okay?

Evie: Much better. Vega put me to bed with some tea. Euca offered what comfort she could.

Zach: Vega's good people. Euca's a good dog. You should get some sleep.

Evie knew he was right, but she could see from the three little dots blinking on her screen that he wasn't done texting her yet.

Zach: We have a wedding this weekend up at the ranch so I'll be tied up, hopefully I can come by and give you a 10 am kiss.

Evie: I think that'll work.

Zach: Goodnight, beautiful.

Evie: Goodnight.

This time when she set down her phone another layer of stress melted away. Zach was still into her, in spite of her little meltdown. She hoped it wouldn't happen again, but if it did, she had Vega here to help her through it, and she had Zach.

Evie stood in the middle of the field, surrounded. The cardboard cutouts, still images of her parents, her grandparents, Mr. and Mrs. Pleasant standing hand in hand without a care in the world, faces she didn't recognize but she knew she should. And Zach. She whipped her head over her shoulder and there he was, over six feet of flat pressed paper and pulp, winking at her like she knew exactly what was happening.

A crashing sound made her jump. She knew she was dreaming and so close to jolting awake, but the dream wouldn't let her go.

In the distance a hole opened in the grass, a gaping hole that seemed to be spreading before it suddenly stopped. A set of hands appeared at the hole's grassy edge. A woman Evie didn't recognize hoisted herself out from the hole. Evie couldn't focus on her face for some reason. Her features were a slowly moving blur, but when she spoke, Evie instantly knew her voice.

"You know the game. I don't know why you're just standing there." Melanie produced a kitchen blowtorch from her pocket. Evie had used them plenty of times. She knew the perfect finishing touch they could add to a dish and the danger they were in clumsy hands.

But Melanie's hands weren't clumsy. They were sure and focused. She stepped to the cardboard cutout of another woman in a chef's coat. Something in the back of Evie's memory knew the name that went with the flat grinning face, but she couldn't bring it to the surface. As if that would do anything to save her.

"I'm not ready!" Evie demanded, but for some reason her voice came out closer to a whisper. It felt like something was sitting on her chest and she didn't have the breath to get her voice to its full volume.

"Just pick one, you dumbass." Melanie pushed the trigger on the torch and lit the grass at the cutout's feet.

Evie glanced around the circle, her eyes settling on the cutout of her parents in their wedding attire.

Suddenly, Zach's fingers wrapped around her wrist. "Here."

"What?" She looked down at the pair of tickets Zach pressed into her palm. She couldn't make out the writing on the golden trimmed paper. "What am I supposed to do with this?"

He looked down the front of his tux and smoothed out his tie, then flashed her a smile. "You ready?"

"For what?! I have to save my parents!" she tried to tell him, but nothing came out. The grass was going up quickly, the flames closing in around them, but Zach seemed completely calm, completely unbothered.

"You've got this, Buck," he said. But she didn't. She didn't at all.

Chapter 14

Zach had a plan. Up at six. Take Steve out for a sunrise stroll. Swing back to his house. Shower. Check on Evie with his own two eyes, then kiss the hell out of her before he went over to the ranch to greet the first wave of the Getlier bridal party.

Weddings at Big Rock ran about the cost of several major organs. He found that whoever was footing the bill appreciated it if the man in charge made an appearance and gave his personal assurance that the bride, groom, and all in tow received the full ranch experience, with all its special touches. This time around, the bride's father was Sebastian Getlier, owner of the Rams. Zach wanted to make this man happy.

At five fifteen the blaring ringer on his phone woke him up. He hit Accept before he really processed the name he saw on his screen. He answered anyway.

"Zach Pleasant."

"Zach, it's Nicole Pruitt."

"Morning, Nicole. How can I help you?" Zach groaned as he rolled over.

"I'm calling about Evie."

Okay, that woke him up. He rubbed his face and sat up in bed. "Is she okay?"

"As far as I know, yeah. Unless she had another head injury under your watch."

"Nope, she's fit as a fiddle. What's up? I figured Jesse would be your point man."

"Well, I tried your brother, but he didn't answer."

"He's probably still asleep. Talk to me."

"I just spoke to Raquelle and she was spiraling out over some messages Evie got on Instagram."

"Yeah, from Melanie Burns? She asked Evie if she knew her. I saw the messages. They were pretty fucked up."

Nicole sighed. "I told Raquelle to run everything by me first."

"Listen, I get it, but I think transparency with Evie might be best. I mean, she needs to know if she's on the outs with someone. There's protecting her and there's keeping her in the dark."

"Yeah, I get that. I—I'm not certain, but I think Chef Burns was at the party. I think. There were a lot industry chefs there."

Okay, Zach was really awake now. He turned on his bedside lamp. "You think maybe she pushed Evie?"

"It's just a hunch. I asked if I could get a look at the guest list, but the person who has it is on vacation with her family and won't be back until Tuesday. But if Melanie was there—"

"No, I hear ya. Those messages were pretty out of control. Even if she wasn't there, she clearly hates Evie enough to threaten her. Does anyone else in your circle know Evie is in California?"

"I don't think so. I'm sure some people think she's still in the hospital."

"Okay, so we put Melanie Burns's wanted poster all over Charming, and if she pops up here we'll take care of it."

"Slow down there, Tex. We don't need to do all of that yet, but I just wanted you and Jesse to know."

"We need to tell Evie."

"Give me a few days. I'm keeping my eye on Melanie either way, and I'm reaching out to her team. There are plenty of people that don't like Evie, but Melanie isn't some rando on the internet. They are colleagues."

"Has she gotten messages like this before, like from strangers?"

"Uh, yes. She's a successful Black female chef. Her nickname is Princess. Just think about how many people would hate that?"

"Yeah, okay."

"Like I said. Give me a few days."

Zach didn't like it, but he knew Nicole was right. They had no proof of anything, and Evie had no memory. Hopefully, Nicole could get some answers and they could fill Evie in. If Melanie wasn't involved, at the very least Nicole could get her off Evie's back and out of her DMs.

Zach set down his phone and turned off his light. It would take a few minutes for the alertness caused by his loud-as-fuck ringer and his call from Nicole to fade. He made a new plan. Talk to Jesse and Evie. Talk to Miss Leona. Then carry on with the rest of his day as planned. But first he needed at least another hour of sleep. Which he would have gotten if his phone hadn't started ringing again.

He looked at the screen. It was the ranch.

Evie tossed and turned all night, waking herself up every time she rolled too hard to her right and agitated her stitches. Each time she'd fall back asleep she'd find herself in the midst of a different, but equally horrible, vivid dream. She couldn't remember them all, just bits and pieces. So many faces she didn't recognize and more strange places, miles and miles of desert and burning fields. And just like before, right by her side or just out of her reach, there was that cowboy with his devastating smile, only this time she knew his name and it only made it more frustrating when her mind had her running through a vine maze, trying to seek him out.

The other bits and pieces of the night that still left her raw? She didn't know what to make of them. Her mind, her memory were still in chaos, and clearly whatever part Melanie Burns had to play in her life wasn't helping with any sort of clarity.

When Vega came in to check on her, waking her just before noon, she realized she'd overslept. She tried to be polite as Vega took her blood pressure, but the weight of her dreams felt like it was still crushing her. She knew if she said anything she might cry, so she waited quietly until Vega was done.

She gave Evie's arm a light squeeze. "You're all set. Miss Leona is waiting for you in the kitchen."

"Oh, crap. She was probably thinking I'd be up in time to make breakfast. I'll get dressed."

"I'm going to take a walk to the end of that seven-mile-long driveway and back," Vega said as she put away her stethoscope. "Then I think I might sit in the garden for a while. I'm sorry, but I love this place."

Evie smiled. "Me too."

When she was alone again, she checked her phone. She had a few text alerts. She braved a look at her conversation with Blaire and Raquelle and saw the messages Vega had sent the night before, politely relaying that Evie was turning in for the night and that she'd talk to them soon. She considered texting them herself, but decided against it. She didn't have the energy to handle Raquelle's well-intentioned apologies. The rest of the texts were from Zach. Early morning fire to put out over at the ranch. Raincheck on that good morning kiss.

The text was sent hours earlier, probably in the middle of Evie's tenth bizarre dream of the night. There's no way she would have been in any condition for a pre-dawn smooch session, but still Evie's heart sank. Her growing feelings for Zach seemed so simple. She was drawn to him, and even with Jesse's warnings something deep down told her that Zach was a man she absolutely wanted in her life. That good-morning kiss would have done a lot to lift her funk. She sat back in her bed and responded to his text. Hope everything's okay. My schedule is very full though. Please check with my assistant to reschedule some kissing.

She reread the message to herself before she hit Send. She wondered if other women put this much effort into texting guys. She'd ask Blaire. She got as far as undressing for a quick shower when her phone vibrated on her sheets. Another text from Zach.

> Zach: Just a broken industrial freezer during a very busy weekend. We got it under control. I'll draft a formal request to your assistant. Shortly.

> Evie: Please do. I am a very busy woman.

> Zach: I'm busy over here thinking about how I'd much rather be spending my day with you.

She knew she was playing with fire, but she drafted one more risky text, just to see how far this could go. A whole day of not doing reverse cowgirl? I told you, I'm all about the face-to-face.

Zach immediately responded with a GIF of a man passionately kissing a woman all along her throat. The expression on the woman's face was so over-the-top, Evie tried to hold in her snort of laughter and failed miserably. But the longer she stared at the GIF the more she thought about the possibilities. Her dreams had ruined her night. Her dreams and some extremely unnerving direct messages from Melanie Burns, but just talking with Zach turned things around. It wasn't as good as a kiss, but flirty texts from Zach Pleasant were something she could get used to. If this was what it was like to be with him all the time, this light buzzy feeling, she might be in trouble, the kind of trouble Nicole had warned her about. She'd worry about that another time. She sent one more text. Yes, just like that. That's what I want. *winky emoji*

* * *

Evie found Miss Leona waiting for her at the kitchen island. She had the framed pictures Evie had set aside, lined up on the counter. Evie's other boxes were stacked near the door.

She wasn't sure if Miss Leona heard her enter the room. She stood there in another one of her flowy, two-piece ensembles in a lovely bright green. She had on a longer wig, the blond-streaked curls falling around her shoulders. Evie wondered for a moment when she would get back to being somewhat fashionable, if ever. For now her jeans and slouchy sweatshirt would have to do.

"Good morning," Evie said.

Miss Leona turned and smiled at her before she turned her attention back to the photos. "Good morning, baby."

Evie joined her at the counter and looked at the black-and-white photo that seemed to have Miss Leona's full attention. She recognized a young Miss Leona sitting at a round table in an elegant scoop-neck gown. Beside her was a much younger version of her own grandmother. In most of the photos she'd seen of her nana she was sporting jeans, a flannel shirt, and some rugged boots. Her hair was pulled back or under a weathered hat, but in this photo she looked downright glamorous, her big, slick curls wrapped in a pretty up-do.

"That's your grandmother Amelia and your grandfather Justice. And that's my Gerald and me in all my postpartum glory." She gestured to her face with a flourish.

"You'd just had a baby?" Evie looked at the picture a little closer. She didn't have any specific memories of any pregnant women in mind, but she had a sense women who just gave birth never looked that good.

"Yes, my oldest son, Gerald Jr. That's Lilah's daddy. He and his Denise live up in wine country. We went out to The Orange Grove that night. A fancy place near the beach. We had to wait until the second show to get in because we were colored," she said with a roll of her eyes. "But we had a blast."

"Were you celebrating anything in particular that night, or just enjoying some time out?"

"Just a night out." Miss Leona fell silent again.

"You were really close?" Evie asked.

"Thick as thieves. Your grandmother and I couldn't be more different. Give me gowns and wigs any day, and Amelia just really loved being around animals, but our friendship just worked. I don't think we would have taken over this ranch without your grandparents' emotional support."

"What do you miss the most about them?"

"Watching your grandfather ride. My Gerald was an amazing horse trainer. He could get a filly to two-step sideways back into her own stall, but your granddaddy was born in the saddle. It was impressive to see. And your grandma? I miss the way she could always make me laugh."

"She was funny?"

"Oh, and she was quick. Girl. When your grandfather proposed, she told him she had no use for a husband, but if he stayed out of her hair she'd let him stick around."

"Did they love each other? Did she love him?" Evie wondered out loud as her fingers touched the edge of the frame.

"They did. Very much. We had our own little bubble. Whatever horrible thing was happening in the world, any bit of bad news any of us got, when we were together, everything was alright. I miss them very much."

Evie looked at the photo: her grandmother's face and her grandfather's hand on her shoulder. She looked at the four of them so happy together. She'd had so much fun spending time with everyone here at Pleasant Lane, and it had only been a few days. What must it be like to have a friendship that lasted years and years and then to lose all of those people? Evie leaned over and wrapped her arms around Miss Leona's shoulders.

"I wish I could remember them."

Miss Leona patted her arm. "You will one day, baby. I'm sure of it."

They stood that way for a few moments, looking at the photos, thinking their own thoughts. What would her grandmother tell her to do now? What would she want for Evie? There was no way of knowing, but Miss Leona was here now, and Evie knew that was a pretty great substitute.

She stepped away, giving the older woman her personal space back. Miss Leona let out a deep sigh, then seemed to reset herself, like she was getting back into character for the next scene of the day.

"Okay, now I usually cook a big Sunday dinner, but I'm going up to Los Angeles tonight for a few days."

"Oh? Alright. So this will be our last lesson for a few days." Evie shouldn't be surprised, but she was. Miss Leona was a literal movie star. Of course she had a life.

"While I'm gone, I want you to try to make one dish a day. You don't need your teacher to practice. Lilah will be here to supervise. And I'm sure Vega knows how to use a fire extinguisher in a pinch," Miss Leona joked. Sort of. "I'd rather keep my hind parts right here, but I need to show my face at an event and I'm overdue for a visit with some of my people. I'll be back on Tuesday. Lilah and Vega will be here with you."

"And Zach and Jesse?" Evie asked before she could stop herself. She'd be more than fine alone with the girls.

"They'll be around, but the ranch is very busy this weekend with it being New Year's Eve, and some fancy so-and-so is having a wedding. And I believe Zachariah is filling in at the exhibition today."

"What's the exhibition?"

"They do a bit of a sample rodeo. Just a few events for the guests. Roping, riding, barrel racing, things like that. Zach does a bit of trick riding."

The thought of Zach doing tricks in the saddle made Evie hot all over for some reason she couldn't explain. She thought it might be best not to fan herself right in front of Miss Leona. "Oh, okay," she said instead.

"For now, girlfriend. We're making French toast."

A wave of relief replaced the pulse of Zach-induced lust heat that rushed over her. She wasn't ready to return to a professional kitchen, not by a long shot, but cooking with Miss Leona gave her more than a comforting distraction from the bizarre reality of her life. It gave her a purpose, a challenge she was eager to face with a delicious payoff.

"I'm ready," Evie said, confidence backing her voice.

"Great. Go get yourself a few eggs."

"Are chickens always this vicious?" Evie asked, eyeing the small nick on her hand as she walked back into the chicken coop. She'd done her best to sweet-talk the fat feathered birds as she entered their coop, but the one with the white and gray feathers had taken real offense at her attempt to gather eggs. Evie caught a beak on the back of her hand.

"Bertie," Mrs. Leona said, making a little tsking noise as she shook her head. "Sorry, I should have warned you. She can be a little moody every now and then. How's your hand?"

Evie stopped and let Miss Leona gently examine the scratch.

"Didn't break the skin. That's good," she said.

"I think my ego is more bruised than anything. She scared me," Evie said with a trembling laugh.

"Next time, I'll show how to sweet-talk little Bertie. Come wash your hands and let's get started."

Miss Leona was more hands-off with this lesson. Taking a seat at the island, she directed Evie as she slowly and carefully moved around the kitchen gathering her ingredients. A thick loaf of brioche, milk, vanilla extract, which Evie was also very fond of, but the striking scent still didn't match the warm kiss and hug she felt from the nutmeg when she first untwisted the lid on its small glass shaker.

She unscrewed the lid and brought the brown powder to her nose. Her eyes fluttered shut as the aroma hit her senses. "Oh, I like that."

"You'll get to know your seasoning and your spices again. Every chef needs their nutmeg. Let's get your dredge going." Miss Leona handed her a plate with raised edges, then nodded toward the milk.

"May I ask a silly question?" Evie asked as she started cracking her eggs. So much had happened in the last few days, but now that she was back in Miss Leona's company, she couldn't help but think of her films.

"No such thing, my dear. Go right ahead."

"When we were watching *Glory in the Night*—never mind." She suddenly felt so silly. There was no way she could talk to Miss Leona about this. She would sound so immature and maybe a little rude. She wasn't the person to help her fill in the cracks of insecurity she was having in her prospective love life.

"Come out with it, girl. This right here, this is part of having your own kitchen. Cooking and talking shit. Out with it."

Laughter sputtered out of Evie.

"Okay. Well." Evie went on, choosing her words wisely. She'd really enjoyed *Seeds in the Sunshine*, but she'd loved *Glory in the Night*. She'd kept her initial reaction to the steamy romance to herself, but now she had questions. "You and the man who played John Daly had such chemistry. How—how did you pull that off? I mean I know you were acting, but I'm just trying to picture what it's like to pretend."

"Baby girl, you don't know just how much acting I did. Wayne Westwood, the man who played John Daly? Horrible, horrible man."

"Really?"

"Oh yes. He treated me like complete dirt during that whole production. I won't repeat some of the things he said, but he had even more choice words for me after I won the Oscar and he wasn't even nominated."

"How did you get through it?" Evie asked.

"I met my Gerald on that shoot. He was the animal wrangler. I'd never ridden a horse before and he helped me learn during preproduction. By the time principal photography began, I was already half in love. During all my scenes with John Daly I would just picture Gerald holding me in his strong arms."

"That's really romantic," Evie said, right before she splashed a bit of the milk mixture over the edge of the bowl. "Shoot."

"Here." Miss Leona was quick to hand her a paper towel. Evie cleaned up her little spill, then grabbed the nutmeg. She held it up to her nose, smelling it again and again, and didn't realize how long she'd been interrupting her own lesson until she turned and saw Miss Leona staring at her with a tiny smirk on her face.

"Sorry."

"Let's heat your pan."

"Which do you like better?" Evie asked as she turned one of the front burners on the Viking range up to medium. "Film or television?"

"Whichever one is paying my bills," she said with a nod. "I'm two hundred and twelve years old and people are still paying to put my name on a call sheet. As long as the work is good, I'm grateful to be there—Now take your bread and dunk it in the milk, just like that."

Evie followed her instructions, soaking the thick pieces of brioche. She wondered how long it would be before she could carry on a conversation and effortlessly move around the kitchen.

"But things are so different now. I love working on *Rory's*. In my day there were so few brown faces running things when you walked on set, and now we have a Black woman producing, a Black show-runner, all kinds of people in the writers' room. Evie, it's wonderful."

Evie glanced over, smiling. "That sounds like fun. It sounds welcoming."

"It is. And it keeps me young, being surrounded by all of these different young people. Watching them work together and learn from each other. I'm a lucky girl."

"I wonder what it was like for me on my show."

"When you're ready, you can watch it."

"I should do that." Evie placed the first piece of bread in the warm pan and watched as the edges started to slowly brown.

"You smell that?" Miss Leona asked.

"It's the nutmeg?"

Miss Leona's wink was all the answer she needed.

Chapter 15

Evie felt like she'd made her first real big decision. Uncertainty and hesitation seemed to follow her around as she waited for everyone around to give her cues and instructions about what she should do next, what she should think, where she should go, but finally she found herself fully in command of the direction her heart and mind wanted her to go.

Evie was in love with nutmeg.

She'd taken note of the way a fry pan could transform the pungent odor of onions or bring out this certain sweetness from butter as it melted and browned, but nutmeg? Whatever her life was like before her accident, Evie knew she'd known no greater love than what she was currently feeling for the wonderful brown spice.

After Evie made enough French toast for her own late breakfast—it was very good, warm and sweet and buttery in the best possible way—and for Miss Leona to taste test, Vega expressed some interest in a second breakfast when she returned from her walk with three of the four dogs, so Evie made some more. And more for Lilah when she appeared from her room and wanted to give Evie's handiwork a try and then *more* with the remaining bread for Corie when she returned from her trip into town.

Vega helped her with cleanup, then Evie found herself drawn back to that nutmeg. She joined Vega and Lilah on the couch, where Lilah brought up the first season of *Supreme Chef*. She suggested they ease Evie into it before jumping to her seasons. Evie watched a dozen chefs from around the country compete for cash prizes and a chance to present an international food festival.

The first timed challenge had the chefs fighting over a variety of produce for a simple tasting course. The pace and the pressure made Evie cringe. She loved cooking with Miss Leona. She couldn't imagine having to come up with a dish on the spot while trying to battle other people for the last of the bell peppers. She also made a mental note to ask Lilah if they could try out bell peppers.

She glanced over and caught Lilah looking at her as she held the open nutmeg just under her nose. "Sorry," Evie said, only mildly embarrassed.

"Don't apologize. I love the smell of nutmeg."

"Right, but you don't want to marry it."

"Maybe it's attached to a memory."

"Oh yeah. Could be," Vega said with a shrug.

"What do you mean?" Evie asked.

"Sometimes scents or sounds or even textures can remind you of something. Like I went with Zach to go have lunch with a new feed supplier a few weeks ago and he was wearing this awful aftershave that my brother Jack used to wear, and immediately, I just remember my mom telling him that he was gonna wilt every grape we had. It was like a memory of my mom just as much as it was a memory of my brother," Lilah said.

"Hmmm," Evie took another whiff. She couldn't walk around with a container of nutmeg in her pocket, but she was strongly considering it.

Later in the afternoon, Miss Leona's driver arrived and they sent her and Corie off for their New Year's Eve adventure. With her official kitchen adviser away, Evie decided to give herself homework for the weekend. Pick a dish per day to make on her own—with Lilah's help and Vega's moral support. For dinner she tried her hand at spaghetti carbonara. She resisted the urge to add nutmeg. The execution was far from smooth. She dropped an egg on the floor. Burned some of the bacon. Luckily there was plenty more in the fridge.

She learned a valuable lesson about cheese graters as she almost took a nice chunk out of her finger while preparing some fresh parmesan. And while there was a big difference between crazed chefs and big dopey dogs, having Sugar Plum follow her back and forth from fridge to sink to stove until Lilah bribed her with treats so she would sit the heck down made managing the space pretty challenging.

She refused to give up, though, and in the end she made enough to feed half a dozen people. It was disappointing when she remembered it would just be their party of three. Vega and Lilah's company was wonderful, but she wanted as much feedback as she could get. Zach was still tied up at the ranch and

Jesse had a standing social engagement that had him going into town. He popped in to say hello before he and Clementine hopped into his truck and took off.

"He plays bingo down at the senior rec center every Saturday," Lilah told them when they finally sat down to eat.

"Oh. I thought he was just sick of us," Evie said. She took a sip of the tiny glass of wine Vega cleared her to try.

"That too," Lilah said with a smile. "Okay. Wait. Have you been photographing any of your meals since you got out of the hospital?"

"No."

"Okay. Hold on." Lilah jumped up and played with the dimmer switch, adjusting the lighting. "Your phone, please." Evie handed over her phone, trying not to notice that there were no new texts from Zach—and watched as she moved her plate around.

"Here, post that."

"My assistant is still in charge of all that. I'll send it to her." She sent the pictures off to Raquelle, and Nicole for good measure, and then to Blaire just because she liked sharing things with Blaire. "Okay. Let's eat." What followed was a few moments of perfect silence as they all took their first bites. Evie didn't want to get ahead of herself, but she thought it wasn't half bad. She loved the creaminess of the sauce and the bite from the parmesan cheese. The bacon added just the right texture to the slick noodles. She wanted to know what Lilah and Vega thought, but figured she could put off grilling them for their opinions for at least a few minutes. Polite conversation seemed like the better move for now.

"Miss Leona said your family lives in wine country?" Evie asked Lilah. Maybe that was the wrong question to ask, because Lilah's expression dropped. "I'm sorry. I didn't mean—"

"No, it's okay. You've had plenty of drama lately. It's only fair if one of us shares ours."

"I mean. I'm technically on the clock so I'm keeping my drama to myself, but you two have at it," Vega said.

Lilah chuckled a bit and shook her head before she went on. "I don't know if Jesse or Zach told you, but I have a bunch of brothers. Six, and I'm the baby."

Evie tried to imagine growing up with Zach, Jesse, and Sam times two, and then being the only girl.

"Okay, that's a lot," Vega said, taking the words right out of Evie's mouth.

"It was great growing up. They are great. I love my brothers. My dad just—he's old-school. Too old-school. He tried to marry me off."

"Wow," Vega and Evie said at once.

"Yeah. To a man twice my age. He wanted me to be taken care of, 'cause it's 1840 in his mind? I don't know." Lilah let out a deep sigh and sat back from the table. "So Jess and Zach have the ranch and my other uncle, Curt, has his medical practice."

"Right," Evie said, encouraging her to go on.

"Well, we have the winery, complete with horseback tours and a bed-and-breakfast. My oldest brother, Jack, helps run the wine business, Brandon and his wife run the bed-and-breakfast. Kelly plays pro football, so he's not involved in any of the businesses right now. The twins, Thomas and Micah, just started their own construction company. They're off to a rough start, but they're doing it. And Walker is in veterinary school. My other cousins are all still in grad school. I wasn't exactly sure what I wanted to do, but I figured I had a little time to figure it out."

"But your dad had other plans?" Evie said.

"Oh yeah. A real estate investor who will not be named. My dad thought he was really doing me a favor when he invited this man over for dinner and pretty much announced our engagement without consulting me at all. I'd met him like twice. My dad didn't think I'd actually leave home. I'm just glad my grandma didn't send me back. And that Jesse trusted me enough to hire me. I was not cut out to be that kind of wife."

"Man, that's a lot. My dad is just happy that I'm employed," Vega said. "That's all he wanted for me."

"Yeah, less unrealistic pressure is better," Lilah replied. "Anyway, I haven't talked to him since I got here. I message my mom, but I'm afraid to call her because I know she'll put my dad on the phone and I know that makes me a horrible child, but I'm still *pissed*."

Evie's thoughts went back to the photos of her own parents. What had they wanted for her? Did they want her to get married and have kids? Would they be happy with the way her life had gone—minus the whole amnesia thing? She liked to think they would be proud of her.

Lilah leaned forward again and took a healthy

bite. Evie watched her face as she sat back and seemed to analyze everything about the dish. Finally she swallowed and took a swig of wine.

"Well?"

"You still got it."

"Don't lie to me, Lilah," Evie teased, even though she was completely serious.

"I'm not," Lilah said, a real smile returning to her face as she laughed.

"She's not. It's good, Evie. Really good," Vega added.

"I just followed the recipe," Evie replied. She took another bite herself and yeah, it was really good. So good she was already planning on having a second helping.

"Listen. There's no place for modesty at this table. I burn ice cubes," Vega said. "And I'm not family. I'll hurt your feelings if I have to. This is delicious." Evie didn't want to get her hopes up too high. Cooking dinner for a few people wasn't the same as cooking in front of cameras or cooking in a restaurant. If she was going to get her life back she was going to have to keep practicing, maybe be a little more careful with the cheese grater, but for now, this really good pasta dish would have to do.

Zach was dead on his feet, but he wasn't turning in before he gave Evie a proper goodnight kiss. The Getlier wedding party was great company, and Zach had been smart to show his face to greet Sebastian and his wife, Marsa. Getlier was a good man and he was very happy with the red carpet treatment Big Rock had rolled out for his daughter and her husband-to-be. That kind of relationship led to repeat business.

There were two full days left of ranch-related entertainment in store for the wedding party. Beyond the rodeo exhibition, Zach had to show his face at the rehearsal dinner and the reception. After losing the industrial freezer and scrambling to help save thousands of dollars' worth of food, he still had to deal with the rest of his Saturday as planned. He needed some solid shut-eye, and that was the reason he jumped in his truck and headed straight for Miss Leona's.

As he drove, the image of Nana Buck popped into his mind. Over the years he thought of her less and less, but still that mixed feeling of pain—and something close to resentment, though Zach was always hesitant to name it—filled his chest. He'd loved Nana Buck almost as much as his own grandmother. His father had taught him the confidence he needed to enter the arena, how to perform, but Nana Buck taught him everything he knew about how to properly care for his animals, how to ride with flare, and the sense he'd need to keep from breaking his neck. He'd never forgotten how clear she'd been when it came to him and Evie. He knew she'd never meant for their friendship to crumble. Still, the power of hindsight was a hell of a thing. Had he stayed away from Evie because of Nana Buck, or his own foolishness?

Now it was as if he'd finally been given permission by the universe to think about Evie again, and now that he wasn't forcing himself to push every thought of her to the back of his mind or forcing himself to avoid her public image, she was all he could think about. All day long, he'd been thinking of ways he could cash in that rain check on that kiss, and maybe more. Getting her into bed was not his focus. He just wanted more time with her, wanted to make up for all the potential moments they'd missed, and, if he was being honest, soak up as much Evie as possible just in case her memory did come back and cussing him smooth-the-fuck-out was the first thing on her agenda. That what-if was still lingering in the back of his mind, but that didn't change the way he felt now, and it didn't change the fact that Evie had kissed him and had plans to do it again. Who was he to disappoint a lady?

It was only a little after nine p.m. when the dogs greeted him at his grandmother's door. If Evie wasn't awake, Zach was sure that all the barking Sugar Plum and Poppy did when he opened the door probably did the trick. But he was glad to see she was still up, watching television with Lilah and Nurse Vega. He was also pleased to see her scribbling in the journal he'd given her for Christmas.

"Evening, ladies," he said with a tip of his hat.

"Hey, you're back." The lightness in Evie's voice inflated Zach's ego a little bit.

"What I miss?"

"Evie made some amazing carbonara," Lilah said.

"Oh yeah?"

"There's leftovers for you and Jesse in the fridge. If you want to try it."

"I think I just might, but I had one question for you first. If it's okay with Nurse Vega."

"Ask away," Vega said with a tilt of her head in Evie's direction.

"You wanna check out the ranch?"

"Yeah." Evie perked up even more. "I'd love to."

"Grab your coat and your boots. The temperature's dropped a bit." Zach had his own wool-lined Carhartt jacket in the truck.

"Okay. One sec." Evie jumped up and headed toward her room. Zach resisted the urge to kiss her as she passed by, but he did follow a few steps behind. They could catch up while she laced up her boots.

"Uh, Mr. Pleasant." Zach turned back around just as Vega looked at her smart watch. "Wellness curfew is eleven p.m."

"Absolutely. I'll have her back at ten fifty."

"Now you're just showing off." Vega smiled, then turned her attention back to the television.

Evie was back, jacket on, boots in her hand, before he could make it down the hallway. Euca was following close at her heels.

"You make some new friends?" Zach joked as Evie took a seat on the front entry bench. She dodged Euca's attempt to lick her face and pulled on her boots.

"Yeah. I think she loves me."

"Can't blame her," Zach said. "You want to bring her along?"

"Sure, I guess. If that's okay."

"The dogs are up at the ranch all the time. They just aren't allowed in the dining areas."

"Sure, let's bring her."

They said their goodbyes to Lilah and Vega, then loaded Euca into the back of Zach's truck. Zach didn't want to fuck around and waste any time he got with Evie alone. She must have felt the same way. A certain heat moved between them as she shyly glanced over at him.

"Hi."

"Hey."

A bright smile touched her face and she turned her whole body toward him in the seat. The heat instantly turned into something else, a deeply familiar warmth. Zach was falling for Evie all over again, but like Jesse, he was happy to have his friend back. He'd kiss the shit out of her another time.

"I also made French toast today," Evie said.

Zach smiled at her triumphant tone. "Oh yeah? How'd that go?"

"Good. I discovered an unhealthy love of nutmeg that I'm learning to cope with, but the execution of the breakfast and dinner went relatively well. None of it was easy, but when I was finished and nothing tasted awful, I guess—I just thought cooking would be harder. I don't know."

Zach let a burst of laughter slip.

"What?"

"Cooking is hard. You're a pro."

"I just wish I could remember. I can't recall any recipes at all, but when I get started my hands just know what to do."

"Well, you lost—I don't know the medical term—event-based memories, but your fine motor skills are intact and clearly there's something to be said about muscle memory. You also clearly held on to your appreciation for quality spices."

"I guess so," Evie said with a sigh. "It's just confusing, I guess."

"Give yourself time. It'll be a'ight."

Zach started the truck, but Evie's hand on his thigh stopped him from releasing the brake. He looked down at her delicate fingers as they slowly flexed across the fabric of his dress pants. Zach took his hands off the wheel and slid his arm along the seat behind Evie's shoulders as he turned in her direction.

"Something I can help you with?" he said, his voice dropping.

"You owe me a kiss."

"I owe you, huh?"

"I mean, I still haven't decided if I want you to be my boyfriend yet. We're just feeling things out right now. It seems like a bad time to start breaking promises."

"Oh, so you're talking about boyfriends now? I thought you just wanted to use me for sex."

"Zach. Shut up."

Zach chuckled a bit, then leaned forward and delivered on the kiss he'd been waiting on all day. Perfectly, their lips moved together and Zach didn't deny Evie as she moved closer, pushing her tongue into his mouth. His hand slid around the back of her neck, careful not to brush the silk scarf she had tied around her hair. She moved closer then, her hand moving higher up his thigh. Blood rushed to his dick and while he knew she still needed time before she could help him out in that department, holding back didn't change how bad he wanted her one bit.

They kept on kissing, and what he figured would be one thorough but quick kiss melted into something more. Her fingers brushed the bulge in his pants and he groaned. No way he was holding that shit in, even if he was still burying most of the emotion that came with it.

They both had their own lives, and Zach knew whether her memory returned or not, Evie would return to hers. Charming wasn't big enough for her shine or her talent. If she was nailing complex flavor profiles less than a week out of the hospital, she's be back at *The Dish* in no time. Still, Zach couldn't help but want this to last. Coming home from a long day at the ranch, seeing Evie's beautiful smile, kissing her perfect lips, holding her close. It was something he could get used to.

When she finally pulled away, Zach was completely hard.

"You smell like nutmeg," he whispered against Evie's lips. The scent was coming up from the inside of her coat.

"I'll explain later." She moved back across the seat and fastened her seat belt. "We should go. Vega will be waiting up."

"You miss Tilde?" Zach asked as he turned his truck around.

"This might be mean, but no. I don't."

Chapter 16

Still dazed by the feeling of Zach's lips on hers, Evie did her best to take in the beautiful winter night as they made their way through the huge iron gates that welcomed guests onto the property of Big Rock Ranch. In the distance the property stretched out in front of them as they pulled up to a large log cabin–style building. She could see the paths that wove their way across the flat terrain, lit by electric lanterns. The ranch seemed to stretch on for miles, and even though it was dark, the moon lit the mountains off in the distance. Zach put the truck in park and gave her a few more moments to take it all in before he hopped out and came around to open her door.

"It's so beautiful," Evie said as he helped her down from the high cab.

"It's not too bad," Zach replied with a smile. "We're on Serrano land. The Spanish came, and then Black people and Chinese people came, then the Mormons showed up. My grandparents bought the place from a Mormon family. Eli Smith. My great-grandfather used to work for him."

"I wish I remembered growing up here."

"We had a good time. Speaking of." Evie watched as Zach reached into the back seat and pulled his wool-lined jacket on over his blazer. He knew how sexy he looked so Evie resisted the urge to tell him, but maybe she could snap a picture on her phone, for the sake of new memories, of course.

"We don't have to go into the kitchen, but Britnay Lim is our head chef and her girlfriend, Delfi Hernandez, is our guest services manager. I think they're both still here right now. They were like your best friends in high school. I know they'd love to see you."

"Oh." It had crossed her mind, but she hadn't given a ton of thought to what might happen if she ran into old friends, mostly because she thought she'd be confined to the high fences of Pleasant Lane during her extended stay. As she thought about it though, it might be nice to meet some new people. If they were cool with retrograde amnesia.

"Do you want to see them?"

"Do they know?" Evie's hand absently rose to her bandage. "About all of this."

"Well, Britnay checks your Instagram, so she knows you had an accident, but they don't know about the memory loss."

Nicole was trying to keep her condition under wraps, so maybe they didn't have to know. "How long has it been since I've seen them?"

"Ten years, I think. They were at Nana Buck's funeral, but you maybe have talked to them since."

"If your friend just got out of the hospital you wouldn't press them for details, right?"

"Nah, not at all. What are you thinking?"

"That maybe we go in and say hello and we don't have to tell them."

"Not a bad idea. Britnay is half Chinese and Delfi's Latina. That should help you tell them apart."

"Okay, got it. Britnay, chef. Delfi, guest services. Got it."

"We'll go in and say hi and then I'll introduce you to the most important person in my life."

"Who?"

"My horse."

"Wait—"

"Come on, Euca." Zach let out two short whistles and sure enough the large brown-and-white dog jumped out of the back of the truck, trotting after them as Zach took Evie's hand and led her around the front of the building. As they came around the corner, Evie spotted a sign welcoming guests to Big Rock Lodge. Just beyond that was a sign pointing toward the Sunrise Spa and another pointing in the direction of the Mercantile.

Zach opened one side of the massive double doors that led into the building and ushered Evie inside with a hand on the small of her back. Euca skipped right inside with them. There was a lot to take in in the large foyer. A fireplace, taller than Evie, stood along the far wall, surrounded by large leather chairs. Evie's eyes were drawn up to the elaborate profile of the mountain carved into the stone above the mantel. Beautiful golden light came from large globed fixtures that hung from the high ceiling every few yards. Zach stood with her while she took it all in. The space was somehow expansive, yet cozy.

"What do you think?" he asked.

"It's beautiful. Jesse told me about it, but he was giving me stats about square footage and how many employees the grounds required." She turned and found herself smiling up at Zach. "How many tons of food the animals eat each year. But he didn't say anything about all of this."

"And this is just the lobby."

"I saw pictures of the lobby, but still."

"Come on." They walked over to the reception desk, where a young woman with light brown skin and shiny black hair pulled back in a tight bun stood behind a computer monitor. She was wearing a well-tailored blue, white, and green plaid button-down top. She greeted them before Evie got close enough to read her name tag.

"Good evening, Mr. Pleasant. Miss."

"Iris, this is Yvonne. She's a good friend of our family."

"Lovely to meet you, Yvonne. Welcome to Big Rock Ranch."

"Likewise. Happy to be here," Evie said.

"Anything crazy happen in the last thirty minutes?" Zach asked.

Iris laughed. "No. Had a brief conversation with a Mr. Canover about how firm we were on the no-smoking rules, but he was a very good sport about it. Said he'd smoke the rest of his pack at the airport. He's staying over in Sparrow."

"Ask Ed to do an extra pass, just to be sure. I met Mr. Canover this morning. Good sport, not much on rules though. "

"Will do."

"Thanks. Just gonna show Yvonne around. We're

gonna head back to the dining room." He pointed to the floor. "Euca is down here."

The woman's professional exterior immediately dropped. "Oh, I love Euca!" She looked over the counter. "Hey, girl. She can hang out back here."

Iris walked around the reception desk and disappeared through what seemed to be a hidden door in the hall. There was a wooden sign hanging just above that said STAFF. She patted her thigh and Euca went right to her, nearly knocking Iris over as she tried to lick her face.

"I missed you too. Don't worry, Mr. Pleasant. I'll keep her company."

"Thanks. We'll be right back."

"Nice to meet you," Evie said, waving with her free hand. Her other hand was suddenly intertwined with Zach's. Iris had her hands full with Euca, but she didn't miss the close contact between Evie and Zach. Evie hoped Zach was okay with the ranch staff knowing that maybe they were more than just friends. Clearly, he didn't care. They walked into the kitchen, where a few employees were still finishing their side work. Zach didn't introduce Evie, but hellos were exchanged and he held on to her hand the whole time.

They went down another short hallway and stopped at a door with a plaque that read EXECUTIVE CHEF BRITNAY LAM. Zach knocked on the door.

"Brit? It's Zach."

"Yep."

Zach cracked open the door, then turned to Evie and said, "One sec." He stepped into the room and pulled the door closed behind him, but Evie could still hear what he said next.

"Evie's with me, but no screaming or grabbing. She's still on the injured list."

"*What?*" Evie heard next.

"What did I just say?"

"We got it. Keep it down and don't be grabby. Move the fuck out of the way."

The door swung open and a beautiful, plump Asian woman in a chef's coat stared up at her, hands on her hips. Behind her was a woman in a black blazer and matching pants. Evie could see the blue, green, and white plaid blouse and the name tags she was wearing. Her dyed red hair was in a long braid over her shoulder.

"Oh my fucking God," Britnay said in a dramatic whisper. She reached forward and just barely touched Evie's hand with her finger tip.

"Can I hug her or will she break?" Britnay asked.

"Hey, I'm just—"

"Shut up, Pleasant. No one was talking to you." Britnay stepped forward and gave Evie a very gentle hug. Delfi was right behind her, pulling her into a tighter embrace. Tears lined her eyes when she pulled back.

"Buck. It's so good to see you."

"Good to see you too," Evie said honestly.

"I like the glasses," Brit said.

"Yeah, me too. Seriously, only you look this good straight out of the hospital. What the hell happened?" Delfi asked.

"Ultra-high heels and a dark staircase," Evie said so easily she almost believed herself.

"Yeeeesh. Well, I'm glad you came home. I can't imagine you can get shit worth of R and R in New York City. It's so tight and noisy," Britnay said.

"I see the appeal," Delfi said. "There's not much to do here. At least in New York there's stuff to do."

"LA is a short drive away."

"Not the same."

Evie felt herself smiling as the two rolled their eyes at each other.

"It's definitely different," she said.

"How long are you in town?" Britnay asked.

She glanced at Zach. "Uh, not sure yet. Just trying to heal up and rest. We'll see."

"Don't you have to get back for the show?" Britnay asked.

"Man, that's a sweet gig," Delfi added. "Heal up quick and go back to those checks."

"Are we not paying you enough?" Zach said. He placed a hand on his chest with exaggerated offense.

"Why is he acting like I wouldn't take more money?"

Evie laughed, enjoying their back-and-forth.

"I'm gonna run Evie over to the barns so she can meet Steve before she turns in for the night."

"Cool, cool. I have a ton of crap to finish up here," Britnay said. "We're both off Tuesday and Wednesday. Let's hang."

"Yeah, okay."

"I'll have her people call your people," Zach replied.

"Don't bring him," Delfi said before she stuck out her tongue at Zach.

"I'll text you," Britnay added. They said their goodbyes and left Britnay to her work.

"That wasn't so bad," Evie whispered when they were back out in the kitchen.

"Shit, you nailed it," Zach replied.

She'd had a conversation with old friends and it felt good and normal. She had no clue who they were, but maybe she had old texts. Maybe even pictures or things in her old journals that could help fill in holes on the relationship. If she spent more time with them, she'd tell them the truth. Britnay and Delfi seemed cool and she wanted to see them again. Eventually Vega would leave, and she was sure Lilah and Corie wouldn't want to babysit her forever. Hanging out with her own friends. Now that was another big step. She made a mental note to text Blaire. She had more to tell her.

Evie looked down the length of the large kitchen and suddenly forgot all about friends and whatever renewed social life might lie before her. She felt Zach as he stepped closer.

"You okay?"

"Yeah," she replied as she looked at his gorgeous face. She glanced back down the open space and saw the last of the kitchen staff turn the corner. "Can I—may I look around just for a sec? I won't touch anything."

"I mean, I trust you not to go around spitting on everything. Have a look around."

Evie let go of his hand and started slowly walking to the far side of the room. It wasn't anything like *Supreme Chef*. Aside from the quiet. It felt, again, overwhelmingly huge and yet somehow tight. There was a faint smell of cleaning products. Every shiny, metal surface was sparkling and clean. She looked at the row of gas burners, the massive deep fryer and the flat grill top. Nothing came to her. Not a sound, a scent, a flicker of a memory, but she somehow felt right at home. It would take time, but she would do it. She'd make her way back to a real kitchen.

She turned and saw Zach leaning against the freezer door. Handsome as all get-out and proud of it too. His mustache lifted at the corner as he smiled at her. She turned and walked right back into his arms. She waited for a wave of sadness to hit her as his hand gently moved up and down her back.

"You okay?"

"Yeah, I just watched a lot of *Supreme Chef* today. Thinking about what it was like to work in a real kitchen."

"You made dinner in a real kitchen today and you had dinner guests."

"But you know what I mean."

"I do, I just don't want you to sell yourself short, Buck. You got this."

"If I stay, like forever, maybe I can tell Britnay the truth and I can come work for her."

"She'd love to have you."

"You called me Buck and I didn't start crying."

"See? That's progress. You wanna meet a horse?"

"Oh my God. More than anything," she teased. "Let's go."

For some reason she expected the barn to be dark. After a quick conversation with Oliver, one of the three night guards who patrolled this portion of the property, he opened the door for her and Zach and they slipped inside. The space was dimly lit, but light enough for Evie to see. A few seconds later though, the lighting design was the last thing on Evie's mind.

She had no idea what she expected a barn to smell like, but this wasn't it. She couldn't describe it. It was a weird smell that made her nose twinge and made her want to inhale to convince her mind that it wasn't smelling things. It was weird.

"Come on. Steve's down here."

They walked down the center of the dirt-covered floor and stopped at a stall about halfway down. Some of the horses poked their heads up to inspect their nighttime visitors. A few horses greeted them with their backsides. Another weird thing Evie remembered from her dream.

"They're all awake."

"Yeah, horses don't sleep that much. They just rock and roll all night and party most of the day. Hey, boy," he said softly, then made an odd clicking noise. The large head of a beautiful gray horse with black patches that almost looked smudged popped his head over the stall door. Zach dropped Evie's hand and started stroking the animal's big jaw.

"Evie, this is Steve. Steve, Evie met you once, but she doesn't remember you, but that's alright. Isn't it, buddy?"

The horse moved his head to the side almost like he was nodding. Evie almost didn't believe it.

"Can I pet him?"

"Sure you can. Here." Zach took her hand and guided it up to the same spot he'd just been stroking.

"Hi, Steve." She copied Zach's gentle tone. "You're softer than I imagined."

"Gotta stay fresh for the ladies," Zach said. "Give me your hand. Evie turned back to him and let him arrange her hand chest high, with her fingers together and her palm flat. He pulled a carrot out of his pocket, broke it in half, and placed the smaller pieces in her upturned palm. "Hold your hand just like that."

Sure enough, Steve took the carrot right out of Evie's hand, his lips tickling her palm. "Oh, that's weird." She giggled as Steve pulled back to chew his treat.

Zach pulled a few more carrots out of his bottomless pockets and they took turns feeding the horse his treats.

"Do you ride him during the exhibition?" Evie asked.

"You bet your boots I do." It was Evie's turn to roll her eyes. "Had him about twelve years. Before that I had a horse named Flex. Won all those trophies with that beast. God, he was the best." Zach let out a little laugh. "You hated him."

"Why?"

"You know that scar on your forearm?"

"Yeah, I was wondering about that."

"That was you thinking you should ride Flex out to the ravine. He threw you and you broke the hell out of your arm. I got in so much trouble."

"Good," Evie said with her own chuckle. "That scar is not small. It must have hurt like hell."

"When you were high on painkillers, you told me you loved me for the first time. You said we had to get married because it's what the baby Jesus would have wanted and I didn't want to disappoint the baby Jesus."

"Sounds like I was on some good drugs. How old was I?"

"Fifteen." Evie did the mental math and made note of the year. She'd have to go back and check her journals. "I feel like you owe me another apology."

"Oh, I'll apology you good." He leaned down and kissed her softly on the mouth. When he pulled back, she was surprised her glasses weren't steamed up. He flashed her that cocky smile, claiming his job well done without saying a word.

"Come down here. Meet Sam's horse, Majesty."

Majesty was a gorgeous all-black horse with a beautiful black mane, but she didn't seem to give a shit about their visit or the fact that Zach had apples.

"Fine, then more for Steve."

Majesty stomped her hooves and blew a breath out of her nose as if she was telling them to fuck off. A sudden wave of fatigue hit Evie. Maybe it was the quiet of the barn or maybe she'd pushed herself too far, socializing and talking to horses. She tried to cover a yawn, but Zach caught it.

"Let's get you home." They stopped once more at Steve's stall and gave him the apples. Evie watched as Zach literally kissed the horse on its face. "Night, bud." If it was possible, Evie was sure Steve would have said goodnight back.

When Zach stepped away, Evie pulled out her phone and snapped a quick picture of Steve. She sent it to Blaire. **No barn sex, but I met a great horse named Steve.**

Chapter 17

"Why is this so hard?" Evie looked down in the pan as her egg yolk started to spill out of the side of the slowly cooking white. There was nothing over-easy about this. "Darn it, I ruined it. I'll eat this one." She reached for the spatula and flipped the egg and finished frying it all the way through.

"I'll eat it. I shouldn't have said anything," Vega said. Evie could hear the regretful wince in Vega's voice even though her back was to her.

Vega had asked a simple question. Did Evie know how she liked her eggs? Evie had no clue. She'd enjoyed the few ways Miss Leona had shown her how to prepare them, but the next thing she knew, she and Vega were going down an internet rabbit-hole of cooking videos. After they watched a woman cook an egg in the dishwasher, Evie realized it was time to get to work. Almost a dozen eggs later and she was starting to know the true meaning of frustration.

"No, no, you were right. I need to know this. If there are four hundred ways to prepare an egg, I should figure out which is my favorite. And if I ever get back to work, I need to know how to make things

the way people want them. I might love a frittata, but
I can't become the frittata champion of the world."

"I mean, true. Or you can be one of those snooty
chefs who sets their menu, and people just take what
they give them. Well, snooty chefs and my mother.
She can make eggs fifty-eleven ways, but if you catch
her cooking before work, its fried or nothing."

"Well, I have that down." Evie looked over at the
pan on the right burner. It looked like the water was
almost ready. "I should have waited for Miss Leona
or Lilah. Ugh! That carbonara recipe was like forty-
eight steps. This is like two. Acquire egg. Cook it."

"Sorry." Vega groaned even louder. "I know my
way around the human body. Not a kitchen."

"No, we're gonna do this. Here." She served up
the egg she'd accidently fried through and through
on a small plate and placed it on the island, then
turned back to the stove. "Okay." She picked up another one of the eggs she'd managed to retrieve in
an incident-free trip to the coop. "You don't like me,
egg, and I don't like you. But I'm going to poach
you and you're going to take it."

"You got this. Poach that egg," Vega said with a
few claps.

Evie pulled up the video on her phone again.
Then went to work. She cracked the egg into the
small saucer she had standing by, then gently poured
it into the simmering water. She had the recommended vinegar on standby, but she wanted to try
one without it. She watched as the clear white began
to thicken.

"Miss Leona mentioned food waste, but it's not

wasteful if we give some eggs to the dogs, is it?" Evie glanced over at Euca and Poppy, who had long grown tired of their unsupervised culinary adventure.

"I mean I won't tell if you don't."

Evie gave herself a little shake and tried to focus. This egg would be perfect. It would not become dog food. A few minutes later she grabbed a large spoon and scooped the warm, soft egg out of the water. A dash of salt and pepper, then she handed it over to Vega. She watched as she used the side of her fork to slice into the egg.

"Well?"

Vega took a bite, then held up her thumb. "Perfect, but you know what it needs?"

"What?"

"More egg."

"Very funny."

"No. It would be perfect with toast." Vega hopped up and threw some of the leftover brioche in the fancy toaster oven.

"Make me some too." Evie said as she cracked another egg.

Nicole was under strict instructions to stay in bed. She'd made it through the holidays, but she hadn't gotten any real rest. When she found herself yawning in the middle of date night, Jane laid down the law. One real day off. No running around Manhattan, no chores, no work calls—with one exception. She could check in on Evie.

Beyond that, they were going to stay in bed and

rely on Postmates for as long as possible. Great plan. Pure genius. It was almost noon and Janie was still snoring away, but Nicole had been staring at the ceiling for hours. She couldn't stop thinking about those completely unhinged messages Chef Melanie Burns had sent Evie.

Nicole had asked around, and sure enough, Melanie Burns had been at *The Dish*'s holiday party, but that didn't mean she'd assaulted Evie. Nicole contacted the library again, and that was a dead end. Their head of security felt for her, but the Holiman Library had a New Year's Eve party for another set of New York's cultural VIPs right around the corner. He didn't have time to focus on Nicole's theory.

She understood. Without a push from the cops or a court order, there was no way he was going to sift through at least three hours' worth of security videos, frame by frame, again. He did take her suggestion to add another security camera near that rear staircase; still, that wouldn't help Evie now.

And even if Melanie hadn't been in the stairwell with Evie that night, what the hell was up with those DMs? Evie was a television personality. Of course, there would be people who didn't like her. Assholes showed up in her Instagram comments and Twitter replies every day, but the things Melanie Burns sent were next level. Melanie probably viewed her as a thorn in her side, since Evie whooped her ass on *Supreme Chef*, but that was years go. Talk about getting a grip. Nicole couldn't protect Evie from everything and everyone, but that didn't stop Nicole from caring. She'd already contacted Nicole's agent but hadn't received a reply. Sure, it was the weekend, but she was going to follow up right after New Year's Day. This kind of shit just couldn't fly.

The suits at *The Dish* had already found a short-term replacement for Evie. They were due back at the studio in three days, and reality star and newly single housewife Montgomery Fent would be there to whip up easy meals and snacks. The camera loved Montgomery, but she wasn't a chef and she didn't have Evie's spark. In that respect Evie's job was most likely safe—for now. Nicole knew she had to be patient, but hoped like hell Evie would start showing signs of at least some memory recovery. The rest she could fake. Maybe.

Nicole picked up her phone and looked at the picture Evie had sent her the night before. Then she sent Raquelle a text. **Anything new from Chef Burns?**

Bless Raquelle. She was responding before Nicole's screen went dim. **Nothing, but I do remember that she had watched all of Evie's Instagram videos.**

Nicole: **Unhealthy obsession, maybe?**

Raquelle: **You could be right.**

Nicole was still reluctant to torment Evie with her theory about what happened that night, but needed to talk to Evie about Melanie. Whether she recovered her memory or not, she needed to keep her guard up when it came to Melanie Burns. Nicole switched over to Evie's Instagram and looked at the photo of the carbonara Raquelle had posted for her. Thousands of likes and nearly as many comments.

Her fans were still with her. She liked the photo and
left her own encouraging comment for good measure.

"Are you texting?" Jane's muffled voice rose up
from the sheets.

"Just checking on Evie." Nicole quickly switched
over to their conversation.

"I'll allow that." Jane slipped out of bed and slowly
made her way to the bathroom.

Nicole had no clue how she was going to sort this
shit out, but if she found out that Melanie Burns had
been the one in the stairwell with Evie that night, if
she found out that asshole laid a hand on her—well,
Nicole was the nonviolent type, but she was going to
be real pissed, and she'd make sure Melanie paid for
what she did. She sent Evie a text. Hey gorgeous.
How's your day going?

Evie replied immediately. Good. Met a horse last
night. A picture of gray and white horse popped up on
the phone. Made some eggs 78 ways. Never want to
look at an egg again. About to watch Supreme Chef.

> Beautiful horse. Sorry about the eggs. That
> Pleasant boy hasn't gotten fresh with you has
> he?

> Yes, ma'am, he has and I'm handling it.

"I should have given her the alk." Nicole groaned
out loud. Pasta looked amazing. I'm proud of you.

Evie sent back a few heart-shaped emojis.

"Just relax," Nicole told herself. "Everything is
gonna be okay." Now if she could only make herself
believe it.

* * *

Evie glanced up at the screen and felt herself cringing. She was stuffed to the brim with various egg dishes, but it wasn't her full stomach that was making her feel off. When Lilah and Jesse came back from church, they joined her and Vega for a marathon of *Supreme Chef*. After a few episodes Evie was ready to watch her season. She knew it would be strange to see herself on screen, competent in the kitchen, unafraid, but she wanted to know everything about her past, not just the parts neatly packed in boxes.

They were halfway through the second episode. Evie had won the first challenge with a shrimp and grits creation which granted her immunity in the final round. The first thing Evie noticed was how good she looked. Fresh faced. Braids piled in a high bun on her head. She looked right in a chef's jacket. Confident, and she moved around the kitchen with the same certainty.

And then there was Chef Burns. Lilah warned Evie that Melanie would be in nearly half the episodes. She'd had plenty to distract her, but those messages were now burned into her new memory. On the screen they were rushing around a farmers' market, searching for ingredients to make a main course dish. They cut to Melanie in the interview chair.

"I don't know what Tiffany thinks she's going to do with all of those mushrooms. This isn't a one-ingredient-dish challenge."

The camera went back to a tall, plus-size Asian who was scrambling to grab onions and carrots. It was her friend, Evie remembered. The one who sent her flowers in the hospital. Evie thought about texting her, but what would she say? Evie stared at the screen, watching as the show went on. The camera wasn't on her much, instead following Tiffany as she cried after cutting her finger. It was painful to watch her hands shake and she struggled to pull her meal together.

They cut to an interview with a guy named Jaren who commented on how Tiffany had the talent, she just needed to up her confidence. She was genuine competition. Once they presented the dishes, they cut back to Evie.

"I feel bad for Tiffany. I've definitely been there. I know how it feels when your nerves knock you off your feet," she said to the camera. They cut back to Tiffany in the back corner of the waiting area. She was holding her hand to her mouth, trying not to cry. Evie went right up to her and pulled her into a hug.

"You're not gonna make it if you can't keep that shit together," Melanie said.

Kate spun around, staring daggers at her while Darren, the only other Black contestant on the show, told Melanie to chill out. They cut back to the judges. Evie knew it was only a TV show. She knew how it all turned out. That didn't stop the sour taste settling in her mouth. Melanie really was an asshole.

"Evie. Evie." She turned toward the concern in Vega's voice.

"Yeah?"

"Hey, you okay?"

"Yeah."

"I just—"

Lilah hit pause on the show. The screen froze on Melanie, mid-interview, saying how she deserved to win. Out of the corner of her eye she saw Jesse lean forward, like he was watching her closely.

"I guess it's just shocking to see myself. And Melanie. Melanie is awful."

"It's what the producers want," Jesse said.

"What do you mean?"

"It's reality TV. The competition isn't enough, they want some drama. If it was just you guys preparing foods, it would be a different kind of show."

"Like *The Dish*?"

"Yeah, kinda," Lilah said.

Evie looked back at the screen and Melanie's sour expression. There were thirteen more episodes to go. She knew she should keep watching, but a strange feeling was eating at her. Suddenly she wanted to see Zach.

"What time does the rodeo start?"

Jesse looked at his smart watch. "About twenty minutes."

"Can we go? I know I can't be seen, but is there somewhere I can watch from the truck?"

"You don't have to stay in the truck. Let's go."

Zach stared at the ground beneath his feet. He'd done this a hundred times before. He'd practiced, took the time to warm himself and Steve up. Steve was ready to go, but he knew to wait for Zach's cue. Their part of the show would be over in less than five minutes. It was the Mendonza twins who really stole the show. He remembered being their age, wowing the crowd with the tricks that a teenager shouldn't be able to pull off. He thought of Sam and the hours they'd put in and how lucky they were that they'd only been concussed a few times and broken a few toes and fingers here and there.

He was only filling in, but Zach thought maybe it was time to give this part of his life up for good. He would never tire of working with Steve. He was a great animal and a great companion, but Zach didn't live for the spectacle anymore.

"All good?"

Zach looked up as Boyd Tillman gave him a firm pat on the back.

"All good. How's it looking out there?"

"Good. Bride and groom are front and center, but you know how I do things."

"I do."

"Let me get out there."

He watched Boyd as he slipped out the side door, microphone in hand as he went. Zach turned and caught Cherry's eye.

"Ready, Mr. Pleasant?" she said with a big smile, her braces gleaming.

"Hey. I'm just here to warm up the crowd. You're the main attraction."

"I know," she replied with a laugh. "I was just trying to be nice."

Zach made a big show of rolling his eyes, making Cherry and her brother laugh even harder. He turned toward the ring doors and gave Steve a gentle pat just before he climbed in the saddle.

"Come on, boy, let's do this."

A few moments later the doors sprung open,

Zach clicked his tongue and Steve took off. They circled the ring once, the faces in the crowd a blur until they slowed to a canter, approaching the announcer's platform. Zach swung his leg over Steve's back and hit the ground in a smooth, effortless stride as Steve continued on, picking up speed. Zach put his hand up in the air, taking in the crowd's cheers as he caught the mic without looking.

"Welcome to Big Rock Ranch, everybody!" he said as he turned to the Getlier wedding party. "We've got an amazing show for you today and for those of you out there in your seats who think you got that true grit, we'll invite you to try your hand at roping and wrastling." Yeah, volunteers would be roping a big wooden block shaped like a sheep, but it was plenty enough to be a part of the fun.

Steve sprinted by. Zach held the smile on his face as he noted Steve's gait. He kept on with his spiel, then introduced the twins. Steve finished his second loop just as Zach handed the mic back to Boyd. He slowed to a trot and then a stop. Zach waved to the crowd, then tipped his hat at Elizabeth Getlier and her groom-to-be, Chuck. Then he turned back and made a move for Steve's reins, moving his hand just in Steve's line of sight. The horse knew his cue. He made a show of skipping forward a few steps, so the horn of the saddle was just out of Zach's reach.

Zach made the move again and Steve skipped forward, then turned to face Zach. The laughter from the crowd told Zach their little bit was landing. Zach stood still, head tilted at Steve, then pointed to the ground, motioning for him to get his big horsey ass back over to him. But Steve wasn't having it. He did a loop around the ring backwards. Zach watched his progress, throwing his hands up in exasperation.

When Steve reached the far side of the corral, Zach saw them. Saw Evie on the other side of the fence, sitting in the flatbed of his brother's truck. Jesse and Vega and Lilah were with her. The dogs too, but all Zach could see was Evie's smile beaming at him from across the ring. He froze for a beat, meeting her eyes before he went back to tracking Steve's movements.

His horse stopped when he reached the main stands. He bowed his head and lightly brushed his lips on the cheek of one of the wedding guests. He moved along the railing, dropping kisses on every face and forehead he could reach until Zach stuck fingers in his mouth and let out a wolf whistle that could be heard on the other side of the mountain. Steve cut across the ring and stopped right in front of Zach. He used his nose to knock Zach's Stetson off as he brushed his mouth against Zach's forehead. The crowd was loving it.

Zach swung back up in the saddle, leaving his hat on the ground. On his cue, Steve took off again, working up to a gallop. Zach swung his leg back over, his feet tapping the ground, before he swung his whole body back over to Steve's right flank. He flipped back on so he was backward in the saddle, then rolled forward and spun back around so he was facing forward. As they completed a final loop, Zach leaned down and snatched his Stetson off the ground and slipped it back on his head.

"Zach Pleasant and his noble steed, Steve!" He

waved to the cheering crowd, letting Steve guide them back into the barn.

One of their stable hands, Emily was waiting to take Steve for his cool-down. Zach dismounted and gave Steve a few firm pats.

"Good boy, buddy. Great job."

"You killed it, huh?" Emily laughed.

"Every time."

He'd planned to cool down himself, then head out to the side of the stands to watch the rest of the show before he went to check on the Getliers. Instead he jogged around the far side of the arena. Evie spotted him before he reached the truck, and hopped down. He thought about all the times she'd been waiting for him and Sam after their events. All the times she hadn't been there. When her grandmother wouldn't let her come on their overnight trips. Nana Buck suggested that Evie would be considered "fast" for even wanting to join them.

He started jogging faster, thinking of the sound of his father's voice telling him how Evie would make a good wife one day. He remembered thinking his dad was nuts. Evie was just his friend, even if she did make him feel things he'd never felt before. There was a time Zach thought Nana Buck was right. Evie wasn't meant for him. She wasn't meant for Charming. But Zach had no clue what that friendship really meant to him then. He didn't understand what he could feel growing between them now.

Evie stopped short and let Zach take her in his arms. He didn't kiss her, but he hugged the shit out of her. She smelled like soap and a little like nutmeg again. When he pulled back she had the prettiest smile on her face.

"What are you doing here? I thought Miss Leona left strict orders lest we risk a celebrity sighting."

"I hit my limit with cooking shows and I wanted to see you ride. Jesse said we'd be away from the guests over here." Which they were. "That was amazing," Evie said.

"Yeah, that was pretty sweet," Vega added.

"Nah," Zach said. "It wasn't much. You should see Sam."

"How're the knees?" Jesse asked.

"Screaming, but I'll live." Zach took Evie's hand and led her back over to the truck.

He leaned back against the edge of the flatbed and pulled Evie back into his arms, her shoulders pressing against his chest. They watched a good chunk of the show this way, Zach breathing in her clean scent, taking in the warmth from her lush body. But as soon as Elizabeth Getlier was chosen from the crowd, it was time for him to head back. Roping her husband-to-be was the last act of the exhibition.

"I have to get back."

"Okay." That bright smile touched her lips again. He wanted to kiss her so badly.

"And I have to do some more networking tonight. A few of Getlier's businesses are coming in for the rehearsal dinner."

"Okay."

"I don't want to ask you to wait up for me," he said quietly.

"Yeah, you do."

A chuckle burst out of his chest. He kissed her quickly on the lips, then took off for the other side of the arena. Evie still needed her rest, but he hoped like hell that when he pulled himself away and got back over to Pleasant Lane that she would still be awake, waiting for him.

Chapter 18

Evie chewed the inside of her lip and reminded herself again that Jesse was not the chatty type. His near stony demeanor bled over into his teaching style. On the way back from the ranch he declared that he would be in charge of dinner. Steaks with a side salad, and a peach cobbler one of the women at church had sent him home with. Evie thought this would be a perfect opportunity to learn how to use a grill. She though Lilah was joking when she said Jesse wouldn't let her touch his grill or the steaks.

She was not.

Still, Evie refused to turn down the chance to at least watch and learn. She followed Jesse and Clementine over to his house and watched in complete silence as he pulled the steaks out of the fridge and then went to turn on the grill.

Forty minutes later, he'd barely said a word, but Evie had learned a thing or two about grilling and Jesse. Jesse's backyard was nearly as big as Miss Leona's, but he had a large pool constructed out of dark stone that gave it the feel of a deep lagoon. Jesse Pleasant was anti-horse, but pro-dog and pro-swimming. The man also took care with his steaks.

She was impressed with the focused way he seasoned each cut with his massive hands. He meticulously arranged each steak on the hot slats, saying—more to himself—that inches between each cut was required for even cooking. He closed the lid on the grill and finally turned to her.

"Now we wait. It won't take long."

"This was better than watching videos on YouTube," Evie admitted.

"How so?"

She explained the egg debacle. "I think I was taking in too much information. Like videos with music and graphics, or the cook just going on about how their kids like their eggs fluffy, but their husbands like them a little dry. Watching you, I could just focus on what you were doing." She smiled up at him.

"Sometimes simple is better."

"Agree. So, tell me something new. About you." She was going to bond with Jesse. That was her mission for the evening.

"I think Miss Leona is seeing someone."

Evie almost choked on her own breath, before laughter came bursting out of her. "Excuse me, what? Also, that has nothing to do with you."

"I can tell you more about next quarter's projections for the ranch," he replied, one dark eyebrow arching up.

"Uh, no, thank you."

"This is all there is to me. My work, my dog, and this grill. I'm not trying to give you the hot goss on my grandmother's love life. It's just something I've noticed and it's been on my mind."

"Okay, tell me."

"Semiretired attorney. He goes to our church."

"And they've been going out? He's been coming around asking to see her?"

"Miss Leona is old-man bait, so I'm not shocked when even married dudes flirt with her, but there's something different here."

"Does she flirt back?" Evie tried to picture it and then immediately tried not to picture it. There was acting and then there was real life. This was a little too real.

"She doesn't flirt, but she doesn't politely blow him off either, or make him look like a fool for even trying. I caught them talking on the phone the other day."

"What's bothering you about it? Besides the part where you have to think about your grandmother dating."

"Not sure yet." He pulled out his phone and appeared to be sending a text. And then he was quiet. Evie had follow-up questions, but she didn't know where to start. She'd gotten a taste of what it was like when he didn't approve of a relationship. Would Jesse hunt down an elderly man and put the fear of God in him if he got too close to Miss Leona?

"They're done," he announced suddenly.

"How do you know?" Evie asked as he lifted up the hood of the grill. A mouthwatering aroma hit her nose.

"I've been doing this a long time. You'll learn more about meat thermometers and the like, but I just know."

"I'm glad to see Zach's not the only cocky one in

the family." Evie looked up and caught the ghost of a smile pass under his mustache. Evie set the table while the steaks were resting and a few moments later Lilah and Vega arrived with the salad and the cobbler.

After Lilah said grace, Jesse made a show of serving his steaks, and gave Evie his first real bit of culinary advice.

"You can make my cousin here like drown hers in A.1., 'cause—"

"Let me live my life," Lilah scoffed.

"But if you season it properly and know your way around the heat the way I do"—geez, it was like Zach had grown a foot and packed on a hundred pounds—"your steak won't need a thing."

Lilah rolled her eyes. "Try it his way. And then next time I'll make garlic-butter sauce. There's more than one way to eat a steak."

"Mine's the best way," Jesse said right before he popped a bite of the meal he'd prepared in his mouth.

Evie shook her head, then followed suit. She managed to hold in a groan of pleasure, but a small breath of pleasure did slip out of her nose.

"See," Jesse muttered with his mouth full.

"It's good," Evie said. Jesse had a different approach, but if Evie paid attention, she could learn a thing or two from him. Including intriguing Pleasant family gossip.

Evie was forever in debt to the people who organized her and her grandmother's belongings. It only took her a few minutes to find her journal from the summer when she turned fifteen. After the four of them had dinner, Evie went for a walk down to the end of the lane with Vega and the dogs.

Lilah didn't have to go back to work for another few days. She asked Evie if she wanted to join her for a late-night movie marathon, but Evie felt drained again. It had been another long day and the excitement from the exhibition had worn her out more than she'd realized. And in the morning, she was off to see the doctor. She'd had enough action for one day. She retreated to her room and started going through her box of journals.

She flipped back and forth through the pages until she found the entry she'd been looking for. Zach had been right about the scar on her arm. In messy handwriting, the twenty-third of June.

Busted my arm. I hate that stupid horse.

The next entry wasn't until late August and it was long. Her fifteen-year-old self, celebrating the removal of her cast, recounting how Nana Buck had grounded her for attempting to even ride Flex, and the tragic account of discovering that Zach had kissed a girl named Katie. She didn't leave any clues as to who Katie was, but Evie made her feelings about the situation very clear. If anyone was kissing Zach Pleasant it should be her. Her fifteen-year-old self would be very pleased with recent developments.

She read on, and saw that sophomore year had been filled with drama. A fight with Delfi and details of how Britnay had planned a sleepover to force them to make up. Something about a couple—Callie and Mitch?—who'd had a messy public breakup in the halls. Lots of entries about Zach. Entries on how she dreamed about him, daydreamed about him, wondered what it would be like to "go all the way with him." And she was *stressed* by the idea. All of it seemed so silly and trivial, especially as most of her grievances seemed to be resolved almost overnight. There was one entry that made her stop. A simple sentence a few days before Halloween: *I miss Mom and Dad.*

Evie stared at the words, her heart aching for her younger self and parents she no longer knew, but when she turned the page, what she read lifted that ache almost instantly.

> *I'm in love with Zach Pleasant.*
> *He found me crying in the library after my family tree presentation and convinced Nurse Baker I was sick and needed to go home. He told her Nana and his parents were in Dallas for Golden Spur so he had to drive me home.*
> *We drove to Sonic instead of going home and we just hung out there until dinner time. I think he wanted to kiss me when we were sitting his truck, but we didn't. I know it sounds dumb, but sometimes he looks at me like he's really thinking about me. I know he tells me all the time we're buddies, but I don't know.*
> *It doesn't help that Mr. Pleasant jokes that I'm his girlfriend all the time either. Zach hates it.*
> *I want to make a move, but I think rejection is literally deadly and I just can't risk it. Also Nana*

*will have me shipped off to a Swiss boarding school
if she finds out any parts of our bodies touched. I
hope she never finds out I saw Jesse's dick by
accident that one time. She'll send me to a convent.*

    *Nana totally busted us 'cause Nurse Baker called
her at the ranch to double check after we left, but
Zach stuck up for me and Nana understood why
I wanted to get out of school. She's kinda pissed,
but she said that I can still go to Britnay's
Halloween party. Maybe I'll dress up as Katie.
He'll kiss me then.*

She dog-eared the page before she set down the
diary, then picked up her phone. Still thinking about
the amazing show you put on today. Are you still up at
the ranch?

Her face heated shamelessly when she saw his
immediate response pop up on her screen. Hey!
Thought you'd be asleep by now. About to head back.

Evie texted, You want some company? When you get
back. She imagined Zach had to be up early the next
day. He seemed to be an early riser, and while she
was tired herself, she wanted to see him. The rodeo
had been a complete tease. Forget the tricks, she
never thought seeing him on horseback would be
such a turn-on. She didn't want to wait a whole
twenty-four hours before she could see him again.

    Zach: If you can sneak away from Nurse Vega.
      Fuck yeah.

    Evie: No sneaking required. I'm grown, as she
      likes to say.

Zach: I knew I liked her. Meet me at my place
   in 10.

Evie: See you soon.

Evie hopped out of her bed and rushed to the
bathroom to brush her teeth and freshen up. She had
ten minutes to figure out how to seduce a cowboy.

Evie never knew how long ten minutes could
stretch on. She found herself sitting on the stone
bench just outside Zach's front door. She wrapped
the plaid wool shawl Blaire had packed for her
tighter around her shoulders and tried to ignore the
cool wind blowing across the cul-de-sac. The anticipation that lit a fire under her ass and had her
practically running from Miss Leona's house was just
enough to keep her warm, when she saw headlights
make their way up Pleasant Lane. She could hear
the dogs barking inside Jesse's house as she ap-
proached, but they quieted just as quickly, probably
hushed by Jesse himself.

It was silly, but just seeing Zach behind the wheel
as he pulled his truck to a stop made Evie's heart
beat faster. Her body warmed all over again. When
he got out of his truck she stood, her body coiled
and ready to pounce.

"Evening, ma'am," he said, touching the brim of
his hat.

Evie rolled her eyes even though heat rushed
between her legs at the sight of his smile and nicely
pressed suit. "Get over here." She'd been in his arms

that afternoon, but that didn't stop her from soaking up every bit of him as he pulled her close. She fell into the shadow of his hat brim, burying her cheek against his neck as both their faces were hidden from the porch light. She breathed him in, expecting a faint hint of the way he'd exerted himself in the ring, but all she got was the scent of fresh soap. He must have showered before he changed. He pulled back, then lightly touched her cheek with the rough pad of his thumb.

"You're spoiling me," he said. Evie couldn't help but watch his full lips when he talked.

"How so?"

"There's a beautiful woman waiting for me on my porch. There's not much more I can ask for," he replied, and then that smug smirk was back. When she woke up in the hospital, part of her wondered how it was possible for his intense good looks to distract her from his over-the-top cockiness, but now she understood. It was all a front, and if she played along she knew she'd reap the rewards of tangling with a cowboy like Zach Pleasant. She smiled to herself and took a step back, loving the way his hands slid down the length of her arms as she moved.

"You really want me to leave, don't you?" she teased.

"Hell, nah."

"Then stop talking and kiss me." She followed his gaze as his eyes roamed over her face, settling on her lips. She needed to send Shanny a thank-you note for the lip balm. She wasn't confident of much these days, but she knew her lips were kissably soft.

Zach's arms slid around her waist, and as she pressed her hands against his chest, Evie prepared herself to be kissed senseless. Instead, the way he pressed his lips to hers was light and gentle, a whisper of the different ways things could be between them. Another kiss, just as sweet as he turned his head just a bit. Evie felt the breath leaving her lungs. She didn't breathe again until he pulled away. She watched his face as she sighed, making a sound dangerously close to a moan.

He had no right to be so handsome. Still, she could see the emotions dancing across his features. She was tempted to smooth away the worry that touched the corners of his dark brown eyes. She wanted to touch his lips, remind him that they still had time. That for now, she wasn't going anywhere, but she kept her hands right where they were, on his perfectly sculpted chest.

"What is it?" She could feel his muscles dance under her fingers through the fabric of his dress shirt.

"Nothing. I've just missed you. That's all. You leave a note for Vega?" he asked, lifting the spell between them, just a little bit.

"She heard me leave my room and came to check on me."

"And she didn't stop you?"

"She just told me to make sure you had protection and not to overexert myself. The doctor has to clear me for sex."

"Hey, listen. We don't have to do anything. We can just—"

"I know. That's what I want. I just want to spend time with you. Not that I don't want to try forward- and reverse-cowgirl with you. That's not the only reason I came over. I mean it is, but—you know what I mean."

"Let's go inside and see what we can do about keeping your heart rate in a safe range." Zach eased by her, pulling his keys from his pocket. She stopped him, though, with a hand on his elbow before he could open the door.

"Wait. Before I come in, who's Katie?"

"Katie. Do you have a last name?"

"I found my diary from the summer, when I broke my arm." Evie looked down as she traced the scar on her skin. "You kissed some girl named Katie? I was pretty pissed about it."

"Woow. Katie Brown." He shook his head, then took off his cowboy hat as if it and the memory were too much to handle at once. "Yes. I kissed Katie Brown that summer. She had a meeting at her house, announcing it to her friends and—fuck, what was that girl's name—Nora Berks told anyone who would listen."

"Sounds dramatic."

"Are you jealous?"

"Of a girl that you kissed when we were in high school? No. I was just looking for some clarity. I had a lot to say in those diaries. A lot of nothing, but some good stuff too."

"Come inside and tell me all about it." He unlocked the door and led her inside with a gentle touch to the small of her back. They went right to his bedroom and slipped under the covers. He'd changed into a shirt and some shorts and she was still fully dressed in her pajamas. Still, that didn't take away from what was happening between them.

He told her about his day with the Getliers. She told him some of the things she'd found in her journal, including a picture of her standing a safe distance from Flex, flicking off the large black horse. She wouldn't tell him about the declaration of love she'd put on the page back then. She had a feeling she'd be back there again, very soon.

Billie, the hairdresser Miss Leona had hired to take care of Evie's destroyed sew-in, asked, "Okay, Miss Thang. We are ready to style. You made your decision yet?"

Evie looked at herself in the handheld mirror, then looked at the collage of hairstyles on her phone for the fiftieth time. She was glad she'd taken the hour-long drive with Jesse and Vega to St. Bernadette's Medical Center. She had her stitches removed. She had her scan, and after Vega saved her the embarrassment and asked Jesse to give them a minute alone with Dr. Zordetski, she was cleared for sexual intercourse. She did recommend that Evie go slowly and not be surprised if she noticed fluctuations in her sex drive, but at the moment she knew there would be no issues.

It was barely two in the afternoon and she was already exhausted, and with it being New Year's Eve, even though there would be no parties on her personal agenda, she wanted to stay awake to see the

clock strike midnight. But right now she had one
very important decision to make.

"Can we text Corie?" She looked over at Lilah,
who was sitting on the counter.

"Sure, why?" Lilah asked.

"I feel like she'll give me the most honest opinion."

"That's true," Billie muttered. She was clearly familiar with Corie's blunt way of moving through life.

"Okay, hold on." Evie watched Lilah as she franti-
cally texted her god-sister.

"She'll respond right away. She—see? She replied.
'I thought we decided on the first one. It's a freaking
haircut not surgery. Just don't give Jesse the clippers
and she'll look great.' I think she just means 'cause
you stay bald, Jess," Lilah said.

"I get it," Jesse replied.

"How do you feel about it? Talk to me," Billie said
with a light squeeze on Evie's shoulder. She'd been
very kind when she'd gently removed Evie's tracks
and washed her hair. Evie trusted her with the cut.
She looked at the picture on her own phone one
more time. Billie called the style a tapered fade.

"Just remember where you are and who you're
staying with," Billie said.

"That's right," Lilah added. "If you don't like it,
I'm sure Miss Leona will buy a lifetime supply of wigs."

Evie took a deep breath. "You're right. Okay. Let's
do it."

Chapter 19

At some point in the future, maybe sometime very soon, Zach knew he'd be thanking himself for giving Sebastian Getlier and his family the gold-star treatment, but at the moment all he wanted to do was fall face-first into his bed. He'd been up late with Evie and up early to take Steve for a ride. He had a few calls that he'd promised to handle while Jesse took Evie to the doctor. Jesse had backed off since the three of them had had their chat, but Evie's health was of course still weighing heavy on Zach's mind when Getlier tracked him down and asked him to join all the men in the wedding party for lunch.

He didn't expect to be the guest of honor, but apparently the groom had been blown away with his riding skills and wanted to know everything about his days on the rodeo circuit. He gave them the short version, leaving out the parts where he'd come up with a brother and father who were now fairly well-known actors, and he definitely didn't mention Miss Leona. Lunch damn near turned into dinner when they finally listened to Zach's tenth reminder that there was an actual wedding to get ready for.

He ducked out the door in the middle of their "Oh shit" and scrambled.

When he realized he'd left his own suit back at the house, he contemplated skipping out on the ceremony and climbing right back in bed with Evie. They'd only talk and sleep, get a little of that sweet make-out action they both clearly loved. A nice, slow way to ring in the New Year. In reality it sounded like a perfect New Year's Eve in. No guests. No calls. No family. Just the two of them.

Wasn't happening though. He had just enough time to shower, change, and floor it back over to Big Rock to check in with Delfi and Brit one more time before the ceremony started. God, they had a long night ahead of them: vows, dinner, a barn dance complete with a live band, and the fireworks at midnight. And Zach was already kicking himself 'cause he knew Evie would be a good three hours into a REM sleep cycle by the time it was all over. For once he wished he could switch places with Jesse, be the money behind the scenes, the silent Prince of Charming instead of the face and the mouthpiece.

Just as he turned down Pleasant Lane, his cell rang. His mom's international number flashed across his dashboard display.

"Shit." He reaches up and hit Accept. "Hey, Mom!"

"Hi, sweetie! Happy New Year!" It sounded like she was a little lit.

"Happy New Year, Mom. I think you caught me a little bit early."

"It's midnight in Prague."

"I thought it was Paris this year." He pulled to a stop in front of his place and double checked the time. He had a whole three minutes to deal with this conversation.

"Change of plans."

"Oh, okay. You with Senior?"

"Of course I am. Jesse, say hi to your son."

"Happy New Year, Zachariah." His dad's booming baritone shook the inside of his truck.

"Happy New Year, Pop. Listen, I hate to rush off the phone but I have maybe ten minutes to get ready for a wedding. Can I call you two tomorrow?"

"Sure, that's fine. We'll talk then."

"Zachariah, wait," his mom said.

"Yes, Mom."

"Is Evie still there?"

Zach closed his eyes and managed not to let an annoyed groan slip out. "Yes, ma'am. She is. She's probably with Lilah right now."

"Oh, good. So you two made up?"

Zach swallowed, knowing what was coming next. They hadn't had this conversation in years. Not since he made it clear that he'd ruined things with Evie and that she wouldn't see him again if she could help it.

"What makes you ask, Mom?"

"Oh, your dad and I were just wondering how long she's staying in town."

"Not sure yet, but you know she had a serious accident. I think she's just happy to have some place quiet to rest."

"Oh. You think she'll be sticking around for a while?"

Zach tried to not to sigh too loud, but failed. The last thing he wanted to think about was Evie leaving

town again. Next on that list of do-not-wants was his
parents trying to get involved in his love life from a
whole hemisphere away. He loved his mom and dad,
but they'd decided to take off and leave him and
Jesse to run the ranch, and lead their own lives. He
wished they'd follow through on the latter.

"What's on your mind, Mom?"

"I just know how busy you and Jesse are and I
know how you two are when you get consumed by
work. I just hoped Evie could convince you to come
up for air for a moment."

"If you are on speaking terms—" his dad chimed
in, but Zach cut him off. A flash of annoyance he
hadn't felt in years rushed over him. His parents had
found each other and fell in love instantly. They
were a good match and set an even better example
for Zach and his brothers for what a healthy partner-
ship could look like. For some reason they couldn't
understand that not every relationship came together
so easily.

"We are on speaking terms again, but things aren't
that simple."

"I don't see why not. You still pretending you don't
love the girl?" his dad said.

"I—"

"You won't let us set you up. You won't get online
and find someone for yourself. What's wrong with
the woman who's right in front of you? Is she seeing
someone?"

"Listen, I gotta go. I love you guys. I'll call you
tomorrow."

"There's no reason to be upset, sweetheart," his

mom said. "We just know how you two used to feel about each other and now that she's back, maybe this is God's way of giving you a second chance."

"I'll keep that in mind. I have to go."

"We love you. Happy New Year," his mom said.

"Love you too." They said their goodbyes. Zach might have hit the End Call button a little too hard. Slammed his door a little hard too when he got out of his truck.

"Hey, what's up?" Jesse called from across the driveway. He jogged over, Clementine at his heels.

"Nothing. Just got off the phone with Regina and Senior. They were on one, talking about Evie. Walk and talk. I gotta change." Zach felt like that's all he'd been doing the last three days. Jumping on and off horses and running back and forth for showers and a change of clothes. He was taking a day off. Soon. He opened his front door and Jesse and Clementine followed him to his room. He toed out of his boots and immediately started loosening his tie.

"What they say this time?" Jesse asked.

"Nothing, they just—what is their deal?! Seriously. We can't just *take a wife*."

"You think I don't know that? They are just a notch above Uncle Gerald with this archaic bullshit. I'd say they want grandchildren, but that's not it."

"This is why—" Zach stopped himself.

"Why what?"

"Nothing. I—" He picked up his Stetson and hung it on the hook beside his bed. "Dad thought he was so cute trying to push me and Evie together, but that's basically the reason Nana Buck told me to stay away from her."

"And she didn't want you to accidentally get her pregnant."

Zach sighed in confirmation. He'd never forget the afternoon Nana pulled him aside in the barn and read him the riot act. He wasn't gonna fuck up Evie's life. Didn't matter how badly her granddaughter had it for him. He thought she was just being protective, keeping them from making teenage mistakes, but the warnings didn't stop.

Finally Nana straight-up told Zach's parents she didn't want the two of them together. She had plans for Evie outside of their small town. His parents thought Nana was overreacting, but the words had sunk in, and Zach feared and respected the old woman too much to cross her. He'd buried his feelings deep and done his best to convince Evie to do the same by putting her deep in the friend zone. And it had worked, for over ten fucking years.

"I know, but shit, man. She just started speaking to me again and she doesn't even remember me. Can we wait five minutes before I ask her if she wants to be a rancher's wife?"

"Is that what you want?" Jesse asked. Zach could tell his brother was holding back from giving him another lecture about playing games with Evie's heart, but it was a valid question.

"Can I take the Fifth for now?" Yeah, they were both old enough to make their own decisions, but there were plenty of reasons for them not to rush.

Jesse shrugged, giving in. "Sure."

"Were you gonna ask me something? Why were you waiting in the driveway?"

"I didn't know if Evie texted you, but she got her hair cut and she's really nervous about it."

"How's it look?"

"Fine. I mean, you've seen Evie. She'd look good in a clown wig. I just figure since you two are, I don't know, a thing, I'd give you a little brotherly advice."

"And what's that?"

"When you see her, don't fuck with her. No sarcasm, no jokes."

Before, Zach would have been annoyed. Now, though, he knew his brother was coming from a good place. He was looking out for him and Evie both, trying to help them protect this thing they were trying to find between them.

"Thanks, man. I hear you. Let me get ready."

Jesse and his dog left him to it. When he was wedding-ready, Zach took a quick detour over to Miss Leona's. He was running crazy late now, but he wanted to see Evie before he went back to work. For once he found her alone in the kitchen, whipping up something that smelled absolutely amazing.

"There's so much cream and cheese in this recipe, I can see why she had it listed on her blog as a main dish." She did a double take when she saw him. "Oh, hi. I thought you were Vega. I'm making macaroni and cheese." She watched him as he crossed the terracotta floor. Evie set down the wooden spoon in her hand and turned to face him. Her delicate fingers touched the side of her head. "What do you think?"

Zach twirled his hand, motioning for her to turn

around. She spun slowly, showing off her fresh fade. He appreciated Jesse's warning. She looked amazing, but Zach wasn't expecting the scar on the side of her head to be so big. God, that must have been one hell of a fall. She faced him again, a hopeful smile touching her lips. "Well?"

Zach closed the distance between them and pulled Evie into his arms. He couldn't help but smile at the adorable way she pushed her glasses up her nose.

"What is it?" she asked.

"You're the most beautiful woman I've ever seen."

"Be serious for a moment, Zach. How does it look? Really."

"I am being serious. It looks perfect. When we were in high school you begged Nana to let you cut your hair this short, like Halle Berry, but she wouldn't let you. I think it looks dope as fuck."

"Thank you. I'm still getting used to it."

"What did the doctor have to say?"

"So far so good. There's obviously still some concern about the whole memory loss thing, but Dr. Zordetski is very happy with where I am physically. She referred me to a therapist. Vega is going to help me make an appointment later this week and I get my MRI results in a couple days, but in the meantime . . ."

"What?"

"I've been cleared for more adult activities."

That was all she had to say for all the blood in Zach's brain to rush to his dick. "I know you need your rest, but man, I'd love to be with you tonight."

"I could wait for you at your house. Like, in your bed."

Zach didn't hesitate slipping the key to his front door off the ring. He pressed it into her palm. "You don't have to wait up for me. I just want to be with you."

"Oh," Evie said, her tone very serious. "I'm waiting up."

Evie couldn't sleep and it wasn't the nervous anticipation that had swirled in her stomach earlier that day when Zach eagerly handed over his key. She'd waited for Jesse and Lilah to leave for a black-tie charity event at the mayor's house before she let Vega know of her plan to spend the night at Zach's. She felt bad for ditching Vega at first, but she handled the news very well.

"Just remember what the doctor said. Take it easy. I'm sure Zach is a wild ride, but keep the sexual acrobatics to a minimum."

"I don't remember what sex is even like. I'm going slow for sure."

When a final wave of exhaustion hit her a little after eight p.m., she changed into her pajamas, packed up some of the leftover mac and cheese, said goodnight to Vega, and made her way over to Zach's house. Once she was settled in bed, she took her time figuring out how his remotes worked. She figured she'd find a movie or another interesting cooking show to binge-watch while she waited for her cowboy to arrive. She clicked a button and brought up what turned out to be his DVR menu.

The menu was filled with only one thing, episodes of *The Dish*. She started to scroll, and when she thought there couldn't be more, there was. Every episode of *Supreme Chef*, season seven. The season she'd won. She'd watched so much *Supreme Chef*, but she hadn't seen a moment of *The Dish*. She pressed Play on the first episode.

The tone was completely different from the chaos of *Supreme Chef*. She watched herself engage in playful back-and-forth with her cohosts, take questions from the audience about the best way to cook steaks. By the time the hour ended, Evie felt strangely numb inside. No memories came to the surface. No recollection of her banter with Troy.

Nothing to explain the expression on her face when she did her best to cover what had to be the horrible taste of Leslie's seasoned snack mix. She thought about being in Miss Leona's kitchen. Cooking with her, cooking with Lilah, sharing the fruits of her labor with Jesse and Vega, and she couldn't help wondering what it would be like to return to *The Dish* after all that had happened and was still happening. Would she have the same enthusiasm for the work?

The sudden and insistent sound of her phone vibrating like crazy shook her out of the trance of it all. It was midnight in New York and it seemed like everyone she knew in her former life was calling or texting to wish her well in the New Year. She'd screenshot the texts in the morning and ask Raquelle and Blaire who she should respond to. She silenced her phone and fell into a marathon of a softer, more pleasant show featuring British amateur bakers competing for a prize. A little before midnight, she heard the front door open. Zach crept into the bedroom. He seemed surprised to find her awake.

"You're back?" she said just as he leaned over the edge of the bed and kissed her on the lips.

"The bride and groom tapped out, so I made my escape. I'll say goodbye to them tomorrow during their brunch. I wanted to ring in the New Year with you." Evie looked into his deep brown eyes before she looked back down at the remote. She brought up the DVR menu.

"Why have you been saving these?" she asked. Zach froze, his hand on his bow tie. After a moment, when the air between them refused to budge an inch, he sank down on the bed beside her. The heat she felt whenever she was near him filled her body again and suddenly she knew whatever he had to say could wait.

"I wasn't ready to watch them. I wasn't ready to watch you."

"Why?"

He shrugged, then ran his thumb just along the strap of her tank top. She could feel the goose bumps springing up all over her skin. "Because I missed you too much. And I knew if I watched them it would mean admitting that I knew you were never coming back."

Evie had no idea what to say.

"How many episodes did you watch?" he asked.

"Just the one. I—I don't . . ." She wanted to tell him about the numb feeling that had washed over her earlier in the night, but something stopped her.

"You don't what?"

"Nothing. Let's talk about it later."

"Can I hold that for a second?"

Evie handed over the remote and watched Zach click to the New Year's Eve countdown show Vega had recommended. A very loud woman and a very shiny man were very excited for midnight, which was just minutes away.

Zach tossed the remote back on the bed and finished undressing, down to his boxers. Evie didn't realize she was staring until he flashed that smile that made her cheeks heat. What seemed like miles of lean muscle covered in dark brown skin she was dying to caress, his body was a thing to behold. And so was the large bulge just aching to push through the slit in his shorts. She wanted him, so badly her core soaked at the thought of taking him inch by inch. At least her body remembered what to do next.

"Do you want me to put my hat back on?" He was joking, but she didn't care.

"Yes."

He chuckled a bit, then grabbed his cowboy hat off the hook near his bedroom door. He slipped it on his head, then climbed in the bed. Evie eased onto her back, grateful for the soft sheets and thick blankets that covered the mattress.

Zach wasted no time climbing over her body and she wasted no time reaching between them so she could slide her underwear down her legs. Zach stopped her though. She held her breath, body shivering as he smoothed the rough palm of his hand over her skin, easing the fabric away, exposing her wet slit to the warm air of his bedroom.

He looked up at her from under that hat, his heated gaze traveling over her face, and he gently spread her lips apart with his thumb. She somehow managed to keep her eyes on him as he teased her clit, teased her opening, spreading her juices around. She wanted this, every slow, deliberate moment. She wanted him to be the one to show her how this could be like the first the time, all over again. All she had were her dreams and her diaries to remind her how long she'd been waiting for this moment, and it didn't seem right to make herself wait any longer.

"Please," she whispered. "Don't make me wait."

"I got you," he replied, his voice thick and rough. He stood from the bed and shed his boxers, exposing the impressive erection between his legs. Evie almost drooled watching Zach stroke himself for a beat as he reached for a box of condoms in his nightstand.

On the TV the countdown began.

He climbed back over her, gently pushing her thighs apart to make room for his perfect hips. She looked up into his face, the light from the TV illuminating his perfect brown skin as his thick length nudged against her clit. She closed her eyes against the sensation for just a moment before gazing back at him again.

"Happy New Year, Zach," she whispered.

"Happy New Year, Buck."

His head dipped down and he pressed his lips to hers. Evie sighed against his mouth, opening up to him so their tongues could meet. She slid her arms around his waist and welcomed him inside.

Chapter 20

If Zach wasn't careful, he was going to pass out from pleasure. He held himself above Evie's amazing body, focusing on the way her lips parted as he moved inside of her. Her wet heat surrounding him was better than Zach had imagined. The slick grip was so tight and inviting, he knew he could easily stay with her like this until the sun came up.

He almost laughed, thinking about how damn foolish he'd been. All those late nights—hell, even some afternoons and early mornings—when he'd thought about what it would be like to be with Evie Buchanan. All of those times he wondered what would happen if he'd just said *fuck it* to the warnings from Nana Buck, and told Evie how he felt. The hours he'd lost thinking about how much he'd screwed up not asking her to be his girl. But she was here now, and before the night was over he'd finally tell her exactly how he felt. No bullshit, no put-on charm. She deserved all of him, including the words he'd been too young and cowardly to say. No more.

He leaned down and pressed a light kiss to the side of her neck. Her head lolled to the side as she let out a soft moan, urging him on. He kissed the same spot again, slowing the motion of his hips. She didn't want to wait, Zach didn't want to rush. He wanted to make love to Evie, slowly. He wanted it to last for the both of them.

He moved carefully, gently withdrawing from the slick warmth that was practically begging him to keep on with his slow and deep back-and-forth. Evie groaned, gripping his back tightly with her fingertips. Her perfect pussy did the same, squeezing around him, pleading him not to let go.

"Hold on," he whispered. He moved back up her body and pressed a soft kiss to her mouth. "I got you. Okay? This isn't over."

She stared back at him through her pink-framed glasses, scanning his eyes before finally giving him a shy nod. Zach took that as the sign he needed to continue a proper exploration of her body. He set aside his Stetson on the bedpost, then went back to kissing his way down her chest. She was still wearing her pajama top. He pulled the thin strap to the side, exposing her hard nipple. Zach drew it into his mouth before gently swirling his tongue over the tip.

He could feel Evie shiver as her fingers moved along the back of his head. He sucked the puckered brown tip again, lightly scraping it with his teeth before he gave her other breast the same attention. His cock was aching, throbbing against her thigh. He wanted to be inside her again, but this was just as good, watching her trembling on the bed beneath him. Zach rolled to the side, but kept close with his body draped over her thigh and his mouth still on her skin.

He played with her breasts for a long time, using his fingers to circle her clit in slow, drawn-out strokes. He teased her entrance, watching the way her neck strained.

Her hand went to his wrist. Zach froze and looked up at her beautiful face.

"Do you want me to stop?"

"No." She shook her head. "Please don't stop." He obeyed, picking up the rhythm of his fingers right where he left off. "That—yeah," Evie moaned.

"Right here?" His fingers were coated now, soaked with her juices as he stroked either side of the tightening bud.

"Yes, please. Just like that."

He kept up with the strokes, watching her face, feeling her grip on his hand grow tighter and tighter. A second later she started coming, her hips rising off the bed. He slowed his strokes, easing her down. Her doctor had cleared her for sex, but Zach still didn't want to push her too hard.

"How we doing?"

"Good. You—you didn't—"

"Not yet." He leaned up and kissed her on the mouth. "Just wanted to check in with you. How's your head?"

"Fine. I feel good." Zach chuckled at the slow smile that eased across her lips. "But I want you to come, too. I need to tell my diary how I finally got Zach Pleasant naked and brought him to his knees."

Zach let out a shout of laughter, then buried his face against Evie's neck. He could feel her body shake as she laughed along with him. His breathing slowed when he felt her lips on the side of his face a moment later. He moved just enough so their lips could meet. His arm looped her waist, and in a careful maneuver, he shifted onto his back, pulling Evie on top of him.

Zach reached down and aligned his still painfully hard dick with her opening. Evie sank down on him like she was meant to be there, right where she belonged. Zach didn't hold back. He let out a guttural moan when he felt every inch of himself pressed deep inside her. Evie sat up for just a moment, just to pull her tank top over her head, and then she was kissing him again. Zach wrapped his arms around her, pulling her close so her breasts pressed against his chest as he started working his hips against her. Fuck, he could do this for days.

Before long though, he felt that telltale tingle in his spine. It shot down to his balls and just before he filled the condom, Evie arched against him, their cries echoing off the vaulted ceiling.

Evie couldn't stop touching Zach. She lay on her stomach at an odd angle across his rumpled sheets, staring at his amazing body, splayed out on his muscled back. His eyes were closed, but he was still awake, breathing deeply. Her fingers traced over his dark brown nipple. Her hand moved down his chest, trailing over the dark hair that led down to his softening erection.

Blaire had mentioned Evie's previous boyfriends and sexual partners, but something told her none of her previous experiences came close to the feeling of having a certain cowboy between her thighs.

Yes, her memory failed her, but she knew no one in her past could compare to Zach. And it wasn't just his gentle skill when it came to pleasuring her, it was the way she was falling for him more and more every minute they were together. The words in her diary made more and more sense. It was easy to fall for Zach Pleasant.

"Were those fireworks earlier?" she asked. She thought she'd heard the booming pops over the sounds of the TV and her own sighs.

"I don't know. You tell me," he replied with a wink.

"Goodbye, Zach." She started to get up, but strong arms pulled her close.

"Come back here." He kissed her face and she realized even his annoying-ass sarcasm couldn't drive her from his bed. "I'm just playin'. Yes, those were fireworks for the guests at the Getlier wedding. I should have taken you out to see them."

"It's okay. I enjoyed being indoors with you much more." Evie paused, wondering if she would regret telling Zach what was on the tip of her tongue. If his ego got too big, one of them would have to sleep on the couch. "I've dreamt about this before," she said. "Well, parts of it. We were in your truck during one of Jesse's football games."

"And how'd we do in real life?"

"It was much better. Mostly because you disappear in the middle of my dreams. And this was, you know, real."

Zach leaned up on his elbow and looked at her, a frown creasing his forehead.

"What do you mean I disappeared in the middle?"

Evie sighed and sat up so she could lean against

the headboard. Zach readjusted and pulled her legs over to his side. She liked having him close. She liked the constant contact. "Ever since I woke up in the hospital, I've been having these dreams where we're together, doing all kinds of things. Riding, hanging in the barn, in a school parking lot. Sometimes we're kissing. Sometimes, there's more. But every single time, I would look away or close my eyes, and when I'd look back you'd be gone. You'd just vanish."

Evie winced, the meaning of these dreams suddenly becoming clear. Some part of her brain felt abandoned by him. "Sometimes I feel like I'm going to cry, in my sleep."

"Jesus, Buck."

"What?"

Zach leaned down and pressed a firm kiss to her knee. "I owe you another apology."

"For what?"

"I wasn't there for you when you needed me. You forgive me, *now*, but I want you to know that I fucked up."

Evie looked at the way his fingers were touching her leg. She'd made plenty of mistakes, probably plenty she was glad she couldn't remember now. "You were a teenager," she told him. "Or you were young, at least. I don't remember my teens, but from my diaries it seems like they were filled with lots of unnecessary drama."

"True—"

"Did I ever tell you how I felt?" Evie asked. She told her diary, but did she tell him?

"No, but I knew."

"Did I ever ask you to be my boyfriend?"

"Well, Nana Buck wouldn't let you have a boyfriend, so that's a no."

"It sounds like I broke plenty of Nana Buck's rules."

"You did."

"Also, it's not true that you weren't there for me. From what I wrote in my diary, you were there for me a lot. There was something about you ditching school with me after my family-tree project."

"Shit, I remember that," Zach said with a chuckle. "Mr. Archuleta was a dick. You straight-up told him that you didn't want to do it because it hurt too much to talk about your parents, and he told you to build a bridge and get over it. He threatened to give you an F if you didn't turn it in."

"Well, apparently I did my presentation and then you stayed with me after."

"We sat in my truck and sang along with that god-awful 'My Humps' song on repeat until you started laughing. I still hate the song," Zach said.

"I've tried to think about what might have been going through my mind the night we had our . . . falling out."

"Yeah?"

"Well, each time I just end up pissed that I can't remember anything. And then I remind myself that all I can focus on is now and the future. I had fights with Delfi and Britnay too and we grew apart, but there doesn't seem to be any bad blood there. I want to move forward. I have too many things to think about, so much stuff that I can't spend energy I don't have, so you don't have to apologize anymore. Not for this."

"Okay, okay. I hear you. Come here." Evie made room for Zach to move and then she was back in his arms, her head resting on his wonderfully sculpted chest. The TV was still on, but Zach had muted it. Some old black-and-white TV show played on the screen. "What's stressing you out?" Zach asked. "Tell me."

"I've been watching myself, on television, and I don't like what I see."

"What do you mean?"

"We watched *Supreme Chef* and obviously it was good that I won because it helped my career, but something about it just made me feel awful. Like it had nothing to do with actual cooking or being an actual chef."

"Yeah, that's kinda the point of those shows. It's the competition and the manufactured drama. Not the food."

"Yeah, that's what Jesse told me. And then I was thinking about how I met that unhinged woman Melanie on that show. Obviously I can't contact her and ask her what happened between us, but it still isn't sitting well with me. When I watched myself on *The Dish*, I thought I would feel—what's the word I'm looking for? *Determined*, maybe? Or *inspired*."

"Yeah?"

"I felt like seeing myself on *The Dish* would give me a good reference point. It would show me what I need to get back to and how much or how little will be asked of me. I also thought it would help me understand how I made the transition from *Supreme Chef* to cohosting a show."

"And what happened instead?" Zach asked.

"I was disappointed in myself. I was thinking about all the hard work I must have put in, and even all the work I've put in since I was released from the hospital. Does all that work lead me back to a show where I'm not even really cooking? I—I don't know if I want to go back." Evie closed her eyes, sudden relief washing over her. It felt good to admit the doubts she was having out loud. "Please don't tell anyone."

"I won't."

"I don't know enough yet to make any decisions, and for as long as I can, I do want to at least try to hold on to my job at *The Dish*, but this feeling, it's just—it's giving me a lot to think about."

"Listen, I'm here, if you just want to bounce around ideas, if you just need a sounding board. If you realize you want something else and *The Dish* ain't it, Miss Leona or Jesse and I, we can all help you. We're with you, whatever you decide. I'm sure Nicole will have your back too."

"I know. Thank you."

On the screen a man and woman were having an animated conversation. "What show is this?"

"It's called *I Love Lucy*."

"Hmm."

"Evie." She looked up at the strange sound in his voice. It made her stomach turn. This bubble they'd created for themselves was about to pop. "Listen, I have to tell you something about Melanie Burns."

"What is it? You didn't sleep with her too, did you?"

"No." Zach laughed. "I've never met the woman. Nicole thinks that Melanie may have had something to do with your accident." Zach paused, and his face contorted a bit before he went on like he was choosing his words very carefully. "She thinks you might have been pushed, but she can't prove it. She—we didn't want to tell you because we didn't want to double down on your stress level on a hunch."

"Oh." Evie thought, pointlessly trying to dig up any memories from that night. She had no memory of Melanie, but considering the way she'd acted on the show and the messages she'd written in Evie's DMs, she wouldn't be surprised if things between them had escalated and gotten physical. It would explain the tone of her messages too. Maybe Melanie really wanted Evie dead, or at least out of the way. Evie sat up and turned to face Zach.

"She doesn't know I'm here, right?"

"No. And we're going to keep it that way. If she did something, we'll figure it out and she'll fucking pay for it. Maybe I should have said something earlier—"

"No, I get it. I've had a lot to process. This is . . . a lot more. But at least I know to keep her at a distance for real."

"It's just a theory Nicole had. It still could have been an accident."

A theory, sure, but the more Evie thought about it, the more sense it made. She's been thrown from a horse and just broken her arm. Would slipping down the stairs be enough to put her in a coma? Maybe. But someone shoving her down a flight of stairs would definitely do the trick. A sudden tightening in Evie's chest made her feel like Nicole may have been right to keep this from her. A possible murder plot was not something Evie was ready to handle.

"Are you okay?" Zach asked before he pressed his lips to her forehead.

"Yeah, I'm okay." She snuggled closer and wrapped her arm around his waist. It was too late now, or too early in the morning on the East Coast to talk to Nicole, but as soon she could she'd ask Nicole to tell her everything about this Melanie Burns theory and figure out exactly what they could do about it.

Evie sat on the edge of Zach's bed, waiting as he finished getting ready for his day. They'd been up most of the night talking and making love. She would have spent the whole day in bed with him, but she had to check in with Vega. Plus Miss Leona would be back eventually and it would be rude for Evie not to show her face.

She looked at the flood of text messages that had hit her phone in the last twelve hours. Television personality Chef Evie was pretty dang popular. She'd ask the girls which Happy New Year greetings she should respond to and which messages she should ignore after she took a shower and got something to eat.

She felt pleasantly worn out. Zach talked a big game, but he also knew how to back it up. So much of her recovery had felt like an uphill battle, but being in Zach's bed made her feel pretty damn good. She could learn how to cook and take care of herself again and she could also be a woman who had amazing sex with an incredibly hot guy. What the future meant for them, she had no clue. But she wanted to give herself the room to enjoy what was happening between them in the present.

Zach came out of his walk-in closet, slipping a tie under his collar. "I was thinking about what you said last night," he said. "About not liking what you saw on *Supreme Chef* and *The Dish*."

"Yeah?"

"Two things. You may not have been really cooking on *The Dish*, but think about the viewers at home, right? You were teaching them to cook. And from what I understand, you were the biggest ratings draw to the show. *Supreme Chef* was bullshit drama, but some people need stuff like that to unwind. Ask Lilah her feelings about the whole *Housewives* franchise. With *The Dish*, people are watching to learn something from someone they like. You. You are a part of something that people want and need. If it's not fulfilling moving forward, I get it, but it's just something to consider."

"I hadn't thought of it that way."

"And you do have to cook a little. You have to demonstrate a good chunk of the steps."

"You're right. What was the second thing?"

"Ask Lilah to put on *The Chef's Corner* for you. I've seen a few episodes and it's about actual chefs and the food they make. I think you might find more of the inspiration you're looking for there."

"Thank you. I'll try that."

"You ready?"

Zach was in another perfectly tailored suit and his cowboy hat. Shiny black boots with swirls carved into the leather finished the look. She gave him a once-over, then cocked her head at him as he adjusted his Stetson.

"You know how good you look in that hat, don't you?"

Zach shrugged, the corner of his mustache lifting in a more earnest smile. "I mean, I feel good in it. That's what matters."

"Uh-huh."

"Come on."

Evie took Zach's hand and let him pull her off the bed. She followed him out to the front door. Just as he opened it for her, she heard the dogs barking. When they stepped outside, Evie could see a car driving up Pleasant Lane.

Zach glanced over his shoulder as he finished locking up. "That's Miss Leona and Corie."

"Oh, they're back already."

"Yeah." Something in Zach's voice was off, but he took her hand. "Let's go say hello." They crossed the property and met the black SUV in front of Miss Leona's house just as Lilah opened the front door. Sugar Plum and Euca came running out to greet Corie as soon as she hopped out of the car. She came around the other side and opened the passenger door for Miss Leona while their driver grabbed their bags.

"Good morning," Miss Leona said, eyeing Evie's pajama pants and her shawl.

Zach bent down and kissed Miss Leona on her cheek.

"You heading over to the ranch?" she asked him.

"Yeah, I have to give my regards to the bride and her family before they leave."

"Okay. This won't take long. Lilah, come help Corie bring my things inside."

"Yes, ma'am," Lilah said. She scrambled to grab her grandmother's large weekend bag.

"You two are in trouuuuuble," Corie sang as she handed the driver a bit of cash. Evie felt her face heat with embarrassment and dread. Miss Leona stood there silently until the SUV pulled around the driveway and headed back down the lane. Then she looked up at the both of them. She was wearing a silver pantsuit with a royal-blue silk blouse. It was a festive look that seemed a little too light for the nearly deadly look on her face. Her finger came up and she pointed a finger right in Zach's direction.

"Now I know ya'll two are full-grown adults, but Evie is under my care, so there will be no more of this."

"Miss Leona, we didn't—" Zach started, but she cut him off with a sharp tilt of her head.

"Was I done speaking?"

"No. Ma'am."

"Thank you. I appreciate that you two waited until I was gone to engage in a little bit of hanky-panky, but there'll be no shacking up under my watch. Do you understand me?"

"Yes, ma'am," they both responded.

"Evie, I know you're feeling a lot of emotions and that's fine, but there is no need to rush anything. And you." Zach failed to hide his chuckle as his grandmother's eyes narrowed in his direction. "If you really care about her, you will court her properly. The poor girl has no memory. Let her get to know you the right way, 'cause the good Lord forbid

you two decide this isn't something you want to
pursue and I have to deal with two heartsick chil-
dren moping around. Do you understand me?"

"Yes, ma'am."

"And as much as I'd love to see more great-
grandchildren before I die, I'm old-fashioned
and I'd like it if you two were married before that.
And don't give me that 'we used protection' crap.
People get sloppy and condoms can fail too."

"Hear you loud and clear," Zach said.

"Good. I'm gonna go sit down and then Evie, we're
making cornbread."

"That sounds wonderful. I wouldn't miss it."

Miss Leona gave them both a firm nod, then strut-
ted into the house. Evie didn't dare breathe until
the front door closed behind her.

"Did she just tell us we're not allowed to have sex
anymore?" she said.

"She said no more overnights. We can get creative
with the sex."

"Oh, thank God."

Zach pulled her into his arms with his hands tight
around her waist. "Why? You don't want me to court
you?"

"To what me?"

"Try to win your love and affection the right and
proper way. You know, take you out, even though you
can't be seen out in public. Buy you gifts and thangs."

"That's exactly what I want."

"Then that's exactly what I'll do. Come on. I'll
walk you to your door," Zach said before employ-
ing the horrible fake Southern accent. "It's what a

gentleman courting a sweet young lady like yourself ought to do."

Evie rolled her eyes, a smile sneaking across her face. Then she did the next logical thing that came to mind. She stood up on her tiptoes and kissed Zach Pleasant right on the lips.

Chapter 21

Nicole made her way up the subway stairs into the unusually balmy morning air. Days ago the city was covered in a good ten inches of snow, and now it was in the high fifties. She tried not to let the obvious signs of global warming mess up her day even more. It was a new day and now she was a few signatures away from signing her first new client of the year. Ursula Simmons, child star turned fashion designer, who was looking for new representation.

The twenty-five-year-old was in talks to star in her own cable reality show following the ins and outs of her growing empire, but talks had stalled when she realized her mom/agent was carrying on negotiations behind her back. She'd decided it was time to dead the professional part of their mother/daughter relationship before they found themselves in a situation where the personal part was unsalvageable.

Nicole had had a good feeling about Ursula and she felt even better after their early morning face-to-face. She'd planned to give herself a few more days before she jumped back into work, but when Ursula had to reschedule a last-minute trip to Paris and asked Nicole if she could move up their meeting, Nicole jumped at the chance.

Jane had been a saint, done her best to get Nicole to relax, distracting her with good food, great sex, and some A-plus quality time. But there was nothing Jane could do to distract Nicole from the accidental group text Evie had sent.

> I slipped and had sex with Zach. We didn't do any cowgirl positions I don't think. But it was amazing.

Nicole's brain hopped offline for just a moment and then her fingers kicked into gear. She typed out the words **Oh Really???** and hit Send. Seconds later Evie responded.

> I am so sorry. That text was just for Blaire. I thought I was just texting her.

Nicole checked the group conversation and saw where Evie had gone wrong. Blaire's name was listed first before her own name and then Raquelle's. *First* being the operative word. She really hoped Evie hadn't texted anyone else anything that could be used as a Page Six hot take.

Nicole: See the three circles at the top of the screen? That's a group text.

Evie: Got it. So sorry. Please don't hate me.

Nicole: I could never. Please tell me he wore a
   condom.

Evie: Yes. The sex was very safe. I promise.

Nicole: Good. And congrats on the sex.

Evie: Thank you.

Evie signed off with a blushing emoji. Nicole was
sure Evie was thoroughly mortified and turned right
to Blaire to discuss what had just happened. Nicole
wanted to ignore it. Evie was allowed to have sex. She
was allowed to have sex with Zach Pleasant. Based
on looks and sheer charisma alone, Nicole couldn't
blame her, but three days later the text was still
burned into her mind.

Evie was now sleeping with a hunky rancher from
Southern California. This was not a part of the plan.
The Pleasant brothers seemed like good guys and
she appreciated how much they'd done for Evie, but
the more time Evie spent with Zach, the more time
Evie had to consider that she might want to stay with
him. And Nicole couldn't honestly say she could
blame her. Evie had been through hell. Busted her
head open and woken up surrounded by strangers
with no clue of who she was or how she'd gotten
there. It was small miracle that she was up and about,
well enough to find time for extracurricular activities
like what Nicole hoped was very gentle missionary-
style sex.

Nicole stopped on the corner and waited for the
light to turn before she crossed. Her apartment was
just a few blocks away, but she took a detour to the

newly constructed Whole Foods not far from her place. Damn gentrification, but neither she or Jane could resist their hot bar.

Everything would be fine, she reminded herself as she made her way up the street. Evie was in good health and doing better every day, but when Nicole woke up that morning and started to get ready for her meeting with Ursula, she couldn't shake this sense of impending doom. Something in her gut was telling her the rug was about to be ripped out from under her and Evie both.

She walked into the Whole Foods, only a little bit grateful the store had switched back to regular adult contemporary music after almost three straight months of Christmas tunes. She was headed right for the mac and cheese in the hot bar when her phone rang. She fished her cell out of her bag and smiled at the name on the screen as she hit Accept.

"Evie, hey. I was just thinking about you. What's up?"

"Nothing, I just—are you busy?" The tone in Evie's voice stopped her in her tracks. "I can call back another time."

"Nope. Not at all. Just doing a little shopping." Nicole stepped out of the way and tucked herself beside the cookie display case. "What's going on?"

"Well, I've been wondering—did I ever tell you why I took the job on *The Dish*? Obviously I needed a paycheck. Blaire explained that I'd been let go from a restaurant called Nighly and this job came along at the right time, but if I was such a good chef why did I take a job that didn't involve any real cooking?"

"Oh. You wanted to open your own restaurant,

but that's an expensive undertaking and you just didn't have the capital yet. Beyond a lack of funds we both thought a successful run on *The Dish* would give you enough name-recognition to start working on making that dream come true."

"So I wasn't planning on being on *The Dish* forever?"

"Of course not. I wouldn't let you stay on *The Dish* forever. This was just part one of a larger plan. I make sure I know what my clients are picturing for the long term, even if those plans change. The goal is always to level up while chasing your dreams, and I'm here to help you get there."

"Thank you, Nicole," Evie said with a sigh. Nicole could feel her relief through the phone. "I guess I just needed a little reassurance."

"No problem. What's going on? What did you think I was going to say?"

"I was afraid you were going to say that I gave up on being a chef, off-camera. I've been cooking with Miss Leona and I absolutely love it. It makes me feel like I have a purpose. Zach pointed out that I was teaching people how to cook on *The Dish*, but I don't know, I just didn't feel passionate about the . . . performance of it all."

"Do you want to back out now? Give your notice to the producers?"

"No, no. I'm trying not to make any rushed decisions, like sending texts without looking first."

"We all have our teachable moments."

"Yes. I just—I just wanted to know where I was coming from before I decided where I was going."

Wise words, but there was a question hanging

on the tip of Nicole's tongue. How did Zach play into all this? Would he want her to stay in Charming forever? Would he be selfish enough to ask? Would Evie give herself the room to say no if that wasn't what she wanted?

"If your dream is still to open your own restaurant, I'm still here to help make that happen any way I can. If you feel like you're headed in another direction, you just let me know." Nicole knew any other agent in her shoes would take this moment to try to steer Evie back toward the clear and easy money-making opportunities. If Evie wasn't about that on-camera life anymore, then what was the point? The point to Nicole was clear.

Evie needed as many people in her corner as possible, especially now, and Nicole would stick with her for as long as she could. This memory loss may have screwed things up, but Evie was still Evie, and if she was waking up every day and getting her butt in that kitchen, then Nicole knew there was plenty to hold on to. She just hoped Zach Pleasant and his "amazing" skills in the bedroom didn't screw things up.

"Wait, tilt the phone down, I can't see." Blaire said.

Evie stood still as Lilah adjusted the angle of her phone. She could see Blaire's face in the tiny box on the screen scrutinizing every inch of her outfit. Thinking it would be eighty degrees, twenty-four hours a day, Blaire had packed Evie a few very cute sundresses, but it was creeping down into the low fifties and the sundress idea was out. Evie looked down at her torn jeans and black boots. Lilah had

picked out a cute long-sleeved blouse that matched
her glasses. They were just heading over to the ranch
for a private dinner, but she wondered if she was
underdressed.

"Lilah, there should be a tan jacket in her bag."
Blaire was the only person in Evie's small circle who
was currently dating, so Evie needed to turn to her
for pre-date guidance. Lilah was still frustrated with
all men after the stunt her dad had pulled, and Corie
had made it clear that she was less than impressed
with what Charming's single scene had to offer. The
date with Dr. David had gone so well, Blaire was seeing
him again that Saturday night. Tonight she was on
best-friend duty.

"I'll grab it," Evie said. She used a bit of the
pent-up energy running through her to dig through
her things. It didn't take long for her to find the
long coat Blaire was thinking of. She pulled on
the tan jacket with large black buttons, then glanced
in the full-body mirror mounted in the bathroom. It
was exactly what her outfit needed. That didn't stop
her from taking a lingering glance at her hair. She
was still getting used to the short cut.

"How's this?" she said as she stepped into the
doorway. She did a little turn so the girls could see
her. Even Euca looked up from her spot on the floor.
"I like the way it makes my butt look."

"You look perfect," Blaire said.

"Are you sure?"

"Lilah agrees with me, right?"

"I do. I think you look very cute. The jacket makes
it," Lilah said with a rigorous nod of her head.

"And you know I'd tell you if you looked fucked

up." Evie look over and rolled her eyes at Corie, but Corie was too busy sitting in the armchair flipping through the latest issue of *People* to catch it.

There was no reason for her to be nervous. She'd already slept with Zach. Their first date should be an absolute breeze, but that didn't mean she didn't want to put together a good outfit. Before she could ask for the twelfth time if she looked okay, she heard the front door open and Zach announce himself. She heard Jesse's deep voice respond, but she couldn't make out exactly what he said.

"Your prince charming is here," Lilah teased as she handed back her phone.

"He's here, Blaire. I gotta go."

"Have tons of fun. Call me tomorrow, 'kay?"

"I will." She said her goodbyes, then hit End on the video call and slid her phone into her jacket pocket.

"Corie, come on."

Corie slapped down the magazine and then strode right past them. "Let's do this." Evie laughed, and followed her down the hall, Lilah trailing behind her. Zach was there, waiting in the kitchen, his tan cowboy hat in hand. When she saw his worn-in jeans and his wool-lined jacket she realized the one gown that Blaire had for some reason slipped in her baggage would have been a little over-the-top. Not that what either of them was wearing mattered. The moment their eyes met, all Evie could think of was how she'd been waiting all week to be alone with him.

Between the ranch and lessons with Miss Leona and Jesse, they'd both had their hands full. They spent their nights as a family. The whole gang gathered around the TV or the kitchen island. She really appreciated Corie's attempts to teach her how to play spades. Still, whenever she caught Zach looking at her, or whenever they were able to sneak in the slightest touch, she knew Miss Leona had been on to something. If they'd had it their way, they would never have left the blissfully naked comfort of Zach's bed.

When Zach asked if he could take Evie out Friday night, she eagerly accepted, with Miss Leona's blessing.

"Hi," Evie said, unable to hide her smile.

"Ma'am," Zach replied with a little nod of his head that made her stomach flutter.

"You two get going," Miss Leona said from the couch. Jesse stood from his spot on the other end of the large sectional and crossed the large space in what seemed like two strides. He lifted his hand and brought it down hard on Zach's shoulder. Evie imagined it felt like having a tree fall on you, but Zach barely flinched. He just looked up at his brother with a bit of *what the hell?* written across his face.

Jesse looked at his smart watch, then back to his brother. Evie tried not to laugh as Zach rolled his eyes and motioned for Jesse to get on with it. "Have her back by eleven. Not eleven-o-five or eleven-o-two. I will be waiting right here at ten fifty-nine, and if I don't see headlights pulling up—"

"Man, shut the hell up." Zach laughed. "We'll be back at eleven. Relax."

"Good." Jesse went back to the couch and sank back into the cushions.

"Have fun, you two," Lilah said with a bright smile.

"Thank you, Lilah. We will."

"Shall we?" Zach nodded toward the door, then slipped his cowboy hat on his head with a subtle confidence that reminded her how good things had been between them just a few nights ago.

"Let's." Evie took his hand and followed him out to his pickup truck. "Such a gentleman," she teased as he opened her door for her. He kept a gentle grip on her hand as he helped her into the high cab.

"Gentleman is my middle name." The wink he tossed her way did nothing to calm the warmth radiating through her body. She knew what she'd promised Miss Leona. Still, as she watched Zach walk around the front of his truck with that stride that yelled *you know you want this*, Evie wondered just how long she'd be able to hold out.

"So what do you have planned for us tonight?"

Evie glanced at the large gate at the end of Pleasant Lane, before she looked back at Zach's handsome profile. The gate swung open and they pulled out onto the main road. In the distance she could see the moon rising over the horizon. A perfect night with even better company. Zach reached over and took her hand. Their fingers laced together on top of his thigh. She tried not to think about how close she was to the impressive bulge hiding behind the worn dark denim.

"I was thinking a little dinner and little dancing. On the ranch, of course."

"I can't wait."

Zach gave her hand a soft squeeze. "I'm sorry I

can't take you into town. Not that Charming has a whole lot to offer in the way of nightlife."

"Where would you take me if you could?"

"This shitty bar called Claim Jumpers. You and Britnay tried to sneak in senior year, but Sheriff Ortega caught you in the parking lot and called Nana. She almost beat your ass to Sunday and back."

Evie laughed. "Did I ever get to go?"

"I don't think so, but Britnay drags us there every year on her birthday. Terrible beer and some garbage food, but the jukebox selection? Tops," he said with a slow chuckle.

"You know what I want to do, when Miss Leona and Jesse think it's okay?"

"What's that?"

"Drive around and see if I remember anything from my dreams. I've only been out to the storage place, and there's not much else over there. I've had a few dreams about a high school."

"Charming High, maybe."

"Maybe. I wonder if it's the same place from my dreams."

"You have any dreams about me lately?"

Evie knew he was only half joking, and she only half hated how much he wanted to occupy her thoughts, whether she was asleep or awake.

"You were in my dream last night, but it wasn't *about* you."

"What were we doing in your dream?"

Evie had to pause a moment and see if she could actually remember the details. Odd images of standing on a fence suddenly came back to her.

"We were at a rodeo, I think, and your dad was there, but there wasn't—oh God, now I remember!" She didn't mean to yell, but the weirdest part of it all came flooding back.

"What is it?"

"We were at a rodeo and we were waiting for your dad to finish because you and I were going to be in some dance competition. God, Corie told me about *Dancing with the Stars* and she made me watch a bunch of clips with that guy Troy, who's on *The Dish* with me. I think she has the hots for him. He is pretty cute."

Zach made a disgusted grunting noise as they neared the entrance of the ranch.

"What?"

"I mean, he's a'ight if you're into that sort of thing."

"Oh, I know you can't be jealous. I know you know what you look like."

"First off, I know how good I look and I know for a fact that Troy and his fumbling-ass hands are lucky he's good in front of a camera so he can keep paying off all those back taxes."

"Do I even want to know?" Evie asked. She glanced ahead as they pulled into the spot behind the main lodge where they'd left the truck the week before.

"Later." Zach put the pickup in park, then leaned over and pressed a long, lingering kiss to Evie's lips. "Don't move. I'll be right back."

"Where are you going?"

"To grab our dinner. For real, I'll be back in a sec. Hold tight." Zach hopped out of the truck and

Evie watched as he went through a back door. She took out her phone and then instantly thought twice, slipping it back in her pocket. She still hadn't recovered from her colossal text screwup New Year's Day. She knew Nicole had forgiven her, but how unprofessional was it to accidentally text your assistant and your agent about your sex life. Raquelle thought it was hilarious. Evie was mortified. Luckily it would be a while before they saw each other face-to-face. It would give her a little time to live down the embarrassment.

A few minutes later Zach was back, carrying a large basket covered in a blue, green-and-white plaid blanket, the same pattern as the shirts the Big Rock employees wore.

"What's that?" Evie asked as he secured the basket behind the driver's seat. A moment later she caught the warm smell coming out of it. It smelled delicious, whatever it was.

"It's a surprise," Zach said before he laughed at Evie's sudden frown. "You can wait the whole minute it'll take us to drive over to the cabin."

"I guess."

Zack backed the truck out of its spot and drove to the main dirt road through the center of the property. Even though the temperature outside was quickly dropping, Evie spotted a small group of guests gathered around a firepit. From the smiles on their faces it didn't seem like they minded the cold too much.

They continued on through the property and then turned up a short rise. Ahead Evie could see a cute cabin up on top of a hill. Zach brought the truck to a stop right beside the wrap-around porch.

"Is this still a part of the ranch?" Evie glanced over her shoulder and looked back down the hill. The main lodge seemed a ways off.

"Sure is. This is our premium honeymoon cabin. For a price you can enjoy the privacy and splendor of nature complete with heat, central air, Wi-Fi, premium cable, and twenty-four-hour room service. It was booked this weekend, but there was a cancellation this afternoon."

"Oh no. What happened?"

"Wasn't as bad as you think. Bride and groom both got cold feet and decided to call the whole thing off right before the wedding march started. Come on."

Instead of waiting for Zach to open her door, Evie climbed down from the high cab on her own. Zach grabbed the picnic basket and took her hand. "You ready?"

"Should I be worried?" she asked as they walked up the half dozen stairs to the cabin's front door.

"About what?"

"You're taking me to the honeymoon suite. That seems pretty serious," she teased.

"It is. There's a reverend inside waiting, two witnesses and everything. I hope you're ready to do this shit 'cause when I said let's go out on a date I meant let's get married."

"Oh, so nothing to be worried about."

"Not a thing."

Evie gave Zach's shoulder a little nudge, then took the picnic basket so he could open the door. Underneath one of the porch lights there was a wooden sign. STARLIGHT.

When she stepped inside, Evie was taken aback by the rustic beauty of the place. The cabin was cozy but large enough for two people to stretch out, or snuggle close in the large four-poster bed against the rear wall.

"This is so beautiful."

"We remodeled it last year, but here." Zach set down the basket on the table for two by the window. "Come look at this." Evie shrugged out of her jacket, then followed Zach over to the fireplace. Beside the mantel was a metal plaque. Evie couldn't stop herself from reading the words out loud.

"'In loving memory of our dear friends Justice and Amelia Buchanan. The Starlight Honeymoon Suite.'"

"Miss Leona insisted upon it."

Evie lifted her fingers and ran them over the engraved letters.

"Apparently when my grandparents bought the place, the four of them came up here to celebrate and Nana thought it would be a good idea to put a private cabin out here. She came up with the name."

"Starlight. I like that."

Evie turned and looked at Zach. "I've been thinking a lot about how I feel like . . . like I'm sort of betraying them with this memory loss. Like I'm failing them because I can't remember what they were like or any of the moments we spent together."

"Hey, come on—"

"I know it's silly. But that's not all I was going to say. It makes me feel better, almost, that I know they were together at one point. Like the four of them had something special. Friendship, love. This amazing

place. They must have had so much *fun*." Evie felt
the tear sting the back of her eyes, but it didn't stop
her from smiling.

"I'm sure of it."

Evie leaned up on her toes and pressed her lips to
his. She soaked in the warmth of his body as his arms
wrapped around her and pulled her closer. She
meant for the gesture to be something small, just a
little reminder that she was happy to be with him
now, in this moment. But it slowly melted into something more—like a declaration of love.

When Zach pulled away, Evie could see it in his
dark brown eyes. He felt what she felt. The future
was so uncertain, but Evie knew one thing: The
more time she spent with Zach Pleasant, the more
certain she was of the fact that she never wanted to
let him go.

Chapter 22

Nicole knew what she was doing was crazy.

No, no it wasn't. Under any other circumstances she would stop herself from following, practically stalking, someone through Midtown, but when she saw Chef Melanie Burns come out of the subway, something told her not to let the woman get away. She didn't think about how bad an idea it was or how she was definitely going to be late meeting Jane and her sister.

Days had gone by, but finally Melanie's agent, Larry, responded to Nicole with a simple "Thank you. We'll handle it." She had no idea how seriously Larry had taken the extreme way his client had popped up in Evie's DMs, but something in her gut told her Larry wasn't going to do what was right or necessary to stop it from happening again.

Maybe the stress finally got to her. Or a desperate need to find some concrete justice for her friend. Whatever it was, she found herself hurrying across the street, hot on Melanie's tail. She followed her for two blocks, and right before she slipped into a

Duane Reade, Nicole called out at the top of her lungs.

"Melanie. Melanie Burns. Chef Burns!"

When Melanie froze, Nicole froze. For a micro-second, regret filled her whole body. Nicole hadn't been in a fight since third grade. She was tough, but she didn't know if she was ready to fight another grown woman in the middle of a busy street. A teen boy pushing past her broke her out of her trance. Just as Melanie turned around, Nicole braced herself. If she had to fight another grown woman in the middle of the street, so be it.

"Melanie!" she repeated.

"Yeah?" Chef Burns stalked toward her, pushing her way through the throng of pedestrians making their way up the street. "Who are you?"

"You're Melanie," Nicole said when they were only a few feet apart.

"Uh, yeah. Who are you? What the fuck do you want?" Okay, yeah. Nicole could definitely see this woman shoving someone down some stairs. She felt herself scowl back at her and then she swallowed, as if it would give her more courage to face down a possible maniac.

"I'm a friend of Evie Buchanan's," she said.

Melanie let her head roll to the side and made a dramatic show of rolling her eyes. "Who isn't a friend of Miss Delightful? In high places only, though, right?" She looked Nicole up and down, sneering at her Burberry coat. It was a gift, damn it.

"I wanted to talk to you about *The Dish* Christmas party and what happened to Evie that night."

"Oh, you wanna talk? Jesus Christ. Pretty princess can't even send someone after me for some real fucking revenge. You push a bitch down some stairs and she sends someone after you for a chat."

"*What?!*" There was no way Nicole heard her correctly.

"God, that bitch is a joke. I can't believe they gave her a show. Tell her I said Happy New Year and I hope she fucks right off." Nicole was so in shock she stood there, blinking after Melanie as she turned and began to walk away. But Nicole reached out and yanked her back by the elbow. Harder than she'd intended. Melanie stumbled and caught herself before she fell off the curb.

"What the hell is your problem?"

"You admit it. You pushed her."

"And she's fine!"

Nicole couldn't believe what she was hearing. All she could see was Evie lying in that dusty stairwell, nearly lifeless, blood pooled around her head. Everything she'd been through in the days that followed. The trauma, the confusion, her damn memory. Evie might never be the same again, and this evil woman was freely admitting her guilt.

Melanie stared back at her, tilting her head and cocking her shoulders like she was daring Nicole to take the first swing, knowing she wouldn't. Then suddenly the look on Melanie's face changed. Nicole watched her features reset to nearly neutral, and then creepiest smile slowly stretched out her cheeks.

"Holy shit," Melanie said, with a sickening laugh. "You didn't know. Un-fucking-believable. What is Evie going for? Gold medal in the morality Olympics?

I mean, I really messed her up and she still didn't rat me out. Tell your friend a little thing about self-preservation. It trumps kindness every now and then."

Nicole closed her mouth, which had apparently been hanging open, and did her best to reclaim her cool. "She did tell me."

"And then what? She told you not to go to the cops 'cause she didn't want me to get in trouble. I know Evie, I just didn't know she could turn the other cheek this hard. Bravo." Melanie took out her phone and checked the time. Somehow this conversation about how she almost killed someone was considered a time suck.

"Listen. Go to the cops or whatever. Who's gonna believe her? There was no one else in the that staircase. Just me and her. It's her word against mine and I'm pretty sure NYPD is not gonna give a shit about a she-said, she-said between two celebrity chefs. Give me a fucking break."

"Why didn't you help her?" Nicole said. Practically yelled it. "How long was she up there?"

"Uh, because I pushed her and why does it matter now? She's fine. Surrounded by flowers from her adoring fans. I know she's getting some sweet paid time off now too."

"Says who?" Nicole demanded.

"Like I'd tell you," Melanie replied, as though naming her possible in at *The Dish* was somehow worse than confessing to attempted murder. Melanie turned on her heels and put her middle finger in the air. "Have a nice day, Evie's friend. Real effective work there."

This time Nicole let her go. Melanie wasn't wrong. Unless Melanie walked into a precinct and confessed, there was no proof of what happened in that stairwell. And no proof of the conversation they'd just had. And even if Nicole went to the police, there was no way for Evie to corroborate her story. Still no timeline, no details as long as Evie was still suffering from this awful amnesia.

Nicole turned and walked back toward the movie theater. She had to tell Jane what had just happened and then she needed to call Jesse Pleasant.

Evie sat on the flatbed of Jesse's truck and watched the horse trailer back into the small paddock behind the barn. She was a good hundred yards away, but that didn't stop her from appreciating Zach's commanding presence as he and their ranch foreman, Felix, directed the arrival of the ranch's newest addition.

Thoughts of the previous night still warmed Evie's whole body. After they'd enjoyed the lovely meal Britnay had made for them, Zach had turned on some music and there was definitely some intimate slow dancing. How they stopped themselves from christening the cabin's large bed was beyond Evie, but they managed to keep their kissing and groping above the belt. For the most part. There may have been a moment or two when they climbed back into the truck and his hand found its way between Evie's legs.

The quick, but mind-blowing orgasm he delivered

made them a few minutes late for Jesse's ridiculous imaginary curfew, but the scowl on his face when Evie walked through the door was worth it. Zach featured heavily in her dreams that night, and this time, wherever Evie went in her dream, he was right there, right by her side. He never left her, never disappeared, and it was his smile that had her waking up the next morning with a smile on her own face instead of a head filled with jumbled thoughts.

Their plans for a thrilling Saturday night involved pizza and a movie at Zach's place, but for now Zach had important business to deal with, getting a new horse acclimated to its surroundings. Miss Leona had to head back to Los Angeles the following day to attend the Golden Globes. When Jesse offered to take Evie and Vega over to see the new colt, they figured it would be a good chance to give Miss Leona a few hours of peace and quiet. Plus, Evie wanted to see this animal Zach was so excited about.

"This is the horse he bought before Christmas?" Evie looked up at Jesse.

"That the ranch bought. Yeah."

"Why do you say it like that?"

"We didn't need another horse."

"But you love your baby brother so you let him get away with anything?" Vega teased.

"Yeah, something like that," Jesse grumbled.

"You don't like horses?" she asked.

"I respect them, but I think a relationship with a horse works best when there's a fence between the horse and me."

"But you own a ranch."

"Coaches don't play, Vega."

"Oh, okay," she said as she and Evie both burst out laughing.

"I got bit once and that was enough for me. Also, I've been about this size since I was twelve and I'm pretty sure our draft horses are the only ones who can comfortably carry three-hundred-and-fifty pounds of pure man."

"Three-fifty?" Vega reached out and grabbed his flannel-covered his biceps. "I know I only come up to your belly button, but damn."

Jesse casually looked at his smart watch before he pointed in the direction of the corral. "You're about to miss the show."

Evie looked up and sure enough, one of the ranch hands was easing the black-and-white horse down the trailer ramp. A female ranch hand led him by the reins and stopped the horse right in front of Zach and Felix. Zach took the reins and started very slowly to lead him around the corral.

"Okay, that's a pretty-ass horse," Vega said.

"Yeah, he's beautiful," Evie added. The young horse was clearly smaller than the other horses, but its black-and-white coat would set it apart from the rest of the horses in the stable.

"Will they use him in the rodeo?" Evie asked.

"No. He's for the guests to ride."

"I'll come up with a few thousand bucks and come for a ride," Vega said.

"We'll let you take him out on the house—Shit."

"What?" Evie noticed a moment later that one of the ranch hands was running toward them.

"That is Evie!" the man said.

"Oh shit." She whipped her head in Jesse's direction. "Do I know him?"

"Yeah, that's Chris Alvarez. His sister Kelly was in your class. Just play it cool. Keep it loose on the details."

Chris closed the distance between them, then hopped the corral fence like it was nothing.

"Evie Buchanan! How are you?"

Evie climbed off the flatbed and stepped into his waiting arms. "Hey, Chris. How are you doing?"

"Good, good. Exciting day. You see that handsome colt?"

"Yeah. It's—uh. Kinda why we came over. Um—this is my friend Vega."

Vega offered him a wave and wary smile, but Chris wasn't having it. He reached out and gave her hand a rough shake.

"Nice to meet you!" He didn't seem to notice she was wearing scrubs under her coat.

"Same."

"Evie. God. It's been forever. What brings you back to town? I have to tell Kelly. She'd love to see you."

"Oh, I'm not in town for long. I just came to visit for a few days."

"Well, you should come out with us tonight to Claim Jumpers."

"Oh, I—"

"She has dinner plans with Miss Leona tonight," Jesse said, coming to her rescue.

"Oh. Yeah, okay." Evie watched as Chris took a small

pack of gum out of his pocket and popped a stick in his mouth. "Miss Leona pulls rank. You want some gum?" He held out the pack, nodding for Evie to take a piece.

"Um, sure, thanks." She took piece and tried to match the bright smile on Chris's face.

"Hey, Alvarez! Little help over here?!" Felix called out.

"I gotta get back, but Jesse has my number. Seriously, we should hang before you leave. Kelly would love to see you. You gotta meet her kids." Chris didn't wait for Evie to respond before he hopped over the fence and jogged back around the corral.

"He's a good guy. Just excitable," Jesse said. "You handled it just fine."

"That was a close call. We really should talk about how much longer I'm gonna be 'hiding,'" Evie said with a sigh. "I can't keep this up."

"I think you handled it just fine, but you're right. I'll text Nicole and ask her when's a good time for us to all get on the phone."

"You should try the gum," Vega said with a smile. "New, overly sweet flavor to add to your profile." Evie knew she was only half joking. She looked down at the flat stick in her hand, wrapped in foil, the word Wrigley's embossed on the wrapper in a diagonal pattern. She lifted it to her nose and inhaled the artificial cinnamon scent.

Across the field, Chris helped the rest of the crew close up the trailer ramp. Evie unwrapped the gum and put the stick in her mouth. She crushed the sugary, chewy substance between her teeth and the sharp flavor flooded over her tongue. The sensation that hit her started in her chest, like a fist gripping her dead center, shaking the memory out of her. She stood there, looking up at her grandmother, and as clear as day she could hear her voice.

"I don't have any candy, I just have gum."

The memory only lasted a moment longer, but she remembered the sun on her face. The smell of horses, the grass under feet, the piece of Big Red gum in her hand and her grandmother by her side.

Evie doubled over, her eyes squeezing shut just as she gripped the middle fence rail.

In the distance she could hear Jesse and Vega saying her name, but everything was muffled. She felt like she was underwater. Through the haze she felt Vega's fingers lifting her chin.

"Look at me," she said.

It was so much harder than it should have been, but she managed to open her eyes.

"Good. Look at me and breathe. In and out, just breathe."

Evie did her best. In and out, and suddenly tears were running down her cheeks. Nana Buck. Her nan. She was gone.

"Can you hear me? Nod yes."

Evie gave her a weak nod.

"Jesse. Help me out here." The next thing Evie knew she was in Jesse's arms. He carried her around the side of the truck and set her down in the passenger seat. A moment later Vega was back in front of her taking her pulse and encouraging her to breathe. She produced a bottle of water and encouraged her to drink. "Okay, just breathe. Good. Can you tell me what happened?"

Evie glanced back toward the corral. It was clear she'd caused a scene. Zach was looking over in her direction.

"I—I—the gum. I remember."

"You remember what?" Vega asked slowly.

"Everything. I remember everything." Her whole life didn't flash before her eyes, no. It was like something had been reset, and instead of feeling lost and unsure, she felt like herself again, buoyed back in her own reality, connected to her own past. She remembered everything. Including how she'd spent the last two weeks growing closer and closer to Zach Pleasant. And then every detail of the conversation that had driven them apart was as clear as that cloudless night she laid her grandmother to rest.

Her finally telling Zach the truth, that she loved him. Her begging him to understand that she just needed some time, but she needed to be with him, to be close to him just to help her get through the crushing pain of losing the last person she had in the world. She could see it, the clarity in his eyes as he almost gave in and pulled her into his arms. But instead he held her at arm's length, begging her to understand that Paris was where she needed to be, that she couldn't give up on her dreams just to be with him. The disappointment and the anger, the realization that Zach didn't understand her. He didn't understand that she knew exactly what was best for her and sadly, he would never be the one to give it to her.

She glanced back again just as he handed off the reins and started jogging in their direction.

"You remember your accident?" Vega asked.

"I have to get out of here. I have to get back to the house."

"What?"

"Jesse. Now. Please take me back to the house. I can't deal with him."

Jesse looked up and saw Zach closing the distance between the far end of the corral and his truck. "Yeah, okay. Vega, get in. And put on your seat belt." Vega rushed around the other side of the truck and climbed in the rear of the cabin.

Evie looked at Zach through the back window. Saw him trying to wave them down. She knew she'd have to deal with him much sooner than later. But now she couldn't. She needed to get back to Miss Leona's. She needed to talk to Nicole.

Zach called three times as they drove back to Miss Leona's house. Each time Jesse hit the Decline button on his dash display. The fourth time he answered.

"Evie's fine. Lunch just didn't agree with her."

"Are you sure?" The sound of Zach's voice made her stomach lurch. She was not ready to speak to him.

"Yeah, she's fine," Jesse said. "We're just heading back so she can lie down. Finish up with the gang and we'll see you later."

"Yeah, okay. See ya."

Just as they pulled up to Pleasant Lane, Jesse's phone rang and Nicole's number flashed across the dashboard. Evie's hand darted out and hit the green Accept button.

"Nicole! Hey! I was just about to call you."

"Evie, hey, are you with Jesse?"

"I'm here. We were just on our way back to the house to call you. I—"

"Wait."

"What?"

"Your voice . . . Evie." Nicole gasped. "Your voice."

"What about my voice?"

"Nothing. For a second it sounded like—"

"Like I was back to normal?"

"Yeah . . ."

"I—I remember, Nicole. My—my memory's back."

"Holy shit! How? Are you okay?"

"Yeah, I think I'm okay. I'm fine, I just—You could tell from my voice?"

"I mean, yeah. You were talking a little like a polite cyborg before. But hold on one second. I just saw Melanie Burns on the street. She confessed to pushing you down the stairs."

"What?" echoed around the cab of the truck. She looked over at Jesse, his shock mirroring hers before a dark cloud of rage passed over his features. Melanie was lucky there were three thousand miles between herself and all three-hundred-plus pounds of him.

"God," Evie sighed. "She just can't—She did. She did push me down the stairs."

"I knew it!" Jesse pulled the truck to a stop right in front of Miss Leona's, and the three of them sat there and listened to Nicole's whole strange encounter with Chef Burns.

"This is insane," Evie said. She was having trouble

breathing again. There were still some gaps in her memory, but parts of that night were very clear.

"What exactly happened?" Jesse asked.

"I don't know if she followed me or what, but she was in the stairwell as I was coming down. We got into an argument about the way she'd treated Tiffany, and then when I tried to walk away, she shoved me."

"We have to go to the police."

"Damn right we do. I'm coming back and we'll go speak to them first thing in the morning."

"Hi. Sorry to interrupt. But can we slow down for a minute here," Vega said from the back seat. "Hi, yeah. You're possibly experiencing spontaneous recovery after a massive head injury. I think you're still in the middle of a pretty intense panic attack. Maybe don't jump on a red-eye tonight."

"She does have a point," Nicole said.

"Nicole, let us call you back," Jesse said, his voice oddly calm.

"Yeah, okay. Call me back soon."

Jesse ended the call. "Thank you," Vega said. "Let's get Evie inside. I'd like to properly examine you and then we need to call Dr. Zordetski. Even if she doesn't need to see you right away, she needs to know. And I'm pretty sure Miss Leona would like to know what's going on as well."

"That's a good idea," Jesse agreed.

Evie knew they were right. Her heart was still beating a mile a minute and her mind was racing. So much was happening, so much had already happened. She had to take a breath, take a moment before she rushed off into the night again. Last thing she needed was to pass out mid-flight from something like undiagnosed internal bleeding.

"Come on." Evie carefully stepped out of the truck and followed Jesse up to the front door.

Chapter 23

Zach knew between his brother, Vega, and Miss Leona they were more than capable of handling Evie's stomachache. That didn't stop him from rushing back to the house as soon as he could. Still, the sun was already starting to set by the time they could get Bam Bam settled in his stall. Clearly date night, part two, was off if Evie wasn't feeling well, but Zach wanted to check on her before she turned in.

Things were oddly quiet when he walked into Miss Leona's. The dogs didn't even bother to greet him. He found his grandmother in the kitchen. Jesse and Corie were standing at the island, with grim looks on their faces.

"Hey. Where's Evie? Is she okay?"

"She's fine, baby," Miss Leona said. "She's down in her room with Vega and Lilah. You should go speak to her."

"Is she alright?"

"She's fine," Jesse said again, but the grave tone of his voice was anything but reassuring.

"Just go talk to her," Corie chimed in.

"Okay. I will." Zach turned and headed down the hall toward Evie's room.

"Do you want us to stay?" he heard Vega say as he got closer. He didn't hear a reply. Just as he reached Evie's door, Lilah and Vega came out and squeezed by him in the hallway. Vega wouldn't look at him as she said her excuse-me, but the expression on Lilah's face matched the grim look that Miss Leona hadn't tried to hide.

Zach came around the corner and found Evie standing near the foot of her bed. Her suitcase was spread open on top of her bedspread, half full of clothes. Euca was curled up in the armchair in the corner. She looked at him before she closed her eyes.

"What are you doing?" Zach said.

"Close the door, will you?"

Zach did as she asked, letting the door gently snick closed behind him before he turned back around. "What's going on?"

"I'm packing."

"Why—" Zach registered it then. Something was different about Evie. Since she'd been in the hospital, she'd been occupying space in a particularly cautious way. But this Evie suddenly seemed possessed with a confidence he hadn't seen in almost ten years. Zach swallowed and watched Evie as she glanced up at him through her eyelashes. She folded a pair of jeans and carefully put them in her suitcase before she reached for another pair of pants. "What happened out at the ranch today? Didn't have anything to do with your stomach, did it?"

Evie moved over to the window seat and sat down.

She crossed her legs, then dragged her teeth over her top lip, letting out one hell of a sigh.

"Dr. Zordetski thinks it was a full, spontaneous recovery of memory brought on by an overwhelming familiar scent or flavor connected to an important person or moment."

"What?"

"Chris Alvarez gave me a piece of Big Red gum and I practically hallucinated Nana right there by the corral. It hit me so hard I thought I was having a stroke."

"Your memory's back?" he asked, a heavy sense of relief flooding through him before the panic rushed right up behind it. Her memory was back and she was skipping town. "No," he said stepping closer to her. "Don't leave like this."

"I have to."

"No, you don't—"

"Zach."

"So, this is over?" he asked, motioning between them.

Evie nodded. "Yeah, I think it is."

"At least talk to me. I don't want a repeat of last time. Where you're pissed at me and then you run anyway and I don't hear from you for another twenty years."

"I'm not running away. I'm just—"

"That's exactly what you're doing. You're—"

"I don't live here!" Evie exploded, shutting him right up. Euca perked up and glanced between them. She didn't settle until Evie let out another deep breath. Zach watched Evie as she closed her eyes, then adjusted her glasses before she went on drilling a hole through the center of his heart. "I'm not trying to be dramatic, Zach. Not everything is about you. I don't live here anymore. I know what we had, but my family isn't here anymore. My life isn't here. And I don't mean that you guys aren't *like* family. I don't mean that all of the Pleasants aren't important to me. I just—"

"I think that's exactly what you mean."

"God, Zach. I have to get back to the city for reasons that have nothing to do with us."

"Nah. You're running. You can make some calls, whatever you have to do. You don't have to bounce like this."

"Can we just *not* right now? Can we not act like this isn't extremely weird and maybe not the best idea?"

"Are the circumstances here a little strange? Yeah, that doesn't mean I want you to take off again," Zach said, knowing immediately that he'd fucked up again. That wasn't how things went down. He knew his father would have backed off if Zach had asked him to stop trying to push them together. He also knew, now, that if he had just been honest with himself and told Nana Buck and Evie how he really felt about her, they might have had something. He'd taken Nana's words to heart and he'd sent Evie away.

"I didn't mean that."

"Yes, you did. And this is why this isn't going to begin to work. Ten years, Zach, and you still think you had no part in me putting three thousand miles between us."

"That's not true. I'm sorry. I admit it. I sent you away. I thought that I knew what was best for you. I thought you were grieving and maybe—"

"You thought that losing my grandmother meant I wanted to throw my life away. Even though you knew I'd finally found my passion and my calling, you thought that just because I got up the courage to finally make a move and tell you how I felt and what I wanted for us that I was really going give it all up."

"I—There was only one way it could work. I had to take over for Senior. It was that or we sell the ranch."

"No, Zach. That was the only way it could work for you. You didn't see it any other way. You're still so arrogant. Jesus. You think I didn't know the pressure Senior had put you under? You think I wasn't paying attention? It didn't have to be all or nothing for either of us, Zach, but you thought it did. You made the call, so I went back to Paris. I finished my training. I saw the world. Without you."

Evie closed her mouth suddenly. Zach didn't miss the way her knuckles tensed as she gripped the edge of the window seat. "Why couldn't you just admit that you felt the same way about me?"

"I don't know. I didn't know until it was too late."

"You did. I think you didn't want to admit it until you realized you could have lost me forever."

Zach swallowed. He didn't want to validate that statement, even if it did have a hint of truth to it. "I'm sorry I don't have a better answer, but I don't know why I didn't tell you a hundred times. Your grandmother made it so clear that she didn't want me for you, and when she died—"

"Listen, I get it. I struggled with the same thing. Doing what she wanted of me, making sure that I focused on myself and built my own dreams. She told you to stay away from me and you took that to mean forever. Well, it worked and now I have to go."

"So all of this is nothing?"

"Zach," she said with a pained laugh. "I know you didn't do it on purpose, but this? This sucks. It stings. It stings knowing that I had to lose my memory and become someone else for you to fall for me."

"You think I only care about you because of a head injury? You think I haven't been thinking about you this whole time? You think I haven't subconsciously kept every woman I meet at arm's length just on the off chance that I'd see you again?"

"Maybe. The more logical answer is that you've been so busy with the ranch, every woman who comes near you knows she can't compete."

"Wow, that's messed up, but no. That's not it. Evie. I have been in love with you my whole life. I told you that almost the moment I set foot in that hospital room. Why do you think I have practically a hundred episodes of *The Dish* just hanging out on my DVR?"

"It's more than that and you know it. I—I never got a chance to see what this was really like. I never got to know what you were like when you weren't giving me shit. I—"

"Say it. Please." This was the worst conversation he'd had in his whole life, but he wanted to know it all. He needed to understand what was really going on before he lost Evie again.

"I never got the satisfaction of knowing I was right. You did have feelings for me and you would never just say it. Do you remember what you said to me that night after Nana's funeral?" Evie asked, her voice cracking a little.

"I told you that I didn't want you to let it set you back—"

"You told me that us *kissing* was a bad idea because you knew I had plans and you didn't want to screw them up."

"I didn't!"

"And then you told me I was too good for this place. Too good for you and you wanted me to keep seeing the world. But you know what I heard?"

Zach sighed, the realization hitting him. "That I never felt that way about you. Ever. I never thought you weren't good enough for me."

"No. All I heard was that you didn't think I was smart enough to think for myself. You had your future planned out and you couldn't possibly conceive of derailing your plans, so you had to make sure *I* stayed on track. Exactly the way *you* envisioned it. You saw me needing you and wanting you as giving up on myself, without even talking to me about it. It was belittling, Zach. And humiliating."

"That wasn't it. I was young, and if you want to know the truth, emotionally unequipped to be there for you the way I thought you really needed me. I hadn't lost anyone close to me at that point. My grandpa died when I was like two. I didn't know how to handle your grief over losing Nana—or mine.

"When you came to live with us right after your parents died, when you came back to me after Nana died, I didn't know how to do anything other than try to make you laugh and try to help you move on. I didn't tell you to go back to Paris because I didn't want you to be here with me. I think this place was the place—"

"Where I come when people leave me."

"Evie. That's not what I meant."

"I know, Zach, but it's true. This was never my home. It was just a place where I ended up until I figured out where I needed to be. And now I know where that is. I'm leaving for the city in the morning."

"I don't want you to leave. Not yet. They found a temporary replacement for you at *The Dish*. You don't need to go back right away."

"That night, after Nana's funeral—I didn't need you to suddenly know how to fix everything or how to fix me. I just wanted you to admit that I wasn't in this alone for one second. I wanted you to admit all that those looks we shared growing up meant something more. I just wanted you to be brave."

"Evie. I'm sorry."

"I know. Listen. I know we've talked and I know you apologized. And I still accept your apology, but this—what I feel for you, all of it. Loving you, wanting to choke you. I've been dealing with that for years and I can't help it, but I'm still pissed. I might be even more pissed than I was before."

"Why?"

"You just said that you've been in love with me your whole life."

"I have."

"You never called once." Her voice sounded like it was splitting in two and suddenly tears started streaming down her cheeks. She lifted her glasses and started to wipe them away, but more kept coming. "You never tried to see me. Jesse and Sam knew I was hurting, and they tried. You loved me so much, but it was so easy for you to let me walk away. You never even asked your brothers to check in on me. I know you thought I was being dramatic, but I had lost the last of my whole family, Zach. And you just let me go."

Zach's mouth opened, but his pitiful defense died in the back of his throat. Yeah, Evie had always been stubborn and quick tempered when it came to him. Still, in this moment she was right. Zach had loved Nana Buchanan, but she was Evie's whole world, and in a flash she was gone. Zach had his brothers, and his grandmother, and even with the distance and a bit of unresolved tension, his parents to fall back on, knowing that they'd love him unconditionally. No matter how close they'd been as kids, Zach had never offered Evie anything close to unconditional love, even with their friendship. When she told him she wanted and needed more, he'd dropped the ball and never even bothered to pick it up.

"I just. I don't trust myself with you. Even right now. I feel fifteen all over again, just trying to get you to see me," Evie said.

"I do see you."

"Yeah, and it only took a coma to get you there."

"I don't know what else to say, but I am sorry."

Evie shrugged, the tears still running down her face. "And I don't know what else to say other than I still need time to be pissed about it and I don't know when I *won't* be pissed about it. I need to finish packing. Vega and I are flying out in the morning."

"Vega's going with you?"

"Yes. I need to get another MRI, but I want to do

it back in New York. Miss Leona and Jesse said they'd feel better sending me off if I had her around just in case. It'll only be for a few days. Oh, and I didn't tell you the best part," she added with a bitter laugh. "I *was* pushed."

"What the fuck?"

"It was Melanie Burns. I have to go back and deal with her."

"Jesus. Okay. Okay." As much as he hated to see her walk away, there was nothing he could do. Evie had a place, she had friends, her own life in New York, and she definitely needed to get back to dole out some stair-related justice on Chef Burns. "Please don't leave without saying goodbye."

"I promise I won't."

"Okay. I'll leave you to it."

"Goodnight, Zach."

It took everything in him not to cross the bedroom and scoop her up into his arms. He wanted to kiss the hell out of her, remind her what they could still have together, but he knew better than to push her in this moment. He turned, and again, walked out of Evie Buchanan's life.

Three hours into their flight back to New York and Evie still couldn't sleep. She'd been up most of the night crying. She was glad Dr. Zordetski recommended that she still follow through with her plan to see a therapist when she got back to the city, because she was sure going to need it. Everything that had happened kept replaying in her head over and over, and when she wasn't thinking about this almost make-believe relationship that she'd finally gotten to share with Zach Pleasant, a relationship that had been circumstantial at best, she was weeping for her parents and her grandparents all over again.

Her recovered memory didn't just dredge up what happened that night with Melanie in the stairwell; it brought up almost thirty years of repressed pain and trauma. When her alarm had gone off, she felt puffy and parched. She managed to hold it together as she said her goodbyes. She would miss Jesse and Lilah, and Corie too. Nothing could replace the moments she'd shared with Miss Leona in her kitchen. And yes, she would miss Zach.

She had to give him credit. He didn't make things harder than they had to be. As Jesse was loading their bags into his truck, Zach came out his house in a gray sweat suit and made his way across the cul-de-sac. When he wrapped his arms around her, she knew she had to go. Her true feelings for Zach had never changed and that was a problem. She'd forgive him anything if she looked at that smile too long, and do nothing to really try and heal herself. When she pulled away she knew she was doing the right thing, putting some distance between them again.

"Just text me when you get back to your place. So I know you're okay," was all he said. She tried not to think of the look on his face when she glanced at him in the rearview mirror. She tried not to think of the bags under his eyes, proof that he'd had an equally sleepless night.

She held it together when Jesse dropped her and Vega off at the airport, but just after they reached their cruising altitude, Evie felt the tears return to the corners of her eyes. She didn't make a sound, but for at least an hour, the tears streamed down her face. Luckily Vega was quick with the tissues.

She felt like hell when they walked back through her apartment door, but thank god for Blaire. Her amazing bestie was waiting for them with hot take-out and chilled wine and fresh linens for Vega.

After she cried on Blaire some more, Vega insisted that she try and get some sleep. Evie took a long, hot shower, reminded anew of the fact that she'd chopped most of her hair off—something else to bring up with her therapist—then climbed into her bed that suddenly felt foreign and cold. She knew it would mold back to her body in a few days, but for now she missed the bright yellow sheets from Miss Leona's guest room. Before she turned off her lights, she plugged in her phone. She'd called Jesse in the Lyft on the way back from the airport so he knew they were home, but she hadn't reached out to Zach.

She pulled up their text conversation, very careful not to scroll and look much at the texts they'd exchanged when things were different between them. She typed out a simple message.

Home. Heading to bed. Thank you for coming to get me.

She set her phone back on her nightstand and turned off the light, but she heard her cell vibrate before she could close her eyes. She rolled over and looked at the text from Zach.

Anytime. And I mean that. Anytime you need me,
    Evie. I'm here.

She didn't reply. She couldn't. It would start a
conversation and at that moment she had nothing
left in her to give. Instead she turned on her light
and dug the diary Zach had given her out of her
carry-on.

January 10
    I had no idea how badly I missed him. I have
no idea how we go back or how we go forward.
I could see myself going back to Charming and
being his girl. Maybe even being his wife, but I have
no idea how I could ever make Zach Pleasant mine.

That night she slept so deeply she didn't dream
at all.

Chapter 24

Zach thought about hitting the bottle, but he knew he'd enjoy the numbed-out bliss that came from being completely faded for exactly ten minutes before Miss Leona gave him an earful about what he was not going to do as long as she was around. So instead of drinking his sorrows away, he spent every moment he could away from the office, with Steve. He'd take him out for some exercise. Practice the dismount he'd almost taken an L on at the last exhibition, but instead they ended up loafing around the back pasture.

Zach lay in the grass, looking up at the blue sky, wondering how he had fucked things up so badly. Steve joined him, lying on his side a few feet away. It was the first big trick he'd taught the large thoroughbred. Fainting on command.

"Is Steve depressed too?"

Zach lifted his head and saw Jesse standing just outside the fence. Clementine was a few yards away, enjoying the midday break from the office.

"No, he's just playing dead. Pull up some grass. Join us."

"I have a meeting in an hour and I'd rather not fuck up this suit."

"Fair enough." Zach stood and dusted himself off, then made his way over to the fence. Steve followed, probably wondering when they would get around to actually doing something that wasn't a sad ride down by the stream. He nudged Zach's shoulder, then made a move to grab Jesse's Stetson. His brother jumped out of the way like he was avoiding a grizzly bear.

"He's not going to bite you."

"You don't know that."

"Hold still. Steve." Zach clicked his tongue twice and lightly tapped his brother's cheek. His trusty steed leaned over the fence and brushed his big horsey lips on Jesse's face, then turned away in search of better things to eat.

"See, you survived. What can I do for you?"

Jesse cleared his throat, seeming to recover from Steve's vicious mauling. "I actually came over here to see what I can do for you."

"What are you getting at? I don't need anything."

"So how long are you going to spend your days lying in a field with a horse? What did Lilah call it? Man pain. She said you're in deep."

Zach couldn't help but laugh. "What the fuck is man pain?"

"She said you're wallowing in a way only a real man can. Deep, bone-deep pain. No tears though."

"Oh, there's been tears. Plenty of weeping and wailing, I've just been doing it behind closed doors."

"So, what do we do, man? Help me out."

"Hell if I know. I just miss her. I spent ten years pretending I didn't and it finally caught up with me."

Zach was trying his best to give Evie space. He'd texted her one more time, to ask if she was doing okay. Her response wasn't bad.

> Dr. Manzo is very happy with my progress.
> Cleared to resume on-camera work in a
> week. Thank you for asking.

But he hadn't heard from her again. Nicole had been keeping them in the loop regarding the Melanie Burns situation. Evie had gone to the police, told them every detail of what happened that night, and filed a restraining order. They'd sent officers to pick up Melanie for questioning, but she was out of the country. On paper it was a simple assault case, so it wasn't like they were going to have Interpol track her down, but at least Evie had put something official on the cops' radar. And once the restraining order was served, she had legal cause to tell Melanie Burns to stay the hell away from her.

He knew if any of that changed, Nicole would be the first to tell him or Jesse. Zach was back in the loop and he appreciated that. It didn't do anything to ease the bone-deep ache that had settled in the center of his chest.

"I don't know. Maybe I just gotta get over it."

"You think you should move on?"

Zach let out a dry chuckle. "No. I don't want to close that door unless I absolutely have to."

"Makes sense."

"I thought you were coming out here to tell me to get over myself."

"Nah. I realized I can give you shit about work, the ranch, getting on Miss Leona's nerves, but I can't give you shit about this."

"Why?"

"'Cause I don't know what it's like. I've never been in love." Jesse looked down and dragged the sole of his boot over the bottom fence rail. "Can't really set an example for you either."

"Eh. It's not on you," Zach said, meaning every word of it. He never pressured Jesse when it came to women. People thought because he was built like a Mack Truck, women threw themselves at his feet. Which was true, but Jesse didn't know exactly how to pick up women. He'd always been shy, and when he found the nerve to talk to a woman, he was too blunt. He'd blown a few chances at a good thing and then he just stopped trying altogether.

And though they'd only talked about it once, Jesse had made it clear that casual sex just wasn't an option for him. He needed a connection with someone who got him. When he loved, Jesse loved hard, and Zach knew any woman would be lucky to have him in their corner. Zach just had no idea how to help him get to that point.

"Should we call Sam? Ask him to give us some pointers?"

"It would be wild if we had a father we could talk to about these things. Oh wait," Jessie said, cracking a ghost of a smile.

"You know exactly what he'd say. 'Just marry her. I don't understand the problem.'"

"I know Evie's upset, but I know she loves you too. Just give her some time."

"It's all I can do."

"Let me get back. If you're still out here after dark, we're staging an intervention."

"I'll be back in a minute." Then something so obvious occurred to him, something his baby cousin would definitely understand. "Actually, can you spare Lilah for a second?"

"Yeah, of course. Text her."

"I will." They executed their elaborate Pleasant brother handshake before Jesse turned and headed back for the office.

"Keep that horse away from me!" he called out. Zach shook his head at his brother's retreating back, watching as Clementine ran to catch up with him. He pulled out his phone a few seconds later and shot Lilah a text. Eager for a break from emails and paperwork, she happily met him out in the corral.

"What's up?" she said as she perched on the top rail of the fence.

Zach watched as Steve ambled over to her and nudged her for some head scratches. "I have to ask you something. I know you might laugh, but I'm asking you cousin to cousin, not to laugh in my face."

"I swear. What's going on?"

"Okay. Here goes. Hi, I'm Zach."

"Hi, Zach," Lilah said with a smile.

"And I don't think I know the first thing about women."

"Oh, I agree with you there."

"Damn, it's that bad?"

Lilah rolled her eyes, moving her hand up to

Steve's mane. "All of you Pleasant men are the same. Great minds for business, great with people when it has to do with business, but when it comes to real relationships? Yeah, you don't know a thing about women."

"You got any advice?"

A bright smile spread out across Lilah's face. She was the baby of the whole bunch, if only by a few years, but when she tilted her chin up Zach knew she might be the wisest. "As a matter of fact. I do."

Evie sat across from Nicole's desk and took the tissue she offered. She had no idea what she had done wrong, but some part of the universe's New Year's resolution seemed to involve kicking her while she was down.

She was set to return to *The Dish*, but when she went in that Friday to talk to Troy and the other producers, they'd all been shocked by her appearance. The short hair and the glasses. They were more than shocked when she explained that she needed Melanie Burns banned from the studio and all *Dish*-related functions. She had the medical records and the restraining order available to back up her claim. She was just eager to get back to work.

Troy had been a little strange toward her as the meeting ended, but she just figured he was processing all of the unbelievable things she'd just told them. The assault, the memory loss. Her hair. But clearly he had done more than process.

She woke up that Monday morning and went down to meet her driver, Octavio, but he wasn't there waiting for her in his usual spot. She figured he was running late, but when fifteen minutes went by she called the production office to see if he was okay. Then she'd been put on hold. She'd never been put on hold. Chelsea, their production manager, finally got on the phone and told her not to come in. She couldn't explain why, but she'd hear from Jacinda May, their executive producer, soon. As soon as she hung up she got a text from Raquelle, who was waiting at the studio with Evie's breakfast and coffee. They wouldn't let her in.

Two hours later she was in Nicole's office, sitting through the third worst call she'd received in her life. They were letting her go. Their official statement: Evie's temporary replacement was crushing it and Troy felt it would be best if she stayed on. They would pay out the rest of her season-one contract, but her days at *The Dish* were done. Evie knew it was more than a bit of on-screen chemistry that had gotten her canned. She and Troy were great together on camera, and she and Ashley and Mitchell had this great back-and-forth that the audience loved. She didn't doubt for one second that Montgomery Fent was doing a great job standing in, but Evie knew what she herself had brought to the table. The viewers and the ratings. She was the reason they'd been renewed for a second season. This wasn't about Montgomery, it was about her.

Nicole tried her best to get them to reconsider, but Evie had yet to actually renew her contract. Nothing was in writing. There was nothing she could do.

"This sucks. I know this sucks, but it's going to be okay," Nicole said.

"I know. I know." She let out a deep breath and lightly dabbed the edge of her new tortoiseshell frames.

"I want you to go home. Take a hot shower—"

"Ugh, I don't want to go home. I've been dying to get out of the house." Cabin fever didn't begin to describe it. Though she'd been a wonderful, essential houseguest, Evie thought Vega leaving would give her a little more breathing room, but what she really wanted was to get back to work and the rest of her normal routine. She needed a break from the constant stream of Zach-related thoughts that would not stop running on a loop in her head. Now the thing that had given her the routine she so desperately craved had been taken away.

"Okay. Well, reschedule that vacation you had on the books. Head down to Barbados. Hell, call your friend Tiffany and see what's going on in Barcelona. You have options. You wanna write a book? Cookbook? Memoir? I'm sure we can get the ball rolling on something."

"Yeah," she said, her voice filled with defeat. She had plans. *The Dish* had been a part of those plans. She might as well light on fire the imaginary blueprints for the restaurant that would never be.

After she gave herself a little shake, Evie stood and grabbed a few more tissues. "I'm sure Oprah and Beyoncé would want me to find the silver lining in this."

"Rihanna too," Nicole said with a shrug.

"I'm going to head home and pull myself together. I'll call you in few days. Maybe I'll drag Blaire to Vermont or somewhere the snow stays pretty for the weekend." If Blaire wasn't busy with Dr. David.

"That sounds amazing."

Evie thanked Nicole, then caught a cab back to her place. Blaire wouldn't be home for a few hours so she had time, too much time, to herself before she could lament losing her job in a less-than-dignified way. She knew she should probably call Raquelle, let her know what had happened, assure her everything would be okay and she definitely still had a job as Evie's assistant. She sat on the edge of her couch, phone in hand, and a sudden need she couldn't explain came over her. Things were not going her way right now, but she didn't have to handle this alone. She called Miss Leona.

"Hey, girl. What up?"

Fresh tears sprang to the corners of her eyes at the sound of Corie's voice. This time Evie laughed. "Hey, Corie. Is Miss Leona around?"

"Yeah, one sec."

A moment later she heard Miss Leona's soothing voice on the other end of the line. "Yvonne. My sweet baby. What's going on in the Big Apple today?"

"Um, not much. Nothing good."

"Oh? Well then, it's a good thing you called me. Tell me what's going on."

At first, Evie told herself that she just wanted to hear Miss Leona's voice. They'd only spoken a few times for a few minutes since she'd left Charming, but the next thing she knew she was telling Miss Leona everything. About *The Dish*, and the fear that Melanie would reappear and violate the restraining order just for kicks. She told her everything. Well, almost everything. She left out the fact that she desperately wanted to share all this with Zack. She didn't tell Miss Leona just how much she missed him and how, for some ridiculous reason, she thought stepping into his arms would make all of this go away. If only for a few minutes.

"I'm sorry I've been rambling on," Evie finally said. She'd have to ask Dr. Manzo if chronic weeping could be a side effect of traumatic brain injury or if her life was that much of a mess.

"I don't mind the rambling. Would you like an old woman's two cents on an industry that's tried to get rid of me more than a few dozen times?"

Instantly, Evie felt so foolish. She'd called Miss Leona for the grandmotherly shoulder to lean on. She'd almost forgotten that the woman also knew her way around an industry deal gone wrong.

"I would love to hear your opinion. Please."

"Fuck 'em," Miss Leona said, her voice stern.

A rough burst of laughter came from Evie's mouth. "What?"

"I said, fuck 'em. From what you've told me, this show is Troy's baby, an ex–football player's fall-back plan. He's calling the shots now. Okay, fine. The question is, what is your dream, your baby? What does Chef Evie Buchanan want to show the world?"

Evie almost lied and said she didn't know, like speaking her dreams out loud would somehow taint them, but the idea of withholding the truth felt so exhausting. She said what was in her heart. "I want to open my own restaurant. That's all I've ever wanted, and truthfully? It's the main reason I took the gig on *The Dish*, but now, I don't know. Now I feel like I'm going to miss being in front of the camera. I'm not sure I'm ready to give it up."

Evie was shocked to hear herself offer up that bit of information, but it wasn't the whole truth. She didn't want to stay at *The Dish* forever, but having the rug pulled out from under her like this was not what she had in mind.

"Hmmm," Miss Leona said. "Well, let me make some calls—"

"No, please—"

"Let me finish."

"Yes, ma'am."

"Let people help you. Let me make some calls and we'll see what we can get going for you next."

"I just—I appreciate that. That's just not why I called, you know, for your connections."

"I know, but that's what I'm going to do. I know you and Zachariah had a rough go of it, but I need to own up to my part in all this too."

"What do you mean?" Evie asked.

"I didn't pull you closer when Amelia died, and I should have. Not that I should have stopped you going back to culinary school, but I should have opened my home to you at every possible turn because you're one of my babies too. You lost your mom and your daddy and then your nana too, and I just let you walk away. I was wrong and I'm sorry."

That was the last thing she'd expected to hear. She figured Miss Leona had just been staying out of their drama. Evie supposed in the back of her mind she could have called her if she needed to. Maybe she hadn't because Miss Leona reminded her too much of her grandmother. Maybe she'd created another reason in her mind to stay away. She never imagined Miss Leona felt like she'd messed up in any kind of way. It was also really strange to hear someone she respected so much apologize to *her*.

"I—I appreciate you saying that. I didn't know how to speak to Zach, but I should have called you."

"I say we call it even."

More tears threatened to fall from Evie's eyes as a small knot made its way up her chest. "I think I can live with that."

Chapter 25

Evie refused to change again. Three times was plenty for a lunch with a man she swore she no longer had feelings for. She refused to get dressed up for Zach Pleasant. She definitely didn't need to dress up for Sam. A week ago Sam had called and said he'd be in the city for a few days and asked if she wanted to meet up for a few hours. He was considering a project and wanted input from someone who didn't share his last name. Evie eagerly agreed and then instantly reconsidered when he mentioned Zach would be with him.

Zach Pleasant had featured prominently in her conversations with her therapist. He also seemed to have taken up permanent residence in her dreams. She wasn't ready to see him, but she knew sooner or later she was going to have to rip the Band-Aid off and face him. She loved his family too much to spend the rest of her life avoiding just him.

She tied her boots and walked out to the living room. Blaire was stretched out on the couch binge-watching *Living Single*.

"How do I look?"

Blaire lifted her head, then reached for the remote and paused the TV. "Cute casual. Perfect outfit. Your boobs look amazing."

Evie looked down at her argyle sweater that was a shade away from skintight. Her jeans weren't exactly loose either, and she may have gone with a full face of makeup. "Not too much? I wanna say *I'm doing fine and yeah, I've thought about sleeping with you literally every day since we've been apart, but I'm not going to sleep with you again.*"

Blaire gave her a swift nod. "Mission accomplished."

"Okay. I'm off." Evie slipped on her parka and had one takeaway from her time back in California: She did not love New York winters. "You and David still on for tonight?"

"Yeah, but change of plans. We're both exhausted, so we're going to watch TV at his place."

"Oooooh, that's hot," Evie teased.

"You jest, my friend, but David said we could lie on top of each other, butt naked, and watch my choice of period drama. Yeah, we could hit up a happening hot spot, but nothing gets my butter churning like a man who gives tax-deductible donations to your local PBS station."

"Okay, that is hot. You and woke bae enjoy yourselves."

"I'll be here till seven if you need to debrief."

"Thank you. You're the best."

Thirty minutes later she walked out of the blistering cold and into T_G. Trekking all the way out to Brooklyn on such a crappy day wasn't the brightest idea, but Donia promised her a private table in the back, in the middle of their midday rush. Nowhere else in all the boroughs could promise that on such short notice.

She shed her coat and stepped up to the hostess stand. The young girl manning the seating chart did a double take, her eyes lighting up the second she recognized Evie.

"Chef Buchanan, hi! Your guests are already here. Let me show you to your table."

"I got this," Donia said as she made her way over from the bar. She gave Evie a warm hug, then took her hand and led her toward the back of the restaurant. The moment she spotted Zach she almost turned and hightailed it out of there. How could he possibly look better than the last time she saw him? Fresh haircut, nicely pressed suit. She could see that Stetson of his on the seat beside him. And then all she could picture was how good he looked wearing nothing but that hat. The corner of his mustache tipped up in a cautious smile. She thought she returned it, but she may have just been drooling.

"After this can you tell me how you know Sam Pleasant?" Donia whispered, snapping her out of her Zach-focused reverie.

"It's a boring story, I swear."

"And his hot brother."

"Now that's where the drama is," she whispered back.

Donia let out a faint snort before she plastered on a professional smile. She stood by as Zach and Sam both stood and greeted Evie with light kisses on the cheek. Donia gave them her VIP spiel, then left them to make their final choices off the menu.

"It's nice to see you guys," Evie said as she slid into

the booth so Sam was seated between her and Zach. It was awkward, but she couldn't be too cautious. He even smelled good.

"Likewise. How are you feeling?" Sam said with his bright smile.

"Good. Great, actually. Still getting used to the hair, but I whipped up a killer three-course dinner for some friends last night, so it's nice to know I can find my way around a kitchen. Again."

"New glasses?" Zach asked.

"Oh yeah." Evie swallowed the nerves rising in her throat. She hadn't been prepared to hear his voice again. "A lot of people on the Gram like them." Evie expected Zach to shoot back with some snarky comment about her adoring fans or some porny comment about how much he liked them too. *Wink, wink. Nudge, nudge.* But he simply gave her another cautious shadow of a smile. She got it. She'd drawn a distinct line in the sand and he was trying to respect it.

"Oh, another bit of good news, before we get started. Melanie Burns got picked up in Italy on aggravated assault charges."

"What?!" Sam and Zach said at the same time.

"She went over there to do a wedding and ended up choking the bride's aunt, who is married to some local politician. Apparently, she'll be a guest of the Italian authorities for a little while."

"Wow."

"Damn."

"Yeah. Locked up abroad seems like a much worse punishment than whatever the Manhattan DA was going to slap her on the wrist with for what she did to me."

"Here, here," Zach said, raising his glass.

"So, Sammy," Evie went on before she stared into Zach's gorgeous brown eyes a bit too long. "Talk to me. What's this project you've got going on?"

"We want to invest in your restaurant."

"'Scuse me, what?"

"Miss Leona told us about your plans pre- and post-*Dish*, and we want to help. I'm kicking in some funds, so are the parents. You'll get a check from Zack and Jesse, and Miss Leona will cover the rest."

"I'm sorry. 'Scuse me? Your parents?"

"I talked to them. Both of them, and they couldn't deny that it would be a good investment," Zach said.

"This is gonna be one hundred percent your show," Sam went on. "We're gonna be silent partners. You won't have any Pleasants following you around, second-guessing your every move. This will be your baby."

"Well—" Zach cut in.

"Well what? Bring on the catch, Pleasant," she said.

"There's no catch. I just want to offer my assistance. I have over ten years' experience in hospitality. More, if you count the years I helped out Granddad."

"What about the ranch? I'm surprised you're here now."

"Jesse and I decided I don't need to be so hands-on day to day. I've been giving a little too much of myself to the guests. We created a position for Delfi. She's now the general manager and we promoted Lilah too. Teaching her more of the business."

"I—that's great. For all of you."

"There's more," Zach said, cautiously.

"Celia Lamontagne wants to make a documentary about the whole process," Sam blurted out.

"How in the—" Evie stopped herself from screaming in the middle of a crowded restaurant. Celia Lamontagne was only her favorite writer/director. She was fairly new on the scene, but she'd already directed five award-winning films and won an Oscar for *A New Day*, a documentary on Black women and midwifery. Evie would do anything just to breathe this woman's air.

"How did Celia Lamontagne get involved in all this?"

"I ran into her after the SAG Awards," Sam explained. "And somehow we got on the subject of you. I brought up your dreams for a restaurant and she pitched me the idea. She told me she actually voted for you as fan favorite when you were on *Supreme Chef*."

"I'm not freaking out, but Celia Lamontagne knows who I am."

"She wants to do a doc about you. She thought the idea of following a young Black female chef trying to break ground in a tough business would make for great material. Say the word and she'll start making some calls."

"Think about how many customers the doc alone could drive through the door," Zach said. She looked over at him and considered everything they were offering. Money and support. She wanted to jump at the chance. It would be foolish to turn down such an amazing, generous offer. Of course, it came with one huge caveat. Even if she turned Zach's part of the bargain down, she would still be working closely with his family. She'd be talking to them more, seeing them more. They would have to deal with each other in one way or another.

Evie cleared her throat and straightened her shoulders. "And what about you? Considering how things are between us? Do you think working with me would be a good idea?"

"Honestly, Buck. That's on you. But here's what I do know. I love you and I want you to be happy. I would do anything to help make your dreams come true."

Sam snickered, then nudged Zach, motioning for him to move out of the way. "I'll give you two a minute." When he was gone Zach stayed on his side of the booth, but the way he looked at Evie became all the more intense. She couldn't remember the last time she'd seen him like this. So straightforward. So serious.

"Like I was saying—"

"Yeah, I have questions."

He cracked that smile then, that real smile that always made Evie's feet feel like they were stuck to the floor.

"You were right. It took a blunt and embarrassing-as-hell conversation with Lilah for me to see it, but you were right. When Senior left me and Jesse in charge, I became so focused on making Big Rock an even bigger success, I didn't stop to think of a lot of things. Mainly what I wanted out of it."

"And you've sorted that out."

"I have. I want the ranch to thrive and I want it to

stay in the family, but then I realized I hadn't stopped to think about what I want for *myself*. I want a life with you. In Charming, in New York, in Paris. Wherever. I love you. Yes, I was putting the ranch before any chance at love, but that's because no one I met compared to you. You're the most important thing in the world to me, Yvonne Buchanan. I would do anything for you. Anything. Okay, Lilah told me to stop there 'cause declarations of love don't mean anything if the other person don't want shit to do with you."

Evie tried to cover her laughter and failed. She owed Lilah big-time.

"I knew you wanted to be a chef and I know you want to open this restaurant, but I never asked what you wanted for your *life*. That's where I went wrong. I was so focused on not derailing your career, I forgot that you—that we—are both so much more than the work we do. That's where I fucked up. For the both of us. And I can't apologize enough. Okay. Now I'll really stop."

"I mean, go on if you have more good points."

"No, I'm good. Please." He sat back against the booth and motioned to the table between them. Evie looked up at the elaborate steel light-fixture and tried to force back the tears that stung at her eyes. She'd spent years fighting against this exact feeling. Ever since her nan died, all that mattered was the work, the drive. She imagined one day she'd pull the money together on her own. She'd open her dream spot in the dream location, and magically the man of her dreams would just appear and they would start their life together. But whenever she closed her eyes and let that dream play out, she saw only one face.

But she couldn't let Zach off that easy. Not right away. Especially when he could not stop talking.

"If you decide to do this restaurant deal, you have me along for the ride. All of my knowledge and resources are yours. You want me completely out of the way, then I'll back off. But I'm here, I don't *want* to go."

"So your love for me? That's it. That's the only reason you're gonna give me a bazillion dollars to take a swing at something I've never done before?"

"That and I inhaled that leftover carbonara you made. If you can cook like that when you can barely remember your name, I know you'll kill it when you're firing on all cylinders. Miss Leona took a gamble, giving me and Jesse the reins of Big Rock when our dad passed on it. She had faith in us and now the ranch is doing better than ever. Now let us have faith in you."

Evie refused to cry. Her tear ducts couldn't take it anymore. And then he had to go and slide closer and take her hand. Evie tilted her head back, willing the tears away.

"What are you doing?" he laughed.

"I used a quality setting powder, but I refuse to screw up this Fenty face." She swallowed and then told him something she'd only spilled in the pages of that hideous diary. "I want a family. A big family. I want dogs, and one cat to rule them all. I want to see the world with my family. The dogs and the cat can stay home. I want to feel loved, like really loved. I want to feel that I have something that is mine for as long as I can hold on to it."

Zach moved closer. "Nana was right. I wasn't ready back then, but I'm ready now. I want to be your man. I want to be wherever you are. I want to be there for you in every way. I have dogs, but we can get more. I don't know too much about cats, but I'll learn. And I will do anything and everything to get started on a family, if you know what I'm saying."

Evie groaned. "Oh my God."

"If you can handle being seen walking around Manhattan with a man in a bad-ass Stetson, I'll be yours forever."

A burst of laughter came from Evie's chest and the tears finally followed. Zach was quick to hand her a napkin. "The cowboy hat is the best part," Evie said.

She didn't know what she was fighting anymore. She couldn't punish Zach forever and she certainly couldn't punish herself. She had waited years to hear him say those words and she couldn't think of a sensible reason not to say them back. Zach Pleasant was it for her, her Prince of Charming, California. And had been since the first day she set foot on Big Rock Ranch.

She moved closer and leaned into his open arms. Zach embraced her, pulling her in closer. She'd been right about the magic of just being in his touch. Being with him wouldn't suddenly fix her whole life, but it would make it a hell of a lot better.

She snuggled in closer still, burying her face against his neck.

"I missed you so much," she confessed.

"I missed you too. I even dreamt about you."

Evie pulled back and looked into his eyes. "You did?"

"Every night since you've been gone. It's the strangest thing, but I can't stop it. Lilah said my subconscious is trying to tell me something. I think she's right."

"I've dreamt about you too."

"Pleasant dreams, I hope."

Evie groaned even louder, her eyes rolling. "See, why'd you have to go and ruin—"

He grabbed her hand mid-shove and pulled her right to his chest. "Kiss me already, Buck."

She didn't hesitate this time. She kissed Zach Pleasant like she'd been wanting to do for years. She kissed him hard and deep, their tongues slowly tangling together, and only when she remembered they were in public did she stop herself from climbing across his lap.

"You've been thinking about the sex."

"Oh my God, yes," Evie said with a sigh. "All the time."

"You can come check out my hotel room later this afternoon, if you like. Talk a bit more about this business plan."

"Yeah. Please give me your whole business plan. All of it."

Zach laughed as he shook his head a bit, then pulled out his phone. "Let me text Sam and tell him to come back. I know he's starving, and then you can tell me what's good on this menu."

"Try the grilled cheese."

"For seventeen dollars?"

Evie leaned over and kissed him on the lips. "It's worth every penny."

Epilogue

Evie could not stop smiling. She'd just sat down with Celia Lamontagne for their third in-person meeting. Nervous didn't begin to describe the way she felt, but slowly things were starting to come together. She'd started working with Lavane Connor, a consultant who would help Evie with all the ins and outs of opening a restaurant. Zach was still available to give his input, but Lavane knew the New York culinary scene better than anyone.

Celia was in the middle of post-production on her latest film. In one month, cameras would start rolling on their documentary. Celia had explained her vision and they'd decided that Evie would go public with her memory loss. She wanted to tell the audience and her fans how and why she'd ended up on this path and hopefully inspire other young women not to give up when the road feels impossibly hard.

Evie had received so much support since leaving *The Dish.* Their ratings had absolutely tanked when viewers realized she wasn't coming back. Since then she'd been offered two hefty endorsement deals. One with FitJade, a women's athletic apparel company, and one for MedHealthChat, an online therapy tool. So many things seemed to be falling into place. Including her relationships with all the Pleasants.

As soon as they heard the good news—about her personal and professional life—Senior and Mrs. Pleasant practically added Evie to their speed dial. It was strange at first, but she liked Senior's kind words of encouragement and the texts Mrs. Pleasant sent just to check in. And Mrs. Pleasant keeping her up-to-date on all of the latest fashion trends out of Paris. They would never replace her mom and dad, or Nana, but Evie valued their support.

Evie pulled her rental SUV to a stop right in front of the main lodge. She pulled out her phone and called Blaire. She had so much to do, but she figured if she was heading to Los Angeles for business, it would be a shame not to stop off in Charming for the weekend. She owed Blaire and Raquelle big-time, so it only made sense to bring them along.

"Where you at?" she said as soon as Blaire picked up.

"Umm, I just left the spa and what the hell, Evie? I can't believe you've kept me from this place for so long."

"I'm sorry. I know. I'm the worst." She climbed out of the driver's seat and reached for her weekend bag. A new staff member named Peter jogged around the front of her car and took her keys.

"Enjoy your stay, Mrs. Buchanan," he whispered.

"Thanks."

"Raquelle's still in the sauna. We're gonna head back to our cabin and take a nap, and then Jesse said there was a barbecue and then a barn dance tonight? You grew up in a freaking movie."

"Well, it's a little different when your grandma is the one leading the trail rides, but this place has always been pretty incredible. I'm just gonna grab my key and find Zach, and then I'll come meet up with you."

"Um, so he took us out on the trails this morning, and I need David to learn how to ride a horse."

"Oh yeah?" Evie laughed.

"Yeah. I get it now. I totally get it."

Evie turned at the sound of a loud wolf whistle, and there was Zach coming up the path from the barns, looking as fine as ever. He was wearing a black-and-white flannel, those jeans that made his thighs look downright sinful, and that cowboy hat that always did something to her insides. She could see that sexy smile of his too, beaming off in the distance. "Speaking of. Just found my man. I'll be over a little later."

"Have fun."

"Well, hey there, little lady," he said in that fake Southern accent that made her laugh and drove her crazy all at the same time. "I haven't seen you around these parts before."

"Howdy, stranger," she replied, stepping into his arms. She leaned up on her tiptoes and pressed a soft kiss to his lips.

"How was your meeting?" he asked.

"Great. Celia has a vision and I am with it. I have some listings I wanted you to take a look at this weekend, if you don't mind."

"I think we can squeeze that in. I got you a little something." Zach reached into his pocket and pulled out a little burlap pouch tied with a blue ribbon. Evie opened it and found a tiny bottle at the end of a silver chain. There was a brown powder inside of it.

"What is this?" she asked.

"Nutmeg. Thought you could use a little something to carry around and huff. Keep you grounded when this whole process really starts getting hectic."

"I wasn't huffing nutmeg. I just found the smell to be comforting."

"Sure. Right. Well, now you can comfort huff all you want."

"Thanks, babe. I love it. I thought I'd check into my private cabin that Miss Leona need know nothing about, and then maybe go see a man about a horse named Steve."

Zach bent down and brushed his lips against hers. "You feel like having some company?"

"With you, cowboy? Anytime."

Keep an eye out for more
Cowboy adventures with
The Pleasant Brothers

Coming soon from
Rebekah Weatherspoon
And
Dafina Books

Connect with Us

Visit us online at
KensingtonBooks.com
to read more from your favorite authors, see books
by series, view reading group guides, and more.

for sneak peeks, chances to win books and prize packs,
and to share your thoughts with other readers.

facebook.com/kensingtonpublishing
twitter.com/kensingtonbooks

Tell us what you think!

To share your thoughts, submit a review,
or sign up for our eNewsletters, please visit:
KensingtonBooks.com/TellUs.